1¾s
5 —
m

ELLERY QUEEN'S
VEILS OF MYSTERY

Volume 39

ELLERY QUEEN'S VEILS OF MYSTERY

Edited by
ELLERY QUEEN

The Dial Press

DAVIS PUBLICATIONS, INC.
380 LEXINGTON AVENUE, NEW YORK, N.Y. 10017

CONTENTS

1 SHORT NOVEL

8   **Rex Stout**   *Eeny Meeny Murder Mo*

2 NOVELETS

151   **Patricia McGerr**   *Hide-and-Seek—Russian Style*

253   **William Bankier**   *Dangerous Enterprise*

18 SHORT STORIES

60   **John D. MacDonald**   *Man in a Trap*

70   **Edgar Wallace**   *Warm and Dry*

78   **Patricia Highsmith**   *The Pond*

94   **James Holding**   *Still a Cop*

107   **Richard Laymon**   *Paying Joe Back*

114   **Michael Gilbert**   *The Merry Band*

     L. E. Behney   *Tales from Home:*

129   *The Man Who Kept His Promise*

135   *Why Don't You Like Me?*

(CONTINUED ON NEXT PAGE)

CONTENTS   *(CONTINUED FROM PAGE 5)*

143   **Douglas Shea**   *Advice, Unlimited*

174   **Jack P. Nelson**   *The Weasel*

181   **Isaac Asimov**   *The Cross of Lorraine*

197   **Jon L. Breen**   *An Evening with the White Divorcees*

203   **Dana Lyon**   *The Living End*

214   **Bill Pronzini & Barry N. Malzberg**   *Problems Solved*

218   **Celia Fremlin**   *The Magic Carpet*

225   **John Ball**   *Full Circle*

238   **Ellery Queen**   *The Odd Man*

246   **Robert L. Fish**   *In the Bag*

Dear Reader:

In his *Poetics,* the Greek philosopher Aristotle wrote that the poet must imitate one of three objects: things as they were or are, things as they are said or believed to be, or things as they ought to be.

This dictum can be applied to all writers, including detective-story writers. But it occurs to us that there may be a fourth object that all writers—and particularly detective-story writers—can use as their creative image: things as the author *imagines* them to be.

Imagining is not always make-believe. You can imagine fantasy, but you can also imagine reality, or a reasonable facsimile. The detective-story writer imagines and creates a world of his own, its origin in reality, its people deriving from observation, its action arising from the needs or urgencies of character, its climax in imaginative necessity. It is these kinds of worlds you will find in the 21 stories selected for this volume—worlds as the authors imagined them to be, worlds that will fascinate you to the last entertaining and exciting denouement.

Let your imagination "pierce the veil" of mystery!

ELLERY QUEEN

Rex Stout

Eeny Meeny Murder Mo

To quote Archie Goodwin, "It was a new kind of hole," and Nero Wolfe had never "looked into one just like it." It also concerned a divorce with a fabulous settlement—$30,000,000 ... A short novel complete in this anthology ...

Detective: NERO WOLFE

I was standing there in the office with my hands in my pockets, glaring down at the necktie on Nero Wolfe's desk, when the doorbell rang.

Since it would be a different story, and possibly no story at all, if the necktie hadn't been there, I had better explain about it. It was the one Wolfe had worn that morning—brown silk with little yellow curlicues, a Christmas gift from a former client. At lunch Fritz, coming to remove the leavings of the spareribs and bring the salad and cheese, had told Wolfe there was a drop of sauce on his tie and Wolfe had dabbed at it with his napkin; and later, when we had left the dining room to cross the hall to the office, he had removed the tie and put it on his desk.

Wolfe can't stand a spot on his clothes, even in private. But he hadn't thought it worth the effort to go up to his room for another tie, since no callers were expected, and when four o'clock came and he left for his afternoon session with the orchids in the plant rooms on the roof his shirt was still unbuttoned at the neck and the tie was still on his desk.

It annoyed me. It annoyed Fritz too when, shortly after four, he came to say he was going shopping and would be gone two hours. His eye caught the tie and fastened on it. His brows went up.

"Schlampick," I said.

He nodded. "You know my respect and esteem for him. He has great spirit and character, and of course he is a great detective, but there is a limit to the duties of a chef and housekeeper. One must

8

draw the line somewhere. Besides, there is my arthritis. You haven't got arthritis, Archie."

"Maybe not," I conceded, "but if you rate a limit so do I. My list of functions from confidential assistant detective down to errand boy is a mile long, but it does not include valeting. Arthritis is beside the point. Consider the dignity of man. He could have taken it on his way up to the plant rooms."

"You could put it in a drawer."

"That would be evading the issue."

"I suppose so." He nodded. "I agree. It is a delicate affair. I must be going." He went.

So, having finished the office chores at 5:20, including a couple of personal phone calls, I had left my desk and was standing to glare down at the necktie when the doorbell rang. That made the affair even more delicate. A necktie with a greasy spot should not be on the desk of a man of great spirit and character when a visitor enters. But by then I had got stubborn about it as a matter of principle, and anyway it might be merely someone with a parcel.

Going to the hall for a look, I saw through the one-way glass panel of the front door that it was a stranger, a middle-aged female with a pointed nose and a round chin, not a good design, in a sensible gray coat and a black turban. She had no parcel.

I opened the door and told her good afternoon. She said she wanted to see Nero Wolfe. I said Mr. Wolfe was engaged, and besides, he saw people only by appointment. She said she knew that, but this was urgent. She had to see him and would wait till he was free.

There were several factors: that we had nothing on the fire at the moment; that the year was only five days old and therefore the income tax bracket didn't enter into it; that I wanted something to do besides recording the vital statistics of orchids; that I was annoyed at him for leaving the tie on his desk; and that she didn't try to push but kept her distance, with her dark eyes, good eyes, straight at me.

"Okay," I told her, "I'll see what I can do," and stepped aside for her to enter. Taking her coat and hanging it on the rack and escorting her to the office, I gave her one of the yellow chairs near me instead of the red leather one at the end of Wolfe's desk.

She sat with her back straight and her feet together—nice little feet in fairly sensible gray shoes. I told her that Wolfe wouldn't be available until six o'clock.

"It will be better," I said, "if I see him first and tell him about you. In fact, it will be essential. My name is Archie Goodwin. What is yours?"

"I know about you," she said. "Of course. If I didn't I wouldn't be here."

"Many thanks. Some people who know about me have a different reaction. And your name?"

She was eyeing me. "I'd rather not," she said, "until I know if Mr. Wolfe will take my case. It's private. It's very confidential."

I shook my head. "No go. You'll have to tell him what your case is before he decides if he'll take it, and I'll be sitting here listening. So? Also I'll have to tell him more about you than that you're thirty-five years old, weigh a hundred and twenty pounds, and wear no earrings, before he decides if he'll even see you."

She almost smiled. "I'm forty-two."

I grinned. "See? I need facts. Who you are and what you want."

Her mouth worked. "It's *very* confidential." Her mouth worked some more. "But there was no sense in coming unless I tell you."

"Right."

She laced her fingers. "All right. My name is Bertha Aaron. It is spelled with two A's. I am the private secretary of Mr. Lamont Otis, senior partner in the law firm of Otis, Edey, Heydecker and Jett. Their office is on Madison Avenue at Forty-first Street. I'm worried about something that happened recently and I want Mr. Wolfe to investigate it. I can pay him a reasonable fee, but it might develop that he will be paid by the firm."

"Were you sent here by someone in the firm?"

"No. Nobody sent me. Nobody knows I'm here."

"What happened?"

Her fingers laced tighter. "Maybe I shouldn't have come," she said. "I didn't realize . . . maybe I'd better not."

"Suit yourself, Miss Aaron. *Miss* Aaron?"

"Yes. I am not married." Her fingers flew apart to make fists and her lips tightened. "This is silly. I've got to. I owe it to Mr. Otis. I've been with him for twenty years and he has been wonderful to me. I couldn't go to him about this because he's seventy-five years old and he has a bad heart and it might kill him. He comes to the office every day, but it's a strain and he doesn't do much, only he knows more than all of the rest of them put together." Her fists opened. "What happened was that I saw a member of the firm with our opponent in a very important case, one of the biggest cases we've ever had, at a place where they wouldn't have met if they hadn't wanted to keep it secret."

"You mean with the opposing counsel?"

"No. The opposing client. With opposing counsel it might possibly have been all right."

"Which member of the firm?"

"I'm not going to say. I'm not going to tell Mr. Wolfe his name until he agrees to take the case. He doesn't have to know that in order to decide. If you wonder why I came, I've already said why I can't tell Mr. Otis about it, and I was afraid to go to any of the others because if one of them was a traitor another one might be in it with him, or even more than one. How could I be sure? There are only four members of the firm, but of course there are others associated—nineteen altogether. I wouldn't trust any of them, not on a thing like this." She made fists again. "You can understand that. You see what a hole I'm in."

"Sure. But you could be wrong. Of course that's unethical, a lawyer meeting with an enemy client, but there could be exceptions. It might have been accidental. When and where did you see them?"

"Last Monday, a week ago today. In the evening. They were together in a booth in a cheap restaurant—more of a lunchroom. The kind of place she would never go to, never. She would never go to that part of town. Neither would I, ordinarily, but I was on a personal errand and I went in there to use the phone. They didn't see me."

"Then one of the members of the firm is a woman?"

Her eyes widened. "Oh. I said 'she.' I meant the opposing client. We have a woman lawyer as one of the associates, just an employee really, but no woman firm member." She laced her fingers. "It couldn't possibly have been accidental. But of course it was conceivable, just barely conceivable, that he wasn't a traitor, that there was some explanation, and that made it even harder for me to decide what to do. But now I know. After worrying about it for a whole week I couldn't stand it any longer, and this afternoon I decided the only thing I *could* do was tell him and see what he said. If he had a good explanation, all right. But he didn't. The way he took it, the way it hit him, there isn't any question about it. He's a traitor."

"What did he say?"

"It wasn't so much what he said as how he looked. He said he had a satisfactory explanation, that he was acting in the interests of our client, but that he couldn't tell me more than that until the matter had developed further. Certainly within a week, he said, and possibly tomorrow. So I knew I had to do something, and I was afraid to go to Mr. Otis because his heart has been worse lately, and I wouldn't go to another firm member. I even thought of going to the opposing counsel, but of course that wouldn't do. Then I thought of Nero Wolfe, and I put on my hat and coat and came. Now it's urgent. You can see it's urgent?"

I nodded. "It could be. Depending on the kind of case involved. Mr. Wolfe might agree to take the job before you name the alleged traitor, but he would have to know first what the case is about—your firm's case. There are some kinds he won't touch, even indirectly. What is it?"

"I don't want . . ." She let it hang. "Does he have to know that?"

"Certainly. Anyhow, you've told me the name of your firm and it's a big important case and the opposing client is a woman, and with that I could—but I don't have to. I read the papers. Is your client Morton Sorell?"

"Yes."

"And the opposing client is Rita Sorell, his wife?"

"Yes."

I glanced at my wrist watch and saw 5:39, left my chair, told her, "Cross your fingers and sit tight," and headed for the hall and the stairs.

Two new factors had entered and now dominated the situation: that if our first bank deposit of the new year came from the Sorell pile it would not be hay; and that one of the kinds of jobs Wolfe wouldn't touch, even indirectly, was divorce stuff. It would take some doing, and as I mounted the three flights to the roof of the old brownstone my brain was going faster than my feet.

In the vestibule of the plant rooms I paused, not for breath but to plan the approach, decided that was no good because it would depend on his mood, and entered. You might think it impossible to go down the aisles between the benches of those three rooms—cool and tropical—without noticing the flashes of color, but that day I did, and was in the potting room.

Wolfe was over at the side bench peering at a pseudo-bulb through a magnifying glass. Theodore Horstmann, the fourth member of the household, who was exactly half Wolfe's weight, 135 to 270, was opening a bag of osmundine.

I crossed over and told Wolfe's back: "Excuse me for interrupting, but I have a problem."

He took ten seconds to decide he had heard me, then removed the magnifying glass from his eye and demanded, "What time is it?"

"Nineteen minutes to six."

"It can wait nineteen minutes."

"I know, but there's a snag. If you came down and found her there in the office with no warning it would be hopeless."

"Find whom?"

"A woman named Bertha Aaron. She came uninvited. She's in a hole, and it's a new kind of hole. I came up to describe it to you so you can decide whether I go down and shoo her out or you come down and give it a look."

"You have interrupted me. You have violated our understanding."

"I know it, but I said excuse me, and since you're already inter-rupted I might as well tell you. She is the private secretary of Lamont Otis, senior partner . . ."

I told him, and at least he didn't go back to the pseudo-bulb. At one point there was even a gleam in his eye. He has made the claim, to me, that the one and only thing that impels him to work is his desire to live in what he calls acceptable circumstances in the old brownstone on West 35th Street, Manhattan, which he owns, with Fritz as chef and Theodore as orchid tender and me as goat (not his word), but the gleam in his eye was not at the prospect of a big fee because I hadn't yet mentioned the name Sorell. The gleam was when he saw that, as I had said, it was a new kind of hole. We had never looked into one just like it.

Then came the ticklish part. "By the way," I said, "there's one little detail you may not like, but it's only a side issue. In the case in question her firm's client is Morton Sorell. You know."

"Of course."

"And the opposing client is Mrs. Morton Sorell. You may remem-ber that you made a comment about her a few weeks ago after you had read the morning paper. What the paper said was that she was suing him for thirty thousand a month for a separation allowance, but the talk around town is that he wants a divorce and her asking price is a flat thirty million bucks, and that's probably what Miss Aaron calls the case. However, that's only a detail. What Miss Aaron wants is merely—"

"No." He was scowling at me. "So that's why you pranced in here."

"I didn't prance. I walked."

"You knew quite well I would have nothing to do with it."

"I knew you wouldn't get divorce evidence, and neither would I. I knew you wouldn't work for a wife against a husband or vice versa, but what has that got to do with this? You wouldn't have to touch—"

"No! I will not. That marital squabble might be the central point of the matter. I will not! Send her away."

I had flubbed it. Or maybe I hadn't; maybe it had been hopeless no matter how I handled it; but then it had been a flub to try, so in any case I had flubbed it. I don't like to flub, and it wouldn't make it any worse to try to talk him out of it, or rather into it, so I did, for a good ten minutes, but it neither changed the situation nor improved the atmosphere.

He ended it by saying that he would go to his room to put on a necktie, and I would please ring him there on the house phone to tell him that she had gone.

Going down the three flights I was tempted. I could ring him not to say that she was gone but that we were going; that I was taking a leave of absence to haul her out of the hole. It wasn't a new temptation; I had had it before; and I had to admit that on other occasions it had been more attractive. To begin with, if I made the offer she might decline it, and I had done enough flubbing for one day.

So as I crossed the hall to the office I was arranging my face so she would know the answer as soon as she looked at me. Then as I entered I rearranged it, or it rearranged itself, and I stopped and stood.

Two objects were there on the rug which had been elsewhere when I left: a big hunk of jade which Wolfe used for a paperweight, which had been on his desk, and Bertha Aaron, who had been in a chair.

She was on her side, with one leg straight and one bent at the knee. I went to her and squatted. Her lips were blue, her tongue was showing, and her eyes were open and popping; and around her neck, knotted at the side, was Wolfe's necktie.

If you get at a case of strangulation soon enough there may be a chance, and I got the scissors from my desk drawer. The tie was so tight that I had to poke hard to get my finger under. When I had the tie off I rolled her over on her back. Nuts, I thought, she's gone, but I picked pieces of fluff from the rug, put one across her nose and one on her mouth, and held my breath for twenty seconds.

She wasn't breathing.

I took her hand and pressed on a fingernail, and it stayed white when I removed the pressure. Her blood wasn't moving. Still there might be a chance if I got an expert quick enough, say in two minutes, and I went to my desk and dialed the number of Doc Vollmer, who lived down the street only a minute away. He was out.

I sat and stared at her a while, maybe a minute, just feeling, not thinking. I was too damn sore to think. I was sore at Wolfe, not at me, the idea being that it had been ten minutes past six when I found her, and if he had come down with me at six o'clock we might have been in time.

I swiveled to the house phone and buzzed his room, and when he answered I said, "Okay, come on down. She's gone," and hung up.

He always uses the elevator to and from the plant rooms, but his room is only one flight up. When I heard his door open and close I got up and stood six inches from her head and folded my arms, facing the door to the hall. There was the sound of his steps, and then him. He crossed the threshold, stopped, glared at Bertha Aaron, shifted to me, and bellowed, "You said she was gone!"

"Yes, sir. She is. She's dead."

"Nonsense!"

"No, sir." I sidestepped. "As you see."

He approached, still glaring, and aimed the glare down at her, for not more than three seconds. Then he circled around her and me, went to his oversized made-to-order chair behind his desk, sat, took in air clear down as far as it would go, and let it out again. "I presume," he said, not bellowing, "that she was alive when you left her to come up to me."

"Yes, sir. Sitting in that chair." I pointed. "She was alone. No one came with her. The door was locked, as always. As you know, Fritz is out shopping. When I found her she was on her side and I turned her over to test for breathing—after I cut the necktie off. I phoned Doc—"

"What necktie?"

I pointed again. "The one you left on your desk. It was around her throat. Probably she was knocked out first with that paper-weight"—I pointed again—"but it was the necktie that stopped her breathing, as you can see by her face. I cut—"

"Do you dare to suggest that she was strangled with *my* necktie?"

"I don't suggest, I state. It was pulled tight with a slipknot and then passed around her neck again and tied with a granny." I stepped to where I had dropped it on the rug, picked it up, and put it on his desk. "As you see. I do dare to suggest that if it hadn't been here handy he would have had to use something else, maybe his handkerchief. Also that if we had come down a little sooner—"

"Shut up!"

"Yes, sir."

"This is insupportable."

"Yes, sir."

"I will not accept it."

"No, sir. I could burn the tie and we could tell Cramer that whatever he used he must have waited until he was sure she was dead and then removed it and took it—"

"Shut up. She told you that nobody knew she came here."

"Bah," I said. "Not a chance and you know it. We're stuck. I put off calling until you came down only to be polite. If I put it off any longer that will only make it worse because I'll have to tell them the exact time I found her." I looked at my wrist. "It's already been twenty-one minutes. Would you rather make the call yourself?"

No reply. He was staring down at the necktie, with his jaw set and his mouth so tight he had no lips. I gave him five seconds, and then went to the kitchen, to the phone on the table where I ate breakfast, and dialed a number.

Inspector Cramer of Homicide West finished the last page of the statement I had typed and signed, put it on top of the other pages on the table, tapped it with a finger, and spoke: "I still think you're lying, Goodwin."

It was a quarter past eleven. We were in the dining room. The gang of scientists had finished in the office and departed, and it was no longer out of bounds, but I had no special desire to move back in. For one thing, they had taken the rug, along with Wolfe's necktie and the paperweight and a few other items.

Of course they had also taken Bertha Aaron, so I wouldn't have to see her again, but even so I was perfectly willing to stay in the dining room. They had brought the typewriter there after the fingerprint detail had finished with it, so I could type the statement.

Now, after nearly five hours, they were gone, all except Sergeant Purley Stebbins, who was in the office using the phone, and Cramer. Fritz was in the kitchen, on his third bottle of wine, absolutely miserable. Added to the humiliation of a homicide in the house he kept there was the incredible fact that Wolfe had passed up a meal. He had refused to eat a bite. Around eight o'clock he had gone up to his room, and Fritz had gone up twice with a tray.

When I had gone up at ten thirty with a statement for him to sign, and told him they were taking the rug, he made a noise but had no words. With all that for background in addition to my personal reactions, it was no wonder that when Cramer told me he still thought I was lying I was outspoken.

EENY MEENY MURDER MO

"I've been trying for years," I said, "to think who it is you remind me of. I just remembered. It was a certain animal I saw once in a cage. It begins with B. Are you going to take me down or not?"

"No." His big round face is always redder at night, making his gray hair look whiter. "You can save the wisecracks. You wouldn't lie about anything that can be checked, but we can't check your account of what she told you. She's dead. Accepting your statement, and Wolfe's, that you have never had any dealings with her or anyone connected with that law firm, you might still save something for your private use—or change something. One thing especially. You ask me to believe that she told—"

"Excuse me. I don't care a single measly damn what you believe. Neither does Mr. Wolfe. You can't name anything we wouldn't rather have done than report what happened, but we had no choice, so we reported it and you have our statements. If you know what she said better than I do, that's fine with me."

"I was talking," he said.

"Yeah. I was interrupting."

"You say that she gave you all those details, how she saw a member of the firm in a cheap restaurant or lunchroom with an opposing client, the day she saw him, her telling him about it this afternoon, all the rest of it, including naming Mrs. Sorell, but she didn't name the member of the firm. I don't believe it." He tapped the statement and his head came forward. "And I'm telling you this, Goodwin. If you use that name for your private purposes and profit, and that includes Wolfe, if you get yourselves hired to investigate this murder and you use information you have withheld from me to solve the case and collect a fee, I'll get you for it if it costs me an eye!"

I cocked my head. "Look," I said. "Apparently you don't realize. It's already been on the radio, and tomorrow it will be in the papers, that a woman who had come to consult Nero Wolfe was murdered in his office, strangled with his own necktie, while he was up playing with his orchids and chatting with Archie Goodwin. I can hear the horse laugh from here. Mr. Wolfe couldn't swallow any dinner; he wouldn't even try. We knew and felt all this the second we saw her there on the floor. If we had known which member of the firm it was, if she had told me his name, what would we have done? You ought to know, since you claim you know us. I would have gone after him. Mr. Wolfe would have left the office, shut the door, and gone to the kitchen, and would have been there drinking beer when Fritz came home. When he went to the office and discovered the body would have depended on when and what he heard from me. With any luck I would have got here with the murderer before you and the scientists arrived. That wouldn't have erased the fact that she had been strangled with his necktie, but it would have blurred it. I give you this just to show you that you don't know us as well as you think you do. As for your believing me, I couldn't care less."

His sharp gray eyes were narrowed at me. "So you would have gone and got him. So he killed her. Huh? How did he know she was here? How did he get in?"

I pronounced a word I'll leave out, and added, "Again? I have discussed that with Stebbins, and Rowcliff, and you. Now again?"

"What the hell," he said. He folded the statement and stuck it in his pocket, shoved his chair back, got up, growled at me, "If it costs me both eyes," and tramped out. From the hall he spoke to Stebbins in the office.

It will give you some idea of how low I was when I say that I didn't even go to the hall to see that they took only what belonged to them. You might think that after being in the house five hours Purley would have stepped to the door to say good night, but no. I heard the front door close with a bang, so it was Purley. Cramer never banged doors.

I slumped farther down in my chair. At twenty minutes to midnight I said aloud, "I could go for a walk," but apparently that didn't appeal to me. At 11:45 I arose, picked up the carbons of my statement, went to the office, and put them in a drawer of my desk. Looking around, I saw that they had left it in fairly decent shape.

I went and brought the typewriter and put it where it belonged, tried the door of the safe, went to the hall to see that the front door was locked and put the chain bolt on, and proceeded to the kitchen. Fritz was in my breakfast chair, humped over with his forehead on the edge of the table.

"You're pie-eyed," I said.

His head came up. "No, Archie. I have tried, but no."

"Go to bed."

"No. He will be hungry."

"He may never be hungry again. Pleasant dreams."

I went to the hall, mounted one flight, turned left, tapped on the door, heard a sound that was half growl and half groan, opened the door, and entered. Wolfe, fully clothed, including a necktie, was in the big chair with a book.

"They've gone," I said. "Last ones out, Cramer and Stebbins. Fritz is standing watch in the kitchen expecting a call for food. You'd better buzz him. Is there any alternative to going to bed?"

"Can you sleep?" he demanded.

"Probably. I always have."

"I can't read." He put the book down. "Have you ever known me to show rancor?"

"I'd have to look in the dictionary. What is it exactly?"

"Vehement ill will. Intense malignity."

"No."

"I have it now, and it is in the way. I can't think clearly. I intend to expose that wretch before the police do. I want Saul and Orrie and Fred here at eight o'clock in the morning. I have no idea what their errands will be, but I shall know by morning. After you reach them sleep if you can."

"I don't have to sleep if there's something better to do."

"Not tonight. This confounded rancor is a pimple on the brain. My mental processes haven't been so muddled in many years. I wouldn't have thought—"

The doorbell was ringing. Now that the army of occupation was gone, that was to be expected, since Cramer had allowed no reporters or photographers to enter the house. I had considered disconnecting the bell for the night, and now, as I descended the stairs, I decided that I would. Fritz, at the door to the kitchen, looked relieved when he saw me. He had switched on the stoop light.

If it was a reporter he was a veteran, and he had brought a helper along, or maybe a girl friend just for company. I was in no hurry getting to the door, sizing them up through the one-way glass panel. He was a six-footer in a well-cut and well-fitted dark gray overcoat, a light gray woolen scarf, and a gray homburg, with a long bony face with deep lines. She could have been his pretty little grand-daughter, but her fur coat fastened clear up and her matching fur cloche covered everything but the little oval of her face. I removed the chain bolt and swung the door open and said, "Yes, sir?"

He said, "I am Lamont Otis. This is Mr. Nero Wolfe's house?"

"Right."

"I would like to see him. About my secretary, Miss Bertha Aaron. About information I have received from the police. This is Miss Ann Paige, my associate, a member of the bar. My coming at this hour is justified, I think, by the circumstances. I think Mr. Wolfe will agree."

"I do too," I agreed. "But if you don't mind—" I crossed the sill to the stoop and sang out, "Who are you over there? Gillian? Murphy? Come here a minute!"

A figure emerged from the shadows across the street. As he crossed the pavement I peered, and as he reached the curb on our side I spoke. "Oh, Wylie. Come on up."

He stood at the foot of the seven steps. "For what?" he demanded.

"May I ask," Lamont Otis asked, "what this is for?"

"You may. A police inspector named Cramer is in danger of losing an eye and that would be a shame. I'll appreciate it if you'll answer a simple question: were you asked to come here by either Mr. Wolfe or me?"

"Certainly not."

"Was your coming entirely your own idea?"

"Yes. But I don't—"

"Excuse me. —You heard him, Wylie? Include it in your report. It will save wear and tear on Cramer's nerves. Much obliged for—"

"Who is he?" the dick demanded.

I ignored it. Backing up, I invited them in, and when I shut the door I put the bolt on. Otis let me take his hat and coat, but Ann Paige kept hers. The house was cooling off for the night. In the office, sitting, she unfastened the coat but kept it over her shoulders.

I went to the thermostat on the wall and pushed it up to 70, and then went to my desk and buzzed Wolfe's room on the house phone. I should have gone up to get him, since he might balk at seeing company until he had dealt with the pimple on his brain, but I had had enough for one day of leaving visitors alone in the office, and one of these had a bum pump.

Wolfe's growl came, "Yes?"

"Mr. Lamont Otis is here. With an associate, Miss Ann Paige, also a member of the bar. He thinks you will agree that his coming at this hour is justified by the circumstances."

Silence. Nothing for some five seconds, then the click of his hanging up. You feel foolish holding a dead receiver to your ear, so I cradled it but didn't swivel to face the company. It was even money whether he was coming or not, and I put my eyes on my wrist watch. If he didn't come in five minutes I would go up after him. I turned and told Otis, "You won't mind a short wait."

He nodded. "It was in this room?"

"Yes. She was there." I pointed to a spot a few inches in front of Ann Paige's feet. Otis was in the red leather chair near the end of Wolfe's desk. "There was a rug but they took it to the laboratory.

Of course they—I'm sorry, Miss Paige. I shouldn't have pointed."
She had pushed her chair back and shut her eyes.

She swallowed, and opened the eyes. They looked black in that
light but could have been dark violet. "You're Archie Goodwin," she
said.

"Right."

"You were—you found her."

"Right."

"Had she been . . . was there any . . ."

"She had been hit on the back of her head with a paperweight,
a chunk of jade, and then strangled with a necktie that happened
to be here on a desk. There was no sign of a struggle. The blow
knocked her out, and probably she—

My voice had kept me from hearing Wolfe's steps on the stairs.
He entered, stopped to tilt his head an eighth of an inch to Ann
Paige, again to Otis, went to his chair behind his desk, sat, and
aimed his eyes at Otis.

"You are Mr. Lamont Otis?"

"I am."

"I owe you an apology. A weak word; there should be a better one.
A valued and trusted employee of yours has died by violence under
my roof. She was valued and trusted?"

"Yes."

"I deeply regret it. If you come to reproach me, proceed."

"I didn't come to reproach you." The lines in Otis' face were furrows
in the better light. "I came to find out what happened. The police
and the District Attorney's office have told me how she was killed,
but not why she was here. I think they know but are reserving it.
I think I have a right to know. Bertha Aaron had been in my confidence for years, and I believe I was in hers, and I knew nothing
of any trouble she might be in that would lead her to come to you.
Why was she here?"

Wolfe, rubbing his nose with a fingertip, regarded him. "How old
are you, Mr. Otis?"

Ann Paige made a noise. The veteran lawyer, who had probably
objected to ten thousand questions as irrelevant, said merely, "I'm
seventy-five. Why?"

"I do not intend to have another death in my office to apologize
for, this time induced by me. Miss Aaron told Mr. Goodwin that the
reason she did not go to you with her problem was that she feared
the effect on you. —Her words, Archie?"

I supplied them. " 'He has a bad heart and it might kill him.' "

Otis snorted. "Bosh! My heart has given me a little trouble and I've had to slow down, but it would take more than a problem to kill me. I've been dealing with problems all my life, some pretty tough ones."

"She exaggerated it," Ann Paige said. "I mean Miss Aaron. I mean she was so devoted to Mr. Otis that she had an exaggerated idea about his heart condition."

"Why did you come here with him?" Wolfe demanded.

"Not because of his heart. Because I was at his apartment, working with him on a brief, when the news came about Bertha, and when he decided to see you he asked me to come with him. I do shorthand."

"You heard Mr. Goodwin quote Miss Aaron. If I tell Mr. Otis what she was afraid to tell him, what her problem was, will you take responsibility for the effect on him?"

Otis exploded. "Damn it, *I* take the responsibility! It's *my* heart!"

"I doubt," Ann Paige said, "if the effect of telling him would be as bad as the effect of *not* telling him. I take no responsibility, but you have me as witness that he insists."

"I not only insist," Otis said. "I assert my right to the information, since it must have concerned me."

"Very well," Wolfe said. "Miss Aaron arrived here at twenty minutes past five this afternoon—now yesterday afternoon—uninvited and unexpected. She spoke for some twenty minutes with Mr. Goodwin and he then went upstairs to confer with me. He was away half an hour. She was alone on this floor. You know what greeted him when he returned. He has given the police a statement which includes his conversation with her." His head turned. "Archie, give Mr. Otis a copy of the statement."

I got it from my desk drawer and handed it to him. I had a notion to stand by, in case Bertha Aaron had been right about the effect it would have on him, but from up there I couldn't see his face, so I returned to my chair; but after half a century of practising law his face knew how to behave. All that happened was that his jaw tightened a little, and once a muscle twitched at the side of his neck. He read it clear through twice, first fast and then taking his time. When he had finished he folded it neatly, fumbling a little, and was putting it in the breast pocket of his jacket.

"No," Wolfe said emphatically. "I disclose the information at my discretion, but that's a copy of a statement given the police. You can't have it."

Otis ignored it. He looked at his associate, and his neck muscle twitched again. "I shouldn't have brought you, Ann," he said. "You'll have to leave."

Her eyes met his. "Believe me, Mr. Otis, you can trust me. On anything. Believe me. If it's that bad you shouldn't be alone with it."

"I must be. I couldn't trust you on *this*. You'll have to leave."

I stood up. "You can wait in the front room, Miss Paige. The wall and door are soundproofed."

She didn't like it, but she came. I opened the door to the front room and turned the lights on, then went and locked the door to the hall and put the key in my pocket. Back in the office, as I was crossing to my desk Otis asked, "How good is the soundproofing?"

"Good for anything under a loud yell," I told him.

He focused on Wolfe. "I am not surprised," he said, "that Miss Aaron thought it would kill me. I am surprised that it hasn't. You say the police have this statement?"

"Yes. And this conversation is ended unless you return that copy. Mr. Goodwin has no corroboration. It is a dangerous document for him to sign except under constraint of police authority."

"But I need—"

"Archie. Get it."

I stood up. The heart was certainly getting tested. But as I took a step his hand went to his pocket, and when I reached him he had it out and handed it over.

"That's better," Wolfe said. "I have extended my apology and regret, and we have given you all the information we have. I add this: first, that nothing in that statement will be revealed to anyone by Mr. Goodwin or me without your consent; and second, that my self-esteem has been severely injured and it would give me great satisfaction to expose the murderer. Granted that that's a job for the police, for me it is my job. I would welcome your help, not as my client; I would accept no fee. I realize that at the moment you are under shock, that you are overwhelmed by what you have just learned; and when your mind clears you may be tempted to minimize the damage by dealing with your intramural treachery yourself and letting the culprit escape his doom. If you went about it with sufficient resourcefulness and ingenuity it is conceivable that the police could be cheated of their prey; but it is not conceivable that I could be."

"You are making a wholly unwarranted assumption," Otis said.

"I am not making an assumption. I am merely telling you my intention. The police hypothesis, and mine, is the obvious one: that a member of your firm killed Miss Aaron. Though the law does not insist that the testimony against him in court must include proof of his motive, inevitably it would. Will you assert that you won't try to prevent that? That you will not regard the reputation of your firm as your prime concern?"

Otis opened his mouth and closed it again.

Wolfe nodded. "I thought not. Then I advise you to help me. If you do, I'll have two objectives: to get the murderer and to see that your firm suffers as little as possible; if you don't, I'll have only one. As for the police, I doubt if they'll expect you to cooperate, since they are not nincompoops. They will realize that you have a deeper interest than the satisfaction of justice. Well, sir?"

Otis' palms were cupping his knees and his head was tilted forward so he could study the back of his left hand. His eyes shifted to his right hand, and when that too had been properly studied he lifted his head and spoke. "You used the word 'hypothesis,' and that's all it is, that a member of my firm killed Miss Aaron. How did he know she was here? She said that nobody knew."

"He could have followed her. Evidently she left your office soon after she talked with him. —Archie?"

"She probably walked," I said. "Between fifteen and twenty-five minutes, depending on her rate. At that time of day empty taxis are scarce, and crosstown they crawl. It would have been a cinch to tail her on foot."

"How did he get in?" Otis demanded. "Did he sneak in unseen when you admitted her?"

"No. You have read my statement. He saw her enter and knew this is Nero Wolfe's address. He went to a phone booth and rang this number and she answered. Here." I tapped my phone. "With me not here that would be automatic for a trained secretary. I had not pushed the button, so it didn't ring in the plant rooms. It would ring in the kitchen, but Fritz wasn't there. She answered it, and he said he wanted to see her at once and would give her a satisfactory explanation, and she told him to come here. When he came she was at the front door and let him in. All he was expecting to do was stall for time, but when he learned that she was alone on this floor and that she hadn't seen Mr. Wolfe he had another idea and acted on it. Two minutes would have been plenty for the whole operation, even less."

"All that is mere conjecture."

"Yeah. I wasn't present. But it fits. If you have one that fits better I do shorthand too."

"The police have covered everything here for fingerprints."

"Sure. But it was below freezing outdoors and I suppose the members of your firm wear gloves."

"You say that he learned she hadn't seen Wolfe, but she had talked with you."

"She didn't tell him that she had told me. It wouldn't take many words for him to learn that she was alone and hadn't seen Mr. Wolfe. Either that, or she did tell him but he went ahead anyhow. The former is more probable. I like it better."

He studied me a while, then he closed his eyes and his head tilted again. When his eyes opened he put them at Wolfe. "Mr. Wolfe. I reserve comment on your suggestion that I would be moved by personal considerations to balk justice. You ask me to help you. How?"

"By giving me information. By answering questions. Your mind is trained in inquiry; you know what I will ask."

"I'll know better when I hear you. Go ahead and we'll see."

Wolfe looked at the wall clock. "It's nearly an hour past midnight, and this will be prolonged. It will be a tiresome wait for Miss Paige."

"Of course," Otis agreed. He looked at me. "Will you ask her to step in?"

I got up and crossed to the door to the front room. Entering, words were at the tip of my tongue, but that was as far as they got.

She wasn't there.

Cold air was streaming in through a wide-open window. As I went to it and stuck my head out I was prepared to see her lying there with one of my neckties around her throat, though I hadn't left one in that room. It was a relief to see that the areaway, eight feet down, was unoccupied.

A roar came from the office: "Archie! What the devil are you up to?"

I shut the window, glanced around to see if there were any signs of violence or if she had left a note, saw neither, and rejoined the conference.

"She's gone," I said. "Leaving no message. When I—"

"Why did you open a window?"

"I didn't. I closed it. When I took her in there I locked the door to the hall so she couldn't wander around and hear things she wasn't supposed to—so when she got tired waiting, the window was the only way out."

"She climbed out a window?" Otis demanded.

"Yes, sir. It's a mere conjecture, but it fits. The window was wide open, and she's not in the room, and she's not outside. I looked."

"I can't believe it. Miss Paige is a level-headed and reliable—" He bit it off. "No. No! I no longer know who is reliable." He rested his elbow on the chair arm and propped his head with his hand. "May I have a glass of water?"

Wolfe suggested brandy, but he said he wanted water, and I went to the kitchen and brought some. He got a little metal box from a pocket, took out two pills, and washed them down.

"Will they help?" Wolfe asked. "The pills?"

"Yes. The *pills* are reliable." He handed me the glass.

"Then we may proceed?"

"Yes."

"Have you any notion why Miss Paige was impelled to leave by a window?"

"No. It's extraordinary. Damn it, Wolfe, I have no notions of anything! Can't you see I'm lost?"

"I can. Shall we put it off?"

"No!"

"Very well. My assumption that Miss Aaron was killed by a member of your firm—let us call him X—rests on a prior assumption, that when she spoke with Mr. Goodwin she was candid and her facts were accurate. Would you challenge that assumption?"

Otis looked at me. "Tell me something. I know what she said from your statement, and it sounded like her, but how was she—her voice and manner? Did she seem in any way . . . well, out of control? Unbalanced?"

"No, sir," I told him. "She sat with her back straight and her feet together, and she met my eyes all the time."

He nodded. "She would. She always did." To Wolfe: "At this time, here privately with you, I don't challenge your assumption."

"Do you challenge the other one, that X killed her?"

"I neither challenge it nor accept it."

"Pfui. You're not an ostrich, Mr. Otis. Next: if Miss Aaron's facts were accurate, it must be supposed that X was in a position to give Mrs. Sorell information that would help her substantially in her action against her husband, your client. That is true?"

"Of course." Otis was going to add something, decided not to, and then changed his mind again. "Again here privately with you, it's not merely her action at law. It's blackmail. Perhaps not technically, but that's what it amounts to. Her demands are exorbitant and preposterous. It's extortion."

"And a member of your firm could give her weapons. Which one or ones?"

Otis shook his head. "I won't answer that."

Wolfe's brows went up. "Sir? If you pretend to help at all that's the very least you can do. If you're rejecting my proposal, say so and I'll get on without you. By noon tomorrow—today—the police will have that elementary question answered. It may take me longer."

"It certainly may," Otis said. "You haven't mentioned a third assumption you're making. You are assuming that Goodwin was candid and accurate in reporting what Miss Aaron said."

"Bah." Wolfe was disgusted. "You are gibbering. If you hope to impeach Mr. Goodwin you are indeed forlorn. You might as well go. If you regain your faculties later and wish to communicate with me I'll be here." He pushed his chair back.

"No." Otis extended a hand. "Good God, man, I'm trapped! It's not my faculties! I have my faculties."

"Then use them. Which member of your firm was in a position to betray its interests to Mrs. Sorell?"

"They all were. Our client is vulnerable in certain respects, and the situation is extremely difficult, and we have frequently conferred together on it. I mean, of course, my three partners. It could have only been one of them, partly because none of our associates was in our confidence on this matter, but mainly because Miss Aaron told Goodwin it was a member of the firm. She wouldn't have used that phrase, 'member of the firm,' loosely. For her it had a specific and restricted application. She could only have meant Frank Edey, Miles Heydecker, or Gregory Jett. And that's incredible!"

"Incredible literally or rhetorically? Do you disbelieve Miss Aaron—or, in desperation, Mr. Goodwin? Here with me privately?"

"No."

Wolfe turned a palm up. "Then let's get at it. Is it equally incredible for all three of those men, or are there preferences?"

During the next hour Otis balked at least a dozen times, and on some details—for instance, the respects in which Morton Sorell was vulnerable—he clammed up absolutely, but I had enough to fill nine pages of my notebook.

Frank Edey, 55, married, with two sons and a daughter, wife

living, got 27% of the firm's net income. (Otis' share was 40%).) He
was a brilliant idea man but seldom went to court. He had drafted
the marriage agreement which had been signed by Morton Sorell
and Rita Ramsey when they got yoked four years ago. Personal
financial condition, sound. Relations with wife and children, so-so.
Interest in other women, definitely yes, but fairly discreet. Interest
in Mrs. Sorell casual so far as Otis knew.

Miles Heydecker, 47, married, wife living but no children, got
22%. His father, now dead, had been one of the original members
of the firm. His specialty was trial work and he handled the firm's
most important cases in court. He had appeared for Mrs. Sorell at
her husband's request two years ago when she had been sued by a
man who had formerly been her agent. He was tight with money
and had a nice personal pile of it. Relations with his wife, uncertain;
on the surface, okay. Too interested in his work and his hobbies,
chess and behind-the-scenes politics, to bother with women, including Mrs. Sorell.

Gregory Jett, 36, single, had been made a firm member and al-
lotted 11% of the income because of his spectacular success in two
big corporation cases. One of the corporations was controlled by
Morton Sorell, and for the past year or so Jett had been a fairly
frequent guest at the Sorell home on Fifth Avenue but had not been
noticeably attentive to his hostess. His personal financial condition
was one of the details Otis balked on, but he allowed it to be inferred
that Jett was careless about the balance between income and outgo
and was in the red in his account with the firm.

Shortly after Jett had been made a member of the firm, about two
years ago, he had dropped a fat chunk—Otis thought about
$40,000—backing a Broadway show that flopped. A friend of his,
female, had been in the cast. Whether he had had other expenses
connected with a female friend or friends Otis either didn't know
or wasn't telling. He did say that he had gathered, mostly from
remarks Bertha Aaron had made, that in recent months Jett had
shown more attention to Ann Paige than their professional association required.

But when Wolfe suggested the possibility that Ann Paige had left
through a window because she suspected, or even knew, what was
in the wind, and had decided to take a hand, Otis wouldn't buy it.
He was having all he could do to swallow the news that one of his
partners was a snake, and the idea that another of his associates
might have been in on it was too much. He would tackle Ann Paige

himself; she would no doubt have an acceptable explanation for her sudden and unconventional departure.

On Mrs. Morton Sorell he didn't balk at all. Part of his information was known to everyone who read newspapers and magazines: that as Rita Ramsey she had dazzled Broadway with her performance in *Reach for the Moon* when she was barely out of her teens, that she had followed that with even greater triumphs in two other plays, that she had spurned Hollywood, that she had also spurned Morton Sorell for two years and then abandoned her career to marry him.

But Otis added other information about Mr. and Mrs. Sorell that had merely been hinted at in gossip columns: that in a year their union had gone sour; that it became apparent Rita had married Sorell only to get her lovely paws on a bale of dough; and that she was by no means going to settle for the terms of the marriage agreement. She wanted much more—more than half—and she had carefully begun to collect evidence of certain activities of Sorell's, but he had got wise and consulted his attorneys, Otis, Edey, Heydecker and Jett, and they had stymied her—or thought they had. Otis had been sure they had, until he had read the copy of my statement. Now he was sure of nothing.

But he was still alive. When he got up to go, at two hours past midnight, he had bounced back some. He wasn't nearly as jittery as he had been when he asked for a glass of water to take the pills. He hadn't accepted Wolfe's offer in so many words, but he had agreed to take no steps until he had heard further from Wolfe, provided he heard within thirty-two hours, by ten o'clock Wednesday morning.

The only action Otis would take during that period would be to instruct Ann Paige to tell no one that he had read my statement and to learn why she had skedaddled. He didn't think the police would tell him the contents of my statement, but if they did he would say that he would credit it only if it had corroboration. Of course he wanted to know what Wolfe was going to do, but Wolfe said he didn't know and probably wouldn't decide until after breakfast.

When I returned to the office after holding Otis' coat for him and letting him out, Fritz was there.

"No," Wolfe was saying grimly. "You know quite well I almost never eat at night."

"But you had no dinner. An omelet, or at least—"

"No! Confound it, let me starve! Go to bed!"

Fritz looked at me. I shook my head, and he went.

I sat down and spoke: "Do I get Saul and Fred and Orrie?"

"No." He took in air through his nose and let it out through his mouth. "If I don't know how I am going to proceed how the deuce can I have errands for them?"

"Rhetorical," I said.

"It is not rhetorical. It's logical. There are the obvious routine errands, but that would be witless. Find the cheap restaurant or lunchroom where they met? How many are there?"

"Oh, a thousand. More."

He grunted. "Or question the entire personnel of that law office to learn which of those three men spoke at length with Miss Aaron yesterday afternoon? Or, assuming that he followed her here, left the office on her heels? Or which one cannot account for himself from five o'clock to ten minutes past six? Or find the nearby phone booth from which he dialed this number? Or investigate their relations with Mrs. Sorell? Those are all sensible and proper lines of inquiry, and by midmorning Mr. Cramer and the District Attorney will have a score of men pursuing them."

"Two score. This is a special."

"So for me to put three men on them, four including you, would be frivolous. A possible procedure would be to have Mr. Otis get them here—Edey, Heydecker, and Jett. He could merely tell them that he has engaged me to investigate the murder that was committed in my own house."

"If they're available. They'll be spending most of the day at the D.A.'s office. By request."

He shut his eyes and tightened his lips. I picked up the copy of my statement which Otis had surrendered, got the second carbon from my drawer, went and opened the safe, and put them on a shelf. I had closed the safe door and was twirling the knob when Wolfe spoke.

"Archie."

"Yes, sir."

"Will they tackle Mrs. Sorell?"

"I doubt it. Not right away. What for? Since Cramer warned us that if we blab what Bertha Aaron told me we may be hooked for libel, which was kind of him, evidently he's going to save it, and going to Mrs. Sorell would spill it."

He nodded. "She is young and comely."

"Yeah, I've never seen her offstage. You have seen pictures of her."

"You have a talent for dealing with personable young women."

"Sure. They melt like chocolate bars in the sun. But you're exaggerating it a little if you think I can go to the specimen and ask her which member of the firm she met in a cheap restaurant or lunchroom and she'll wrap her arms around me and murmur his name in my ear. It might take me an hour or more."

"You can bring her here."

"Maybe. Possibly. To see the orchids?"

"I don't know."

He pushed his chair back and raised his bulk. "I am not myself. Come to my room at eight o'clock." He headed for the hall.

At 10:17 that Tuesday morning I left the house, walked north fourteen short blocks and east six long ones, and entered the lobby of the Churchill. I walked instead of flagging a taxi for two reasons: because I had had less than five hours' sleep and needed a lot of oxygen, especially from the neck up, and because eleven o'clock was probably the earliest Mrs. Morton Sorell, born Rita Ramsey, would be accessible. It had taken only a phone call to Lon Cohen at the *Gazette* to learn that she had taken an apartment at the Churchill Towers two months ago, when she had left her husband's roof.

In my pocket was a plain white envelope, sealed, on which I had written by hand:

Mrs. Morton Sorell
Personal and Confidential

and inside it was a card, also handwritten:

We were seen that evening in the lunchroom as we sat in the booth. It would be dangerous for me to phone you or for you to phone me. You can trust the bearer of this card.

No signature. It was twelve minutes to eleven when I handed the envelope to the chargé d'affaires at the lobby desk and asked him to send it up, and it still lacked three minutes of eleven when he motioned me to the elevator.

Those nine minutes had been tough. If it hadn't worked, if word had come down to bounce me, or no word at all, I had no other card ready to play. So as the elevator shot up I was on the rise in more ways than one, and when I stepped out at the thirtieth floor and saw that she herself was standing there in the doorway my face wanted to grin at her but I controlled it.

She had the card in her hand. "You sent this?" she asked.

"I brought it."

She looked me over, down to my toes and back up. "Haven't I seen you before? What's your name?"

"Goodwin. Archie Goodwin. You may have seen my picture in the morning paper."

"Oh." She nodded. "Of course." She lifted the card. "What's this about? It's crazy! Where did you get it?"

"I wrote it." I advanced a step and got a stronger whiff of the perfume of her morning bath—or it could have come from the folds of her yellow robe, which was very informal. "I might as well confess, Mrs. Sorell. It was a trick. I have been at your feet for years. The only pictures in my heart are of you. One smile from you, just for me, would be rapture. I have never tried to meet you because I knew it would be hopeless, but now that you have left your husband I might be able to do something, render some little service, that would earn me a smile. I had to see you and tell you that, and that card was just a trick to get to you. I made it up. I tried to write something that would make you curious enough to see me. Please forgive me!"

She smiled the famous smile, just for me. "You overwhelm me, Mr. Goodwin, you really do. You said that *so* nicely. Have you any particular service in mind?"

I had to hand it to her. She knew darned well I was a double-breasted liar. She knew I hadn't made it up. She knew I was a licensed private detective and had come on business. But she hadn't batted an eye—or rather, she had. Her long dark lashes, which were homegrown and made a fine contrast with her hair, the color of corn silk just before it starts to turn, had lowered for a second to veil the pleasure I was giving her. She was as good offstage as she was on, and I had to hand it to her.

"If I might come in?" I suggested. "Now that you've smiled at me?"

"Of course." She backed up and I entered. She waited while I removed my hat and coat and put them on a chair, then led me through the foyer to a large living room with windows on the east and south, and across to a divan.

"Not many people ever have a chance like this," she said, sitting. "An offer of a service from a famous detective. What shall it be?"

"Well." I sat. "I can sew on buttons."

"So can I." She smiled. Seeing that smile, you would never have dreamed that she was a champion bloodsucker. I was about ready to doubt it myself. It was pleasant to be on the receiving end of it.

"I could walk along behind you," I offered, "and carry your rubbers in case it snows."

"I don't walk much. It might be better to carry a gun. You mentioned my husband. I honestly believe he is capable of hiring someone to kill me. You're handsome—*very* handsome. Are you brave?"

"It depends. I probably would be if you were looking on. By the way, now that I'm here, and this is a day I'll never forget, I might as well ask you something. Since you saw my picture in the paper, I suppose you read about what happened in Nero Wolfe's office yesterday. That woman murdered. Bertha Aaron. Yes?"

"I read part of it." She made a face. "I don't like to read about murders."

"Did you read who she was? Private secretary of Lamont Otis, senior partner of Otis, Edey, Heydecker and Jett, a law firm?"

She shook her head. "I didn't notice."

"I thought you might because they are your husband's attorneys. You know that, of course."

"Oh." Her eyes had widened. "Of course. I didn't notice."

"I guess you didn't read that part. You would have noticed those names, since you know all four of them. What I wanted to ask, did you know Bertha Aaron?"

"No."

"I thought you might, since she was Otis' secretary and they have been your husband's attorneys for years and they handled a case for you once. You never met her?"

"No." She wasn't smiling. "You seem to know a good deal about that firm and my husband. You said that *so* nicely, about being at my feet and my pictures in your heart. So they sent you, or Nero Wolfe did, and he is working for my husband. So?"

"No. He isn't."

"He's working for that law firm, and that's the same thing."

"No. He's working for nobody but himself. He—"

"You're lying."

"I only allow myself so many lies a day and I'm careful not to waste them. Mr. Wolfe is upset because that woman was killed in his office, and he intends to get even. He is working for no one, and he won't be until this is settled. He thought you might have known Bertha Aaron and could tell me something about her that would help."

"I can't."

"That's too bad. I'm still at your feet."

"I like you there. You're *very* handsome." She smiled. "I just had an idea. Would Nero Wolfe work for me?"

"He might. He doesn't like some kinds of jobs. If he did he'd soak you. If he has any pictures in his heart at all, which I doubt, they are not of beautiful women—or even homely ones. What would you want him to do?"

"I would rather tell him."

"For that," I said, "you would have to make an appointment at his office. He never leaves his house on business." I got a card from my case and handed it to her. "There's the address and phone number. Or if you'd like to go now I'd be glad to take you, and he might stretch a point and see you. He'll be free until one o'clock."

"I wonder." She smiled.

"You wonder what?"

"Nothing. I was talking to myself." She shook her head. "I won't go now. Perhaps . . . I'll think it over." She stood up. "I'm sorry I can't help but I had never met that—what was her name?"

"Bertha Aaron." I was on my feet.

"I had never heard of her." She glanced at the card, the one I had handed her. "I may ring you later today. I'll think it over."

She went with me to the foyer, and as I reached for the doorknob she offered a hand and I took it. There was nothing flabby about her clasp.

When you leave an elevator at the lobby floor of the Churchill Towers you have three choices. To the right is the main entrance. To the left and then right is a side entrance, and to the left and left again is another. I left by the main entrance, stopped a moment on the sidewalk to put my cap on and pull at my ear, and then turned downtown, in no hurry.

At the corner I was joined by a little guy with a big nose who looked, at first sight, as if he might make forty bucks a week waxing floors. Actually Saul Panzer was the best operative in the metropolitan area and his rate was ten dollars an hour.

"Any sign of a dick?" I asked him.

"None I know, and I think none I don't know. You saw her?"

"Yeah. I doubt if they are on her. I stung her and she may be moving. The boys are covering?"

"Yes. Fred at the north entrance and Orrie at the south. I hope she takes the front."

"So do I. See you in court."

He wheeled and was gone, and I stepped to the curb and flagged a taxi. It was 11:40 when it rolled to the curb in front of the old brownstone on 35th Street.

Mounting the seven steps to the stoop, using my key to get in, and putting my hat and coat on the rack in the hall, I went to the office. Wolfe would of course be settled in his chair behind his desk with his current book, since his morning session in the plant rooms ended at eleven o'clock. But he wasn't. His chair was empty, but the red leather one was occupied, by a stranger. I kept going for a look at his front, and said good morning. He said good morning.

He was a poet above the neck, with deep-set dreamy eyes, a wide sulky mouth, and a pointed modeled chin, but he would have had to sell a lot of poems to pay for that suit and shirt and tie, not to mention the Parvis of London shoes. Having given him enough of a glance for that, and not caring to ask him where Wolfe was, I returned to the hall and turned left, toward the kitchen; and there, in the alcove at the end of the hall, was Wolfe, standing at the hole.

The hole was through the wall at eye level. On the office side it was covered by a picture of a waterfall. On this side, in the alcove, it was covered by nothing, and you could not only hear through it but also see through it.

I didn't stop. Pushing the two-way door to the kitchen, I held it for Wolfe to enter and then let it swing back.

"You forgot to leave a necktie on your desk," I told him.

He grunted. "We'll discuss that some day, the necktie. That is Gregory Jett. He has spent the morning at the District Attorney's office. I excused myself because I wanted to hear from you before talking with him, and I thought I might as well observe him."

"Good idea. He might have muttered to himself, 'By golly, the rug is gone.' Did he?"

"No. Did you see that woman?"

"Yes, sir. She's a gem. There is now no question about Bertha Aaron's basic fact, that a member of the firm was with Mrs. Sorell in a lunchroom."

"She admitted it?"

"No, sir, but she confirmed it. We talked for twenty minutes, and she never mentioned the card after the first half a minute, when she merely said it was crazy and asked me where I got it. She told me I was handsome twice, she smiled at me six times, she said she had never heard of Bertha Aaron, and she asked if you would work for her. She may phone for an appointment. Do you want it verbatim now?"

"Later will do. The men are there?"

"Yes, I spoke with Saul when I left. That's wasted. She's not a

fool, anything but. Of course it was a blow to her to learn that her
meeting in the lunchroom is known, but she won't panic. Also, of
course, she doesn't know how we got onto it. She may not have
suspected that there was any connection between that meeting and
the murder of Bertha Aaron. It's even possible she doesn't suspect
it now, though that's doubtful. If and when she does, she will also
suspect that the man she was with in the lunchroom killed Bertha
Aaron, and that will be hard to live with, but even then she won't
panic. She is a very tough article and she is still after thirty million
bucks. Looking at her as she smiled at me and told me I was handsome, which may have been her honest opinion in spite of my flat
nose, you would never have guessed that I had just sent her a card
announcing that her pet secret had been spilled. She's a gem. If I
had thirty million I'd be glad to buy her a lunch. What's biting
Gregory Jett?"

"I don't know. We shall see." He pushed the door open and passed
through and I followed.

As Wolfe detoured around the red leather chair Jett spoke: "I said
my business was urgent. You're rather cheeky, aren't you?"

"Moderately so." Wolfe got his mass adjusted in his seat and swiveled to face him. "If there is pressure, sir, it is on you, not on me.
Am I concerned?"

"You are involved." The deep-set dreamy eyes came to me. "Is
your name Archie Goodwin?"

I said yes.

"Last night you gave a statement to the police about your conversation with Bertha Aaron, and you gave a copy of it to Lamont
Otis, the senior member of my firm."

"Did I?" I was polite. "I only work here. I only do what Mr. Wolfe
tells me to. Ask him."

"I'm not asking, I'm telling." He returned to Wolfe. "I want to
know what is in that statement. Mr. Otis is an old man and his
heart is weak. He was under shock when he came here, from the
tragic news of the death of his secretary, who was murdered here
in your office, in circumstances which as far as I know them were
certainly no credit to you or Goodwin. It must have been obvious
that Mr. Otis was under shock, and it was certainly obvious that
he is an old man. To show him that statement was irresponsible and
reprehensible. I want to know what is in it."

Wolfe had leaned back and lowered his chin. "Well. When cheek
meets cheek. You are manifestly indomitable and I must buckle my

breastplate. I choose to deny that there is any such statement. Then?"

"Poppycock. I know there is."

"Your evidence?" Wolfe wiggled a finger. "Mr. Jett. This is fatuous. Someone has told you the statement exists or you would be an idiot to come and bark at me. Who told you, and when?"

"Someone who . . . in whom I have the utmost confidence."

"Mr. Otis himself?"

"No."

"Her name?"

Jett set his teeth on his lower lip. After chewing on it a little he shifted to the upper lip. He had nice white teeth.

"You must be under shock too," Wolfe said, "to suppose you could come with that demand without disclosing the source of your information. Is her name Ann Paige?"

"I will tell you that only in confidence."

"Then I don't want it. I will take it as private information entrusted to my discretion, but not in confidence. I am still denying that such a statement exists."

"Damn you!" Jett hit the arm of his chair. "She was here with him! She saw Goodwin hand it to him! She saw him read it!"

Wolfe nodded. "That's better. When did Miss Paige tell you about it? This morning?"

"No. Last night. She phoned me."

"At what hour?"

"Around midnight. A little after."

"Had she left here with Mr. Otis?"

"You know damn well she hadn't. She had climbed out a window."

"And phoned you at once." Wolfe straightened up. "If you are to trust my discretion you must give it ground. I may then tell you what the statement contains, or I may not. I reject the reason you have given, or implied, for your concern—solicitude for Mr. Otis. Your explanation must account not only for your concern but also for Miss Paige's flight through a window. You—"

"It wasn't a flight! Goodwin had locked the door!"

"He would have opened it on request. You said your business is urgent. How and to whom? You are trying my patience. With your trained legal mind, you know it is futile to feed me inanities."

Jett looked at me. I set my jaw and firmed my lips to show him that I didn't care for inanities either. He went back to Wolfe.

"Very well," he said. "I'll trust your discretion, since there is no alternative. When Otis told Miss Paige she had to leave, she suspected that Miss Aaron had told Goodwin something about me. She thought—"

"Why about you? There had been no hint of it."

"Because he said to her, 'I couldn't trust you on *this*.' She thought he knew that she couldn't be trusted in a matter that concerned me. That is true—I hope it is true. Miss Paige and I are engaged to marry. It has not been announced, but our mutual interest is probably no secret to our associates, since we have made no effort to conceal it. Added to that was the fact that she knew that Miss Aaron might have had knowledge, or at least suspicion, of a certain—uh—episode in which I had been involved. An episode of which Mr. Otis would have violently disapproved. You said my explanation must account both for my concern and for Miss Paige's leaving through a window. It does."

"What was the episode?"

Jett shook his head. "I wouldn't tell you that even in confidence."

"What was its nature?"

"It was a personal matter."

"Did it bear on the interests of your firm or your partners?"

"No. It was strictly personal."

"Did it touch your professional reputation or integrity?"

"It did not."

"Was a woman involved?"

"Yes."

"Her name?"

Jett shook his head. "I'm not a cad, Mr. Wolfe."

"Was it Mrs. Morton Sorell?"

Jett's mouth opened, and for three breaths his jaw muscles weren't functioning. Then he said, "So that was it. Miss Paige was right. I want—I demand to see that statement."

"Not yet, sir. Later, perhaps—or not. Do you maintain that the episode involving Mrs. Sorell had no relation to your firm's interests or your professional integrity?"

"I do. It was purely personal, and it was brief."

"When did it occur?"

"About a year ago."

"When did you last see her?"

"About a month ago, at a party. I didn't speak with her."

"When were you last with her tête-à-tête?"

"I haven't been since—not for nearly a year."

"But you are still seriously perturbed at the chance that Mr. Otis has learned of the episode?"

"Certainly. Mr. Sorell is our client, and his wife is our opponent in a very important matter. Mr. Otis might suspect that the episode is—was not merely an episode. He has not told me of the statement you showed him, and I can't approach him about it because he has ordered Miss Paige not to mention it to anyone, and she didn't tell him she had already told me. I want to see it. I have a right to see it!"

"Don't start barking again." Wolfe rested his elbows on the chair arms and put his fingertips together. "I'll tell you this: there is nothing in the statement, either explicit or allusive, about the episode you have described. That should relieve your mind. Beyond that—"

The doorbell rang.

I was wrong about them. As soon as I got a look at them through the one-way panel I guessed who they were, but I had the labels mixed.

My guess was that the big broad-shouldered one in a dark blue chesterfield tailored to give him a waist, and a homburg to match, was Edey, 55, and the compact little guy in a brown ulster with a belt was Heydecker, 47; but when I opened the door and the chesterfield said they wanted to see Nero Wolfe, and I asked for names, he said, "This gentleman is Frank Edey and I am Miles Heydecker. We are—"

Since age has priority I helped Edey off with his ulster, putting it on a hanger, and let Heydecker manage his chesterfield, then took them to the front room and invited them to sit. If I opened the connecting door to the office Jett's voice could be heard and there was no point in his trusting Wolfe's discretion if he couldn't trust mine; so I went around through the hall, crossed to my desk, wrote *Edey and Heydecker* on my memo pad, tore the sheet off, and handed it to Wolfe. He glanced at it and looked at Jett.

"We're at an impasse. You refuse to answer further questions unless I tell you the contents of the statement, and I won't do that. Mr. Edey and Mr. Heydecker are here. Will you stay or go?"

"Edey?" Jett stood up. "Heydecker? Here?"

"Yes, sir. Uninvited and unexpected. You may leave unseen if you wish."

Evidently he didn't wish anything except to see the statement.

He didn't want to go and he didn't want to stay. When it became apparent that he wasn't going to decide, Wolfe decided for him by giving me a nod, and I went and opened the connecting door and told the newcomers to come in. Then I stepped aside and looked on, at their surprise at seeing Jett, their manners as they introduced themselves to Wolfe, the way they handled their eyes.

I had never completely squelched the idea that when you are in a room with three men and you know that one of them committed a murder, especially when he committed it in that room only eighteen hours ago, it will show if you watch close enough. I knew from experience that the idea wasn't worth a damn, that if you did see something that seemed to point, you were probably wrong, but I still had it and still have it. I was so busy with it that I didn't go to my desk and sit until Jett was back in the red leather chair and the newcomers were on two of the yellow ones, facing Wolfe, and Heydecker, the big broad-shouldered one, was speaking.

His eyes were at Jett. "We came," he said, "for information, and I suppose you did too, Greg. Unless you got more at the D.A.'s office than we did."

"I got damn little," Jett said. "I didn't even see Howie, my old schoolmate. They didn't answer questions, they asked them. A lot of them I didn't answer and they shouldn't have been asked—about our affairs and our clients. Naturally I answered the relevant ones, the routine stuff about my relations with Bertha Aaron and my whereabouts and movements yesterday afternoon. Not only mine, but others'. Particularly if anyone had spoken at length with Bertha, and if anyone had left the office with her or soon after her. Obviously they think she was killed by someone connected with the firm, but they don't say why—at least, not to me."

"Nor to me," Edey said. He was the compact undersized one and his thin tenor fitted him fine.

"Nor to me," Heydecker said. "What has Wolfe told you?"

"Not much. I haven't been here long." Jett looked at Wolfe.

Wolfe obliged. He cleared his throat. "I presume that you gentlemen have come with the same purpose as Mr. Jett. He asks for any information that will give light, with emphasis on the reason for Miss Aaron's coming to see me. He assumes—"

"That's it," Heydecker cut in. "What was she here for?"

"If you please. He assumes from the circumstances that she was killed to prevent a revelation she meant to make, and that is plausible. But surely the police and the District Attorney haven't withheld *all* the details from you. Haven't they told you that she didn't see me?"

"No," Edey said. "They haven't told me."

"Nor me," Heydecker said.

"Then I tell you. She came without an appointment. Mr. Goodwin admitted her. She asked to see me on a confidential matter. I was engaged elsewhere, upstairs, and Mr. Goodwin came to tell me she was here. We had a matter under consideration and discussed it at some length, and when we came down her dead body was here." He pointed at Heydecker's feet. "There. So she couldn't tell me what she came for, since I never saw her alive."

"Then I don't get it," Edey declared. The brilliant idea man was using his brain. "If she didn't tell you, you couldn't tell the police or the District Attorney. But if they don't know what she came to see you about, why do they think she was killed by someone in our office? It's conceivable that they got that information from someone else—but so soon? They started in on me at seven o'clock this morning. And I conclude from their questions that they don't merely think it, they think they know it."

"They do, unquestionably," Heydecker agreed. "Mr. Goodwin. You admitted her. She was alone?" That was the brilliant trial lawyer.

"Yes." Since we weren't before the bench I omitted the "sir."

"You saw no one else around? On the sidewalk?"

"No. Of course it was dark. It was twenty minutes past five. On January fifth the sun sets at 4:46." By gum, he wasn't going to trap me.

"You conducted her to this room?"

"Yes."

"Leaving the outer door open perhaps?"

"No."

"Are you certain of that?"

"Yes. If I have one habit that's totally automatic, it's closing that door and making sure it's locked."

"Automatic habits are dangerous things, Mr. Goodwin. Sometimes they fail you. When you brought her to this room did you sit?"

"Yes."

"Where?"

"Where I am now."

"Where did she sit?"

"About where you are. About three feet closer to me."

"What did she say?"

"That she wanted to see Nero Wolfe about something urgent. No, she said that at the door. She said her case was private and very confidential."

"She used the word 'case'?"

"Yes."

"What else did she say?"

"That her name was Bertha Aaron and she was the private secretary of Mr. Lamont Otis, senior partner in the law firm of Otis, Edey, Heydecker and Jett."

"What else did she say?"

Naturally I had known that the time would come to lie, and decided this was it. "Nothing," I said.

"Absolutely nothing?"

"Right."

"You are Nero Wolfe's confidential assistant. He was engaged elsewhere. Do you expect me to believe that you did not insist on knowing the nature of her case before you went to him?"

The phone rang. "Not if you'd rather not," I said, and swiveled, lifted the receiver. "Nero Wolfe's residence, Archie Goodwin speaking."

I recognized the voice: "This is Rita Sorell, Mr. Goodwin. I have decided—"

"Hold it please. Just a second." I pressed a palm over the transmitter and told Wolfe, "That woman you sent a card to. The one who told me I was handsome." He reached for his receiver and put it to his ear and I returned to mine. "Okay. You have decided—?"

"I have decided that it will be best to tell you what you came this morning to find out. I have decided that you were too clever for me, not mentioning at all what you had written on the card, when that was what you came for. Your saying that you made it up, that you tried to write something that would make me curious—you didn't expect me to believe that. You were too clever for me. So I might as well confess, since you already know it. I did sit with a man in a booth in a lunchroom one evening last week—what evening was it?"

"Monday."

"That's right. And you want to know who the man was?"

"It would help."

"I want to help. You are *very* handsome. His name is Gregory Jett."

"Many thanks. If you want to help—"

She had hung up.

I cradled the receiver and rotated my chair. Wolfe pushed his phone back and said, "She is a confounded nuisance."

"Yes, sir."

"I suppose we'll have to humor her."

"Yes, sir. Or shoot her."

"Not a welcome option." He arose. "Gentlemen, I must ask you to excuse us. Come, Archie."

He headed for the hall and I got up and followed. Turning left, he pushed the door to the kitchen. Fritz was there at the big table, chopping an onion. The door swung shut.

Wolfe turned to face me. "Very well. You know her. You have seen her and talked with her. What about it?"

"I'd have to toss a coin. Several coins. You have seen Jett and talked with him. It could be that she merely wanted to find out if we already knew who it was, and if so she might have named the right one and she might not. Or it might have been a real squeal; she decided that Jett killed Bertha Aaron, and either she loves justice no matter what it costs her, or she was afraid Jett might break and her spot would be too hot for comfort. I prefer the latter. Or it wasn't Jett, it was Edey or Heydecker, and she is trying to ball it up—and she may be sore at Jett on account of the episode. If it backfires, if we already know it was Edey or Heydecker, what the hell. Telling me on the phone isn't swearing to it on the stand. She can deny she called me. Or she might—"

"That's enough for now. Have you a choice?"

"No, sir. I told you she's a gem."

He grunted. He reached for a piece of onion, put it in his mouth, and chewed. When it was down he asked Fritz, "Ebenezer?" and Fritz told him no, Elite. He turned to me: "In any case, she has ripped it open. Even if she is merely trying to muddle it we can't afford to assume that she hadn't communicated with him—or soon will."

"She couldn't unless he phoned her. They've been at the D.A.'s office all morning."

He nodded. "Then we'll tell him first. You'll have to recant."

"Right. Do we save anything?"

"I think not. The gist first and we'll see."

He made for the door. In the hall we heard a voice from the office, Edey's thin tenor, but it stopped as we appeared.

When Wolfe was settled in his chair he said, "Gentlemen, Mr. Goodwin and I have decided that you deserve candor. That was Mrs. Morton Sorell on the phone. What she said persuaded us—"

"Did you say *Sorell?*" Heydecker demanded. He was gawking and so was Edey. Evidently Jett never gawked.

"I did. —Archie?"

I focused on Heydecker. "If she had called twenty seconds earlier," I told him, "I wouldn't have had to waste a lie. I did insist on knowing the nature of Bertha Aaron's case before I went to Mr. Wolfe, and she told me. She said she had accidentally seen a member of the firm in secret conference with Mrs. Morton Sorell, the firm's opponent in an important case. She said that after worrying about it for a week she had told him about it that afternoon, yesterday, and asked for an explanation, and he didn't have one, so she concluded he was a traitor. She said she was afraid to tell Mr. Otis because he had a weak heart and it might kill him, and she wouldn't tell another firm member because he might be a traitor too. So she had come to Nero Wolfe."

I had been wrong about Jett. Now he was gawking too. He found his tongue first: "This is incredible. I don't believe it!"

"Nor I," Heydecker said.

"Nor I," Edey said, his tenor a squeak.

"Do you expect us to believe," Heydecker demanded, "that Bertha Aaron would come to an outsider with a story that would gravely damage the firm if it became known?"

Wolfe cut in. "No more cross-examination, Mr. Heydecker. I indulged you before, but not now. If questions are to be asked I'll do the asking. As for Mr. Goodwin's bona fides, he has given a signed statement to the police, and he is not an ass. Also—"

"The police?" Edey squeaked.

"It's absolutely incredible," Jett declared.

Wolfe ignored them. "Also I allowed Mr. Otis to read a copy of the statement when he came here last night. He agreed not to divulge its contents before ten o'clock tomorrow morning, to give me till then to plan a course—a course based on the natural assumption that Miss Aaron was killed by the man she had accused of treachery—an assumption I share with the police. Evidently the police have preferred to reserve the statement, and so have I, but not now—since Mrs. Sorell has named the member of your firm she was seen with. On the phone just now. One of you."

"This isn't real," Edey squeaked. "This is a nightmare."

Heydecker sputtered, "Do you dare to suggest—"

"No, Mr. Heydecker." Wolfe flattened a palm on his desk. "I will not submit to questioning; I will choose the facts I'm willing to share. I suggest nothing; I am reporting. I neglected to say that Miss Aaron did not name the member of the firm she had seen with Mrs. Sorell. Now Mrs. Sorell has named him, but I am not satisfied of her veracity. Mr. Goodwin saw her this morning and found her devious. I'm not going to tell you whom she named, and that will make the pressure on one of you almost unendurable."

The pressure wasn't exactly endurable for any of them. They were exchanging glances, and they weren't glances of sympathy and partnership. In a spot like that the idea I mentioned might be expected to work, but it didn't. Two of them were really suspicious of their partners and one was only pretending to be, but it would have taken a better man than me to pick him; better even than Wolfe, whose eyes, narrowed to slits, were taking them in.

He was going on: "The obvious assumption is that one of you followed Miss Aaron when she left your offices yesterday after she had challenged you, and when you saw her enter my house your alarm became acute. One of you sought a telephone and rang this number. In Mr. Goodwin's absence she answered the phone, and consented to admit you. If you can—"

"But it was pure chance that she was alone," Edey objected. The idea man.

"Pfui. If I'm not answering questions, Mr. Edey, neither am I debating trifles. With your trained minds that is no knot for you. Speaking again to one of you: if you could be identified by inquiry into your whereabouts and movements yesterday afternoon the police would have the job already done and you would be in custody. All that they have been told by you and by the entire personnel of your office is being checked by men well qualified for the task. But since they have reserved the information supplied by Mr. Goodwin, I doubt if they have asked you about Monday evening of last week. Eight days ago. Have they?"

"Why should they?" It was Jett.

"Because that was when one of you was seen by Miss Aaron in conference with Mrs. Sorell. I'm going to ask you now—but first I should tell you of an understanding I had with Mr. Otis last night. In exchange for information he furnished I agreed that in exposing the murderer I would minimize, as far as possible, the damage to the reputation of his firm. I will observe that agreement—so man-

ifestly, for two of you, the sooner this is over the better. —Mr. Jett.
How did you spend Monday evening, December 29th, from six o'clock
to midnight?"

Jett's eyes were still deep-set, but they were no longer dreamy.
They had been glued on Wolfe ever since I had recanted, and he
hadn't moved a muscle. He said, "If this is straight, if all you've said
is true, including the phone call from Mrs. Sorell, the damage to
the firm is done and you can do nothing to minimize it. No one can."

"I can try. And I intend to."

"How?"

"By meeting contingencies as they arise."

Heydecker put in, "You say Mr. Otis knows all this? He was here
last night?"

"Yes. I am not a parrot and you are not deaf.—Well, Mr. Jett?
Monday evening of last week?"

"I was at a theater with a friend."

"The friend's name?"

"Miss Ann Paige."

"What theater?"

"The Drew. The play was *Practice Makes Perfect*. Miss Paige and
I left the office together shortly before six and had dinner at Rus-
terman's. We were together continuously until after midnight."

"Thank you. Mr. Edey?"

"That was the Monday before New Year's," Edey said. "I got home
before six o'clock and ate dinner there and was there all evening."

"Alone?"

"No. My son and his wife and two children spent the holiday week
with us. They went to the opera with my wife and daughter, and
I stayed home with the children."

"How old are the children?"

"Two and four."

"Where is your home?"

"An apartment. Park Avenue and 69th Street."

"Did you go out at all?"

"No."

"Thank you. Mr. Heydecker?"

"I was at the Manhattan Chess Club watching the tournament.
Bobby Fischer won his adjourned game with Weinstein in fifty-eight
moves. Larry Evans drew with Kalme, and Reshevsky drew with
Mednis."

"Where is the Manhattan Chess Club?"

"West 65th Street."

"Did play start at six o'clock?"

"Certainly not. I was in court all day and had things to do at the office. My secretary and I had sandwiches at my desk."

"What time did you leave the office?"

"Around eight o'clock. My secretary would know."

"What time did you arrive at the chess club?"

"Fifteen or twenty minutes after I left the office." Heydecker suddenly moved and was on his feet. "This is ridiculous," he declared. "You may be on the square, Wolfe, I don't know. If you are, God help us." He turned. "I'm going to see Otis. You coming, Frank?"

He was. The brilliant idea man, judging from his expression, had none at all. He pulled his feet back, moved his head slowly from side to side to tell hope goodbye, and arose. They didn't ask the 11% partner to join them, and apparently he wasn't going to, but as I was reaching for Edey's ulster on the hall rack here came Jett, and when I opened the door he was the first one out.

I stood on the stoop, getting a breath of air, and watched them heading for Ninth Avenue three abreast, a solid front of mutual trust and understanding, in a pig's eye.

In the office Wolfe was leaning back with his eyes closed. As I reached my desk the phone rang. It was Saul Panzer, to report that there had been no sign of Mrs. Sorell. I told him to hold the wire and relayed it to Wolfe, and asked if he wanted to put them on the alibis we had just collected. "Pfui," he said, and I told Saul to carry on.

I swiveled. "I was afraid," I said, "that you might be desperate enough to try it, checking their alibis. It's very interesting, the different ways there are of cracking a case. It depends on who you are. If you're just a top-flight detective, me for instance, all you can do is detect. You'd rather go after an alibi than eat. When you ask a man where he was at eleven minutes past eight you put it in your notebook and then wear out a pair of shoes looking for somebody who says he was somewhere else. But if you're a genius you don't give a damn about alibis. You ask him where he was only to keep the conversation going while you wait for something to click. You don't even listen—"

"Nonsense," he growled. "They have no alibis."

I nodded. "You didn't listen."

"I did listen. Their alibis are worthless. One with his fiancée, one watching a chess tournament, one at home with young children in

bed asleep. Bah. I asked on the chance that one of them, possibly
two, might be eliminated, but no. There are still three."

"Then genius is all that's left. Unless you have an idea for another
card I could take to Mrs. Sorell. I wouldn't mind. I like the way she
says *very*."

"No doubt. Could you do anything with her?"

"I could try. She might possibly make another decision—for instance, to sign a statement. Or if she has decided to hire you I could
bring her, and you could have a go at her yourself. She has marvelous
eyelashes."

He grunted. "It may come to that. We'll see after lunch. It may
be that after they have talked with Mr. Otis—yes, Fritz?"

"Lunch is ready, sir."

I never got to check an alibi, but it was a close shave. Who made
it close was Inspector Cramer.

Since Wolfe refuses to work either his brain or his tongue on
business at table, and a murder case is business even when he has
no client and no fee is in prospect, no progress was made during
lunch, but when we returned to the office he buckled down and tried
to think of something for me to do.

The trouble was, the problem was too damn simple. We knew that
one of three men had committed murder, and how and when. Okay,
which one? Eeny meeny murder mo.

Even the why was plain enough: Mrs. Sorell had hooked him with
an offer, either of a big slice of the thirty million she was after or
of more personal favors.

Any approach you could think of was already cluttered with cops,
except Mrs. Sorell, and even if I got to her again I had nothing to
use for a pry. What it called for was a good stiff dose of genius, and
apparently Wolfe's was taking the day off. Sitting there in the office
after lunch I may have got a little too personal with him or he
wouldn't have bellowed at me to go ahead and check their alibis.

"Glad to," I said, and went to the hall for my hat and coat, and
saw visitors on the stoop, not strangers. I opened the door just as
Cramer pushed the bell button, and inquired, "Have you an appointment?"

"I have in my pocket," he said, "a warrant for your arrest as a
material witness. Also one for Wolfe. I warned you."

There were two ways of looking at it. One was that he didn't mean
to shoot unless he had to. If he had really wanted to haul us in he

would have sent a couple of dicks after us instead of coming himself with Sergeant Purley Stebbins. The other was that here was a good opportunity to teach Wolfe a lesson. A couple of the right kind of impolite remarks would have made Cramer sore enough to go ahead and serve the warrants, and spending several hours in custody, and possibly all night, would probably cure Wolfe of leaving neckties on his desk.

But I would have had to go along, which wouldn't have been fair, so I wheeled and marched to the office, relying on Purley to shut the door, and told Wolfe, "Cramer and Stebbins with warrants. An inspector to take you and a sergeant to take me, which is an honor."

He glared at me and then transferred it to them as they entered.

Cramer said, "I warned you last night," draped his coat on the arm of the red leather chair, and sat.

Wolfe snorted. "Tommyrot."

Cramer took papers from his pocket. "I'll serve these only if I have to. If I do I know what will happen: you'll refuse to talk and so will Goodwin, and you'll be out on bail as soon as Parker can swing it. But it will be on your record and that won't close it. Held as a material witness is one thing, and charged with interfering with the operation of justice is another. In the interest of justice we were withholding the contents of the statements you and Goodwin gave us, and you know it, and you revealed them. To men suspected of murder. Frank Edey has admitted it. He phoned an Assistant D. A."

The brilliant idea man again.

"He's a jackass," Wolfe declared.

"Yeah. Since you told them in confidence."

"I did not. I asked for no pledges and got none. But I made it plain that if I put my finger on the murderer before you do I'll protect that law firm from injury as far as possible. If Mr. Edey is innocent it was to his interest not to have me interrupted by you. If he's guilty, all the worse."

"Who's your client? Otis?"

"I have no client. I am going to avenge an affront to my dignity and self-esteem. Your threat to charge me with interference with the operation of justice is puerile. I am not meddling in a matter that does not concern me. I cannot escape the ignominy of having my necktie presented in a courtroom as an exhibit of the prosecution; I may even have to suffer the indignity of being called to the stand to identify it; but I want the satisfaction of exposing the culprit who used it. In telling Mr. Otis and his partners what Miss Aaron said

to Mr. Goodwin, in revealing the nature of the menace to their firm,
I served my legitimate personal interest and I violated no law."

"You knew damn well we were withholding it!"

Wolfe's shoulders went up an eighth of an inch. "I am not bound
to respect your tactics, either by statute or by custom. You and I
are not lawyers; ask the District Attorney if a charge would hold."
He upturned a palm. "Mr. Cramer. This is pointless. You have a
warrant for my arrest as a material witness?"

"Yes. And one for Goodwin."

"But you don't serve them, for the reason you have given, so they
are only cudgels for you to brandish. To what end? What do you
want?"

A low growl escaped Sergeant Purley Stebbins, who had stayed
on his feet behind Cramer's chair. There is one thing that would
give Purley more pleasure than to take Wolfe or me in, and that
would be to take both of us. Wolfe handcuffed to him and me cuffed
to Wolfe would be perfect. The growl was for disappointment and
I gave him a sympathetic grin as he went to a chair and sat.

"I want the truth," Cramer said.

"Pfui," Wolfe said.

Cramer nodded. "Phooey is right. If I take Goodwin's statement
as it stands, if he put nothing in and left nothing out, one of those
three men—Edey, Heydecker, Jett—one of them killed Bertha
Aaron. I don't have to go into that. You agree?"

"Yes."

"But if a jury takes Goodwin's statement as it stands it would be
impossible to get one of those men convicted. She got here at 5:20,
and he was with her in this room until 5:39, when he went up to
you in the plant rooms. It was 6:10 when he returned and found the
body. All right, now for them. If one of them had a talk with her
yesterday afternoon, or if one of them left the office when she did,
or just before or just after, we can't pin it down. We haven't so far
and I doubt if we will. They have private offices; their secretaries
are in other rooms. Naturally we're still checking on movements
and phone calls and other details, but it comes down to this. —That
list, Purley."

Stebbins got a paper from his pocket, handed it over, and Cramer
studied it briefly. "They had a conference scheduled for 5:30 on some
corporation case, no connection with Sorell. In Frank Edey's office.
Edey was there when Jett came in a minute or two before 5:30. They
were there together when Heydecker came at 5:45. Heydecker said

he had gone out on an errand which took longer than he expected. The three of them stayed there, discussing the case, until 6:35. So even if you erase Edey and Jett and take Heydecker, what have you got? Goodwin says he left her here, alive, at 5:39. They say Heydecker joined the conference at 5:45. That gives him six minutes after tailing her here to phone this number, come and be admitted by her, kill her, and get back to that office more than a mile away. Phooey. And one of them couldn't have come and killed her after the conference. On that I don't have to take what Goodwin says; he phoned in and reported it at 6:31, and the conference lasted to 6:35. How do you like it?"

Wolfe was scowling at him. "Not at all. What was Heydecker's errand?"

"He went to three theaters to buy tickets. You might think a man with his income would get them through a ticket broker, but he's close. We've checked that. They don't remember him at the theaters."

"Did either Edey or Jett leave the office at all between 4:30 and 5:30?"

"Not known. They say they didn't, and no one says they did, but it's open. What difference does it make, since even Heydecker is out?"

"Not much. And of course the assumption that one of them hired a thug to kill her isn't tenable."

"Certainly not. Here in your office with your necktie? Nuts. You can take your pick of three assumptions. One." Cramer stuck a finger up. "They're lying. That conference didn't start at 5:30 and/or Heydecker didn't join them at 5:45. Two." Another finger. "When Bertha Aaron said 'member of the firm' she merely meant one of the lawyers associated with the firm. There are nineteen of them. If Goodwin's statement is accurate I doubt it. Three." Another finger. "Goodwin's statement is a phony. She didn't say 'member of the firm.' God knows what she did say. It may be *all* phony. I admit that can never be proved, since she's dead, and no matter what the facts turn out to be when we get them he can still claim that's what she said. Take your pick."

Wolfe grunted. "I reject the last. Granting that Mr. Goodwin is capable of so monstrous a hoax, I would have to be a party to it, since he reported to me on his conversation with Miss Aaron before she died—or while she died. I also reject the second. As you know, I talked with Mr. Otis last night. He was positive that she would not have used that phrase, 'member of the firm,' in any but its literal sense."

"Look, Wolfe." Cramer uncrossed his legs and put his feet flat. "You admit you want the glory of getting him before we do."

"Not the glory. The satisfaction."

"Okay. I understand that. I can imagine how you felt when you saw her lying there with your own necktie around her throat. I know how fast your mind works when it has to. It would take you two seconds to realize that Goodwin's report of what she had told him could never be checked. You wanted the satisfaction of getting him. It would take you maybe five minutes to think it over and tell Goodwin how to fake his report so we would spend a couple of days chasing around getting nowhere. With your damn ego that would seem to you perfectly all right. You wouldn't be obstructing justice; you would be bringing a murderer *to* justice. Remembering the stunts I have seen you pull, do you deny you would be capable of that?"

"No. Given sufficient impulse, no. But I didn't. Let me settle this. I am convinced that when Mr. Goodwin came to the plant rooms and told me what Miss Aaron had said to him he reported fully and accurately, and the statement he signed corresponds in every respect with what he told me. So if you came, armed with warrants, to challenge it, you're wasting your time and mine. —Archie, get Mr. Parker."

Since the number of Nathaniel Parker, Wolfe's lawyer, was one of those I knew best and I didn't have to consult the book, I swiveled and dialed. When I had him Wolfe got on his phone.

"Mr. Parker? Good afternoon. Mr. Cramer is here waving warrants at Mr. Goodwin and me . . . No. Material witnesses. He may or may not serve them. Please have your secretary ring my number every ten minutes. If Fritz tells you that we have gone with Mr. Cramer you will know what to do . . . Yes, of course. Thank you."

As he hung up, Cramer left his chair, spoke to Stebbins, got his coat from the chair arm, and tramped out, with Purley at his heels. I stepped to the hall to see that both of them were outside when the door shut.

When I returned, Wolfe was leaning back with his eyes closed, his fists on his chair arms, and his mouth working. When he does that with his lips, pushing them out and pulling them in, out and in, he is not to be interrupted, so I crossed to my desk and sat. That can last anywhere from two minutes to half an hour.

That time it wasn't much more than two minutes. He opened his eyes, straightened up, and growled, "Did he omit the fourth assumption deliberately? Has it occurred to him?"

"I doubt it. He was concentrating on us. But it soon will."

"It has occurred to you?"

"Sure. From that timetable it's obvious. When it does occur to him he'll probably mess it up. It's not the kind he's good at."

He nodded. "We must forestall him. Can you get her here?"

"I can try. I supposed that was what you were working at. I can make a stab at it on the phone, and if that doesn't work we can invent another card trick. When do you want her? Now?"

"No. I must have time to contrive a plan. What time is it?" He would have had to twist his neck to look up at the wall clock.

"Ten after three."

"Say six o'clock. We must also have all the others."

I dialed and asked for Mrs. Morton Sorell, and after a wait heard a voice I had heard before.

"Mrs. Sorell's apartment. Who is it, please?"

"This is Archie Goodwin, Mrs. Sorell. I'm calling from Nero Wolfe's office. A police inspector was here for a talk with Mr. Wolfe and just left. Before that three men you know were here—Edey and Heydecker and Jett. There have been some very interesting developments, and Mr. Wolfe would like to discuss them with you before he makes up his mind about something. You were asking this morning if he would work for you, and that's one possibility. Would six o'clock suit you?"

Silence. Then her voice: "What are the developments?"

"Mr. Wolfe would rather tell you himself. I'm sure you'll find them interesting."

"Why can't he come here?"

"Because as I told you, he never leaves his house on business."

"You do. You come. Come now."

"I would love to, but some other time. Mr. Wolfe wants to discuss it with you himself."

Silence. Then: "Will the policeman be there?"

"Certainly not."

Silence, then: "You say at six?"

"That's right."

"Very well. I'll come."

I hung up, turned, and told Wolfe, "All set. She wants me to come there but that will have to wait. You have less than three hours to cook up a charade, and for two of them you'll be up with the orchids. Anything for me?"

"Get Mr. Otis," he muttered.

I felt then, and I still feel, that it was a waste of money to have Saul and Fred and Orrie there; and since we had no client it was Wolfe's money. When Saul phoned in at five o'clock I could just as well have told him to call it a day. I do not claim that I can handle five people all having a fit at once, even if one of them is seventy-five years old and another one is a woman; but there was no reason to suppose that more than one of them would really explode, and I could certainly handle him. But when Saul phoned I followed instructions, and there went sixty bucks.

They weren't visible when, at eight minutes after six, the bell rang and I went and opened the door to admit Rita Sorell, nor when I escorted her to the office, introduced her to Wolfe, and draped her fur coat, probably milky mink, over the back of the red leather chair. No one was visible but Wolfe. The fact that she gave Wolfe a smile and fluttered her long dark lashes at him didn't mean that she was a snob; I had got mine in the hall.

"I'm not in the habit," she told him, "of going to see men when they send for me. This is a new experience. Maybe that's why I came; I like new experiences. Mr. Goodwin said you wanted to discuss something?"

Wolfe nodded. "I do. Something private and personal. And since the discussion will be more productive if it is frank and unreserved, we should be alone. —If you please, Archie? No notes will be needed."

I objected. "Mrs. Sorell might want to ask me—"

"No. Leave us, please."

I went. Shutting the door as I entered the hall, I turned right, went and opened the door to the front room, entered, shut that door too, and glanced around.

All was in order. Lamont Otis was in the big chair by a window, the one Ann Paige had left by, and she was on one side of him and Edey on the other. Jett's chair was tilted back against the wall to the right. On the couch facing me was Heydecker, in between Fred Durkin and Orrie Cather. Saul Panzer stood in the center of the room. Their faces all came to me and Edey started to speak.

I cut him off. "If you talk," I said, "you won't hear, and even if you don't want to hear, others do. You can talk later. As Mr. Wolfe told you, a speaker behind the couch is wired to a mike in his office, and he is there talking with someone. Since you'll recognize her voice, I don't need to name her."

Saul, who had moved to the rear of the couch, flipped the switch and Wolfe's voice sounded: ". . . and she described her problem to Mr. Goodwin before he came up to me. She said that on Monday evening of last week she saw a member of the firm in a booth in a lunchroom in secret conference with you; that she had concluded he was betraying the interests of one of the firm's clients to you, the client being your husband; that for reasons she thought cogent she would not tell another member or members of the firm; that she had finally, yesterday afternoon, told the one she was accusing and asked for an explanation, and got none; that she refused to name him until she had spoken with me; and that she had come to engage my services. Mr. Goodwin has of course reported this to the police."

MRS. SORELL: "She didn't name him?"

WOLFE: "No. As I said, Mrs. Sorell, this discussion should be frank and unreserved. I am not going to pretend that you have named him and are committed. You told Mr. Goodwin on the phone today that you were with a man in a booth in a lunchroom last Monday evening, and you said his name is Gregory Jett; but you could have been merely scattering dust."

Jett had caused a slight commotion by jerking forward in his tilted chair, but not enough to drown the voice, and a touch on his arm by me had stopped him.

MRS. SORELL: "What if I don't deny it and name Gregory?"

WOLFE: "I wouldn't advise you to. If in addition to scattering dust you were gratifying an animus you'll have to try again. It wasn't Mr. Jett. It was Mr. Heydecker."

Heydecker couldn't have caused any commotion even if he had wanted to, with Fred at one side of him and Orrie at the other. The only commotion came from Lamont Otis, who moved and made a choking noise.

MRS. SORELL: "That's interesting. Mr. Goodwin said I would find it interesting, and I do. So I sat in a booth with a man and didn't know who he was? Really, Mr. Wolfe!"

WOLFE: "No, madam. I assure you it won't do. I'll expound it. I assumed that one of three men—Edey, Heydecker, or Jett—had killed Bertha Aaron. In view of what she told Mr. Goodwin it was more than an assumption, it was a conclusion. But three hours ago I had to abandon it, when I learned that those three were in conference together in Mr. Edey's office at 5:45. It was 5:39 when Mr.

Goodwin left Miss Aaron to come up to me. That they were lying, that they were in a joint conspiracy, was most unlikely, especially since others on the premises could probably impeach them. But though none of them could have killed her, one of them could have provoked her doom, wittingly or not. Of the three, only Mr. Heydecker was known to have left the offices around the same time as Miss Aaron—he had said on a personal errand, but his movements could not be checked. My new assumption, not yet a conclusion, was that he had followed her to this address and seen her enter my house, had sought a phone and called you to warn you that your joint intrigue might soon be exposed, and then, in desperation, had scurried back to his office, arriving fifteen minutes late for the conference."

It was Edey's turn to make a commotion and he obliged. He left his chair, moved to the couch, and stood staring down at Heydecker.

WOLFE: "Now, however, that assumption is a conclusion, and I don't expect to abandon it. Mr. Heydecker does not believe, and neither do I, that on receiving his phone call you came here determined to murder. Indeed, you couldn't have, since you could have no expectation of finding her alone. Mr. Heydecker believes that you merely intended to salvage what you could—at best to prevent the disclosure, at worst to learn where you stood. You called this number and she answered and agreed to admit you and hear you. Mr. Heydecker believes that when you entered and found that she was alone and that she had not yet seen me, it was on sudden impulse that you seized the paperweight and struck her. He believes that when you saw her sink to the floor, unconscious, and then noticed the necktie on this desk, the impulse carried you on. He believes that you—"

MRS. SORELL: "How do you know what he believes?"

That would have been my cue if I were needed. I had been instructed to use my judgment. If Heydecker's reaction made it doubtful I was to get to the office with a signal before Wolfe had gone too far to hedge. It was no strain at all on my judgment. Heydecker was hunched forward, face covered by his hands.

WOLFE: "A good question. I am not in his skull. I should have said, he *says* he believes. You might have known, madam, that he couldn't possibly stand the pressure. Disclosure of his treachery to his firm will end his professional career, but concealment of guilty knowledge of a murder might have ended his life."

MRS. SORELL: "If he says he believes I killed that woman he's lying. He killed her. He's a rat and a liar. He phoned me twice yesterday, first to tell me that we had been seen in the lunchroom, to warn me, and again about an hour later to say that he had dealt with it, that our plan was safe. So he killed her. When Mr. Goodwin told me there had been developments I knew what it was—I knew he would lie. He's a rat. That's why I came. I admit I concealed guilty knowledge of a murder, and I know that was wrong, but it's not too late. Is it too late?"

WOLFE: "No. A purge can both clean your conscience and save your skin. What time did he phone you the second time?"

MRS. SORELL: "I don't know exactly. It was between five and six. Around half-past five."

WOLFE: "What was the plan he had made safe?"

MRS. SORELL: "Of course he has lied about that too. It was his plan. He came to me about a month ago and said he could give me information about my husband that I could use to make . . . that I could use to get my rights. He wanted—"

Heydecker jerked his head up and yapped, "That's a lie! I didn't go to her, she came to me!" That added to my knowledge of human nature. He hadn't uttered a peep when she accused him of murder.

MRS. SORELL: ". . . he wanted me to agree to pay him a million dollars for it, but I couldn't because I didn't know how much I would get, and I finally said I would pay him one-tenth of what I got. That was that evening at the lunchroom."

WOLFE: "Has he given you the information?"

MRS. SORELL: "No. He wanted too much in advance. Of course that was the difficulty. We couldn't put it in writing and sign it."

WOLFE: "No, indeed. A signed document is of little value when neither party would dare to produce it. I presume you realize, Mrs. Sorell, that your purge will have to include your appearance on the stand at a murder trial. Are you prepared to testify under oath?"

MRS. SORELL: "I suppose I'll have to. I knew I would have to when I decided to come to see you."

WOLFE (in a new tone, the snap of a whip): "Then you're a dunce, madam."

Again that would have been my cue if I were needed. The whole point of the set-up—having the four members of the firm in the front room listening in—was to get Heydecker committed before witnesses. If his nerve had held it would have been risky for Wolfe to crack the whip. But Heydecker was done for.

MRS. SORELL: "Oh, no, Mr. Wolfe. I'm not a dunce."

WOLFE: "But you are. One detail alone would pin the murder on you. After you rang this number yesterday afternoon, and Miss Aaron answered, and you spoke with her, you got here as quickly as possible. Since you were not *then* contemplating murder, there was no reason for you to use caution. I don't know if you have a car and chauffeur, but even if you have, to send for it would have meant delay, and minutes were precious. There is no crosstown subway. Buses, one downtown and one crosstown, would have been far too slow.

So unquestionably you took a cab. In spite of the traffic that would have been much faster than walking. The doorman at the Churchill probably summoned one for you, but even if he didn't it will be a simple matter to find it. I need only telephone Mr. Cramer, the police inspector who was here this afternoon, and suggest that he locate the cab driver who picked you up at or near the Churchill yesterday afternoon and drove you to this address. In fact, that is what I intend to do, and that will be enough to sink you, madam."

Ann Paige stood up. She was in a fix. She wanted to go to Gregory Jett, where her eyes already were, but she didn't want to leave Lamont Otis, who was slumped in his chair. Luckily Jett saw her difficulty, went to her, and put an arm around her. It scored a point for romance that he could have a thought for personal matters at the very moment his firm was getting a clout on the jaw.

WOLFE: "I shall also suggest that he send a man here to take you in hand until the cab driver is found. If you ask why I don't proceed to do this, why I first announced it to you, I confess a weakness. I am savoring a satisfaction. I am getting even with you. Twenty-five hours ago, in this room, you subjected me to the severest humiliation I have suffered for many years. I will not say it gives me pleasure, but I confess it—"

There was a combination of sounds from the speaker behind the couch: a kind of cry or squeal, presumably from Mrs. Sorell, a sort of scrape or flutter, and what might have been a grunt from Wolfe.

I dived for the connecting door and went with it as I swung it open, and kept going; but two paces short of Wolfe's desk I halted to take in a sight I have never seen before and never expect to see again—Nero Wolfe with his arms tight around a beautiful young woman in his lap, pinning her arms, hugging her close. I stood paralyzed.

"Archie!" he roared. "Confound it, get her!"

I obeyed . . .

I would like to be able to report that Wolfe got somewhere with his effort to minimize the damage to the firm, but I have to be candid and accurate. He tried, but there wasn't much he could do, since Heydecker was the chief witness for the prosecution at the trial and was cross-examined for six hours. Of course that finished him professionally.

Wolfe had better luck with another effort: the D.A. finally conceded that I was competent to identify Exhibit C, a brown silk necktie with little yellow curlicues, and Wolfe wasn't called. Evidently the jury agreed with the D.A., since it took them only three hours to bring in a verdict of guilty.

At that, the firm is still doing business at the old stand, and Lamont Otis still comes to the office five days a week. I hear that since Gregory Jett's marriage to Ann Paige he has quit being careless about the balance between income and outgo. I don't know if his 11% cut has been boosted. That's a confidential matter.

John D. MacDonald

Man in a Trap

*"There was a curiously unreal flavor about the situation. It was
something you knew could happen. But it never did. Until right
now"... A cool crisp crime story by the creator of Travis
McGee...*

When Joe Conroy walked from the supermarket to his parked
car with the bag of groceries on a late Saturday afternoon, he
looked at the black sky in the west and hoped the rain would hold
off until he could get the grass cut. He was a gangling, freckled
man, part owner and manager of a small and profitable trucking
line. He put the groceries in the back on the floor and got behind
the wheel.

As he looked back over his left shoulder, preparing to back out,
the car door on the other side opened. He turned his head in time
to see a big man step into the car quickly and pull the door shut.

The man was blond and in his twenties. His forehead and nose
were peeling from recent sunburn. His features were heavy and
brutal. He wore jeans, a pale blue sports shirt, and a cheap-looking
dark blue corduroy jacket. He held a small automatic pistol in his
right hand. He held it low, with the barrel aimed at Joe Conroy's
waist. He brought a whisky smell into the car, and a smell of perspiration.

"What do you want?" Joe asked, and was pleased because his voice
sounded a lot more calm than he felt.

The man moved closer and suddenly slapped the barrel against
the point of Joe's knee. It hurt.

"Hey!"

"This is real, ole buddy. You just drive. Go west on Oak and turn
north at the boulevard light. Take it nice and easy and careful. I'm
a nervous man today."

"You can get in a lot of—"

"No talk. Drive."

Joe did as he was told. He had long since decided he was not the
hero type. When they said hands up, Joe's hands would go up. When

they said turn around, he'd turn around. A big dead hero would be no help to Marty and the kids.

There was a curiously unreal flavor about the situation. It was something you knew could happen. But it never did. Until right now. Bang on the brakes and bust his head against the windshield. Sure. And if you lived maybe they'd let you keep the slugs they took out of you. On the mantel, mounted in plastic.

"How far?"

The gun barrel hit him on the knee again. "Just drive, dad." The blond man was as tensely alert as an animal.

Joe saw where he had made a mistake when he had dreamed up such an incident. You imagined the criminal would be somebody you could reason with. This man was big, ugly, irrational, and unpredictable.

Ten miles north of the city he said, "Turn in up there on the right. That Sundown Motel." After Joe had turned in, he said, "Now all the way to the end. Park on the far side of that Ford. Take the keys out and put them in my little hot hand. Okay. Now pick up your groceries. Use both hands. Now walk ahead of me right to that door. Number 20. Good. Now stand still. And don't try any funny stuff."

He rapped on the door, five sharp raps, closely spaced.

"Ray?" It was a woman's voice.

"Open up."

The door opened inward. Ray prodded him at the base of the spine with the gun barrel. "Go on in."

The woman backed away from the door, staring at Joe Conroy with surprise and, he thought, alarm. She was a lean-faced, full-mouthed blonde with a short hairdo. She wore a white blouse, and dark-red, shiny bullfighter pants. She was barefoot, and her ankles looked soiled. She had a very slim waist, long, heavy legs.

A man bounded off one of the beds and pushed the woman out of the way roughly. Ray had kicked the door shut. The man was about the same age as Ray. He had glossy black hair worn full and long, and sideburns down to the corners of a narrow jaw. He was in blue and white plaid underwear shorts. There was a half crescent of lipstick on his chin. His chest was hairless. His arms were long and powerful.

"Is there anything you can't foul up?" he demanded of Ray. "Just one lousy little thing?"

"Get off my back, Diz. I figured it all out."

"You're a big brain now, already."

"Look, Diz. I found a couple I could have took easy, so what happens? The car gets listed as hot maybe ten minutes later, and every prowl in town has it on the list and with the luck we've been running, they grab us off. So I figure this way. Take the car and the driver too. See? That means it isn't reported stole. Isn't that using the old head?"

Diz gave Ray a look of intense disgust. "That's using the old head," he said. He sat down on the bed, heavily, reached the bottle on the night stand and splashed whiskey into a glass.

"So what's the matter?" Ray demanded, looking from the girl to the man.

"Tell him, Lauralee," Diz said.

"This is the matter, lambie pie. Suppose it doesn't go real, real smooth. Suppose somebody has to go bang-bang. Then your new friend has a long talk with the fuzz. Descriptions, stupid."

Ray turned and stared indignantly at Joe Conroy. After a time his expression cleared. "So okay, then. Who's stupid? If the deal goes sour, then it don't make any difference we kill this one, too, does it?"

"If it's any help to you . . ." Joe said.

"Shut up!" Diz said. "Throw me his wallet, stupid."

"You stop climbing on my back," Ray grumbled. He took the identification cards out, and the photographs Joe carried. "Joseph T. Conroy," he said. "Hello, Joe. Wife and kids. And about two hours from now the wife gets so itchy she calls the cops. What the hell is the car? A thirty-seven jalopy or something?"

"No, it's a good car, Diz, honest. Look out the window. It's a new four-door job with five thousand on it and a full tank. It ought to roll."

"Says here you're manager of Pyramid Trucking Lines, Conroy. Ever get called back to the office?"

"Sometimes."

Diz turned to Lauralee. "You hold stupid's hand while Joe and I wander up to the booth and make us a phone call." He put on trousers, shoes, and a jacket, slipped a gun into the jacket pocket. "Put that sack down someplace, Joe. Let's go."

Once they were outside he said, "Nothing funny now. I'm going to hear both ends of this little chat. You met a guy from the office. Something has come up. Make up something logical. You'll have to work late." The booth was outside the motel office. Diz crowded in with Joe. The phone rang three times before Marty answered.

"Yes?"

"It's Joe, honey. Look, something came up. I checked at the terminal and I've got to go back for a while."

"Will you kids hush! I can't hear your father. Did you say you have to go back to work? What's the trouble?"

"Usual thing. Too many rigs down, and we'll have to dig up a lease someplace to keep from faulting on a contract."

"Did you get the groceries?"

"Yes."

"Well, can't you bring them home before you go back?"

"This is sort of an emergency, hon."

"You sound funny, Joe. Is anything wrong?"

"No. Everything is fine."

"Danny, stop screeching! Mommie can't hear. Will you be late?"

"I guess so."

"The Shermans were coming over after dinner."

"Well, you better call Liz and cancel, hon."

"You make sure you get something to eat, now. You're sure everything is all right?"

With enormous false heartiness he said, "Everything is dandy. I'm just a little worried about the contract. See you, honey."

"Goodbye, darling."

He was sweating as he hung up. The conversation had been like a little window open on a sane and normal world. As soon as he hung up he was back in a fantasy place inhabited by Diz, by Ray, and by Lauralee. He wiped his brow, waiting.

"That was just fine, Joe boy. You're being real cool. Now suppose she tries to phone you at the terminal? Think she will?"

"I . . . I guess she might. To remind me to eat."

"Then they better be ready to say you stepped out for a couple of minutes. Who can you call there?"

"Henry Gluckman, the dispatcher."

"Well, leave us do so, ole Joe."

Henry seemed baffled by Joe's request at first, and then he suddenly seemed to understand. "I get it, Mr. Conroy. Sure thing. Have a ball, Mr. Conroy."

Joe hung up and said, "He thinks I've got a woman lined up."

"It happens every day, Uncle Joe. Let's go back. I like you about a half step in front of me. Good."

They went back into the room. It was a setup usually called family accommodations. Two rooms and a bath. Ray was scowling down into a stiff highball. Diz went over and took it lightly out of his hand, and when Ray looked up in sharp annoyance, reaching to retrieve the glass, Diz said, "No more sauce, stupid. You might get another genius-type idea."

"I told him to lay off," Lauralee said.

"Shut up!" Ray barked at her.

"Watch Uncle Joe," Diz said. He went into the next room and came back with a roll of black tar tape. Joe Conroy was instructed to sit on the floor by the radiator, encircle a pipe with his arms, and clasp his hands. Diz wound his wrists and hands with the tape. Each encirclement made tighter pressure.

They don't do this, Joe thought. They tie you to a chair and you work the ropes loose. Nobody works this stuff loose. This is going to be a long day.

Once he was secure, they ignored him. They unfolded a road map on the bed and went over it carefully. Diz was the leader. He gave the orders. There was another piece of paper. Joe judged from the conversation that it was a sketch of a building.

"We stop the car here, motor running, lights out, Lauralee at the wheel. They close at eleven. They have the night deposit made up by midnight. Two of them take it in, the manager and some kind of clerk. They come out the back. Their car is parked here. We'll be between the car and the hedge.

"Now get this, Ray. The minute we hit is when the fat one shoves the key in the car door. The other one will be holding the money bag. You come around the front, fast, gun in the left hand, blackjack in the right. And for God's sake, hit him right, not too hard and not too soft. I'll take the fat one.

"Then we unlock the car and dump them in so nobody sees them laying around. We throw the car keys into the yard and walk—get that—walk to Conroy's car. I'll take the wheel, Lauralee. You be ready to shove over. Ray, you'll have the money. You get in the back."

"How much do you think there'll be?" Lauralee asked with a husky wistfulness.

"From the business they do, someplace between fifteen and twenty-five thousand."

"It's about time," Ray mumbled.

"Six weeks and all we've done is pay expenses," Diz said. "Somebody is a jinx."

"Don't look at me," Ray said. "We did good until you picked her up, Diz."

"If I drop anybody, I drop you. Maybe I drop you after we split this one, stupid."

"I can do good by myself."

"You do fine. Big operations. Mug jobs."

Ray shrugged. "How about dads?"

"If it's smooth we leave him here and they find him when they come to change the sheets. If it goes sour . . . we decide later."

"I feel all empty in the middle," Lauralee said.

Diz rumpled her hair. "That's the name of the game, sweetheart. That's the kick."

She kissed him thoroughly, kneading his back. "How'll I look in mink?" she said.

"Like any other mink," Ray said.

Diz and the girl got up and went into the other room, arms around each other's waists. The door closed softly behind them. Ray got the bottle and poured himself a drink.

"From what I've heard—"

"Shut up, dad."

"I've heard that when you people team up with a woman, things go bad for you."

Ray got up and came around the bed. Holding his drink carefully so as not to spill it, he kicked Joe in the ribs with a full hard swing of his leg. Joe felt the bone go and the pain sickened him. It shamed him to sit on the floor and be kicked like an animal. And for the first time he felt a true and genuine anger.

Ray sat on the bed again. "Just don't talk," he said. "Just don't say word one."

Each time Joe drew breath pain was a knife in his side. I should have started being a man when I had the chance, Joe thought. That kick could have killed me. It could have driven a splintered edge of bone into the lungs. Then Diz would have been very happy with Ray. Delighted with him.

And he began to have a vague idea. As it took more definite shape, he liked it better. If he merely endured, the choice was not good. The men with the money would be armed and wary. This trio had the smell of defeat about them. If they killed one of the men, they would kill the other and come back and kill him. It would not go smoothly for them. Not with Ray drinking heavily. And the only chance seemed to be to increase the dissension between them.

He found the first step of his plan astoundingly hard to accomplish.

He caught a fold of the inside of his cheek between his teeth, and for long moments he did not have the courage to do as he wished. Finally, bracing himself against the expected pain, he bit down as powerfully as he could and tasted the flow of blood into his mouth.

He chewed again and again, and then slumped over against the floor and made himself breathe in a heavy rasping way and let the blood run onto the floor. He kept his eyes closed. He heard Ray come over to him. The big hand took him by the shoulder and shook him roughly.

"Hey! Hey! Wake up!" Ray whispered.

Joe breathed in the same way. There was a long silence. Ray moved away from him.

"Hey, Diz."

"Go away, stupid."

"Diz, come here a minute."

"Shut up, Ray."

"Diz, you got to come here a minute."

Joe heard the door open finally and knew that they had come over to him.

"What the hell happened?" Diz demanded, his voice taut with anger.

"I just kicked him a little. One time. Honest. He was talking too much."

"Oh, you slob! Oh, you stupid, crazy jerk!"

Joe heard the quick suck of breath and knew the girl had come over and seen him. "He's . . . bleeding."

"The genius kicked him. He probably busted up his insides. The guy may be dying."

"I . . . I don't like this," Lauralee said. "I don't like it."

"A nice juicy kidnap murder," Diz said. "In this state they gas you. They drop it in a bucket under a chair."

"Honest, Diz, I only—"

There was a sudden brutal splat of fist on flesh and something heavy fell against a bed and slid sideways.

"You didn't have to do that," Ray said, his voice muffled.

"What're we gonna do?" Lauralee said, and Joe detected hysteria in her voice. He made his breathing more ragged.

"Lemme think," Diz said. "He may be going out right now."

"We ought to get a doctor," Lauralee said.

"That's a wonderful idea. That's a real good idea. The kind Ray has all the time."

"Maybe we ought to anyway cut him loose and put him on the bed," the girl said. "Look at him bleed!"

They unwound the tape from his hands. He kept himself utterly limp. They carried him to the bed and put him down clumsily.

"Go get a towel or something," Diz said.

"I just gave him one little kick in the ribs," Ray said wonderingly.

"Shut up. I got to think. If he dies, we'll have to get him out of here. He'll have to be dumped someplace."

"I didn't know I was going to get into anything like this. I don't like this," Lauralee whined.

"Maybe he's faking," Ray said.

"Give me that cigarette, honey," Diz said.

Joe Conroy braced himself. He did not know where the pain would begin. It began on the back of his left hand. It was bright pain, fierce and sharp. He fought against the instinctive reflex. It lasted a little longer than forever, and finally stopped.

"He's not faking," Diz said. "He's in bad shape."

"If it's going to happen anyway, let's finish it," Ray said.

"No!" Lauralee cried.

"Shut up, honey. Who says it's going to happen anyway? I'm no doctor. You want a murder rap against you, Ray? Stop having ideas. Give me a chance to think."

"It's driving me nuts, listening to him," Ray said.

"Go in the other room and shut the door."

"I want to know what—"

"Move, will you!"

"Okay, okay, okay." Joe heard the door slam.

"What are you going to do?" the girl whispered nervously.

"Ray goofed it up. But I need him tonight. We can get along without you. You stay here with Conroy. Then we'll come back here. Dead or not, we'll take Conroy along. We'll find a side road and I'll have Ray help me drag him off in the brush. And . . . when I come back to the car, I'll be alone."

"No, Diz!"

"Think of a better way. I can leave the gun in Conroy's hand. It'll confuse the law. And we'll switch cars as soon as we can."

"I'm scared."

"Don't be scared. Diz will fix everything nice for baby."

It was a sizable slice of eternity before the two men left. He heard his car drive away. Diz, before he left, had taped Joe's wrists and ankles. Joe opened his eyes and groaned.

The girl came over to the bed. "Water," he gasped.

"Okay. I'll get some." She came back with a glass. She held his head up and held the glass to his lips. "You know, I was a nurse's aide once. I was going to go into nurse training, but it was too tough, you know what I mean? I'm sorry about Ray kicking you."

He clasped his fingers together. "Fix the pillow. Please," he gasped.

"Sure thing." She put the empty glass aside. Joe felt vastly guilty about what he was about to do. He had never struck a woman in his life. And he knew he could not be half-hearted about it.

His wrists were fastened together in front of him. She reached around him to tug at the pillow. He watched her chin carefully. When he judged it was in perfect position, he brought his clasped hands up as hard and as quickly as he could.

The force of the blow straightened her up and she fell against the other bed and bounced onto the floor. He swung his legs over the side of the bed and sat up. She came up onto her hands and knees, face bleared and dazed. As she started to push herself up, he struck her again, swinging his clasped hands sideways, striking the angle of her jaw.

He tried to hop to the door, but he lost his balance and fell. He wriggled the rest of the way, knelt and caught the knob, pulled himself up, unlocked the door, and hopped out into the night yelling as loudly as he could. He hopped four times and fell into the driveway, still hollering, as doors opened, and people were running . . .

At one in the morning, after the police surgeon had taped his cracked rib and packed the wound on the inside of his mouth, Detective Lieutenant Halverson, small and trim, came in as Joe Conroy was putting his shirt back on.

"Delivered the car to your wife. Told her I'd bring you home, but she's going to get a sitter somehow and come down for you."

"You got them, then."

Halverson leaned against a file cabinet and lit a cigarette. "Wouldn't have, if you hadn't overheard the name of the supermarket they were going to knock off. When we put the floods on them they got rattled. So the girl is in a cell, and the big blond punk is in the police morgue, and the one with the sideburns is on the operating table. We don't have the history yet, but it will be coming through soon. Now I've got time for your end of the story."

Joe told him—and the words came hard.

Halverson nodded when he finished. "Smart," he said.

"I'm a real hero," Joe said. "She was being a roadshow Florence Nightingale and I sucker-punched her beautifully."

"So you wish you'd tried to climb the boys instead, so Monday your wife could be picking out a box with bronze handles?"

"Not that. But . . ."

"I know what you mean. Both papers want to talk to you. How will you handle it?"

"I managed to get away. That's enough."

And that's all he told them. But he told Marty all of it. And he didn't start to shake with reaction until he was at last home and safe, and then he took the pills he hadn't thought he would need.

Sunday, except for all the phone calls, was like any other Sunday. Almost like any other Sunday. Just like every day from now on would be almost like the days that had gone before. With one little exception. For Joe Conroy life had become a little more valuable because it would not so readily be taken for granted.

There was evil loose in the world, random and brutal as summer lightning. And this time his luck had been like a coin found in the street. He read the funnies to the kids, and, with an awkward gladness, kissed Marty more often than was his habit.

"Q"

Edgar Wallace

Warm and Dry

The Sooper—Superintendent Minter of Scotland Yard—tells another tale out of his busy professional life. The trouble with most criminals, according to the Sooper, is they've got no originality. Each has his own modus operandi, and he sticks to it. Now, Nippy—acronym for Norman Ignatius Percival Philipson Young—was an exception to the rule. He'd try anything once . . .

Detective: SUPERINTENDENT MINTER

I went down to see Superintendent Minter just before the election began. He heard I was going to participate in the fray with a visible sneer on his homely face. "Politics!" he said. "Good Lord! At your time of life! Well, well, well! I've known a lot of fellows who took up that game, but nobody that ever made it pay, except Nippy the Nose, who used to travel the country and burgle the candidates' rooms when they were out addressing meetings.

"You know a lot about the hooks and the getabits of life, and you know that they're all specialists. If a man's a lob crawler—"

"What's a lob crawler? I've forgotten."

The Superintendent shook his head sadly. "You're forgetting everything," he said. "I suppose it's these politics. A lob crawler's a man who goes into a little shop on his hands and knees, passes round the counter, and pinches the till. There's not much of it nowadays, and anyway in these bad times there's nothing in the till to pinch.

"But once a lob crawler, always a lob crawler. If you go on the whizz—and I don't suppose you want me to tell you that whizzing is pocket-picking—you spend your life on the whizz. If you're a burglar, you're always a burglar. I've never yet met a burglar who was also a con man.

"That's the criminal's trouble—he's got no originality, and thank the Lord for it! If they didn't catch themselves, we'd never catch 'em.

70

Nippy was an exception. He'd try anything once. If you went into the Record Office at Scotland Yard and turned up his M.O. card, which means—"

"I know what a *Modus Operandi* card is," I said.

The Superintendent nodded his head approvingly.

"That's right. Don't let these politics put business out of your mind. As I say, if you turned up his M.O. card you'd have a shock. He's been convicted of larceny, burglary, obtaining money by a trick, pocket-picking, luggage pinching—everything except blackmail. It's a funny thing that none of the regulars will ever admit they've committed blackmail, and there's not one of them that wouldn't if he had the chance.

"I used to know Nippy—in fact, I got two of his convictions. Nothing upsets a police officer more than these general practitioners, because we are always looking for specialists. We know there are about six classes of burglars. There's a class that never attempts to break into a live shop, by which I mean a shop where people are living in the rooms upstairs; and there's a class that never goes into a dead joint, which, you will remember, is a lock-up shop with nobody on the premises.

"And naturally, when we get a burglary with any peculiar features, we go through the M.O. cards and pick out a dozen men who are likely to have done the job, and after we've sorted 'em out and found which of 'em are in stir and which of 'em are out of the neighborhood, we'll pull in the remainder one by one and give them the once-over.

"So that when there was a real big bust in Brockley, and we went over the M.O. cards, we never dreamed of looking for Nippy, because he hadn't done that sort of thing before; and we wouldn't have found him, but we got the office from a fence in Islington that Nippy had tried to sell him a diamond brooch. When you get a squeak from a fence it's because he has offered too low a price for the stolen property, and the thief has taken it elsewhere.

"Nippy got a stretch, and the next time he came into our hands it was for something altogether different—trying to persuade a Manchester cotton man to buy a one-tenth share in a Mexican oil field. Nippy would have got away with the loot, but unfortunately he knew nothing about geography, and when he said that Mexico was in South Africa the cotton man got a little suspicious and looked up the map.

"Nippy was a nice fellow, always affable, generally well dressed, and a great favorite with the ladies. When I say 'ladies' I mean anybody that wore stockings and used lipstick.

"Nippy used to do a bit of nosing, too, but I didn't know he was making a regular business of it. Now, a nose is a very useful fellow. Without a nose the police wouldn't be able to find half the criminals that come through their hands. I suppose I'm being vulgar and ought to call them police informers, but 'nose' has always been good enough for me, because, naturally, I'm a man without any refinement.

"I happened to be walking down Piccadilly towards Hyde Park Corner one day when I saw Nippy. He tipped his hat and was moving on when I claimed him. 'Good morning, Sooper,' he said. 'I'm just on me way to the office. I'm going straight now. I'm an agent, you see, and everything's warm and dry. I've opened a little business in Wardour Street,' he said.

"Nippy had opened lots of businesses, mostly with a chisel and a three-piece jimmy, but I gathered that he had opened this one by paying the rent in advance. All criminals tell you they're going straight. Usually they're going straight from one prison to another. There are exceptions, but I've never heard of 'em.

"We had a few minutes' conversation. He told me where his office was, and I promised to look him up. He was so happy about me calling that I thought he was lying, but when I dropped in a few days afterwards I found that he had a room on the third floor.

"I expected to find that he was the managing director of the Mountains in the Moon Exploration Company, or else the secretary of a new invention for getting gold out of the sea. It was a bit surprising to find his real name, Norman Ignatius Percival Philipson Young, on the glass panel. It was now that I found what he was agent for. He was standing in with the very fence who had given him away on his last conviction, and I suspected he was doing the same job.

"Anyway, he was full of information about various people, and he gave me a tip that afternoon to prove his—what's the phrase? yes, *bona fides*—that's French, isn't it? I made a pretty good capture—a man called Juggy Jones, who did a lot of automobile pinching, and was in with a big crowd up at Shadwell, who took the cars, repaired them, and shipped them off to India. There's many a grand family car running round Madras, loaded to the waterline with little Eurasians.

"Anyway, Juggy was a very sensible man, and if ever a thief could be described as intelligent, Juggy was that man. He didn't talk much.

"He was a big fellow, about six feet two, with a face as cheerful as the ace of spades. But if he didn't say much he did a lot of thinking.

"I took him out of a café, where he was having dinner with a lady friend, and we walked down to the station together and I charged him.

"He said nothing, but when he came up before the magistrate and heard the evidence and was committed for trial, he asked me to see him in his cell.

" 'I shouldn't be at all surprised, Sooper,' he said, 'if I know the name of the man who shopped me.'

" 'And I shouldn't be surprised either, Juggy,' I said, 'because you've known me for years.'

"But he shook his head and said nothing else. Somebody got at the witnesses for the Crown, and when they went into the box at the Old Bailey they gave the sort of evidence that wouldn't bring about a conviction, and it looked as if he was going to get an acquittal and something out of the poor box to compensate him for his wounded feelings, when the prosecuting counsel took a pretty strong line with one witness who, after he had changed his evidence three times, said just enough to convict Juggy on the count.

"He went down for a carpet. Am I being vulgar? Let me say he went down for six months, and a very lucky man he was. If we could have convicted him on the other indictments he'd have taken a dose of penal servitude.

"Naturally Nippy didn't appear in court, and I wondered what he was getting out of it.

"It was a long time afterwards that I found out there was a quarrel between the two rings as to who the stuff should be shipped to, and Nippy had been put in to make the killing. Nippy gave me one of two bits of information which were useful, but you could see that he was just acting for the fence. I made a few inquiries up Islington way, and I found out that whenever the police went to him to find out about stolen property, he referred them to the gentleman in Wardour Street who'd be able to tell them something.

"Now a thief who's earning a regular living has never got enough money, and I was pretty certain Nippy was doing something on the side, because he began to have his old prosperous look and started attending the races. As a matter of fact, though I didn't know it, he was working up a connection with a gang of luggage thieves. I found this out when he came on to my manor—into my division, I mean. I found him at a railway station acting in a suspicious manner, and

I could have pinched him but, being naturally very kind-hearted with all criminals if I haven't enough evidence to get a conviction, I just warned him. Nippy was very hurt.

" 'Why, Sooper,' he said, 'I've got a good job. I'm warm and dry up in Wardour Street. Why should I lower myself to go back to my old sinful life? I haven't had a drink for three months, and I never pass the Old Bailey without taking off me hat to it.'

" 'There are two ways of being warm and dry, Nippy,' I said. 'One is to be honest, and the other is to get to Dartmoor, where I understand there is a fine system of central heating.'

"While this was going on, Juggy Jones came out of stir and reported to me. He'd got out with his usual remissions and I had a little chat with him.

" 'It's all right, Sooper,' he said. 'I'm going straight. I've had enough of the other game. How's Nippy—warm and dry?'

" 'Do you know him?' I asked.

"He thought a long time. 'I've heard about him,' he said.

"I should imagine he'd been doing a lot of thinking while he was in prison, and when I heard that he and Nippy had been seen together having a drink in the long bar, I thought it advisable to see Nippy and give him a few words of fatherly advice. But you couldn't tell anything to Nippy. He knew it all, and a lot more. He just smiled. 'Thank you, Sooper,' he said, 'but Juggy and I have always been good pals, and you couldn't wish to meet a nicer man.'

"According to his story, they had met by accident in the Haymarket. They'd had a drink together. I think Nippy was a bit jealous of Juggy, because he was one of the few crooks I have met who had saved money. He had enough money, anyway, when he was at the Old Bailey to engage a good mouthpiece, and he'd got a nice little flat in Maida Vale.

"One of my men shadowed Nippy and found he was in the habit of calling there, so if Nippy disappeared and his right ear was found on the Thames Embankment, I knew where the rest of the body would be. Not that crooks are that kind—they never commit murder.

"I only heard the rest of the story in scraps and pieces. But so far as I could make out, Nippy had been trying to get the man into the luggage crowd, which was silly because, as I have said before, a man who knocks off automobiles doesn't knock off anything else.

"Juggy said he would like to try the business, and he must have looked it over pretty thoroughly and taken an interest in it because one day he sent for Nippy to come to his flat and put him on an easy job that came off and brought him about £150.

"It's a simple trick. You have a car outside the station, and in it a little hand stamp and a case of type. You hang about the cloakroom till you see a man coming along carrying a bag in and taking his ticket. You've got a little bag of your own, containing a few well-worn bricks wrapped up in your favorite newspaper. You edge up behind him, and when he takes a ticket you check your bag and you receive a ticket. Now, suppose you receive Number 431. You know the ticket just before you was 430.

"You go outside to your little car. You have got a lot of blank tickets of all colors—they sometimes change the color—and you just make up the stamp to Number 430 and you stamp it. About three or four hours later along comes a gentlemanly-looking person, hands in the phony ticket Number 430 and claims the bag, and that's the end of it.

"One night, just as Nippy was going to bed, Juggy rang him up and asked him to come round to see him. When he got to the flat he told Nippy a grand story. It was about a man who traveled in jewelry and who was in the habit of taking one over the eight, and sometimes two. This fellow, according to Juggy, when he felt the inebriation, if you'll excuse the word, overtaking him, used to go to the nearest cloakroom and deposit all his samples in a bag which was kept in a case that you could open with a blunt knife or a celluloid card.

"According to Juggy, this fellow was coming to London from Birmingham, and the two arranged to shadow him. They picked him up at a railway station—a large fat man, who was slightly oiled. You may not have heard the expression before, but it means a man who has been lubricating—which is also a foreign expression, but you must go with the times.

"They tailed him till he went into a restaurant and met another man. He carried a bag, and he took out of this bag, and showed to the world, a large leather roll which he opened on the table. There were more diamonds in that roll than Nippy had ever heard of. When he saw it he began to breathe heavily through his nose.

"When they got outside the restaurant Nippy said to Juggy, 'Can't we get him in a quiet place and convert him to free trade? It's warm and dry.'

"But Juggy wouldn't have it. He said that this man, because he was in the habit of getting soused—which is another expression you may not have heard before, but it means the same thing—was always followed by a detective to watch him. Apparently, he wasn't an ordinary traveler—he was the head of the firm.

"So Nippy and Juggy followed him for a bit. He went into a bar and when he came out he couldn't have driven a car without having his license suspended for ten years. Sure enough he made for a railway station in the Euston Road, handed over the stock, and they watched it being locked in the safe.

" 'He'll do that every day this week,' said Juggy, 'but no time's like the present. You're a peterman, I'm not.'

"And then he told Nippy his plan. It was to put him in a packing case and deposit him in the cloakroom. 'It's Saturday night. They close the office at twelve, and all you've got to do is to get out during the night, open the safe, get the stuff, and I'll be down to collect you in the morning.'

"Nippy wasn't what I might describe as keen on the job, but he'd seen the diamonds and he couldn't keep his mind off them. Juggy took him down to a little garage off the Waterloo Bridge Road and showed him the packing case he'd had made.

" 'If you don't like to do it, I can get one of my lads who'll do the job for a pony and be glad of the chance. It's going to be easy to get, and we'll share fifty-fifty.'

"Nippy was still a bit uncertain. 'Suppose they put me upside-down?'

" 'Don't be silly,' said Juggy. 'I'll put a label on it: *This Side Up—Glass.*'

"Nippy had a look at the case. It was all lined, there was a nice seat, and although it was going to be a little uncomfortable there was a neat little pocket inside, with a flask of whiskey and a little tin of sandwiches.

" 'You won't be able to smoke, of course, but you won't be there more than seven hours. I'll notify the left-luggage people that I'm bringing the case in, and I'll slip the fellow a dollar and tell him not to put anything on top. All you've got to do is open the side of the case and step out. It'll be like falling off a log.'

"Nippy had a good look at the case. The side opened like a door. It didn't look hard at all. The only danger was that when they came in the morning to the cloakroom they'd find out that the safe had been opened.

" 'That's all right,' said Juggy. 'You needn't bust it. I've got a squeeze of the key.' He took it out of his pocket.

" 'That's all right,' said Nippy. 'It's an easy job. We'll be warm and dry on this.'

"About seven o'clock that night Nippy got inside the packing case and tried it out. The air holes all worked beautifully, so everything was as the heart could desire. He bolted the door on the inside, then heard somebody putting in screws on the outside.

" 'Hi!' said Nippy, 'what's the idea?'

" 'It's all right,' said Juggy. 'They're only fakes. They come out the moment you push the side out.'

"I don't know what happened to Nippy in the night, and I can't describe his feelings, because I'm not a novel writer. He heard cranes going and people shouting, felt himself lifted up in the air, heard somebody say, 'Lower away!' and he went down farther than he thought it was possible to go. And then Nippy began to realize that something had to be done.

"It was two hours before anybody heard his shouts, and at last the stevedores broke open the case and got him out. He was in the hold of a ship, and the packing case was labeled on the top: *Bombay. Stow away from boilers. Keep warm and dry.*

"It broke Nippy's nerve. He's in Parkhurst now, recuperating."

"Q"

Patricia Highsmith

The Pond

*Elinor, newly widowed, and her four-year-old son Chris were
living in a rented house in Connecticut. The house had a garden
and a pond—a strange sinister pond. This is a peculiarly haunt-
ing story, and the image of the pond will stay in the back of your
mind, on the screen of your memory, for a long time, perhaps
forever . . .*

E linor Sievert stood looking down at the pond. Was it safe? For
Chris? The real-estate agent had said it was four feet deep. It
was certainly full of weeds, its surface nearly covered with algae or
whatever they called the little oval green things that floated. Well,
four feet was enough to drown a four-year-old. She must warn Chris.

She lifted her head and walked back toward the white two-story
house. She had just rented the house, and had been here only since
yesterday. She hadn't entirely unpacked. Hadn't the agent said
something about draining the pond, that it wouldn't be too difficult
or expensive? Was there a spring under it? Elinor hoped not, because
she'd taken the house for six months.

It was two in the afternoon, and Chris was having his nap. There
were more kitchen cartons to unpack, also the record player in its
neat taped carton. Elinor fished the record player out, connected it,
and chose an LP of New Orleans jazz to pick her up. She hoisted
another load of dishes up to the long drainboard.

The doorbell rang.

Elinor was confronted by the smiling face of a woman about her
own age.

"Hello. I'm Jane Caldwell—one of your neighbors. I just wanted
to say hello and welcome. We're friends of Jimmy Adams, the agent,
and he told us you'd moved in here."

"Yes. My name's Elinor Sievert. Won't you come in?" Elinor held
the door wider. "I'm not quite unpacked as yet—but at least we
could have a cup of coffee in the kitchen."

Within a few minutes they were sitting on opposite sides of the

78

wooden table, cups of instant coffee before them. Jane said she had two children, a boy and a girl, the girl just starting school, and that her husband was an architect and worked in Hartford.

"What brought you to Luddington?" Jane asked.

"I needed a change—from New York. I'm a freelance journalist, so I thought I'd try a few months in the country. At least I call this the country, compared to New York."

"I can understand that. I heard about your husband," Jane said on a more serious note. "I'm sorry. Especially since you have a small son. I want you to know we're a friendly batch around here, and at the same time we'll let you alone, if that's what you want. But consider Ed and me neighbors, and if you need something, just call on us."

"Thank you," Elinor said. She remembered that she'd told Adams that her husband had recently died, because Adams had asked if her husband would be living with her. Now Jane was ready to go, not having finished her coffee.

"I know you've got things to do, so I don't want to take any more of your time," said Jane. She had rosy cheeks, chestnut hair. "I'll give you Ed's business card, but it's got our home number on it too. If you want to ask any kind of question, just call us. We've been here six years.—Where's your little boy?"

"He's—"

As if on cue Chris called, "Mommy!" from the top of the stairs.

Elinor jumped up. "Come down, Chris. Meet a nice new neighbor."

Chris came down the stairs a bit timidly, holding onto the banister.

Jane stood beside Elinor at the foot of the staircase. "Hello, Chris. My name's Jane. How are you?"

Chris's blue eyes examined her seriously. "Hello."

Elinor smiled. "I think he just woke up and doesn't know where he is. Say 'How do you do,' Chris."

"How do you do," said Chris.

"Hope you'll like it here, Chris," Jane said. "I want you to meet my boy Bill. He's just your age. Bye-bye, Elinor. Bye, Chris." Jane went out the front door.

Elinor gave Chris his glass of milk and his treat—today a bowl of applesauce. Elinor was against chocolate cupcakes every afternoon, though Chris at the moment thought they were the greatest food ever invented. "Wasn't she nice? Jane?" Elinor said, finishing her coffee.

"Who is she?"

"One of our new neighbors." Elinor continued her unpacking. Her article-in-progress was about self-help with legal problems. She would need to go to the Hartford library, which had a newspaper department, for more research. Hartford was only a half hour away. Elinor had bought a good second-hand car. Maybe Jane would know a girl who could baby-sit now and then. "Isn't it nicer here than in New York?"

Chris lifted his blond head. "I want to go outside."

"But of course. It's so sunny you won't need a sweater. We've got a garden, Chris. We can plant—radishes, for instance." She remembered planting radishes in her grandmother's garden when she was small, remembered the joy of pulling up the fat red and white roots—edible. "Come on, Chris." She took his hand.

Elinor looked at the garden with different eyes, Chris's eyes. Plainly no one had tended the garden for months. There were big prickly weeds between the jonquils that were beginning to open, and the peonies hadn't been cut last year. But there was an apple tree big enough for Chris to climb in.

"Our garden," Elinor said. "Nice and sloppy. All yours to play in, Chris, and the summer's just beginning."

"How big is this?" Chris asked. He had broken away and was stooped by the pond.

Elinor knew he meant how deep was it. "I don't know. Not very deep. But don't go wading. It's not like the seashore with sand. It's all muddy there." Elinor spoke quickly. Anxiety had struck her like a physical pain. Was she still reliving the impact of Cliff's plane against the mountainside—that mountain in Yugoslavia that she'd never see? She'd seen two or three newspaper photographs of it, blotchy black and white chaos, indicating, so the print underneath said, the wreckage of the airliner on which there had been no survivors of 107 passengers plus eight crewmen and stewardesses.

No survivors. And Cliff among them. Elinor had always thought air crashes happened to strangers, never to anyone you knew, never even to a friend of a friend. Suddenly it had been Cliff, on an ordinary flight from Ankara. He'd been to Ankara at least seven times before.

"Is that a snake? Look, Mommy!" Chris yelled, leaning forward as he spoke. One foot sank, his arms shot forward for balance, and suddenly he was in water up to his hips. "Ugh! Ha-ha!" He rolled sideways on the muddy edge and squirmed backward up to the level of the lawn before his mother could reach him.

Elinor set him on his feet. "Chris, I told you not to try wading! Now you'll need a bath. You see?"

"No, I won't!" Chris yelled, laughing, and ran off across the grass, his bare legs and sandals flying, as if the muddy damp on his shorts had given him a special charge.

Elinor had to smile. Such energy! She looked down at the pond. The brown and black mud swirled, stirring long tentacles of vines, making the algae undulate. It was at least seven feet in diameter, the pond. A vine had clung to Chris's ankle as she'd pulled him up. Nasty! The vines were even growing out onto the grass to a length of three feet or more.

Before five p.m. Elinor phoned the rental agent. She asked if it would be all right with the owner if she had the pond drained. Price wasn't of much concern to her, but she didn't tell Adams that.

"It might seep up again," said Adams. "The land's pretty low. Especially when it rains and—"

"I really don't mind trying it. It might help," Elinor said. "You know how it is with a small child. I have the feeling it isn't quite safe."

Adams said he would telephone a company tomorrow morning. "Even this afternoon, if I can reach them."

He telephoned back in ten minutes and told Elinor that the workmen would arrive the next morning, probably quite early.

The workmen came at eight a.m. After speaking with the two men, Elinor took Chris with her in the car to the library in Hartford. She deposited Chris in the children's book section, and told the woman in charge there that she would be back in an hour for Chris, and in case he got restless she would be in the newspaper archives.

When she and Chris got back home, the pond was empty but muddy. If anything, it looked worse, uglier. It was a crater of wet mud laced with green vines, some as thick as a cigarette. The depression in the garden was hardly four feet deep. But how deep was the mud?

"I'm sad," said Chris, gazing down.

Elinor laughed. "Sad?—The pond's not the only thing to play with. Look at the trees we've got! What about the seeds we bought? What do you say we clear a patch and plant some carrots and radishes—now?"

Elinor changed into blue jeans. The clearing of weeds and the planting took longer than she had thought it would, nearly two hours. She worked with a fork and a trowel, both a bit rusty, which

she'd found in the toolshed behind the house. Chris drew a bucket
of water from the outside faucet and lugged it over, but while she
and Chris were putting the seeds carefully in, one inch deep, a roll
of thunder crossed the heavens. The sun had vanished. Within seconds rain was pelting down, big drops that made them run for the
house.

"Isn't that wonderful? Look!" Elinor held Chris up so he could see
out a kitchen window. "We don't need to water our seeds. Nature's
doing it for us."

"Who's nature?"

Elinor smiled, tired now. "Nature rules everything. Nature knows
best. The garden's going to look fresh and new tomorrow."

The following morning the garden did look rejuvenated, the grass
greener, the scraggly rosebushes more erect. The sun was shining
again. And Elinor had her first letter. It was from Cliff's mother in
Evanston. It said:

"Dearest Elinor,

"We both hope you are feeling more cheerful in your Connecticut
house. Do drop us a line or telephone us when you find the time,
but we know you are busy getting settled, not to mention getting
back to your own work. We send you all good wishes for success
with your next articles, and you must keep us posted.

"The color snapshots of Chris in his bath are a joy to us! You
mustn't say he looks more like Cliff than you. He looks like both
of you . . ."

The letter lifted Elinor's spirits. She went out to see if the carrot
and radish seeds had been beaten to the surface by the rain—in
which case she meant to push them down again if she could see
them—but the first thing that caught her eye was Chris, stooped
again by the pond and poking at something with a stick. And the
second thing she noticed was that the pond was full again. Almost
as high as ever!

Well, naturally, because of the hard rain. Or was it naturally? It
had to be. Maybe there was a spring below. Anyway, she thought,
why should she pay for the draining if it didn't stay drained? She'd
have to ring the company today. Miller Brothers, it was called.

"Chris? What're you up to?"

"Frog!" he yelled back. "I *think* I saw a frog."

"Well, don't try to catch it!" Damn the weeds! They were back in
full force, as if the brief draining had done them good. Elinor went
to the toolshed. She thought she remembered seeing a pair of hedge

clippers on the cement floor there.

Elinor found the clippers, rusted, and though she was eager to attack the vines she forced herself to go to the kitchen first and put a couple of drops of salad oil on the center screw of the clippers. Then she went out and started on the long grapevine-like stems. The clippers were dull, but better than nothing, and still faster than scissors.

"What're you doing that for?" Chris asked.

"They're nasty things," Elinor said. "Clogging the pond. We don't want a messy pond, do we?" *Whack whack!* Elinor's espadrilles sank into the wet bank. What on earth did the owners, or the former tenants, use the pond for? Goldfish? Ducks?

A carp, Elinor thought suddenly. If the pond was going to stay a pond, then a carp was the thing to keep it clean, to nibble at some of the vegetation. She'd buy one.

"If you ever fall in, Chris—"

"What?" Chris, stooped on the other side of the pond now, flung his stick away.

"For goodness' sake, don't fall in, but if you do"—Elinor forced herself to go on—"grab hold of these vines. You see? They're strong and growing from the edges. Pull yourself out by them." Actually, the vines seemed to be growing from underwater as well, and pulling at those might send Chris deeper into the pond.

Chris grinned, sideways. "It's not deep. Not even deep as I am."

Elinor said nothing.

The rest of that morning she worked on her law article, then telephoned Miller Brothers.

"Well, the ground's a little low there, ma'am. Not to mention the old cesspool's nearby and it still gets the drain from the kitchen sink, even though the toilets've been put on the mains. We know that house. Pond'll get it too if you've got a washing machine in the kitchen."

Elinor hadn't. "You mean, draining it is hopeless?"

"That's about the size of it."

Elinor tried to force her anger down. "Then I don't know why you agreed to do it."

"Because you seemed set on it, ma'am."

They hung up a few seconds later. What was she going to do about the bill when they presented it? She'd perhaps make them knock it down a bit. But she felt the situation was inconclusive. And Elinor hated that.

While Chris was taking his nap, Elinor made a quick trip to Hartford, found a fish shop, and brought back a carp in a red plastic bucket which she had taken with her in the car. The fish flopped about in a vigorous way, and Elinor drove slowly, so the bucket wouldn't tip over. She went at once to the pond and poured the fish in.

It was a fat silvery carp. Its tail flicked the surface as it dove, then it rose and dove again, apparently happy in wider seas. Elinor smiled. The carp would surely eat some of the vines, the algae. She'd give it bread too. Carps could eat anything. Cliff had used to say there was nothing like carp to keep a pond or a lake clean. Above all, Elinor liked the idea that there was something *alive* in the pond besides vines.

She started to walk back to the house and found that a vine had encircled her left ankle. When she tried to kick her foot free, the vine tightened. She stooped and unwound it. That was one she hadn't whacked this morning. Or had it grown ten inches since this morning? Impossible.

But now as she looked down at the pond and at its border, she couldn't see that she had accomplished much, even though she'd fished out quite a heap. The heap was a few feet away on the grass, in case she doubted it. Elinor blinked. She had the feeling that if she watched the pond closely, she'd be able to see the tentacles growing. She didn't like that idea.

Should she tell Chris about the carp? Elinor didn't want him poking into the water, trying to find it. On the other hand, if she didn't mention it, maybe he'd see it and have some crazy idea of catching it. Better to tell him, she decided.

So when Chris woke up Elinor told him about the fish.

"You can toss some bread to him," Elinor said. "But don't try to catch him, because he likes the pond. He's going to help us keep it clean."

"You don't want ever to catch him?" Chris asked, with milk all over his upper lip.

He was thinking of Cliff, Elinor knew. Cliff had loved fishing. "We don't catch this one, Chris. He's our friend."

Elinor worked. She had set up her typewriter in a front corner room upstairs which had light from two windows. The article was coming along nicely. She had a lot of original material from newspaper clippings. The theme was to alert the public to free legal advice from small-claims offices which most people didn't know existed. Lots of people let sums like $250 go by the board, because they thought it wasn't worth the trouble of a court fight.

Elinor worked until 6:30. Dinner was simple tonight, macaroni and cheese with bacon, one of Chris's favorite dishes. With the dinner in the oven, Elinor took a quick bath and put on blue slacks and a fresh blouse. She paused to look at the photograph of Cliff on the dressing table—a photograph in a silver frame which had been a present from Cliff's parents one Christmas.

It was an ordinary black-and-white enlargement showing Cliff sitting on the bank of a stream, propped against a tree, an old straw hat tipped back on his head. The picture had been taken somewhere outside of Evanston, on one of their summer trips to visit his parents. Cliff held a straw or a blade of grass lazily between his lips. His denim shirt was open at the neck. No one, looking at the hillbilly image, would imagine that Cliff had had to dress up in white tie a couple of times a month in Paris, Rome, London, and Ankara. Cliff had been in the diplomatic service, assistant or deputy to American statesmen, and had been gifted in languages, gifted in tact.

What had Cliff done exactly? Elinor knew only sketchy anecdotes that he had told her. He had done enough, however, to be paid a good salary, to be paid to keep silent, even to her. It had crossed her mind that his plane had been wrecked to kill him, but she assured herself that was absurd. Cliff hadn't been that important. His death had been an accident, not due to the weather but to a mechanical failure in the plane.

What would Cliff have thought of the pond? Elinor smiled wryly. Would he have had it filled in with stones, turned it into a rock garden? Would he have filled it in with earth? Would he have paid no attention at all to the pond? Just called it "nature"?

Two days later, when Elinor was typing a final draft of her article, she stopped at noon and went out into the garden for some fresh air. She'd brought the kitchen scissors, and she cut two red roses and one white rose to put on the table at lunch. Then the pond caught her eye, a blaze of chartreuse in the sunlight.

"Good Lord!" she whispered.

The vines! The weeds! They were all over the surface. And they were again climbing onto the land. Well, this was one thing she could and would see to: she'd find an exterminator. She didn't care what poison they put down in the pond, if they could clear it. Of course she'd rescue the carp first and keep him in a bucket till the pond was safe again.

An exterminator was someone Jane Caldwell might know about. Elinor telephoned her before she started lunch. "This *pond*," Elinor began and stopped, because she had so much to say about it. "I had it drained a few days ago, and now it's filled up again . . . No, that's not really the problem. I've given up the draining, it's the unbelievable vines. The way they grow! I wonder if you know a weed-killing company? I think it'll take a professional—I mean, I don't think I can just toss in some liquid poison and get anywhere. You'll have to see this pond to believe it. It's like a jungle!"

"I know just the right people," Jane said. "They're called 'Weed-Killer,' so it's easy to remember. You've got a phone book there?"

Elinor had. Jane said Weed-Killer was very obliging and wouldn't make her wait a week before they turned up.

"How about you and Chris coming over for tea this afternoon?" Jane asked. "I just made a coconut cake."

"Love to. Thank you." Elinor felt cheered.

She made lunch for herself and Chris, and told him they were invited to tea at the house of their neighbor Jane, and that he'd meet a boy called Bill. After lunch Elinor looked up Weed-Killer in the telephone book and rang them.

"It's a lot of weeds in a pond," Elinor said. "Can you deal with that?"

The man assured her they were experts at weeds in ponds and promised to come over the following morning. Elinor wanted to work for an hour or so until it was time to go to Jane's, but she felt compelled to catch the carp now, or try to. If she failed, she'd tell the men about it tomorrow, and probably they'd have a net on a long handle and could catch it. Elinor took her vegetable sieve which had a handle some ten inches long, and also some pieces of bread.

Not seeing the carp, Elinor tossed the bread onto the surface. Some pieces floated, others sank and were trapped among the vines. Elinor circled the pond, her sieve ready. She had half filled the plastic bucket and it sat on the bank.

Suddenly she saw the fish. It was horizontal and motionless, a couple of inches under the surface. It was dead, she realized, and kept from the surface only by the vines that held it under. Dead from what? The water didn't look dirty, in fact was rather clear. What could kill a carp? Cliff had always said—

Elinor's eyes were full of tears. Tears for the carp? Nonsense. Tears of frustration, maybe. She stooped and tried to reach the carp with the sieve. The sieve was a foot short, and she wasn't going to muddy her tennis shoes by wading in. Not now. Best to work a bit this afternoon and let the workmen lift it out tomorrow.

"What're you doing, Mommy?" Chris came trotting toward her.

"Nothing. I'm going to work a little now. I thought you were watching TV."

"It's no good. Where's the fish?"

Elinor took his wrist and swung him around. "The fish is fine. Now come back and we'll put on the TV again." Elinor tried to think of something else that might amuse him. It wasn't one of his napping days, obviously. "Tell you what, Chris, you choose one of your toys to take to Bill. Make him a present. All right?"

"One of *my* toys?"

Elinor smiled. Chris was generous enough by nature and she meant to nurture this trait. "Yes, one of yours. Even one you like—like your paratrooper. Or one of your books. You choose it. Bill's going to be your friend, and you want to start out right, don't you?"

"Yes." And Chris seemed to be pondering already, going over his store of goodies in his room upstairs.

Elinor locked the back door with its bolt, which was on a level with her eyes. She didn't want Chris going into the garden, maybe seeing the carp. "I'll be in my room, and I'll see you at four. You might put on a clean pair of jeans at four—if you remember to."

Elinor worked, and quite well. It was pleasant to have a tea date to look forward to. Soon, she thought, she'd ask Jane and her husband for drinks. She didn't want people to think she was a melancholy widow. It had been three months since Cliff's death. Elinor thought she'd got over the worst of her grief in those first two weeks, the weeks of shock. Had she really? For the past six weeks she'd been able to work. That was something. Cliff's insurance plus his pension made her financially comfortable, but she needed to work to be happy.

When she glanced at her watch it was ten to four. "Chris!" Elinor called to her half-open door. "Changed your jeans?"

She pushed open Chris's door across the hall. He was not in his room, and there were more toys and books on the floor than usual, indicating that Chris had been trying to select something to give to Bill. Elinor went downstairs where the TV was still murmuring, but Chris wasn't in the living room. Nor was he in the kitchen. She saw that the back door was still bolted. Chris wasn't on the front lawn either. Of course he could have gone to the garden by the front door. Elinor unbolted the kitchen door and went out.

"Chris?" She glanced everywhere, then focused on the pond. She had seen a light-colored patch in its center. *"Chris!"* She ran.

He was face down, feet out of sight, his blond head nearly submerged. Elinor plunged in, up to her knees, her thighs, seized Chris's legs and pulled him out, slipped, sat down in the water and got soaked as high as her breasts. She struggled to her feet, holding Chris by the waist. Shouldn't she try to let the water run out of his mouth? Elinor was panting.

She turned Chris onto his stomach, gently lifted his small body by the waist, hoping water would run from his nose and mouth, but she was too frantic to look. He was limp, soft in a way that frightened her. She pressed his rib cage, released it, raised him a little again. One had to do artificial respiration methodically, counting, she remembered. She did this . . . fifteen . . . sixteen . . . Someone should be telephoning for a doctor. She couldn't do two things at once.

"Help!" she yelled. "Help me, *please!*" Could the people next door hear? The house was twenty yards away, and was anybody home?

She turned Chris over and pressed her mouth to his cool lips. She blew in, then released his ribs, trying to catch a gasp from him, a cough that would mean life. He remained limp. She turned him on his stomach and resumed the artificial respiration. It was now or never, she knew. Senseless to waste time carrying him into the house for warmth. He could've been lying in the pond for an hour—in which case, she knew it was hopeless.

Elinor picked her son up and carried him toward the house. She went into the kitchen. There was a sagging sofa against the wall, and she put him there.

Then she telephoned Jane Caldwell, whose number was on the card by the telephone where Elinor had left it days ago. Since Elinor didn't know a doctor in the vicinity, it made as much sense to call Jane as to search for a doctor's name.

"Hello, *Jane!*" Elinor said, her voice rising wildly. "I think Chris has drowned!—Yes! *Yes!* Can you get a doctor? Right away?" Suddenly the line was dead.

Elinor hung up and went at once to Chris, started the rib pressing again, Chris now prone on the floor with his face turned to one side. The activity soothed her a little.

The doorbell rang and at the same time Elinor heard the latch of the door being opened. Then Jane called, "Elinor?"

"In the kitchen!"

The doctor had dark hair and spectacles. He lifted Chris a little, felt for a pulse. "How long—how long was he—"

"I don't know. I was working upstairs. It was the pond in the garden."

The rest was confused to Elinor. She barely realized when the needle went into her own arm, though this was the most definite sensation she had for several minutes. Jane made tea. Elinor had a cup in front of her. When she looked at the floor, Chris was not there.

"Where is he?" Elinor asked.

Jane gripped Elinor's hand. She sat opposite Elinor. "The doctor took Chris to the hospital. Chris is in good hands, you can be sure of that. This doctor delivered Bill. He's our family doctor."

But from Jane's tone Elinor knew it was all useless, and that Jane knew this too. Elinor's eyes drifted from Jane's face. She noticed a book lying on the cane bottom of the chair beside her. Chris had chosen his dotted-numbers book to give to Bill, a book that Chris rather liked. He wasn't half through doing the drawings. Chris could count and he was doing quite well at reading too. *I wasn't doing so well at his age,* Cliff had said not long ago.

Elinor began to weep.

"That's good. That's good for you," Jane said. "I'll stay here with you. Pretty soon we'll hear from the hospital. Maybe you want to lie down, Elinor?—I've got to make a phone call."

The sedative was taking effect. Elinor sat in a daze on the sofa, her head back against a pillow. The telephone rang and Jane took it. The hospital, Elinor supposed. She watched Jane's face, and knew. Elinor nodded her head, trying to spare Jane any words, but Jane said, "They tried. I'm sure they did everything possible."

Jane said she would stay the night. She said she had arranged for Ed to pick up Bill at a house where she'd left him.

In the morning Weed-Killer came, and Jane asked Elinor if she still wanted the job done.

"I thought you might've decided to move," Jane said.

Had she said that? Possibly. "But I do want it done."

The two Weed-Killer men got to work.

Jane made another telephone call, then told Elinor that a friend of hers named Millie was coming over at noon. When Millie arrived, Jane prepared a lunch of bacon and eggs for the three of them. Millie had blond curly hair, blue eyes, and was very cheerful and sympathetic.

"I went by the doctor's," Millie said, "and his nurse gave me these pills. They're a sedative. He thinks they'd be good for you. Two a day, one before lunch, one before bedtime. So have one now."

They hadn't started lunch. Elinor took one. The workmen were just departing, and one man stuck his head in the door to say with a smile, "All finished, ma'am. You shouldn't have any trouble any more."

During lunch Elinor said, "I've got to see about the funeral."

"We'll help you. Don't think about it now," Jane said. "Try to eat a little."

Elinor ate a little, then slept on the sofa in the kitchen. She hadn't wanted to go up to her own bed. When she woke up, Millie was sitting in the wicker armchair, reading a book.

"Feeling better? Want some tea?"

"In a minute. You're awfully kind. I do thank you very much." She stood up. "I want to see the pond." She saw Millie's look of uneasiness. "They killed those vines today. I'd like to see what it looks like."

Millie went out with her. Elinor looked down at the pond and had the satisfaction of seeing that no vines lay on the surface, that some pieces of them had sunk like drowned things. Around the edge of the pond were stubs of vines already turning yellow and brownish, wilting. Before her eyes one cropped tentacle curled sideways and down, as if in the throes of death. A primitive joy went through her, a sense of vengeance, of a wrong righted.

"It's a nasty pond," Elinor said to Millie. "It killed a carp. Can you imagine? I've never heard of a carp being—"

"I know. They must've been growing like blazes. But they're certainly finished now." Millie held out her hand for Elinor to take. "Don't think about it."

Millie wanted to go back to the house. Elinor did not take her hand, but she came with Millie. "I'm feeling better. You mustn't give up all your time to me. It's very nice of you, since you don't even know me. But I've got to face my problems alone."

Millie made a polite reply.

Elinor really was feeling better. She'd have to go through the funeral next, Chris's funeral, but she sensed in herself a backbone, a morale—whatever it was called. After the service for Chris—surely it would be simple—she'd invite her new neighbors, few as they might be, to her house for coffee or drinks or both. Food too.

Elinor realized that her spirits had picked up because the pool was vanquished. She'd have it filled in with stones, with the agent's and also the owner's permission, of course. Why should she retreat from the house? With stones showing just above the water it would look every bit as pretty, maybe prettier, and it wouldn't be dangerous for the next child who came to live here.

The service for Chris was held at a small local church. The preacher conducted a short nondenominational ceremony. And afterward, around noon, Elinor did have a few people to the house for sandwiches and coffee. The strangers seemed to enjoy it. Elinor even heard a few laughs among the group, which gladdened her heart.

She hadn't, as yet, phoned any of her New York friends to tell them about Chris. Elinor realized that some people might think that "strange" of her, but she felt that it would only sadden her friends to tell them, that it would look like a plea for sympathy. Better the strangers here who knew no grief, because they didn't really know her or Chris.

"You must be sure and get enough rest in the next days," said a kindly middle-aged woman whose husband stood solemnly beside her. "We all think you've been awfully brave."

Elinor gave Jane the dotted-numbers book to take to Bill.

That night Elinor slept more than twelve hours and awoke feeling better and calmer.

She began to write the letters that she had to write—to Cliff's parents, to her own mother and father, and to three good friends in New York. Then she finished typing her article.

The next morning she walked to the post office and sent off her letters, and also her article to her agent in New York. She spent the rest of the day sorting out Chris's clothing, his books and toys, and she washed some of his clothes with a view to passing them on to Jane for Bill, providing Jane wouldn't think it unlucky. Elinor didn't think Jane would. Jane telephoned in the afternoon to ask how she was.

"Is anyone coming to see you? From New York? A friend, I mean?"

Elinor explained that she'd written to a few people, but she wasn't expecting anyone. "I'm really feeling all right, Jane. You mustn't worry."

By evening Elinor had a neat carton of clothing ready to offer Jane, and two more cartons of books and toys. If the clothes didn't fit Bill, then Jane might know a child they would fit. Elinor felt better for that. It was a lot better than collapsing in grief, she thought. Of course it was awful, a tragedy that didn't happen every day—losing a husband and a child in hardly more than three months. But Elinor was not going to succumb to it. She'd stay out the six months in the house here, come to terms with her loss, and emerge strong, someone able to give something to other people, not merely to take.

She had two ideas for future articles. Which to do first? She decided to walk out into the garden and let her thoughts ramble. Maybe the radishes had come up? She'd have a look at the pond. Maybe it would be glassy smooth and clear. She must ask the Weed-Killer people when it would be safe to put in another carp—or two carps.

When she looked at the pond she gave a short gasp. The vines had come *back*.

They looked stronger than ever—not longer, but more dense. Even as she watched, one tentacle, then a second, actually moved, curved toward the land and seemed to grow an inch. That hadn't been due to the wind.

The vines were growing visibly. Another green shoot poked its head above the water's surface. Elinor watched, fascinated, as if she beheld animate things, like snakes. Every inch or so along the vines a small green leaf sprouted, and Elinor was sure she could see some of these unfurling.

The water looked clean, but she knew that was deceptive. The water was somehow poisonous. It had killed a carp. It had killed Chris. And she could still detect, she thought, a rather acid smell of the stuff the Weed-Killer men had put in.

There must be such a thing as digging the roots out, Elinor thought, even if Weed-Killer's stuff had failed. Elinor got the fork from the toolshed, and the clippers. She thought of getting her rubber boots from the house, but was too eager to start to bother with them. She began by hacking all round the edge with the clippers. Some fresh vine ends cruised over the pond and jammed themselves amid other growing vines. The stems now seemed tough as plastic clotheslines, as if the herbicide had fortified them. Some had put down roots in the grass quite a distance from the pond.

Elinor dropped the clippers and seized the fork. She had to dig deep to get at the roots, and when she finally pulled with her hands, the stems broke, leaving some roots still in the soil. Her right foot slipped, she went down on her left knee and struggled up again, both legs wet now. She was not going to be defeated.

As she sank the fork in, she saw Cliff's handsome, subtly smiling eyes in the photograph in the bedroom, Cliff with the blade of grass or straw between his lips, and he seemed to be nodding ever so slightly, approving. Her arms began to ache, her hands grew tired. She lost her right shoe in dragging her foot out of the water yet again, and she didn't bother trying to recover it. Then she slipped again and sat down, water up to her waist.

Tired, angry, she still worked with the fork, trying to pry roots loose, and the water churned with a muddy fury. She might even be doing the damned roots good, she thought. Aerating them or something. Were they invincible? Why should they be? The sun poured down, overheating her, bringing nourishment to the green, Elinor knew.

Nature knows. That was Cliff's voice in her ears. Cliff sounded happy and at ease.

Elinor was half blinded by tears. Or was it sweat? *Chun-nk* went her fork. In a moment, when her arms gave out, she'd cross to the other side of the pond and attack there. She'd got some roots out. She'd make Weed-Killer come again, maybe pour kerosene on the pond and light it.

She got up on cramped legs and stumbled around to the other side. The sun warmed her shoulders though her feet were cold. In those few seconds that she walked, her thoughts and her attitude changed, though she was not at once aware of this. It was neither victory nor defeat that she felt.

She sank the fork in again, again slipped and recovered. Again roots slid between the tines of the fork, and were not removed. A tentacle thicker than most moved toward her and circled her right ankle. She kicked, and the vine tightened, and she fell forward.

She went face down into the water, but the water seemed soft. She struggled a little, turned to breathe, and a vine tickled her neck. She saw Cliff nodding again, smiling his kindly, knowing, almost imperceptible smile. It was nature. It was Cliff. It was Chris.

A vine crept around her arm—loose or attached to the earth she neither knew nor cared. She breathed in, and much of what she took in was water. *All things come from water,* Cliff had said once. Little Chris smiled at her with both corners of his mouth upturned. She saw him stooped by the pond, reaching for the dead carp which floated out of range of his twig. Then Chris lifted his face again and smiled.

James Holding

Still a Cop

*Is it possible for a detective to solve a mystery without knowing
the solution? Is it possible for a detective to bring a case to a
successful conclusion without really knowing what it's all about?
You don't think so? Well, try this Hal Johnson investigation for
size—Hal Johnson, the library cop, the book bloodhound, the
overdue avenger ...*

Detective: HAL JOHNSON

Lieutenant Randall telephoned me on Tuesday, catching me in
my cell-sized office at the public library just after I'd finished
lunch.

"Hal?" he said. "How come you're not out playing patty-cake with
the book borrowers?" Randall still resents my leaving the police
department to become a library detective—what he calls a "sissy
cop." Nowadays my assignments involve nothing more dangerous
than tracing stolen and overdue books for the public library.

I said, "Even a library cop has to eat, Lieutenant. What's on your
mind?"

"Same old thing. Murder."

"I haven't killed anyone for over a week," I said.

His voice took on a definite chill. "Somebody killed a young fellow
we took out of the river this morning. Shot him through the head.
And tortured him beforehand."

"Sorry," I said. I'd forgotten how grim it was to be a Homicide cop.
"Tortured, did you say?"

"Yeah. Cigar burns all over him. I need information, Hal."

"About what?"

"You ever heard of *The Damion Complex*?"

"Sure. It's the title of a spy novel published last year."

"I thought it might be a book." There was satisfaction in Randall's
voice now. "Next question: you have that book in the public library?"

"Of course. Couple of copies, probably."

"Do they have different numbers or something to tell them apart?"

"Yes, they do. Why?"

"Find out for me if one of your library copies of *The Damion Complex* has this number on it, will you?" He paused and I could hear paper rustling. "ES4187."

"Right," I said. "I'll get back to you in ten minutes." Then, struck by something familiar about the number, I said, "No, wait, hold it a minute, Lieutenant."

I pulled out of my desk drawer the list of overdue library books I'd received the previous morning and checked it hurriedly. "Bingo," I said into the phone, "I picked up that book with that very number yesterday morning. How about that? Do you want it?"

"I want it."

"For what?"

"Evidence, maybe."

"In your torture-murder case?"

He lost patience. "Look, just get hold of the book for me, Hal. I'll tell you about it when I pick it up, okay?"

"Okay, Lieutenant. When?"

"Ten minutes." He sounded eager.

I hung up and called Ellen on the checkout desk. "Listen, sweetheart," I said to her because it makes her mad to be called sweetheart and she's extremely attractive when she's mad, "can you find me *The Damion Complex,* copy number ES4187? I brought it in yesterday among the overdues."

"*The Damion Complex?*" She took down the number. "I'll call you back, Hal." She didn't sound a bit mad. Maybe she was softening up at last. I'd asked her to marry me seventeen times in the last six months, but she was still making up her mind.

In two minutes she called me back. "It's out again," she reported. "It went out on card number 3888 yesterday after you brought it in."

Lieutenant Randall was going to love that. "Who is card number 3888?"

"A Miss Oradell Murphy."

"Address?"

She gave it to me, an apartment on Leigh Street.

"Telephone number?"

"I thought you might be able to look that up yourself." She was tart. "I'm busy out here."

"Thank you, sweetheart," I said. "Will you marry me?"

"Not now. I told you I'm busy." She hung up. But she did it more gently than usual, it seemed to me. She *was* softening up. My spirits lifted.

Lieutenant Randall arrived in less than the promised ten minutes. "Where is it?" he asked, fixing me with his cat stare. He seemed too big to fit into my office. "You got it for me?"

I shook my head. "It went out again yesterday. Sorry."

He grunted in disappointment, took a look at my spindly visitor's chair, and decided to remain standing. "Who borrowed it?"

I told him Miss Oradell Murphy, Apartment 3A at the Harrington Arms on Leigh Street.

"Thanks." He tipped a hand and turned to leave.

"Wait a minute. Where you going, Lieutenant?"

"To get the book."

"Those apartments at Harrington Arms are efficiencies," I said. "Mostly occupied by single working women. So maybe Miss Murphy won't be home right now. Why not call first?"

He nodded. I picked up my phone and gave our switchboard girl Miss Murphy's telephone number. Randall fidgeted nervously.

"No answer," the switchboard reported.

I grinned at Randall. "See? Nobody home."

"I need that book." Randall sank into the spindly visitor's chair and sighed in frustration.

"You were going to tell me why."

"Here's why." He fished a damp crumpled bit of paper out of an envelope he took from his pocket. I reached for it. He held it away. "Don't touch it," he said. "We found it on the kid we pulled from the river this morning. It's the only damn thing we *did* find on him. No wallet, no money, no identification, no clothing labels, no nothing. Except for this he was plucked as clean as a chicken. We figure it was overlooked. It was in the bottom of his shirt pocket."

"What's it say?" I could see water-smeared writing.

He grinned unexpectedly, although his yellow eyes didn't seem to realize that the rest of his face was smiling. "It says: *PL Damion Complex ES4187.*"

"That's all?"

"That's all."

"Great bit of deduction, Lieutenant," I said. "You figured the *PL* for Public Library?"

"All by myself."

"So what's it mean?"

"How do I know till I get the damn book?" He sat erect and went on briskly, "Who had the book before Miss Murphy?"

I consulted my overdue list from the day before. "Gregory Hazzard. Desk clerk at the Starlight Motel on City Line. I picked up seven books and fines from him yesterday."

The Lieutenant was silent for a moment. Then, "Give Miss Murphy another try, will you?"

She still didn't answer her phone.

Randall stood up. My chair creaked when he removed his weight. "Let's go see this guy Hazzard."

"Me, too?"

"You, too." He gave me the fleeting grin again. "You're mixed up in this, son."

"I don't see how."

"Your library owns the book. And you belong to the library. So move your tail."

Gregory Hazzard was surprised to see me again so soon. He was a middle-aged skeleton, with a couple of pounds of skin and gristle fitted over his bones so tightly that he looked like the object of an anatomy lesson. His clothes hung on him—snappy men's wear on a scarecrow. "You got all my overdue books yesterday," he greeted me.

"I know, Mr. Hazzard. But my friend here wants to ask you about one of them."

"Who's your friend?" He squinted at Randall.

"Lieutenant Randall, City Police."

Hazzard blinked. "Another cop? We went all through that with the boys from your robbery detail day before yesterday."

Randall's eyes flickered. Otherwise he didn't change expression. "I'm not here about that. I'm interested in one of your library books."

"Which one?"

"The Damion Complex."

Hazzard bobbed his skull on his pipestem neck. "That one. Just a so-so yarn. You can find better spy stories in your newspaper."

Randall ignored that. "You live here in the motel, Mr. Hazzard?"

"No. With my sister down the street a ways, in a duplex."

"This is your address on the library records," I broke in. "The Starlight Motel."

"Sure. Because this is where I read all the books I borrow. And where I work."

"Don't you ever take library books home?" Randall asked.

"No. I leave 'em here, right at this end of the desk, out of the way. I read 'em during slack times, you know? When I finish them I take 'em back to the library and get another batch. I'm a fast reader."

"But your library books were overdue. If you're such a fast reader, how come?"

"He was sick for three weeks," I told Randall. "Only got back to work Saturday."

The Lieutenant's lips tightened and I knew from old experience that he wanted me to shut up. "That right?" he asked Hazzard. "You were sick?"

"As a dog. Thought I was dying. So'd my sister. That's why my books were overdue."

"They were here on the desk all the time you were sick?"

"Right. Cost me a pretty penny in fines, too, I must say. Hey, Mr. Johnson?"

I laughed. "Big deal. Two ninety-four, wasn't it?"

He chuckled so hard I thought I could hear his bones rattle. "Cheapest pleasure we got left, free books from the public library." He sobered suddenly. "What's so important about *The Damion Complex*, Lieutenant?"

"Wish I knew." Randall signaled me with his eyes. "Thanks, Mr. Hazzard, you've been helpful. We'll be in touch." He led the way out to the police car.

On the way back to town he turned aside ten blocks and drove to the Harrington Arms Apartments on Leigh Street. "Maybe we'll get lucky," he said as he pulled up at the curb. "If Murphy's home, get the book from her, Hal, okay? No need to mention the police."

A comely young lady, half out of a nurse's white uniform and evidently just home from work, answered my ring at Apartment 3A. "Yes?" she said, hiding her dishabille by standing behind the door and peering around its edge.

"Miss Oradell Murphy?"

"Yes." She had a fetching way of raising her eyebrows.

I showed her my ID card and gave her a cock-and-bull story about *The Damion Complex* having been issued to her yesterday by mistake. "The book should have been destroyed," I said, "because the previous borrower read it while she was ill with an infectious disease."

"Oh," Miss Murphy said. She gave me the book without further questions.

When I returned to the police car Lieutenant Randall said, "Gimme," and took the book from me, handling it with a finicky delicacy that seemed odd in such a big man. By his tightening lips I could follow his growing frustration as he examined *The Damion Complex.* For it certainly seemed to be just an ordinary copy of another ordinary book from the public library. The library name was stamped on it in the proper places. Identification number ES4187. Card pocket, with regulation date card, inside the front cover. Nothing concealed between its pages, not even a pressed forget-me-not.

"What the hell?" the Lieutenant grunted.

"Code message?" I suggested.

He was contemptuous. "Code message? You mean certain words off certain pages? In that case why was this particular copy specified—number ES4187? Any copy would do."

"Unless the message is in the book itself. In invisible ink? Or indicated by pin pricks over certain words?" I showed my teeth at him. "After all, it's a spy novel."

We went over the book carefully twice before we found the negative. And no wonder. It was very small—no more than half an inch or maybe five-eighths—and shoved deep in the pocket inside the front cover, behind the date card.

Randall held it up to the light. "Too small to make out what it is," I said. "We need a magnifying glass."

"Hell with that." Randall threw his car into gear. "I'll get Jerry to make me a blowup." Jerry is the police photographer. "I'll drop you off at the library."

"Oh, no, Lieutenant. I'm mixed up in this. You said so yourself. I'm sticking until I see what's on that negative." He grunted.

Half an hour later I was in Randall's office at headquarters when the police photographer came in and threw a black-and-white 3½" by 4½" print on the Lieutenant's desk. Randall allowed me to look over his shoulder as he examined it.

Its quality was poor. It was grainy from enlargement, and the images were slightly blurred, as though the camera had been moved just as the picture was snapped. But it was plain enough so that you could make out two men sitting facing each other across a desk. One was facing the camera directly; the other showed only as part of a rear-view silhouette—head, right shoulder, right arm.

The right arm, however, extended into the light on the desk top and could be seen quite clearly. It was lifting from an open briefcase on the desk a transparent bag of white powder, about the size of a pound of sugar. The briefcase contained three more similar bags. The man who was full face to the camera was reaching out a hand to accept the bag of white powder.

Lieutenant Randall said nothing for what seemed a long time. Then all he did was grunt noncommittally.

I said, "Heroin, Lieutenant?"

"Could be."

"Big delivery. Who's the guy making the buy? Do you know?"

He shrugged. "We'll find out."

"When you make him, you'll have your murderer. Isn't that what you're thinking?"

He shrugged again. "How do you read it, Hal?"

"Easy. The kid you pulled from the river got this picture somehow, decided to cut himself in by a little blackmail, and got killed for his pains."

"And tortured. Why tortured?" Randall was just using me as a sounding board.

"To force him to tell where the negative was hidden? He wouldn't have taken the negative with him when he braced the dope peddler."

"Hell of a funny place to hide a negative," Randall said. "You got any ideas about that?"

I went around Randall's desk and sat down. "I can guess. The kid sets up his blackmail meeting with the dope peddler, starts out with both the negative and a print of it, like this one, to keep his date. At the last minute he has second thoughts about carrying the negative with him."

"Where's he starting out from?" Randall squeezed his hands together.

"The Starlight Motel. Where else?"

"Go on."

"So maybe he decides to leave the negative in the motel safe and stops at the desk in the lobby to do so. But Hazzard is in the can, maybe. Or has stepped out to the restaurant for coffee. The kid has no time to waste. So he shoves the little negative into one of Hazzard's library books temporarily, making a quick note of the book title and library number so he can find it again. You found the note in his shirt pocket. How's that sound?"

Randall gave me his half grin and said, "So long, Hal. Thanks for helping."

I stood up. "I need a ride to the library. You've wasted my whole afternoon. You going to keep my library book?"

"For a while. But I'll be in touch."

"You'd better be. Unless you want to pay a big overdue fine."

It was the following evening before I heard any more from Lieutenant Randall. He telephoned me at home. "Catch any big bad book thieves today, Hal?" he began in a friendly voice.

"No. You catch any murderers?"

"Not yet. But I'm working on it."

I laughed. "You're calling to report progress, is that it?"

"That's it." He was as bland as milk.

"Proceed," I said.

"We found out who the murdered kid was."

"Who?"

"A reporter named Joel Homer from Cedar Falls. Worked for the *Cedar Falls Herald*. The editor tells me Homer was working on a special assignment the last few weeks. Trying to crack open a story on dope in the Tri-Cities."

"Oho. Then it *is* dope in the picture?"

"Reasonable to think so, anyway."

"How'd you find out about the kid? The Starlight Motel?"

"Yeah. Your friend Hazzard, the desk clerk, identified him for us. Remembered checking him into Room 18 on Saturday morning. His overnight bag was still in the room and his car in the parking lot."

"Well, it's nice to know who got killed," I said, "but you always told me you'd rather know who did the killing. Find out who the guy in the picture is?"

"He runs a ratty café on the river in Overbrook, just out of town. Name of Williams."

"Did you tie up the robbery squeal Hazzard mentioned when we were out there yesterday?"

"Could be. One man, masked, held up the night clerk, got him to open the office safe, and cleaned it out. Nothing much in it, matter of fact—hundred bucks or so."

"Looking for that little negative, you think?"

"Possibly, yeah."

"Why don't you nail this Williams and find out?"

"On the strength of that picture?" Randall said. "Uh, uh. That was enough to put him in a killing mood, maybe, but it's certainly not enough to convict him of murder. He could be buying a pound of sugar. No, I'm going to be sure of him before I take him."

"How do you figure to make sure of him, for God's sake?"

I shouldn't have asked that, because as a result I found myself, two hours later, sitting across that same desk—the one in the snapshot—from Mr. Williams, suspected murderer. We were in a sizable back room in Williams' café in Overbrook. A window at the side of the room was open, but the cool weed-scented breeze off the river didn't keep me from sweating.

"You said on the phone you thought I might be interested in a snapshot you found," Williams said. He was partially bald. Heavy black eyebrows met over his nose. The eyes under them looked like brown agate marbles in milk. He was smoking a fat cigar.

"That's right," I said.

"Why?"

"I figured it could get you in trouble in certain quarters, that's all."

He blew smoke. "What do you mean by that?"

"It's actually a picture of you buying heroin across this desk right here. Or maybe selling it."

"Well, well," he said, "that's interesting all right. If true." He was either calm and cool or trying hard to appear so.

"It's true," I said. "You're very plain in the picture. So's the heroin." I gave him the tentative smile of a timid, frightened man. It wasn't hard to do, because I felt both timid and frightened.

"Where is this picture of yours?" Williams asked.

"Right here." I handed him the print Lieutenant Randall had given me.

He looked at it without any change of expression I could see. Finally he took another drag on his cigar. "This guy does resemble me a little. But how did *you* happen to know that?"

I jerked a thumb over my shoulder. "I been in your café lots of times. I recognized you."

He studied the print. "You're right about one thing. This picture might be misunderstood. So maybe we can deal. What I can't understand is where you found the damn thing."

"In a book I borrowed from the public library."

"A book?" He halted his cigar in midair, startled.

"Yes. A spy novel. I dropped the book accidentally and this picture fell out of the inside card pocket." I put my hand into my jacket pocket and touched the butt of the pistol that Randall had issued me for the occasion. I needed comfort.

"You found this print in a book?"

"Not this print, no. I made it myself out of curiosity. I'm kind of an amateur photographer, see? When I found what I had, I thought maybe you might be interested, that's all. Are you?"

"How many prints did you make?"

"Just the one."

"And where's the negative?"

"I've got it, don't worry."

"With you?"

"You think I'm nuts?" I said defensively. I started a hand toward my hip pocket, then jerked it back nervously.

Mr. Williams smiled and blew cigar smoke. "What do you think might be a fair price?" he asked.

I swallowed. "Would twenty thousand dollars be too much?"

His eyes changed from brown marbles to white slits. "That's pretty steep."

"But you'll pay it?" I tried to put a touch of triumph into my expression.

"Fifteen. When you turn over the negative to me."

"Okay," I said, sighing with relief. "How long will it take you to get the money?"

"No problem. I've got it right here when you're ready to deal." His eyes went to a small safe in a corner of the room. Maybe the heroin was there, too, I thought.

"Hey!" I said. "That's great, Mr. Williams! Because I've got the negative here, too. I was only kidding before." I fitted my right hand around the gun butt in my pocket. With my left I pulled out my wallet and threw it on the desk between us.

"In here?" Williams said, opening the wallet.

"In the little pocket."

He found the tiny negative at once.

He took a magnifying glass from his desk drawer and used it to look at the negative against the ceiling light. Then he nodded, satisfied. He raised his voice a little and said, "Okay, Otto."

Otto? I heard a door behind me scrape over the rug as it was thrust open. Turning in my chair, I saw a big man emerge from a closet and step toward me. My eyes went instantly to the gun in his hand. It was fitted with a silencer, and oddly, the man's right middle finger was curled around the trigger. Then I saw why. The tip of his right index finger was missing. The muzzle of the gun looked as big and dark as Mammoth Cave to me.

"He's all yours, Otto," Williams said. "I've got the negative. No wonder you couldn't find it in the motel safe. The crazy kid hid it in a library book."

"I heard," Otto said flatly.

I still had my hand in my pocket touching the pistol, but I realized I didn't have a chance of beating Otto to a shot, even if I shot through my pocket. I stood up very slowly and faced Otto. He stopped far enough away from me to be just out of reach.

Williams said, "No blood in here this time, Otto. Take him out back. Don't forget his wallet and labels. And it won't hurt to spoil his face a little before you put him in the river. He's local."

Otto kept his eyes on me. They were paler than his skin. He nodded. "I'll handle it."

"Right." Williams started for the door that led to his café kitchen, giving me an utterly indifferent look as he went by. "So long, smart boy," he said. He went through the door and closed it behind him.

Otto cut his eyes to the left to make sure Williams had closed the door tight. I used that split second to dive headfirst over Williams' desk, my hand still in my pocket on my gun. I lit on the floor behind the desk with a painful thump and Williams' desk chair, which I'd overturned in my plunge, came crashing down on top of me.

From the open window at the side of the room a new voice said conversationally, "Drop the gun, Otto."

Apparently Otto didn't drop it fast enough because Lieutenant Randall shot it out of his hand before climbing through the window into the room. Two uniformed cops followed him.

Later, over a pizza and beer in the Trocadero All-Night Diner, Randall said, "We could have taken Williams before. The Narc Squad has known for some time he's a peddler. But we didn't know who was supplying him."

I said stiffly, "I thought I was supposed to be trying to hang a murder on him. How did that Otto character get into the act?"

"After we set up your meeting with Williams, he phoned Otto to come over to his café and take care of another would-be blackmailer."

"Are you telling me you didn't think Williams was the killer?"

Randall shook his head, looking slightly sheepish. "I was pretty sure Williams wouldn't risk Murder One. Not when he had a head-lock on somebody who'd do it for him."

"Like Otto?"

"Like Otto."

"Well, just who the hell *is* Otto?"

"He's the other man in the snapshot with Williams."

Something in the way he said it made me ask him, "You mean you knew who he was *before* you asked me to go through that charade tonight?"

"Sure. I recognized him in the picture."

I stopped chewing my pizza and stared at him. I was dumfounded, as they say. "Are you nuts?" I said with my mouth full. "The picture just showed part of a silhouette. From behind, at that. Unrecognizable."

"You didn't look close enough." Randall gulped beer. "His right hand showed in the picture plain. With the end of his right index finger gone."

"But how could you recognize a man from that?"

"Easy. Otto Schmidt of our Narcotics Squad is missing the end of his right index finger. Had it shot off by a junkie in a raid."

"There are maybe a hundred guys around with fingers like that. You must have had more to go on than that, Lieutenant."

"I did. The heroin."

"You recognized that, too?" I was sarcastic.

"Sure. It was the talk of the department a week ago, Hal."

"What was?"

"The heroin. Somebody stole it right out of the Narc Squad's own safe at headquarters." He laughed aloud. "Can you believe it? Two kilos, packaged in four bags, just like in the picture."

I said, "How come it wasn't in the news?"

"You know why. It would make us look like fools."

"Anyway, one bag of heroin looks just like every other," I said, unconvinced.

"You didn't see the *big* blowup I had made of that picture," the lieutenant said. "A little tag on one of the bags came out real clear. You could read it."

All at once I felt very tired. "Don't tell me," I said.

He told me anyway, smiling. "It said: Confiscated, such and such a date, such and such a raid, by the Grandhaven Police Department. That's us, Hal. Remember?"

I sighed. "So you've turned up another crooked cop," I said. "Believe me, I'm glad I'm out of the business, Lieutenant."

"You're *not* out of it." Randall's voice roughened with some emotion I couldn't put a name to. "You're still a cop, Hal."

"I'm an employee of the Grandhaven Public Library."

"Library fuzz. But still a cop."

I shook my head.

"You helped me take a killer tonight, didn't you?"

"Yeah. Because you fed me a lot of jazz about needing somebody who didn't *smell* of cop. Somebody who knew the score but could act the part of a timid greedy citizen trying his hand at blackmail for the first time."

"Otto Schmidt's a city cop. If I'd sent another city cop in there tonight, Otto would have recognized him immediately. That's why I asked you to go."

"You could have told me the facts."

He shook his head. "Why? I thought you'd do better without knowing. And you did. The point is, though, that you *did* it. Helped me nail a killer at considerable risk to yourself. Even if the killer wasn't the one you thought. You didn't do it just for kicks, did you? Or because we found the negative in your library book, for God's sake?"

I shrugged and stood up to leave.

"So you see what I mean?" Lieutenant Randall said. "You're still a cop." He grinned at me. "I'll get the check, Hal. And thanks for the help."

I left without even saying good night. I could feel his yellow eyes on my back all the way out of the diner.

"Q"

Richard Laymon

Paying Joe Back

"You don't catch me arguing with an armed woman"—not with an old gal packing one of those long-barreled .38's and hellbent on—well, she called it justice . . .

Folks say everything changes, but that's not so. I've lived in Windville all my life, and Joe's Bar & Grill looks just the same to me as always.

It has the same heavy steel grill, the same counter, the same swivel stools. Those long tables sticking out of the walls aren't much different than they were 30 years back, when Joe opened up—just older and more beaten up. The booth cushions got new upholstery seven years back, but Joe had them fixed up in the same red vinyl stuff as before, so you can't hardly tell the difference.

Only one thing has changed about Joe's place. That's the people. Some of the old-timers keep dropping by, regular as clockwork. But time has changed them considerably. Lester Keyhoe, for instance, fell to pieces after his wife kicked over. And old Gimpy Sedge lost his conductor job, so he just watches the train pull in and leave without him, then comes by here to tie one on with Lester.

Joe's gone, too. Not *gone,* just retired. I've kept the place going for the past three years, since I turned 21. When Joe isn't shooting deer in the mountains, he comes in for coffee and a cinnamon bun every morning. He likes to keep an eye on things.

I sure wish he'd been after deer the morning Elsie Thompson blew in.

The place was empty except for me and Lester Keyhoe, who was sitting down the bar where he always does, getting a start on the day's drinking.

I was toweling down the counter when the car pulled up. I could see it plain through the window. It was an old Ford that looked like somebody'd driven it a dozen times back and forth through Hell. It sputtered and whinnied for a minute after the ignition key was turned off.

I stopped toweling and just stared. The old gal who jumped out of the Ford was a real sight—short and round, dressed in khakis, with gray hair cut like Buster Brown, and wearing big wire-rimmed glasses. She chewed on some gum like she wanted to kill it. A floppy wicker handbag hung from her arm. I said, "Get a load of this," to Lester, but he didn't even look up.

The screen door opened and she stumped towards the counter in her dusty boots. She hopped onto the stool in front of me. Her jaw went up and down a few times. One time when it was open, the word "coffee" came out.

"Yes, ma'am," I said, and turned away to get it.

"Does this establishment belong to Joseph James Lowry from Chicago?" she asked.

"Sure does," I said, looking at her.

Behind the glasses her round eyes opened and shut in time with her chewing mouth. She gave me a huge grin. "That's mighty good news, young man. I've been driving through every one-horse town west of Chicago looking for this place, looking for Joe Lowry and his damned tavern. There's a place called Joe's in every single one of them. But I knew I'd find Joe Lowry's place sooner or later. Know why? Because I've got will power, that's why. When do you expect him in?"

"Well . . . what did you want to see him about?"

"He *is* coming in?"

I nodded.

"Good. I expected as much. I'm only surprised not to find him behind the counter."

"You know him, huh?"

"Oh, yes. My, yes." Her eyes turned sad for a second. "We used to know each other very well, back in Chicago."

"How about if I give him a ring, tell him you're here?"

"That won't be necessary." Snapping her gum and grinning, she opened the handbag on her lap and pulled out a revolver. Not a peashooter, either—one of those long-barreled .38's. "I'll surprise him," she said. Her stubby little thumb pulled back the hammer and she aimed the thing at me. "We'll surprise him together."

I didn't feel much like talking, but I managed to nod my head.

"What time will Joe be in?" she asked.

"Pretty soon." I took a deep breath and asked, "You aren't planning to shoot him, are you?"

She pretended like she didn't hear me, and asked, "How soon?"

"Well . . ." Far away, the 10:05 from Parkerville let loose its whistle. "Well, pretty soon, I guess."

"I'll wait for him. Who's that slob over there?"

"That's Lester."

"Lester!" she called.

He turned his head and looked at her. She waved the gun at him, grinning and chewing, but his face didn't change. It looked the same as always, long and droopy like a bloodhound's, but more gloomy.

"Lester," she said, "you just stay right on that stool. If you get up for any reason, I'll shoot you dead."

His head nodded, then turned frontwards again and tipped down at his half-empty glass.

"What's your name?" she asked me.

"Wes."

"Wes, keep Lester's glass full. And don't do anything to make me shoot you. If some more customers come in, just serve them like everything is normal. This revolver has six loads, and I can take down a man with each. I don't want to. I only want Joe Lowry. But if you drive me to it, I'll make this place wall-to-wall corpses. Understand?"

"Sure, I understand." I filled Lester's glass, then came back to the woman. "Can I ask you something?"

"Fire away."

"Why do you want to kill Joe?"

She stopped chewing and squinted at me. "He ruined my life. That's enough reason to kill a man, I think. Don't you?"

"Nothing's a good enough reason to kill Joe."

"Think so?"

"What'd he do to you?"

"He ran off with Martha Dipsworth."

"Martha? That's his wife—was."

"Dead?"

I nodded yes.

"Good." Her jaw chomped, and she beamed. "That makes me glad. Joe made a mistake, not marrying me—I'm still alive and kicking. We'd be happily married to this day if he'd had the sense to stick with me. But he never did have much sense. Do you know what his great ambition was? To go out west and open up a tavern. Martha thought that was a *glorious* idea. I said, 'Well, *you* marry him, then. Go out west and waste your lives in the boondocks. If Joe's such a romantic fool as to throw his life away like that, I don't want him.

There're plenty of fish in the sea.' That's what I said. More than thirty years ago."

"If you said that—" I stopped. You don't catch me arguing with an armed woman.

"What?"

"Nothing."

She shifted her chewing gum over to one corner of her mouth and drank some coffee. "What were you going to say?"

"Just . . . well, if you said they could get married, it doesn't seem very fair of you to blame them."

She put down the cup and glanced over at Lester. He still sat there, but he was staring at the gun. "When I said that about the sea being full of fish, I figured it'd only be a matter of time before I'd land a good one. Well, it didn't work out that way."

She chewed a few times, gazing up at me with a funny distance in her eyes as if she was looking back at all the years. "I kept on waiting. I was just sure the right man was around the next corner—around the next year. It finally dawned on me, Wes, that there wasn't ever going to be another man. Joe was it, and I'd lost him. That's when I decided to gun him down."

"That's—"

"What?"

"Crazy."

"It's justice."

"Maybe the two of you could get together. He's unattached since Martha died. Maybe—"

"Nope. Too late for that. Too late for babies, too late for—"

All at once Lester flung himself away from the bar and made a foolish run for the door. The old gal swiveled on her stool, tracked him for a split second, then squeezed off a shot. The bullet took off Lester's earlobe. With a yelp he swung around and ran back to his stool, cupping a hand over what was left of his ear.

"You'd better pray nobody heard that shot," she said to both of us.

I figured nobody would. We were at the tail end of town, so the closest building was a gas station half a block away. The cars passing by on the highway kicked up plenty of noise. And around here, with all the hunting that goes on, nobody pays much attention to a single gunshot unless it's right under his nose.

But I was nervous, anyway. For five minutes we all waited without saying a word. The only sound was her gum snapping.

She finally grinned and squinted as if she'd just won a raffle. "We're in luck."

"Joe's not," I said. "Neither's Lester."

Lester said nothing. He was pinching his notched ear with one hand and draining his glass with the other.

"They shouldn't have run," the woman said. "That was their mistake—they ran. You aren't going to run, are you?"

"No, ma'am."

"Because if you do I'll shoot you for sure. I'll shoot anyone today. Anyone. This is my day, Wes—the day Elsie Thompson pays Joe back."

"I won't run, ma'am. But I won't let you shoot Joe. I'll stop you one way or another." I went over to fill Lester's glass.

"You can't stop me. No one can stop me. Nothing can. Do you know why? Because I've got will power, that's why."

Grinning mysteriously, she chomped three times on her gum and said, "Today I'm going to die. That gives me all the power in the world. Understand? As soon as I gun down Joe, I'll drive out of this burg. I'll get that old Ford up to seventy, eighty, then I'll pick out the biggest tree—"

I made a sick laugh, and came back to her.

"Think I'm fooling?" she said.

"No, ma'am. It's just kind of funny, you talking like that about crashing into a tree. Not funny ha-ha, funny weird. You know what I mean?"

"No."

"That's 'cause you don't know about Joe. He crashed into a tree—an aspen, just off Route 5. That was about three years back. Martha was with him. She got killed, of course. Joe was in real bad shape, and Doc Mills didn't give him much chance. But he pulled through. His face got so broken up he doesn't look quite right, and he lost the use of an eye. His left eye, not his aiming eye. He wears a patch over it, you know. And sometimes when he gets feeling high, he flaps it up and gives us all a peek underneath."

"You can stop that."

"He lost a leg, too."

"I don't want to hear about it."

"Yes, ma'am. I'm sorry. It's just that . . . well, everyone that crashes into a tree doesn't die."

"I will."

"You can't be sure. Maybe you'll just end up like Joe, hobbling around half blind on a fake leg, with your face so scarred up that your best friends won't recognize you."

"Shut up, Wes."

She stuck the pistol into my face, so I slowed down and said quietly, "I just mean, if you want to make sure you die, there's a concrete bridge abutment about a mile up the road."

"Warm up my coffee and keep your mouth shut."

I turned around to pick up the pot. That's when I heard the footsteps outside. Boots against the wood planks out front, coming closer. I faced Elsie. She grinned at me. Her jaw worked faster on the gum. Her eyes squinted behind her glasses as the unsteady clumping got louder.

Through the window I saw his mussy gray hair, his scarred face with the patch on his left eye. He saw me looking, smiled, and waved.

I glanced at Lester, who was holding a paper napkin to his ear and the glass to his mouth.

Elsie pushed the pistol close to my chest. "Don't move," she whispered.

The screen door swung open.

Elsie spun her stool.

"Duck, Joe!" I cried out.

He didn't duck. He just stood there looking perplexed as Elsie leaped off the stool, crouched, and fired. The first two bullets smacked him square in the chest. The next hit his throat. Then one tore into his shoulder, turning him around so the last shot took him in the small of the back.

All this happened in a couple of seconds as I dived at Elsie. I was in mid-air when she wheeled on me and smashed me in the face with the barrel. I went down.

While I was trying to get up, she jumped over the body and ran out. I reached the door in time to see her car whip backwards. It hit the road with screeching brakes, then laid rubber and was gone from sight.

I went back inside.

Lester was still sitting at the bar. His stool was turned around, and he was staring at the body. I sat down at one of the booths, lit a cigarette, and kept Lester company staring.

We spent a long time like that. After a while I heard the sheriff's siren. Then an ambulance's. The cars screamed by and faded up the road in the direction of the bridge abutment.

"Guess that's Elsie," I said.

Lester just kept staring.

Then the screen door swung open.

"My God!" The big man looked at me, then at Lester, and knelt down over the body. He turned it over. "Gimpy," he muttered. "Poor old Gimpy." He patted the dead conductor on the back, and stood up. His eyes questioned me.

I shook my head. "Some crazy woman," I muttered. "She came in here dead set to kill you, Dad."

Michael Gilbert

The Merry Band

"But the boy had a gun on him and he was running away from the scene of the crime."
In some ways, one of Petrella's most unhappy cases. . .
"It took another whole day for Petrella to finish his inquiries, but now that the clue was in his hand it was not difficult to find the heart of the maze."
In some ways, one of Petrella's happiest cases. . .

Detective: SERGEANT PATRICK PETRELLA

The late-afternoon sun, shining through the barred skylight, striped the bodies of the four boys sprawled on the floor. Nearby the Sunday traffic went panting down the Wandsworth High Street, but in this quiet, upper back room the loudest noise was the buzzing of a bluebottle. The warm, imprisoned air smelled of copperas and leather and gun oil.

The oldest and tallest of the boys was sitting up, with his back propped against the wall. In one hand he held a piece of cloth, something that might once have been a handkerchief, and he was using it to polish and repolish a powerful-looking air pistol.

"They're beauties, ent they, Rob?" said the fat boy. He and the red-haired boy both had guns like their leader's. The smallest boy had nothing. He couldn't take his eyes off the shining beauties.

"Made in Belgium," said Rob. "See that gadget?" He put the tip of his finger on the telltale at the end of the compression chamber. "You don't just open it and shut it, like a cheap air gun. You pump this one up slowly. That gadget shows you when the pressure's right. It's accurate up to fifty yards."

"*It* may be accurate," said the fat boy. "What about us? I've never had a gun before."

"We'll have to practise. Practise till we can hit a penny across the room."

114

"Why don't we start right now, Rob?" said the red-haired boy.
"These things don't make any noise. Not to notice. We could chalk
up a target on the wall—"

"Yes?" said Rob. "And when the geezer who owns this shop comes
up here tomorrow morning, or next week, or whenever he does
happen to come up here, and he finds his wall full of air-gun pellets,
he's going to start thinking, isn't he? He's going to check over his
spare stock and find three guns missing. Right?"

"That's right," said the fat boy. "Rob's got it figured out. We put
everything else back like we found it, it may be months before he
knows what's been took. He mayn't even know anyone's broke in."

The leader turned to the smallest of his followers. "That's why
you can't have one, Winkle," he said. "There's plenty of guns in the
front of the shop, but we touch one of them, he'll miss it."

"That's all right, Rob," said Winkle. But he couldn't keep the
longing out of his voice. To own a big bright gun! A gun that went
phtt softly, like an angry snake, and your enemy fifty yards away
crumpled to the ground, not knowing what had hit him!

"What about Les?" said the red-haired boy.

"What about him?"

"He'll want a gun when he sees ours."

"He'll have to go on wanting. If he's not keen enough to come with
us on a job like this."

" 'Tisn't that he's not keen," said the fat boy. "It's his old man.
He's pretty strict. He locks his bedroom door now. Where can we
practise, Rob?"

"I've got an idea about that," said the tall boy. "You know the old
Sports Pavilion? The Home Guard used it in the war, but it's been
shut up since."

The boys nodded.

"I found a way in at the back, from the railway. I'll show you.
There's a sort of cellar with lockers in it. That'll do us fine. We'll
have our first meeting there tomorrow. Right?"

"Right," they all said. The red-haired boy added, "How did you
know about this place, Rob?"

"My family used to live round here," said the tall boy. "Before my
Ma died, when we moved up to Highside. As a matter of fact, I was
at school about a quarter mile from here."

The fat boy said, "I bet I get a strapping from my old man when
I get home. He don't like me being away all day."

"You're all right," said Winkle. "You're fat. It don't hurt so much when you're fat." He looked down with disgust at his own slender limbs.

It was nine o'clock at night nearly a month after that talk and in quite another part of London that Fishy Codlin was closing what he called his Antique Shop. This was a dark and rambling suite of rooms, full of dirt, woodworm, and the household junk of a quarter of a century. Codlin was in the front room, locking away the day's take when the two boys came in.

"You're too late," he growled. "I'm shut."

He noticed that the smaller of the boys stayed by the door, while the older came toward him with a curiously purposeful tread. He had a prevision of trouble and his hand reached out for the light switch.

"Leave it alone," said the boy. He was a half-seen figure in the dusk. All the light seemed to concentrate on the bright steel weapon in his hand. "Slip the bolt, Will," he added, but without taking his eyes off Codlin. "Now you stand away from the counter."

Codlin stood away. He thought for a moment of refusing, for there was nearly £25 in the box, the fruits of a full week's trading. But he was a coward as well as a bully and the gun looked real. He watched the notes disappearing in the boy's pocket. When one of the notes slipped to the floor the boy bent down and picked it up, but without ever removing his steady gaze from the old man.

When he had finished, the boy backed away to the door. "Stay put," he said. "And keep quiet for five minutes or you'll get hurt."

Then he was gone. Codlin breathed out an obscenity and jumped for the telephone. As he picked it up, "I warned you," said a gentle voice from the door. There was a noise like a small tire bursting and the telephone twisted round and clattered to the floor.

Codlin stood, staring stupidly at his hand. Splinters of vulcanite had grooved it, and the blood was beginning to drip. He cursed, foully and automatically. Footsteps were pattering away along the road outside. He let them get to the corner before he moved. He was taking no further chances. Then he lumbered across to the door, threw it open, and started bellowing.

Three streets away Detective Sergeant Petrella, homeward bound, heard two things at once. Distant shouts of outrage and, much closer at hand, light feet pattering on the pavement. He drew into the shadow at the side of the road and waited.

The two boys came round the corner, running easily, and laughing. When Petrella stepped out, the laughter ceased. Then the boys spun around and started to run the other way.

Petrella ran after them. He saw at once that he could not catch both, so he concentrated on the younger and slower boy. After a hundred yards he judged himself to be in distance and jumped forward in a tackle. It was high by the standards of Twickenham, but it was effective, and they went down, the boy underneath. As they fell, something dropped from the boy's pocket and slid, ringing and spinning, across the pavement.

"Of course you've got to charge him," said Haxtell later that night. "It's true Codlin can't really identify him, but the boy had a gun on him and he was running away from the scene of the crime. Who is he, by the way?"

"His name's Christopher Connolly. His father's a shunter at the goods depot. I've left them together for a bit, to see if the old man can talk some sense into him."

"Good idea," said Haxtell. "Can we get anything on the gun?"

"It's an air pistol. Therefore no registration number. And foreign. Newish. And a pretty high-powered job. If it's been stolen we might have it on the lists."

"Check it," said Haxtell. "What about his pockets?"

"Nothing except this." Petrella pushed across a scrap of paper. It had penciled on it: WILL BE AT USUAL PLACE 8 TONIGHT.

"What do you make of it?" said Haxtell.

"It depends," said Petrella cautiously, "if you think the dot after the first word is a full stop or just an accident."

Haxtell tried it both ways. "You mean it could be a plain statement: 'I will be at the usual place at eight o'clock tonight.' Or it could be an order, to someone called Will."

"Yes. And Codlin did say that he thought he heard the bigger boy address the smaller one as Will."

"Is Connolly's name William?"

"No, sir. It's Christopher George. Known to his friends as Chris."

"What does he say about the paper?"

"Says I planted it on him. And the gun, of course."

"I often wonder," said Haxtell, "where the police keep all the guns they're supposed to plant on criminals. What about the other boy?"

"He says that there was no other boy. He says he was alone, and had been alone, all the evening."

"I see." Haxtell stared thoughtfully out of the window. He had a sharp nose for trouble.

"One bright spot," he said at last. "Codlin always marked his notes. Ever since he caught an assistant trying to dip into his till. He puts a letter C in indelible pencil on the back."

"That might be a help if we can catch the other boy," agreed Petrella. He added, "Haven't I heard that name Codlin before? Something about a dog."

"He tied his dog up," said Haxtell. "A nice old spaniel. And beat him with a golf club. Fined forty shillings. It was before your time."

"I must have read about it somewhere," said Petrella.

"And if you think," blared Haxtell, "that's any reason for not catching these–these young bandits–then I dare you to say it."

"Why, certainly not," said Petrella hastily.

"This is the third holdup in a fortnight. The third that's been reported to us. All with guns–or what looked like guns. Now we've caught one of them. We've *got* to get the names of the other boys out of him. For their sake as much as anything. Before someone really gets hurt."

"I expect the boy'll talk," said Petrella.

Haxtell nodded. Given time, boys usually talked.

But Christopher Connolly was an exception. For he said nothing, and continued to say nothing.

The next thing that happened, happened to old Mrs. Lightly, who lived alone in a tiny cottage above the waterworks. Her husband had been caretaker and she had retained the cottage by grace of the management as long as she paid the rent of ten shillings a week. Lately she had been getting irregular in her payments and she was now under notice to move.

The evening after the capture of Connolly, just after dark, she heard a noise down in her front hall. She was a spirited old lady and she came right out, carrying a candle to see what it was all about.

On the patched linoleum lay a fat envelope. Mrs. Lightly picked it up gingerly and carried it back to the sitting room. She got very few letters, and, in any case, the last mail had come and gone many hours earlier.

On the envelope, in penciled capital letters, were the words:

EIGHT WEEKS RENT FROM SOME FRIENDS.

Mrs. Lightly set the candle down on the table and with fingers that trembled tore open the flap. A little wad of notes slid out. She counted them. Two pound notes and four ten-shilling notes. There was no shadow of doubt about it. It was four pounds. And that was eight weeks' rent.

Or, looked at in another way, suppose it was seven weeks' rent. That would have the advantage of leaving ten shillings over for a little celebration. The whole thing was clearly a miracle; and miracles are things which the devout are commanded to commemorate.

Mrs. Lightly placed the notes in the big black bag, folded the envelope carefully away behind a china dog on the mantelshelf, and got her best black hat out of the closet.

On the same evening, shortly after Mrs. Lightly left her cottage, four boys were sitting in the basement changing room of the old Sports Pavilion. A storm lantern, standing on a locker, shed a circle of clear white light around it, leaving the serious faces of the boys in shadow. The windows were carefully blacked out on the inside with cardboard and brown paper.

"I don't like it, Rob," the black-haired boy was saying. He was evidently repeating an old argument.

"What's wrong with it?" said the tall boy. He had a curiously gentle voice.

"Old Cator's what's wrong with it. He's a holy terror."

"He's a crook," said the fat boy.

The small boy said nothing. His eyes turned from one to the other as they spoke, but when no one was speaking they rested on the tall boy, full of trust and love.

"Isn't it crooks we're out to fix?" said the tall boy. "Isn't that right, Busty?"

"That's right," said the fat boy.

The black-haired boy said, "Hell, yes. But not just any crooks. Cator's got a night watchman. And he's a tough, too. As likely as not, they both carry guns."

The tall boy said, "Are you afraid?"

"Of course I'm not afraid."

"Then what are we arguing about? There's four of us. And we've got two guns. There's two of them. When we pull the job, maybe only one'll be there. This is something we've *got* to do. We need the money."

"Another thing," said the black-haired boy. "Suppose we don't give quite so much away this time."

"You mean, keep some for ourselves?"

"That's right."

"What for?"

"I could think of ways to use it," said the black-haired boy, with a laugh. He looked round, but neither of the others had laughed with him. "All right," he said. "All right. I know the rules. Let's get this planned out."

"This is how it is, then," said the tall boy. "I reckon we'll have to wait about a week–" He demonstrated, on sheets of paper, with a pencil, and the four heads came close together, casting long shadows in the lamplight.

Next morning Petrella reported to Superintendent Haxtell the minor events of the night. There was a complaint from the Railway that some boys had broken a hole in the fence below the Sports Pavilion.

"Apart from that," said Petrella, "a beautiful calm seems to have fallen on Highside. Oh–apart from Mrs. Lightly."

"Mrs. Lightly?"

"Old Lightly's widow. The one who lives in the cottage next to the waterworks."

"Was that the one there was a bit in the papers about how she couldn't pay her rent?"

"That's right," said Petrella. "Only she got hold of some money and that's what the drinking was about. It was a celebration. She seems to have drunk her way steadily along the High Street. Mostly gin, but a certain amount of stout to help it down. She finished by busting a shop window with an empty bottle."

"Where'd she got the money from?"

"That's the odd thing. She was flat broke. Faced with eviction, and no one very sympathetic, because they knew that as soon as she got any money she'd drink it up. Then an angel dropped in, with four quid in an envelope."

"An angel?"

"That's what she says. A disembodied spirit. It popped an envelope through the letter box with four ten-shilling notes and two pound notes in it."

"How much of it was left when you picked her up?"

"About two pounds ten," said Petrella.

"I don't see anything odd in all that," said Haxtell. "Some crackpot reads in the papers that the old girl's short of money and how her landlord's persecuting her, and he makes her an anonymous donation, which she promptly spends on getting plastered."

"Yes, sir," said Petrella. He added gently, "I've seen the notes she *didn't* spend. They're all marked on the back with a C in indelible pencil."

"They're *what?*"

"That's right, sir."

"It's mad."

"It's a bit odd, certainly," said Petrella. Something, a note almost of smugness in his voice, made the Superintendent look up. "Have you got some line on this?"

"I think I might be able to trace those notes back to the boy who's been running this show."

"Then we don't waste any time talking about it," said Haxtell. "We need results and we need 'em quickly." He added, with apparent inconsequence, "I'm seeing Barstow this afternoon."

Petrella's hopes, such as they were, derived from the envelope, which he had duly recovered from behind the china dog on Mrs. Lightly's mantelshelf. The name and address had been cut out, but two valuable pieces of information had been left behind. The first was the name *Strangeway's* printed in the top left-hand corner. The second was the postmark, the date on which was still legible.

Petrella knew Strangeway's. It was a shop that sold cameras and photographic equipment, and he guessed that its daily output of letters would not be large. There was a chance, of course, that the envelope had been picked up casually. But equally, there was a chance that it had not.

Happily, the manager of Strangeway's was a methodical man. He consulted his daybook and produced for Petrella a list of names and addresses. "I think," he said, "that those would be all the firm's letters that went out that day. They would be bills or receipts. I may have written one or two private letters, but I'd have no record of them."

"But they wouldn't be in your firm's envelope."

"They might be. If they went to suppliers."

"I'll try these first," said Petrella.

There were a couple of dozen names on the list. Most of the addresses were in Highside or Helenwood.

It was no use inventing an elaborate story. He was too well known locally to pretend to be an insurance salesman. He decided on a simple lie.

To the gray-haired old lady who opened the door to him at the first address he said, "We're checking the election register. The lists

are getting out of date. Have you any children in the house who might come of age in the next five years?"

"There's Jimmy," said the woman.

"Who's Jimmy?"

She explained about Jimmy. He was a real terror. Aged about nineteen. Just as Petrella was getting interested in Jimmy she added that he'd been in Canada for a year.

Petrella took down copious details about Jimmy. It all took time, but if you were going to deal in lies, it was well to act them out.

That was the beginning of a long day's work. Early in the evening he came to Number 11 Parham Crescent. The house was no different from a million others of the brick boxes that encrust the surface of London's northern heights.

The door was opened by a gentleman in shirtsleeves, who agreed that his name was Brazier and admitted having a sixteen-and-a-half-year-old son named Robert.

"Robert Brazier?"

"Robert Humphreys. He's my sister's son. She's been dead two years. He lives here—*when* he's home."

Petrella picked up the lead with the skill of long experience. Was Robert often away from home?

Mr. Brazier obliged with a discourse on modern youth. Boys nowadays, Petrella gathered, were very unlike what boys used to be when he—Mr. Brazier—had been young. They lacked reverence for their elders, thought they knew all the answers, and preferred to go their own ways. "Sometimes I don't see him all day. Sometimes two days running. He could be out all night for all I know. It's not right—Mr.—um—"

Petrella agreed that it wasn't right. Mr. Brazier suffered from bad breath, which made listening to him an ordeal. However, he elicited some details. One of them was the name of the South London school that Robert had left eighteen months before.

Petrella did some telephoning, and the following morning he caught a bus and trundled down to Southwark to have a word with Mr. Wetherall, the headmaster of the South Borough Secondary School for Boys. Mr. Wetherall was a small spare man with a beaky nose and he had been wrestling for a quarter of a century with the tough precocious youths who live south of the river. The history of his struggles was grooved into his leathery face. He cheerfully took time off to consider Petrella's problems; all the more so when he discovered what was wanted.

"Robert Humphreys," he said. "I had a bet with my wife that I'd hear that name again before long."

"Now you've won it, sir."

"Yes," said Mr. Wetherall. He gazed reflectively round his tiny overcrowded study, then said, "This is a big school, you know. And I've been here, with one short break, for more than ten years. Maybe two thousand boys. And out of all that two thousand I could count on the fingers of one hand–without using the thumb–the ones whom I call natural leaders. And of those few I'm not sure I wouldn't put Robert Humphreys first."

Mr. Wetherall added, "I'll tell you a story about him. While he was here, we were planning to convert a building into a gymnasium. I'd got all the governors on my side except the Chairman, Colonel Bond. He was opposed to spending the money, and until I'd won him over I couldn't move.

"One day the Colonel disappeared. He's a bachelor who spends most of his time at his Club. No one was unduly worried. He missed a couple of governors' meetings, which was unusual.

"Then I got a letter. From the Colonel. It simply said that he had been thinking things over and had decided that we ought to go ahead with our gym. He himself wouldn't be able to attend meetings for some time, as his health had given way."

Petrella goggled at him. "Are you telling me–?" he said.

"That's right," said Mr. Wetherall calmly. "The boys had kidnaped him. Robert organized the whole thing. They picked him up in a truck, and kept him in a loft, over an old stable. Guarded him, fed him, looked after him. And when they'd induced him to write that letter they let him out."

"How did they disguise themselves?"

"They made no attempt to disguise themselves. They calculated, and rightly, that if the Colonel made a fuss people would never stop laughing at him. The Colonel had worked the sum out too, and got the same answer. He never said a word about it. In fact, it was Humphreys who told me. It was then that I made my confident prediction. Downing Street or the Old Bailey."

"I'm afraid it may be the Old Bailey," said Petrella unhappily.

"It was an even chance," said Mr. Wetherall. "He was devoted to his mother. If she hadn't died, I believe there's hardly any limit to what he might have done. He's with an uncle now. Not a very attractive man."

"I've met him," said Petrella. As he was going he said, "Did you get your gym?"

"I'll show it to you as we go," said Mr. Wetherall. "One of the finest in South London."

It took another whole day for Petrella to finish his inquiries, but now that the clue was in his hand it was not difficult to find the heart of the maze. It had been a day of blazing heat; by nine o'clock that night when he faced Superintendent Haxtell, hardly a breath was moving.

"There are four of them," he said. "Five with Chris Connolly, the one we caught. First, there's a boy called Robert Humphreys. His first lieutenant's Brian Baker, known as Busty."

"A fat boy," said Haxtell. "Rather a good footballer. His father's a pro."

"Correct. The third one is Les Miller."

"Sergeant Miller's boy?"

"I'm afraid so, sir."

The two men looked at each other. Sergeant Miller was Petrella's opposite number at Pond End Police Station.

"Go on," said Haxtell grimly.

"The fourth, and much the youngest, is one of the Harrington boys. The one they call Winkle. His real name's Eric, or Ricky. There seems to be no doubt that the air guns they've been using were stolen from a shop in Southwark, which is, incidentally, where Humphreys went to school."

"And Humphreys is the leader?"

"I don't think there's any doubt about that at all, sir. In fact, the whole thing is a rather elaborate game made up by him."

"A game," said Haxtell, pulling out a handkerchief and wiping the sweat from his forehead.

"Of Robin Hood. That's why they used those names. Fat Brian was Friar Tuck, red-headed Chris was Will Scarlet, Les was the Miller's son. And Ricky was Allen-a-Dale. Robert, of course, was Robin. I believe that historically—"

"I'm not interested in history. And you can dress it up what way you like. It doesn't alter the fact that they're gangsters."

"There were two points about them," said Petrella. "I'm not suggesting it's any sort of mitigation. But they really did adhere to the ideas of their originals. They didn't rob old women or girls—and they're usually the number-one target for juvenile delinquents."

Haxtell grunted.

"They chose people they thought needed robbing." Petrella caught the look in his superior's eye and hurried on. "And they didn't spend the money on themselves. They gave it away. All of it, as far as I can make out. To people they thought needed it. More like the real Robin Hood than the synthetic version. Hollywood's muddled it up for us.

"You hear the kids saying, 'Feared by the bad. Loved by the good.' But that wasn't really the way of it. Robin Hood didn't rob people because they were bad. He assumed they were bad because they were rich. He was an early Communist."

Petrella stopped, aware that he had outrun discretion.

"Go on," said Haxtell grimly.

"Of course, he's got idealized now," Petrella concluded defiantly. "But I should think the authorities thought *he* was a pretty fair nuisance—when he was actually operating—wouldn't you?"

"And you suggest, perhaps, that we allow them to continue their altruistic work of redistributing the wealth of North London?"

"Oh, no, sir. We've got to stop them."

"Why, if they're doing so much good?"

"Before they get hurt. As you said yourself."

Haxtell was spared the necessity of answering by a clatter of feet in the corridor and a resounding knock at the door. It was Detective Sergeant Miller, and he had his son with him.

"Good evening, Miller," said Haxtell. "I was half expecting you."

"I've brought my boy along," said Sergeant Miller. He was white with fury. "He's got something he's going to tell you."

The boy had been crying, but was calm enough now. "It's Humphreys and the others," he said. "They're going to do Cator's Garage tonight. I wouldn't agree to it. So they turned me out of the band. So I told Dad."

Just so, thought Petrella, had all great dynasties fallen. He was aware of a prickling sensation, a crawling of the skin, not entirely accounted for by the onrush of events. He looked out of the window and saw that a storm had crept up on them. Even as he watched, the first thread of lightning flicked out and in, like an adder's tongue, among the banked black clouds.

Les Miller was demonstrating something on the table.

"They've found a way in round the back. They get across the canal on the old broken bridge, climb the bank, and get in a window of an outhouse, which leads into the garage. There's a watchman, but they reckon they can rush him from behind and get his keys off him. Cator keeps a lot of his money in the garage."

Petrella said, "I expect that's right, sir. We've had our eyes on that gentleman for some time. If he's in the hot-car racket he'd have no use for checks or a bank account."

"We'd better warn Cator," said Haxtell, "and get a squad car round there quick. What time's the operation due to start?"

Before the boy could answer, the telephone sounded. Haxtell picked off the receiver, listened a moment, and said, "Don't do anything. We'll be right around," and to the others, "It has started. That was the watchman. He's knocked one boy out cold."

As Petrella ran for the car the skies opened and he was wet to the skin before he reached the car.

Outside Cator's Garage, a rambling conglomeration of buildings backing on the canal, they skidded to a halt, nearly ramming a big green limousine coming from the opposite direction. Herbert Cator jumped out, pounded up the cinder path ahead of them, and thumped on the door.

The man who opened the door looked like a boxer gone badly to seed. The right side of his face was covered with blood, from a badly torn ear and a scalp wound. He was holding a long steel poker in one hand. "Glad you've got here," said the man. "Three of the little scum. I got one of 'em."

He jerked his head toward the corner where fat Friar Tuck lay on his face, on the oil-dank floor.

"Where are the others?" said Haxtell.

"In there." He pointed to the heavy door that led through to the main workshop. "Don't you worry. They won't get out of there in a hurry. The windows are all barred."

Haxtell walked across, slipped the bolt, and threw the door open.

It was a big room, two stories tall. The floor space was jammed with cars in every stage of dismemberment. The top was a clutter of hoisting and lifting tackle, dim above the big overhead lights.

"Come out of there, both of you."

"The big one's got a gun," said the watchman. "He nearly shot my ear off."

"Keep away then," said Haxtell. He turned back again and said in a booming voice, "Come on, Humphreys. And you, Harrington. The place is surrounded."

As if in defiant answer came a sudden deafening crash of thunder. And then all the lights went out.

"Damnation," said Haxtell. Over his shoulder to Petrella and Miller he said, "Bring all the torches we've got in the car. And the spotlight, if the flex is long enough—"

Cator said, "Hold it a moment. Something's alight." A golden-white sheet of flame shot up from the back of the room. Cator said thickly, "They've set fire to the garage, the devils."

In the sudden light Petrella saw the boys. They were crouching together on an overhead latticework gantry. Cator saw them, too. His hand went down and came up. There was the roar of a gun, once, twice, before anyone could get at him. Then Petrella was moving.

The light showed him the iron ladder that led upward. He flung himself at it and went up. Then along the narrow balcony. When he reached the place where he had seen them, the boys had gone. He stood for a moment. Already the heat was becoming painful. Then, ahead of him, he saw the door to the roof. It was swinging open.

As he reached it the whole of the interior of the room went up behind him in a hot white belch of flame.

Out on the roof he found the boys. Ricky Harrington was on his knees, beside Humphreys. The flames, pouring through the opening, lit the scene with cruel light.

Petrella knelt down beside him. One look was enough.

"He's dead, ent he?" said Ricky, in a curiously composed voice.

"Yes," said Petrella. "And unless the fire engine comes damned quick, he's going to have company in the next world."

The boy said, "I don't want no one to rescue me." He ran to the side of the building, vaulted the low coping, and disappeared. Petrella hurled himself after him.

He was just in time to see the miracle. Uncaring what happened to him, Ricky had landed with a soft splash in the waters of the North Side Canal.

"If he can do it, I can," said Petrella. "Roast or drown." He jumped. The world turned slowly in one complete fiery circle, and then his mouth was full of water.

He rose to the surface, spitting. There was no sign of the boy. Petrella tried to think. They had jumped from the same spot. There was no current. He must be there. Must be within a few yards.

He took a deep breath, turned over, and duck-dived. His fingers scrabbled across filth, broken crockery, and the sharper edges of cans. When he could bear it no longer he came up.

At the third attempt his fingers touched clothing. He slithered for a foothold in the mud and pulled. The small body came with him, unresisting.

A minute later he had it on the flat towpath. He was on the far side of the river, but even so he had to stagger twenty or thirty yards and turn the corner of the wall to escape the searing blast of the heat.

Then he dumped his burden and started to work, savagely, intently fighting for the life under his hands.

It was five minutes before Ricky stirred. Then he rolled onto his side and was sick.

"What's happened?" he said.

"You're all right," said Petrella. "We'll look after you."

"Not me, him." Then he seemed to remember, and sat still.

In the sudden silence Petrella heard a distant and plaintive bugle note. He knew that it was only the hooter, from the goods depot, but for a moment it had sounded like a horn being blown in a lonely glade; blown for the followers who would not come.

L. E. Behney

Tales from Home

*Two poignant and compelling "tales from home" . . . Kendricks
promised his Ma he'd look after his younger brother . . .*

1: The Man Who Kept His Promise

Long evening shadows of live oak and chaparral stretched across
the rutted wheel tracks as Kendricks rode his tired mare down
the hill into town.

He was a tall square-shouldered man, rimed with dust and sweat,
and he held himself stiffly erect in the saddle as the mare picked
her way down the main street through a confusion of riders, buggies,
and wagons.

Except for the crowd of farmers, cowboys, and mill men that filled
the street, Oak Flat might have been any one of the dozens of small
towns that Kendricks had ridden into in the past few weeks—a clus-
ter of frame houses, a string of high-fronted stores, a mingled smell
of dust, manure, and smoke.

Kendricks reined the mare over to the town's livery stable and
swung stiffly from the saddle. He peered into the dark interior of
the frame building, then rapped sharply on the open door. A balding
man wearing a leather apron came limping out.

"We got no more room—full up," he said, grinning.

"Is there another stable in town?" Kendricks asked.

"No, ya just bet there ain't," the man said, "but fer a buck ya can
turn yer hoss out in the corral back of the stable."

"For five could you find her a stall, a measure of oats, and give
her a rubdown?"

"Fer five—silver—I could do a lot of things," the man said, suddenly
respectful. He took the mare's reins as Kendricks fished the coins
out of his pocket. "When'll ya be wantin' her? Tomorrow, I guess,
after the show's over, huh?"

The tall man untied his saddlebags and slung them over his shoulder.

"Is there a hotel in town?"

"Yes, sir, ya bet there is, right down the street. The Antlers–but I'll bet they're full up too. It ain't every day business is this good. Ya just bet it ain't."

Kendricks walked down the board sidewalk, his boot heels thumping hollowly. Teams and wagons lined the hitch rails in a yellowish haze of dust. Some of the farmers had brought their families with them. They had unhitched their horses and fed them hay. The women were busy spreading quilts in the wagon beds and handing out food to their noisy youngsters.

Kendricks stepped into the first saloon he came to. He put his saddlebags on the bar, pulled off his dusty hat, wiped his sweaty face on his shirt sleeve, and ordered a beer. No need to ask the usual questions this time. Aching with weariness, he let his body sag against the stained and polished wood.

The beer was warm and flat, but it quenched his thirst. He drank slowly, listening to the boisterous flood of talk and laughter that swept around him. The bartender wore a broad happy grin–it was a great day for business. Abruptly Kendricks paid for his drink and left.

The hotel lobby was crowded. Kendricks pushed his way to the desk and asked for a room.

"You gotta be kidding," the clerk said, cleaning his fingernails with a penknife. "There ain't been a room here since this morning."

"Any other hotel in town?"

"Nope," the clerk shrugged. He glanced slyly at Kendricks. "'Course, if ya don't mind payin' a little extra, I mought just manage to squeeze ya in with a feller in Room Twelve."

"I don't mind."

"In that case it'll be four dollars–in advance, that is."

Kendricks paid him and laid his saddlebags on the desk.

"I'm going out for a while. Put these up for me."

"Well, I dunno as I want–"

"Do it, and I'd not like to see anything happen to them."

"All right. Yes, sir."

Kendricks went back to the busy street. In the middle of the square formed by the town's only crossroads a wooden structure towered stark and raw. Men were still working on it, clinging like flies to the two uprights, lifting a heavy cross beam into place.

Kendricks walked across the square and looked up at it. One of the onlookers nudged him with a bony elbow.

"Stranger here, ain't ya? Never seen no better lookin' gallows, now did ya? By golly, we don't have many hangin's, but when we do we fix things up good and proper."

The thud of workmen's hammers echoed back from the store fronts.

"Where's the Sheriff's office?" Kendricks asked.

"Right down there," the man pointed with a gap-toothed grin. "Ol' Matt Starrett, he don't go much for fancy hangin's, but Geary had a lot of friends in these parts, and there ain't a hell of a lot Ol' Matt ken do about it."

The Sheriff was sitting alone in his office behind a battered oak desk. As Kendricks entered he swung around, grimly alert, a small man with the toughness of worn leather and sharp, cold gray eyes.

"I'm Bill Kendricks," the tall man said slowly. "I've come a long ways."

The Sheriff stood up. He wore a heavy revolver in a low-slung holster and he moved as though the weapon were a natural part of him.

"Kendricks," he said. "Any relation of the boy's?"

"Brother."

A flicker of light touched the Sheriff's cold eyes. "Sorry about the mess out there," he said. "Some fools'll make a circus out of any-thing—even a hanging."

"Yes," Kendricks said.

"The boy got any other kinfolks?"

"Folks are both dead."

"I suppose you wanta see him?"

"Yes."

Kendricks stood stolidly while the Sheriff ran his hands over his tall body.

"You'd be more of a fool than you look if you tried to break him out."

"Yes," Kendricks said again.

"Come along," the Sheriff said. He took a large ring of keys from his desk drawer and led the way out the back of his office into a debris-littered alley.

The jail stood by itself—a small squat building of stone with a metal roof and a heavy ironbound door. The Sheriff, watching Kendricks steadily, fumbled with the keys, then opened the door. It swung back on protesting hinges and a hot, fetid smell curled out of the darkness inside.

"You stand right there in the door where I can see you," the Sheriff said, and stepped aside.

Kendricks stood in the doorway and peered into the dark. The only light and air came from a small barred window up near the ceiling, and in spite of the thick stone walls the heat was stifling. The room was divided by a grille of iron bars into a narrow hallway and two cells. Each cell contained a bunk, a rusty pail, and a heavy chain riveted to an iron ring set into the stone floor.

One cell was empty. In the one next to the door the chain was padlocked around the bare ankle of a man lying on his face on the narrow bunk, his blond head buried in his arms. In the sticky heat he was shivering, and his sweat-soaked clothing clung to his thin body.

"Tod," Kendricks said.

The man on the bunk jerked. He leaped to his feet and flung himself against the bars. The chain on his leg clattered across the rough floor. His young face was gray and waxy beneath the soft, pale stubble of his beard. As his startled eyes fixed on Kendricks they glittered with a sudden wild hope.

"Bill!" he cried shrilly. "I knew you'd come! You couldn't let me die like this! I sent you word—weeks ago. What took you so damn long? Tomorrow they're gonna hang me. Tomorrow—" His thin gray fingers clutched the bars.

"I happened to hear," the older man said. "I haven't been home since you run off. I been looking for you."

The boy tried to smile. Tears trickled down his cheeks and his mouth twisted grotesquely. "Sure I left," he said. "I wanted to see something—to do something—'fore I got so old and settled down. You can understand that, can't you, Bill?"

"I can't understand you killing a man."

"I never killed nobody!"

"A couple of witnesses and the judge and jury thought you did. They said you bushwhacked a man named Abe Geary—shot him down after he licked you in a fair fight."

"It weren't a fair fight! The damned bully!" The boy's reddened eyes narrowed. "I tell you I didn't kill him. But anyway, what difference does it make?" His thin, high-pitched voice dropped to a whisper. "You gotta get me out of here. You got no time to do it legal. The Sheriff's got the keys. Half the time there ain't even a guard. I don't give a damn how you do it, Bill—but you gotta get me outta here!"

"I think you did kill Geary."

"What if I did? He had it comin'. You swore to Ma you'd look after me. When she was dyin' you swore to her on the Bible that you'd take care of me. You never broke a promise in your life, Bill."

"I don't aim to break my word now, Tod," the older man said heavily. "I looked after you for years—getting you out of scrapes, trying to see to it you did what was right and honorable."

"You get me out of this," the boy panted. "You get me out of here and I'll do like you say. You won't never have no more trouble with me again—I swear I won't."

"You can't give a man back his life." Kendricks turned away slowly, his square shoulders sagging.

"Wait!" the boy shouted. "Bill, you can't leave me here! Bill!" He pressed his face against the bars and stretched out his hands with desperate appeal. The older man looked at him, seeing the bony wrists, the thin white arms, the frightened childish face, the mop of straw-colored hair.

"You done talkin' to him?" the Sheriff called out.

"Yes," Kendricks said. As he walked down the alley he heard the Sheriff slam the heavy door shut and lock it and he heard his brother's hysterical screaming.

Kendricks walked back to the hotel, got his saddlebags, and went upstairs to Room 12.

It was empty and he pulled off his boots and lay down on the bed. After a time the town grew quiet and a small plump man in a checked suit stumbled happily into the room, undressed, and tumbled into bed beside Kendricks where he fell instantly asleep, snoring loudly and smelling of cheap whiskey.

Kendricks, awake in the dark, thought of his brother. Not the Tod who was a sniveling wretched man in the jail cell, but the boy he once was, bright-eyed and laughing. The daydream was so real that the older man groaned and buried his face in the hard pillow.

Toward morning he slept fitfully and awoke as the sky grew light in the east. He slid off the bed quietly so that he would not disturb his snoring companion and went to the window. Already the people camped in the streets were stirring. The smoke of a small campfire rose across the bright sky, and a horse stamped and whickered.

Kendricks pulled on his boots, splashed water into the basin, and washed his face. He took his razor from his saddlebags and shaved carefully, using the hotel's cracked and smelly bar of soap. He emptied the basin into the slop pail, rinsed the basin, wiped it dry, and hung the towel neatly in place. He put on a clean shirt and combed his thick hair.

On the street, beneath the hotel window, people were beginning to pass, their shoes drumming on the boards, their voices low-pitched and full of nervous excitement.

Kendricks took a .45 Colt revolver from his saddlebags. He checked the action, loaded it, and put it inside the waistband of his pants under his shirt. He went down the stairs and joined the crowd as it moved like a fast-flowing river toward the square.

The gallows towered overhead, the splintery green lumber glistening with pitch drops in the early morning sunlight. As Kendricks stepped into the open square, the crowd that had been pushing and shoving and fighting for the best view grew suddenly silent and intent.

The door of the Sheriff's office opened and a small procession emerged. A pale young preacher came first, his hands clasped in prayer. After him came the Sheriff and a grim-faced deputy supporting between them the prisoner in a white shirt and dark trousers, his hands bound behind him. Two other men, solemn and dressed in black suits, followed.

Kendricks walked slowly forward. The street was silent except for the soft sluff-sluff of shoes in the powdery dust. The stumbling prisoner, his mouth hanging slack, his face beaded with sweat, stared with unbelieving horror up at the waiting noose.

The tall man reached the procession.

"Out of the way, Kendricks," the Sheriff said sharply. "There's nothing you can do now."

The boy's terrified eyes fixed on his brother's face. "Bill!" he screamed. "Help me! Don't let them!"

He flung himself toward Kendricks, dragging the Sheriff and the deputy with him.

"Help me!"

With one smooth quick motion the tall man drew the Colt from his shirt front, cocked it, and fired point-blank into the boy's chest.

The prisoner's thin body jerked back and a bright fountain of blood gushed from the wound. The boy's childish face lost its sudden look of incredulous bewilderment and took on the blank and impersonal stare of death.

Kendricks dropped the revolver in the blood-spattered dust. "I promised Ma I'd look after him," he said. "I promised her he'd never hang like his Pa did."

The Sheriff warned her: "Man broke out of jail last night. We were holding him for murdering a couple of women with a knife. He's dangerous" . . .

II: Why Don't You Like Me?

Lying on her back under the old truck and tightening the last of the oil pan bolts, Luddy didn't hear the Jeep drive into the yard until it pulled up close to the machine shed and stopped.

She wiggled out from under the truck as Sheriff Fred Kyle swung his big booted feet to the ground.

"Hello, Luddy," he said politely enough. He ought to be polite—after all she had a vote the same as anyone else in the county; but she could see in the way his gray eyes passed over her coolly, indifferently, what he thought—like all the others—that if a woman worked with her hands and didn't stay dressed up pretty with her hair curled and her face painted—

"Hello, Fred," she said, making her voice deep and still. She picked up a rag and wiped her grease-blackened hands.

"Thought I'd better come by and tell you," he said. "Man broke out of jail last night. We were holding him for murdering a couple of women with a knife. He's dangerous. I'm not trying to scare you, Luddy, but it would be a good idea if you stayed in town nights till we get him."

She laughed harshly. "No man 'ud bother me, Sheriff," she said. "Besides I got a twelve-gauge shotgun in there and I know how to use it." Probably better'n you do, Sheriff—little Freddie Kyle she'd gone to school with and licked at everything, even baseball and arithmetic. Now he was the Sheriff acting smart and wearing a tin badge, and telling her to go stay in town.

The late afternoon sun shone on his short blond hair, on his tanned skin, on the bulge of muscles under his neatly pressed khaki shirt. At least the soft-skinned, cow-eyed Eva Petrie he'd married kept his shirts ironed.

"You've been running this place nearly ten years, haven't you,

Luddy? Ten years since your Pa died?" He looked around at the straight, tight fences, the painted barns, the fat cattle grazing in the lush pasture, the newly mown hayfields. "You're doing a fine job. A man couldn't do better."

"Thanks," she said wryly, "and I'm nearly thirty and I've never been kissed!" She knew she had said the sudden, almost irrational thought aloud when he looked at her sharply. That's what came of being alone so much, of never having anyone to talk to; thoughts became words, and words thoughts, without reason or purpose.

She felt her whole body grow stiff and hot with embarrassment. She looked away from the sharp-eyed Sheriff and saw one of his deputies sitting in the Jeep, a beefy, round-faced man grinning contemptuously at her.

"Get out of here," she said thickly, "and take that gawking ape with you."

Fred Kyle was frowning at her. "We came here to warn you, Miss Vadick," he said with cold formality. "This man we're looking for seems harmless. He's only twenty and he looks as sweet and innocent as a young angel, but he's a psychotic killer and he'd as soon shove a knife into you as eat breakfast. I'd be within my duty to order you into town until we catch him—you living alone this way, miles from anyone."

"You don't order me anywhere, Fred Kyle. I won't go. I've got my stock to look after and my work to do. Now get out, both of you!"

Kyle shrugged. "All right," he said. "If you see anyone suspicious you let me know."

"I'll do better'n that. I'll catch him for you and deliver your killer all tied up neat with pink ribbons."

"If you see him, you call us, Miss Vadick. He's tall and thin, has black hair and eyes, and as far as we know he's still wearing the county's blue shirt and jeans. And let me warn you again that he's dangerous."

Kyle got into the Jeep and drove rapidly out of the yard.

Luddy stood with her hands on her hips watching them until they were out of sight up the winding road across the hillside. She let her rigidly held body slump. "Fred Kyle always was a fool," she said angrily.

She pulled her watch out of her pocket and looked at it. Five o'clock—time to start the chores. She rinsed her rough, greasy hands in stove oil and washed with soap at the hand pump in the yard. She fed the chickens and gathered the eggs. She got the two milk pails in the house and went to the barn. She drove the cows in from pasture and milked, she fed the calves and turned the cows out, and gave hay and water to the big white bull in his strong log pen.

She carried a pail of milk to the spring house and strained the foamy liquid into graniteware pans. She went to the field and fueled the engine that ran the pump and changed the water into three checks in the hayfield for the night. It was dark when she came into the house.

She lighted a lamp, set it on the table, opened a can of beans, fried a slab of bacon, and heated the coffee left in the pot from breakfast. She ate her supper, piled the dishes in the dish pan, poured a dipper of water over them, and wiped out the crusted frying pan with a piece of newspaper.

She picked up the lamp and paused to look around the kitchen. It was cluttered and dirty; cobwebs festooned the walls and the once white curtains were stiff with dust. She thought of Fred Kyle and his scrubbed pink neck and freshly ironed shirt. Eva—she'd been the most helpless little thing, squealing at bugs and looking up at Fred through her eyelashes—

"She got him, didn't she?" Luddy said. She stumped down the hall to her bedroom, blew out the light, undressed in the dark and crawled into her bed.

Sleep with its welcome oblivion wouldn't come. Outside in the dark the pump engine throbbed and crickets and frogs chorused. Her mind churned, her tortured thoughts like sparks from a fire that brightened and dimmed and twisted in bitter remembrance. She saw herself as a child always alone, always left out of the others' games and parties, shy, painfully self-conscious of her homely face and plain ill-fitting clothing.

Memory was like a rasping of sharp fingers across a raw wound. She twisted in anguish remembering her cringing, her fawning, her begging—who wants the candy out of my lunch?—do you want my doll, I don't want her any more—I'll do your homework for you—can't I go too?—oh, Fred, why don't you like me?—why don't you like me?—

She flung herself out of bed, lighted the lamp, and stared at herself in the mirror above the dresser. Her face peered back at her from the fly-specked dark, a gargoyle face, wrinkled, weathered, with hooded glaring eyes—

With a sudden moan she picked up her heavy shoe and beat it against the glass. The mirror shattered into a cascade of silvery fragments. Sobbing convulsively, she put out the light, threw herself back on the bed, and at last slept . . .

In the morning the torment of the night seemed like a dream. She dressed—careful not to look at the shattered mirror—and did her morning chores. She changed the water, ate breakfast, and worked on the old truck. By noon she had it running. In the afternoon she cleaned out ditches, finished the irrigating, and built another calf corral.

That evening as she brought in the cows she thought she saw a movement in the willows along the creek that divided her farm from her nearest neighbor.

"A big dog," she said, "or one of Milt's calves. He better not say I stole it. I'll take a club to him."

She watched the willows furtively as she went about her chores. At sundown she saw with a quick surge of excitement the figure of a man standing just inside the brushy cover. He was tall and thin; his hair was dark and he was staring intently up toward the farm buildings.

"He's hungry," she said. "He'll come."

When she had finished the chores she went into the house and got her shotgun down from the bedroom shelf, wiped it with an oily rag, and loaded it with buckshot.

She didn't eat. Holding the cocked weapon she sat on the front porch and waited. The quartering moon made a faint light. After a while she saw a movement near the barn and a tall, thin figure came stealthily toward the house.

"Hold it!" she called. "I've got you covered!"

The man turned and leaped away. She fired both barrels at his wispy shadow, but he vanished without an outcry. She reloaded the shotgun and got a flashlight. There were tracks in the soft dust, but no drops of blood.

Luddy didn't think of calling the Sheriff. She sat all night on the porch with the shotgun across her knees, but by the light of dawn he had not appeared again. She kept the weapon handy as she went about her work, but she saw no trace of the fugitive.

At noon, when she went into the house, he was sitting at her kitchen table with his hands quietly folded, looking up at her. She knew him instantly. He had *Kings County Jail* stenciled in black across the front of his worn blue shirt.

She felt a moment's wild panic. Then she pointed the shotgun at him and he smiled.

"You don't need that, Luddy," he said. "I won't hurt you. I'm your friend."

His lips barely moved when he talked. It was as if his mind talked to her mind—but she could hear his voice as deep and clear as a great bronze bell. The voice soothed her and she was no longer afraid. Her knees felt as weak and wobbly as a newborn calf's. She leaned the shotgun against the wall and sat down across the table from him.

He sat quietly, still smiling at her. His crisp dark hair curled on his high forehead; his eyes were large and as liquid and deep as the dark still pools beneath the willows along the creek; his skin was the silken gold of fall leaves; his features were perfectly molded and the perfection of his smiling mouth made her shiver. Even his hands, with their tracery of blue veins, were beautiful—with long tapering fingers and just a dusting of black hairs on the backs.

"You must be hungry," she said breathlessly. "Let me get you something to eat."

"Thank you, Luddy," he said. "You are very kind."

It wasn't strange that he knew her name. Everything about him was as familiar and real as her own being. She heard herself babbling as she stoked the stove and got out her pots and pans.

"The Sheriff was here—did you know that? He said you were dangerous, that I should call him if I saw you." She laughed, glancing at him, then pulled her lips down over her uneven teeth, knowing that she was especially hideous when she laughed; but his face did not turn from her. He watched her, smiling gently, his eyes warm and bright.

She put on fresh coffee to boil, sliced bacon, diced potatoes with onions for frying, brought cold fresh milk and a bowl of cream from the spring house, picked a colander of strawberries from the neglected garden. Each time she went out of the house she hurried back, her heart pounding, cold with the fear that he would be gone; but he remained at the table and watched her with his black liquid eyes.

When the food was ready they ate. Luddy kept right on talking. It was wonderful to have someone to talk to. She knew he must hate her, that she must sound like a fool, but still the words bubbled out of her mouth like an inexhaustible spring.

"It wasn't always like this," she said, gesturing at the dirt-encrusted room. "When Papa was alive and I kept house for him I had

everything so neat and clean you wouldn't believe it. I had everything so tidy."

He nodded. "Of course you did, Luddy."

"It's different now," she said. "I don't have time. Something has
to go."

"You're very wise, Luddy."

When they had finished eating she fell silent as she stacked the
dishes. He'd been hungry; he'd come to eat, and in a few moments
he'd be gone.

She said, "They're looking for you everywhere. They want to kill
you."

He nodded and his eyes looked sad.

"You could stay here," she said. "You'd be safe. I'd look after you
and hide you."

He shook his head. "I must go."

"No!" she cried, "I won't let you! You don't know how much they
hate you—how much they want to kill you!"

"Dear Luddy," he said sadly, "how good you are. But I must go."

He stood up. He moved with a sinuous grace and ease that seemed
effortless. He seemed to flow across the floor toward the door.

She snatched up the shotgun. "Don't leave me!" she cried.

He stopped and looked at her with the faintest smile on his curved
lips.

She held the shotgun steady. Where could she put him? It had to
be a safe place, a strong place, one that he couldn't get out of and
where they'd never find him. The grain bin in the barn. It was built
of two layers of tongue-and-groove siding, sheathed with tin and
bolted to a concrete foundation. It had a heavy door and two small
heavily screened windows for ventilation.

He made no objection as she ordered him across the yard to the
big barn. He went quietly into the small, square, dark little room
and he sat on the floor watching her with his faint little smile as
she brought him bedding and a jar of water. She put a heavy padlock
through the hasp of the door.

"It's for your own good," she called, "so's you'll be safe. They won't
find you here."

She hung the key on a nail in the barn wall and leaned the shotgun
in the corner beside the grain bin. She felt strange, almost dizzy and
light-headed. The afternoon sunlight that poured in through the
barn's wide door seemed unbearably bright.

She went to the house and spent the rest of the afternoon cleaning it. By evening the floors shone, the windows were clean, the curtains washed. After the chores were done that evening, she fixed a tray of food and carried it out to the barn. She unlocked the grain bin in a sudden panic that he would be gone, but he was there sitting quietly in a corner on his bedding.

The next day she went into town and recklessly bought meats and vegetables and canned goods and even a carton of ice cream wrapped in newspapers to keep it cold. She went to a store and bought him a fancy shirt and a pair of slacks and a belt with a gold buckle.

When she got back to the farm she carried the clothes and the ice cream out to the barn and they ate the ice cream and while she turned her back he changed into the new clothes and flung his old ones into a corner.

The next few days were the happiest of Luddy's life. She seemed to live for the times when she could sit on an old apple box in the grain bin talking to the stranger. She poured out her heart to him, telling him everything that had ever happened to her, and he listened sympathetically. He never scolded or seemed shocked or repulsed. He sat as still as a carved wax figurine, his head tilted a little forward, his bright dark eyes fixed on her face.

Her thoughts centered on her prisoner. What could she fix for him that he would like? What could she think to tell him that he would find amusing? What small comfort would he enjoy? But he asked for nothing. He seemed content.

A week after Luddy had locked the fugitive in the grain bin, Sheriff Fred Kyle drove into the farm yard. Luddy was carrying the milk pails out to the barn to start her evening chores. She stopped as Kyle swung down from his Jeep. He was alone this time. He looked fat and coarse, not handsome at all, in the reddish evening sunlight.

Luddy watched him coldly. "Well," she called, "what do you want?"

He grinned and seemed pleased about something. "I just came in to tell you, Miss Vadick. We caught that killer, so you can relax."

"You caught him?" she asked stupidly.

"Sure—that fellow I was telling you about—the one that killed those women."

"Oh," Luddy said.

"Caught him between here and town—just this afternoon. Thought you'd want to know. You don't have to worry any more."

Luddy screamed. Her limp fingers dropped the milk pails. She ran across the yard toward the barn. Kyle stared after her with a puzzled frown. Then he shrugged and followed her.

She ran to the grain bin, snatched the key from the nail, and fumbled with the padlock. Her fingers were so clumsy that it took her a long time to get the lock open and throw back the door.

He was there. He sat on the bed and smiled at her. His eyes were luminous in the gloom, like the eyes of a cat. The gold buckle on his belt glimmered in the faint light.

Then she understood. Fred Kyle had tricked her with his lies and she, like the poor stupid fool she was, had led him straight to the fugitive.

She turned blindly toward the door and, whimpering like a mortally wounded animal, seized the shotgun that leaned against the wall. As the Sheriff stood silhouetted against the light, peering into the dark barn from the wide doorway, she shot him. His heavy body jerked back as though he had been struck by a huge fist. He fell and twitched a little, then lay with his astonished face staring sightlessly up into the bright evening sky.

Luddy dropped the shotgun and ran back to the grain bin.

In the shadowy dark she called, "Come! Come quick! We gotta—"

He was gone. The bin was empty.

She dropped to her knees and lighted the lamp with shaking fingers. There was nothing in the tiny square room—nothing but a pile of neatly folded blankets, a gray plaid shirt still in its cellophane envelope, a pair of slacks with pristine creases, and a gold-buckled belt in an unbroken plastic holder. On the floor around the bedding were plates and bowls of food in varying stages of decay.

Luddy cried out wildly. She crawled across the floor to the corner where he had discarded his clothing. Only two ragged burlap sacks lay crumpled in the dust.

"Q"

Douglas Shea

Advice, Unlimited

This is the 453rd "first story" published by Ellery Queen's Mystery Magazine . . . a real chuckler . . .

Mr. Gihon Gore
% Chutney & Chives, Inc., Publishers
New York, N.Y.
Dear Mr. Gore:
Although your mystery stories have not been exactly unheard of by me, last week was the first occasion I had to pick one up and read it. I am speaking of *Brent's First Case*. Generally speaking I found the book adequate but there were two errors in Chapter 21. You speak of the killer African bees navigating to the bedroom of elderly pig-iron heiress Harriet Heald (a) by polarized light from the sky and (b) by being attracted to the interior of the bedroom by the phlox-scented room-freshener spray used by Miss Heald. I'll take the easy one first.

Bees are *never* attracted to phlox, Mr. Gore. Their tongues are too short to reach the nectar deeply buried within the flowers. The bees know this and you might say that they wouldn't even stick out their tongues (ha, ha) at phlox scent. Try cyclamen scent. Your bees will go bananas over that one.

Now about that polarized light bit. It is true that bees do navigate by polarized light from the sky but never (I repeat, *never*) on cloudy days. You have to have blue sky in order to detect polarized light at certain angles to the sun. Cloud particles destroy the effect by scattering the light.

What to do?

The cloudy day seems necessary in order to give Miss Heald her attack of sinus migraine, an attack which brings old Dr. Physick tottering to her bedside so that they can be killed by bee venom together. On the other hand, if the sun isn't shining, forget the polarized light.

Thinking the matter through, I believe that skilled replotting of Chapters 21, 22, 23, and 24 might turn the trick. You might want to consider this in your next edition of *Brent's First Case.*

Very truly yours,
George Ohm
Associate Professor of Science
Dimwiddie University
Glen Cove, L.I., N.Y.

From: Quentin Quarles, Editor
Chutney & Chives, Inc., Publishers
New York, N.Y.

As Mr. Gore now receives several thousand items of mail a year, it is not possible for him to answer you personally. Hence this form letter designed to answer 95% of the questions he is asked.

His home address is Waldorf Towers, New York, N.Y.; his London office % Cratchit and Marley, Solicitors, 54 Dewlap Road, London N22, 4PP.

Biographical details will be found in *Who's Who, Contemporary Authors, Contemporary Novelists, Dictionary of International Biography, Celebrity Register, Britannica 3.* See also profile in *Time* of September 12, 1972.

Mr. Gore has now written 37 books. See above references, or the list in any recent edition.

Permission to quote should be directed to Chutney & Chives, Inc.

Mr. Gore *never* supplies photos or autographs. Also he cannot autograph and mail back books.

Lecture requests are no longer accepted. Nor can questions be answered about how to plot good mystery stories. The only advice he can give to beginners is this: Read, read, read. Read at least one book a day. Also write, write, write. And remember one thing about getting fresh ideas; there is no substitute for living. As Ernest Hemingway said, "Writing is not a full-time occupation."

Mr. Quentin Quarles, Editor
Chutney & Chives, Inc., Publishers
New York, N.Y.

Dear Quentin, Quentin, Quentin:

I return your form letter herewith, having studied it carefully. I took your advice, Quentin: you told me to read, read, read, and to write, write, write.

Please refer to page 209 of *The Case of the Undertaker's Hat.* See where Gore sends the hemophiliac crashing through a thin sheet of invisible glass blocking the garden path? Another no-no, Quentin. Fact is, there's no such thing as "invisible" glass. Gore means non-reflective glass, sometimes called invisible glass by tyros. Such glasses have the light that they would reflect at normal incidence almost completely suppressed by interference.

But the condition for said destructive interference can be fulfilled for only one wave length. This is usually chosen to be near the middle of the visible spectrum. The reflection of red and violet light is then somewhat larger and these two colors combine to form purple.

Take a look at a coated lens in a camera. See the purplish hue? A sheet of glass that color across anybody's path would stand out like your ears, ears, ears, old friend. No matter what wave length you try to suppress, others will be reflected. And that's the name of the game. That seems to knock out Chapters 11 and 12, also pages 209 through 218, also Chapters 23, 24, and 25. I don't know how you fix up *that* mess. Sorry about that.

George Ohm

Mr. Quentin Quarles, Editor
Chutney & Chives, Inc., Publishers
New York, N.Y.
Dear Quentin:

Where are you: I miss those little inspirational words of yours.

Incidentally, I found some more boo-boos—in *The Slim Man*. Say please and I'll tell you what they are. Pretty please, Quentin?

George Ohm

Memo: From the suite of Gihon Gore
To: George Ohm
Get lost.

Gihon Gore

GG: Louise L'Erotique
cc: Quentin Quarles

Memo: From George Ohm
To: Gihon Gore

I have your little note. Gore, you need help and I'm here to give it to you. Let's begin with *The Slim Man*.

In one scene you have The Slim Man, astronomer Herschel Skyanier, look through the eyepiece of the Hale Telescope on Palomar Mountain while the tube of the instrument is lowered for routine inspection. If I read you correctly, and I believe I do, Skyanier thereby witnesses a murder being committed five miles down the mountain slope. Gore, there's so much wrong with that that I hardly know where to begin—but I'll try.

In the first place, you can't even deflect the tube of a modern astronomical telescope to the horizon, let alone point it down a mountain slope. Take a look at a picture of any observatory anywhere in the world, Gore. Notice the position of the slit in the dome. In the case of the Hale Telescope of which you write, the floor on which the mountain of the instrument rests is 75 feet below the level of the slit. What I'm saying is that with one of these big babies you can only look up at the sky—never down.

And another thing: the field of view of any large telescope is so small that even if you could look at a murderer five miles away about all you'd see would be a nose or an eyebrow. Finally, Gore, the image would be *inverted*. You see, they don't bother with erecting eyepieces on astronomical telescopes. It's an absolutely unnecessary refinement. Ask yourself the question: what's up, what's down in the case of the heavenly bodies? and you'll have the answer why.

You slipped up badly in *The Slim Man*, Gore. Tonight I'm going to riffle through *The Affair at Byles* to see if I can be of use to you there. Don't lose heart.

Yours for Science,

George Ohm

Mr. Gihon Gore
Waldorf Towers
New York, N.Y.
Dear Mr. Gore:

You have scarcely had time to digest the information I sent you re *The Slim Man*, but I wanted you to know that I have finished *The Affair at Byles* and I think we are in *real* trouble this time.

As you tell it, Thedabara Gam, spoiled, filthy-rich heiress to the Gam millions, is giving a lawn party at Byles, her family estate, for a small gathering of 200 persons come to honor her engagement to Herman Opdyke, polo-playing scion of her father's business associate. Meanwhile, unbeknown to all, Shamus McGillicuddy, Miss Gam's jilted ex-suitor, just back from the Amazon, has secreted himself in the third cook's tent, murder burning in his black heart.

At an opportune moment McGillicuddy sticks the tip of an Orinoco blowgun through the tent fly and lets Opdyke have it full in the chest with a curare-dipped dart. In the resulting confusion he thereupon escapes through the back of the tent, disguised as an attendant bearing a tray of petits fours, ladyfingers, and strawberry preserves.

Oh, this is dreadful! How shall I begin?

Item Number One. Curare is a highly unreliable poison, its toxicity varying greatly with its source and method of preparation. See *The Merck Index* or any of the several pharmacopoeias. More than that, curare isn't nearly strong enough or quick-acting enough. I myself would prefer to use sodium cyanide. Sodium cyanide is freely soluble in water. It can also be readily obtained since it is widely used in extracting gold and silver ores, in electroplating baths, in fumigating citrus and other fruit trees, and in disinfecting ships, railroad cars, warehouses, etc. Only four to eight grams of this chemical would prove lethal to a horse.

Dissolve a thimbleful of the crystals in a tablespoonful of water when your murderer is ready to go and you've got it made. Have him carry the solution to the scene of the crime in a small plastic-capped vial. The victim who receives a shot of this will die in seconds.

Item Number Two. The blowgun. Do you have any idea how long an Orinoco Indian blowgun is? Well, it would reach from the ground almost to a man's armpit. Try sawing it off to a more practical length and you destroy its accuracy. How did McGillicuddy carry that monstrosity to Byles?—tucked down his pants' leg and up his shirt? Really, Gore, you'd have a veritable stiff before you ever got to the murder. May I suggest replacing the blowgun with a tranquilizing gun and a tranquilizing dart? It seems so obvious to me.

Yours for Science,

George Ohm

Look, Ohm:

I've had you pegged for some time. You're a medical school dropout with a useless smattering of sixth-grade science. You have such a gnawing sense of inferiority that it gives you a compulsion to pester famous people with your paranoid prattle. If Einstein were living, I'll swear you would be deluging him with a one-sided tirade about his mistakes in the theory of relativity. Now don't bother me any further with your puerile disquisitions, Ohm.

Be sure you hang onto my letters, though. The autographs may bring you a buck or two when you come to a decrepit old age.

Gihon Gore

GG: Louise L'Erotique

Dear Mr. Gore:

"Puerile disquisitions," eh? Hoity-toity now!

As for saving your letters, be informed that I use them for a very special purpose. I do find that 20-pound bond paper a little abrasive, though. How much would you want to switch to a 9-pound weight?

Well, Gore, I've prayed with you and I've wrestled in spirit with you and I finally see that I've wasted my time. *En garde* now, Gore!

I see you don't know about my fall and winter Saturday night lectures on popular science. Yes, pompous one, I circulate up and down a good part of the Atlantic seaboard, stopping off at many of the smaller colleges where I have an invitation to speak. I kick off this season's series this coming Saturday night right here in Peter Piper Hall at good old Dimwiddie.

Guess what this season's topic is, Gore? "Scientific Boo-boos in the Works of a Famous Mysterymonger." Do you like the title? Well, guess who I'm going to talk about?

Do you know how popular you are on college campuses, Gore?—almost as popular as Tolkien with his Hobbit stories. Think of the rage and disgust of all those students when the word starts to pass that their idol has typewriter keys of clay.

I'll bury you, buster!

Yours for Science.

George Ohm

INTERIM REPORT
From: Seymour Kravitz, Detective
To Inspector Attila Hund, Homicide
(on cassette tape)

I arrived at Peter Piper Hall, Dimwiddie University, at 8:52 P.M. approximately 25 minutes after the commission of the crime. The body of the victim, George Ohm, white, 34, had not been touched, being still in place on the platform where it had fallen. Death was due to a hypodermic dart which still protruded from the upper left quadrant of the victim's chest. The Medical Examiner reports that the dart, of the type used to tranquilize animal subjects, had been filled with a concentrated aqueous solution of either potassium or sodium cyanide. (Details later on receipt of report of analysis from Departmental chemist.)

A quick-witted student, Gary Cooper Rabinowitz, white, 21, had taken temporary charge pending my arrival and no one had left the theater.

"A Chinese detective with a Jewish name!" exclaimed Gary when I introduced myself. "Welcome, *landsman!*"

"Yes. And you should be a good Jewish boy and help me further so that we may find the murderer and give him such a hurt that he will pray for the death of ten thousand tickling nightingales' tongues."

My words seemed to strike a responsive chord in Gary who I later learned is an exchange student from Sweden.

There were 47 persons in the theater—36 students and 11 senior citizens who excitedly explained to me that they were receiving Social Security benefits and didn't want any further trouble with the government. All 47 persons were eventually released.

The theater is a small one, seating approximately 300 persons. The front platform on which Ohm was standing is elevated about three feet above floor level. Entry to the theater is gained by means of two sets of double doors, right and left, leading in from a spacious corridor. Between the two entrances is a single door leading to a projection booth. As seen from within the theater, the projection booth is a mat-black boxlike structure closed on three sides except for the usual small projection ports which in this case are about eight feet above theater floor level.

An important witness was Willie Crumble, black, 21, who was sitting in the center of the theater two rows from the back and just under the line of sight from the projection ports. Willie was anxiously awaiting the arrival of his girl friend and kept turning and glancing toward first one entrance, then the other. Willie is prepared to swear that no one entered or left the theater after Professor Ohm—Associate Professor of Science at the institution—began to speak.

Only about a half dozen sentences of Ohm's lecture were delivered when the tragedy occurred. No one knows the import of the lecture except that it had to do with technical or scientific mistakes in the writing of mystery fiction. No notes were found, either on the platform or in Ohm's bachelor apartment.

According to a majority of witnesses, Ohm had just uttered the partial sentence, "And so tonight I want to tell you about—" when there was a very faint *throop* sound whose point of origin in the theater could not be determined. Ohm fell backward, flung his arms wide, and emitted a single unintelligible guttural groan that sounded like *Gorrr-r-r!*

And that was it. He died immediately after.

Ohm seems to have been a man of catholic tastes. On the night stand beside his bed were three paperbacks by Mickey Spillane; in the library-study the complete set of Beilstein's *Organischen Chemie*. Over the desk hung framed pictures of Olga Korbut and Thomas A. Edison. He evidently had no enemies, according to the consensus of all students interviewed.

You know my methods, Inspector. I was able to deduce that the lethal dart had come from one of the two projection ports and such indeed proved to be the case. The booth door in the corridor was secured, but I was easily able to open it with a picklock. Inside I found a dart gun on the floor just under the right port. Against it was propped a 3-by-5-inch unlined white index card bearing the legend in block letters: STOLEN FROM THE NASSAU COUNTY SPCA. PLEASE RINSE THOROUGHLY AND RETURN.

According to our handwriting expert the card was lettered by a right-handed person using his left hand. No fingerprints were found anywhere except for some smudged repetitions on the cylindrical sides of the projection lenses, obviously accumulated there by the projectionist. There was a faint fragrance of Brut cologne pervading the air.

There was a curious circular smudge on the end of the dart gun barrel and I was almost immediately able to deduce what it was. The gun was used with an appurtenance which had been tossed or had rolled into one corner. It is probably the first time in history that a tranquilizer gun was used with a silencer.

Inspector, there is really nothing by which to get hold of this case. The Saturday night cultural events at the University are largely informal affairs, no admission being charged, and it is this very informality that allowed the murderer to come and go as he chose.

The homicide itself has the simple line that marks the hand of a master. Hsi Tz'u Chuan says that what is easy is easy to know; what is simple is easy to follow. One part of me wants to believe this—to keep delving and triumph—but another part remembers what the Talmud says: Much talk, much foolishness.

Inspector Hund, I reluctantly have to report to you that at last we seem to have stumbled on The Perfect Crime.

"Q"

Patricia McGerr

Hide-and-Seek— Russian Style

Selena Mead, now Mrs. Hugh Pierce, was (to quote her creator) "born a widow." The earliest published story about Selena, which appeared in "This Week Magazine" in October 1963, began with her first husband's murder. He was knifed by an enemy agent on a dark street in Washington, D.C. while on an assignment from the branch of security known as Section Q. Selena trapped the assassin, and in the succeeding stories became herself a link in the counterspy network.

The Wall Street Journal dubbed Selena "the female James Bond," but it is not an apt comparison. Unlike Bond, Selena's methods are always nonviolent—she prefers wit and wile to fist and gun.

In this novelet Selena, as an undercover Q-agent, again undertakes a secret mission—this time to Russia. Join her and become a 'tec tourist in Moscow and Leningrad . . .

Detective: SELENA MEAD

It was almost time to leave for the airport. Hugh stowed her suitcase in the trunk of the car, slammed down the lid. He was waiting on the sidewalk when Selena came out of the house. She closed the door, made sure the lock was engaged, and turned back to her husband. His artist's eye took in the belted black coat, soft leather boots, black handbag, black gloves. She was a study in quiet chic—from the neck down. But on her head, incongruously garish, was a stocking cap bordered with wide orange, green, and purple stripes.

"What—" His brows drew together in a scowl. "What's that on your head?"

"Moscow in January," she said demurely, "is very cold. This will keep my ears warm."

"And make you visible from a block away. That chewing gum you bought aroused my suspicions. The signal flag on your head confirms them. You're up to something, Selena. Why are you taking this trip?"

"I told you that two weeks ago." She moved past him, got in the car. He walked round to the driver's side and settled himself behind the wheel.

"Two weeks ago," he resumed, "you told me that a heart attack had forced an old school chum of yours to drop out of an alumni association tour and you'd decided to take her place. It had a false ring then and the longer I think about it, the more preposterous it gets." He started the engine, eased the car out of the parking space.

"Funny coincidence," she said. "That's exactly how I reasoned last month when you suddenly took off for the Middle East to paint the portrait of an Arab prince. It lacked credibility."

"Of course it did. I was on a job for Section Q and the portrait commission was my cover story. So you were right not to believe me. Am I right too? Are you hiding a secret mission?"

"How could I be? The only Intelligence work I've ever done were assignments you gave me. And that stopped as soon as we were married. Do you think I got bored after eight years and found employment with some competing spy network?"

"I don't know what to think." He looked again at her gaudy headgear. "But I've a feeling you're involved in something and I'd like to know what it is."

"Maybe that's good," she retorted. "Now you'll understand how I feel when you go off to God-knows-where to do God-knows-what and I lie awake wondering if you'll ever come back."

"That's how it has to be. You know—wait a minute!" His voice sharpened in alarm. "This trip—whatever it's about—you're not walking into danger, are you?"

"Of course not."

"How can I be sure of that?"

"I'll make a bargain with you. I'll give you an honest answer if you give your word that in the future you'll always answer truthfully when I ask the same question."

"That's blackmail!"

"I call it a fair exchange. Oh, I know you think you're saving me worry by hiding the risks you run. The opposite is true. When I'm in the dark I imagine the worst. But if I can believe you when you say a job is routine, without physical danger, then I'll worry only when there's real cause. Agreed?"

"I'm beginning to suspect," he said, "that you planned the whole thing—including that crazy hat—just to make me trade off my right to lie to you."

"It's possible," she returned. "It's also possible that you've been a spymaster so long that you see agents behind every bush. If I choose to defy fashion when I'm thousands of miles from home, why should that upset you?"

"Why indeed?" He was silent while they crossed Key Bridge from Georgetown to the Virginia side of the Potomac. "You're right," he said at last. "When the shoe is on the other foot it rubs blisters. Okay, it's a deal."

"Then I'll tell you as much as I can without betraying a confidence. I'm going to Moscow to do an errand for a friend. It's a private family matter and doesn't involve any government agencies. The only danger is from one of those viruses that lie in wait for tourists. To put your mind at rest I promise not to drink the water."

"All right," he conceded, "it appears I'll have to be content with that."

"I'll be home in eight days," she assured him, "and tell you all about it."

The Moscow-bound 707 took off from Dulles Airport at eight p.m. It was a charter flight packed to the limit with the alumni of two colleges. Selena, buckled into an aisle seat, pulled the cap from her head and stared at the clashing colors.

That was careless, she thought, to put it on before I left home. Hugh's been in the business too long not to recognize an identification device when he sees one. But I couldn't pack it in my suitcase. I've no idea when contact will be made. It may happen at the airport. So I must wear the cap when I step off the plane.

I wish, though, I could have told Hugh the whole story. If only I hadn't let Trinka swear me to secrecy. But in view of the precarious state of her health what choice did I have?

Two weeks earlier the husband of a college classmate had phoned Selena to say that his wife was in the hospital recovering from a coronary and urgently wanted Selena to visit her. The request was puzzling but one she could not refuse. Driving that same afternoon to the hospital in a Washington suburb, she pieced together memories of the woman she was going to see.

Caterina Rodinova, class of '55. They had not been special friends in school, but she remembered well the shy girl whose Russian birth and illustrious ancestry had made her a campus celebrity. Something to do with her grandfather. A novelist? No, a poet. Yes, of course. It came back in a rush. Leonid Korodin, known as the Poet of the Revolution. His verses had been a rallying cry for Communists round the world. There was a square named after him in Moscow. And Trinka's mother had been his only child.

Trinka's mother escaped from Russia with the little girl a few days before the Nazis attacked. They spent the war years in England, then came to the United States. Trinka had married Robert Hudson soon after graduation and they'd moved to the West Coast where they'd lived until a few months ago when, as Robert explained briefly on the phone, his company transferred him to Washington. And now, after being out of touch for nearly twenty years, Trinka wanted to see Selena. Why?

She was no closer to an answer when she walked into the yellow-walled hospital room and stood beside the narrow bed. Long, softly waved flaxen hair spread over the pillow, framing a pale face whose delicate features were nearly eclipsed by a pair of enormous brown eyes.

"Selena?" The eyes were questioning, then the lips curved in a tremulous smile. "Yes, it is you. Oh, thank you! Thank you for coming."

"I was surprised when your husband called. I didn't know you'd moved back east."

"Yes." The woman in the bed shook her head, impatient with small talk. "I need help desperately and I didn't know where to turn. Then I remembered that you lived in Washington. In school you were always so resourceful, someone to trust and rely on. You will help me, won't you?"

"Of course." Selena moved a chair close to the bed and sat down. "I'll do whatever I can."

"It's terribly important. But first you must promise that what I say will be just between the two of us. Even Robert doesn't know. I must be sure you will not give away my secret."

"You know I won't."

"Will you swear?"

"On my word of honor," Selena said solemnly. "But Trinka dear, you must not become so agitated. You'd better rest now. I'll come back tomorrow and we'll talk again."

"No!" She tried to raise herself from the pillow. "I can't rest until

I know you'll help me."

"Very well." Selena held the other woman's hand in both of hers—the hand felt like a small bird that needed quieting. "Talk slowly, without excitement. You must not strain your heart."

"You're right." She lay back and was silent for almost a minute while her breath grew smooth and even. Then she smiled faintly. "I can be calm now, since you'll solve my problem. Did you know our alumni association is sponsoring a tour of Moscow and Leningrad?"

"I probably received a notice. Why? Did you sign on?"

"Yes, but it goes in the middle of January, so I have to cancel. The doctor says it will be many weeks before I can do anything strenuous."

"What a shame! Have you not been back in all these years?"

"No, my father was killed defending Leningrad and my mother was not in sympathy with the régime, which made a coldness between her and her father. So she never wanted to return."

"But you still have relatives there?"

"Only a great-aunt, the sister of my grandfather. He died three years ago."

"Yes, I remember reading the obituaries. He was a great poet."

"Very great." The words were emphatic. "I wish I had known him. But now he is dead and my great-aunt, with whom he lived in Moscow, is old and far from well. So I seized the chance to join the alumni tour. In a large group it is easier to be inconspicuous."

"There'll be other tours," Selena comforted. "Since Soviet-American relations have improved, it seems almost every organization is taking its members to Russia. As soon as you've recovered—"

"That may be too late. You must go now, in my place."

"To Russia?" She was startled. "Oh, Trinka, I don't see how—"

"It is for my grandfather. You know of him what the world knows. When he was young he wrote against the tyranny of the Czar and in favor of the people. His poetry inspired the men who made the Revolution. Afterwards he wrote many poems to celebrate the victory and the new world that was being made. Every schoolboy learned by heart the major works of Leonid Korodin. During his life he was greatly honored and when he died he was given a state funeral. The President of the Supreme Soviet gave the eulogy and the Party Chairman laid a wreath on the grave. Those are the public facts. What I tell you now you must keep secret until after you have returned. You understand?"

"Yes," Selena said. "I've given you my word."

"For some years before his death he was silent. There were new editions of his old work, but not one new poem. Well, he was old, perhaps his mind was failing. That's what everyone believed. Then, soon after we moved to Washington, there came to see me a man who had been my grandfather's close friend—or I should say his protégé, for Mikhail is much younger and also a poet, though not famous.

"He told me that my grandfather had, little by little, year after year, lost his illusions, begun to see in the new government many of the evils he had denounced in the old. He wrote poems of criticism that the Committee disapproved of and, when nothing he wrote could be published, he finally lost the will to write. Of course, none of this was made public. He was a hero of the Soviet and the authorities did not wish to label him a dissident.

"So he remained in seclusion and few people learned of his changed opinions. Even Mikhail was not allowed to see him—he thought it was because he himself held unorthodox views. But before Mikhail got out of the country he visited my great-aunt. She showed him a poem my grandfather wrote before his final illness. All the others, the ones the Committee rejected, had been destroyed, but this one he wrote in secret. It is a kind of last testament, and Mikhail said it is his greatest work. His sister has kept it hidden, but she fears that when she dies—which may be soon—it will be lost forever."

"And that's why you planned to go to Moscow," Selena concluded. "To save your grandfather's poem. Is it so important?"

"A work of art," Trinka answered, "is always important. And truth is more important still. But for me there is a stronger personal reason. I have two sons. I want them to be proud of their great-grandfather, to honor his memory. Now they know only what my mother, in her bitterness, taught them—that he helped to overthrow one oppressor to put a worse one in its place. Publication of his last poem will show them, show all the world, that he was, in the end as in the beginning, a defender of freedom. You will get it for me, Selena? You are my only hope."

The large eyes were fixed on Selena's in anguished entreaty. Selena hesitated only an instant before saying, "Yes, Trinka. I will bring back your grandfather's poem."

She phoned the travel agency at once and was told she was in luck. The Soviet tour was fully booked, but there had been a single cancellation, due to illness. Since time was so short, she could bring her check to the office and fill out the necessary forms. When she had done so, the agency head examined her visa application and nodded approval.

"It all seems in order," he said. "We'll have to press a bit to get it through in time, but we'll manage. Maybe you'll do us a favor in return."

"A favor?"

"Nothing big." He smiled genially. "This group will make up seven busloads and we need one person on each bus to act as leader. Will you be responsible for bus Number One?"

"Oh, I don't think—"

"It's no work," he assured her. "You merely check the list of names each day to make sure nobody is left behind. Since you're traveling alone, it will help you get acquainted. Then that's settled." He was out of his chair, ushering her to the door before she could demur further. "Thank you for coming in, Mrs. Pierce. I'm sure you'll enjoy the trip."

She saw Trinka again on the day before departure. Home from the hospital, though still in bed, she looked much better.

"I told Mikhail you were taking my place," she explained. "But he doesn't think you should go to see my great-aunt. For me, as a member of the family, it would have been natural. But if a strange American visits her, the powers will become suspicious."

"Then I can't get the poem? In that case there's no point in my going."

"Yes, you must go. Mikhail has made arrangements. The writers and artists who are out of favor have an underground organization. The poem speaks for all of them and they are determined that it reach the outside world. Many will work together to put it into your hands. Mikhail told me to give you this."

From the drawer of her bedside table she pulled out the orange, green, and purple cap. "You must wear it at all times and they will know you are my friend. And you must take with you many packs of chewing gum."

"Chewing gum?"

"It is not made in the Soviet Union. So always, Mikhail says, wherever American tourists go, there are youngsters asking for it. The one who recognizes your cap will come close and say 'gum chew' instead of 'chewing gum.' You will give him a package and he will give you a pin or medal. They are not beggars, these boys—they exchange some small souvenir for the gum, though, of course, the gum can be sold for a much higher price.

"In each tour city the daily schedule is posted in the hotel, so they will know where to look for you, but other information—like your room number—you should write on the gum wrapper. And their instructions will come to you with the pin. It sounds complicated, I know, but Mikhail said his friends must always be on guard against spies. Can you handle it, Selena?"

"I'll do my best," she promised. "Don't worry. Next week I'll bring you your grandfather's poem."

The Washington-to-Moscow flight, with a stopover at Shannon to change crews, took nearly twelve hours. With clocks turned forward eight hours, it was mid-afternoon when Selena's plane landed. Buses carried the tourists to the main airport building where they lined up to walk past solemn young men in uniform who stared hard at each passenger's face while checking passports and visa photos. They filled out forms listing currency and valuables and then, having claimed their luggage, carried it through customs.

The formalities over, Selena stood near the door with one hand in her coat pocket clutching a package of chewing gum. From now on, she thought, I must be constantly alert, ready to make contact. She stiffened as a high-booted young woman in a fox fur hat came close and spoke her name.

"You are Mrs. Pierce, yes?"

"Yes." The hand that held the gum relaxed. That was not the password.

"I am your Intourist representative." Her English was precise, only slightly accented. "You are leader of bus Number One, yes?"

"Yes, I am."

"Here is the list." She gave Selena a paper with two columns of typed names. "You can all go to your buses. Please check the names and do not let the driver leave until everyone is aboard. Also please collect from each person his passport to have ready when you arrive at the hotel."

It was the first hint that the job of bus leader was not the sinecure the American agent had made it seem. Selena accepted the list and promised to follow orders. The buses, seven of them, were lined up outside the door. Each had in its left front window a two-foot square card on which was printed in bright blue letters: INTOURIST-MOS-COW—and the name of the travel agency. Beneath the printing, the bus numbers—from 1 to 7—had been added in heavy crayon.

Soon, with 28 passengers and a plump rosy-cheeked guide named Olga, bus Number 1 left the airport for the 35-kilometer ride to the center of the city where it deposited them at the huge modern Hotel Rossia. There Selena turned over the passports to the Intourist representative and waited with the others for their luggage and room assignments.

It was six o'clock when she was at last alone in her room where the single bed with its linen-encased blanket was almost irresistibly inviting. Flying into the sun had cut short the night and telescoped mealtimes, so there had been a surfeit of food and little sleep. She would gladly have skipped supper to take a long hot bath and sleep the clock round. But she could not depart from the formal program. Only by following it exactly could she be sure to be in place when Trinka's allies came to seek her.

So she left her coat in the room but still wore the stocking cap when she descended to the below-lobby restaurant where her group was scheduled to eat all its Moscow meals. Ready in her handbag was a package of chewing gum with her room number on the wrapper. But no one accosted her on the way to the dining room and the meal proved uneventful. Before returning to her room she stopped to copy the tour schedule which was posted at the restaurant entrance:

FRIDAY

8:30 Breakfast
9:30 Kremlin Museum and Armory
1:00 Lunch
2:30 Qs & As
5:30 Dinner
6:15 Bolshoi Ballet

SATURDAY

9:00 Breakfast
10:00 City Tour
1:00 Lunch
2:00 National Fair & Space Museum
5:30 Dinner
6:15 Siberian Folk Dance

SUNDAY

```
 9:00  Breakfast
10:00  Troika Rides
 1:30  Lunch
 2:30  Subway Tour
 9:30  Lv for Railway Station
10:40  Train to Leningrad
```

"What's that mean?"

A fellow tourist, also studying the poster, pointed to the fourth item under Friday.

"Questions and answers, I imagine," Selena said.

"Well, of course I figured that out," the woman said irritably. "But what does it mean? You're our bus leader. Aren't you supposed to know these things?"

"It's a propaganda session." A tall man from another bus came to her rescue. "They bring in experts in various fields. We ask the questions and they give the party-line answers."

"Sounds dull. I think I'll go shopping instead." The woman looked again at Selena. "Don't hold the bus for me."

She moved away and the man gave Selena a companionable wink. "It begins to appear," he said, "that leading a bus isn't all prestige and perquisites, the way they made it sound back in Washington."

"You're a bus leader too?"

"Number Four. Bill Parsons." He offered his hand. "When the going gets rough, maybe we can swap miseries over a vodka or two."

In her own room again she studied the schedule, trying to guess where and when contact would be made. Soon, she hoped. Once the poet's papers were passed over and packed safely away, she could begin to enjoy the sights like an ordinary tourist. Except for her responsibilities as bus leader.

She smiled, remembering the exchange at the dining-room door. Qs and As. "Questions and Answers." Like the chicken-egg enigma, she'd never known—perhaps no one did—which came first? Did Section Q get its name from the fact that its agents established identity with sentences beginning with the letter Q? Or did the name of the section give rise to the device? If I were on an agency assignment instead of a private errand, that conversation would have been loaded with significance. And the woman would be my contact. She put the schedule away and got ready for bed.

How do our Russian-speaking agents meet, she wondered drowsily. The Cyrillic alphabet has no letter Q. But it had been a long day—two days, in fact, with Wednesday running unseparated into Thursday—and sleep put an effective end to her curiosity.

The first onslaught of chewing-gum seekers came the next morning as they waited in the icy wind outside the Kremlin Museum. About a dozen neatly dressed boys paced the lines and many of the Americans exchanged packages for square pins decorated with pictures of the Kremlin tower, the Soviet flag, and other emblems. None of them singled out Selena or spoke the magic phrase, "gum chew."

Another group met them when they left the Museum, and a third pounced as they entered a church. By the time the bus returned to the hotel the tourists had begun to be selective about the souvenirs for which they would trade the coveted merchandise. But the orange, green, and purple headcovering remained unremarked except by their guide, who called it a useful beacon to help straying Number 1 bus riders find their way back to the fold.

During the lunch break Selena was given 28 ballet tickets to distribute. Keeping one for herself, she added the theater-seat location to the hotel-room number on the chewing-gum wrapper. But, though many teenagers asked for gum outside the Hall of Friendship where the question-and-answer session was held, none said "gum chew" and the marked package stayed in her pocket.

That night the Bolshoi troupe danced *Giselle* and Selena almost forgot her anxiety in the beauty of the performance. Trinka didn't say contact would be made the first day, she reminded herself. It could happen tomorrow. Or even on Sunday. The transfer of a few sheets of paper would take only an instant. There was no reason to assume that delay meant something had gone wrong.

It was about 10:30 when the ballet ended. They reclaimed their coats and came out of the theater to see a large segment of the audience moving rapidly on foot in one direction. When they asked their bus driver for an explanation, he tapped his watch, summoned his small store of English to say, "On the hour. The tomb of Lenin."

"The changing of the guard?" Selena asked.

"Yes," he said. "Guard change."

"The hotel's just across Red Square," someone said. "We can walk."

So bus Number 1 returned to the hotel half empty. Selena joined the hardier travelers to follow the swarm who, like lemmings, were moving toward Lenin's tomb.

A crowd of several hundred, mostly Russians, were standing in the Square. They waited with almost breathless anticipation, their eyes fixed on the two soldiers who stood motionless guarding the tomb. Then the clock began to strike and an officer, leading two other soldiers, marched smartly past the crowd. Like Arlington, Selena thought with an odd sense of recognition. It's almost the same ceremony as at the Tomb of the Unknowns.

Then, when she had stopped expecting it, a voice close to her ear said softly, "Gum chew." She almost jumped, almost exclaimed. The words were so out of keeping with the moment's solemnity. But her control held and she made no sound, did not even look round to see the speaker. Instead, moving slowly, she put her hand in her pocket, drew out the gum, and held it in half-open palm behind her back.

A hand took it from her, then slid a folded paper inside her glove. That's not how it was planned, she thought. And he's a man, not a boy.

She waited impatiently for the ceremony to end so that she could get back to the hotel. Some of her group went on to the bar for a warm-up drink, but she declined the invitation and hurried instead to her room to pull the slip of paper from her glove. It had written on it in block letters a single word: QUIT.

She stared at it, unbelieving. That was not a message from the friends of Trinka's grandfather. The word, with its revealing initial letter, could have had only one source. It was an order from Section Q. An order, more specifically, from her husband. But how—why?

Her mind was aswirl with questions. How did Hugh learn about her mission, about the "gum-chew" code? And why had he sent an emissary to warn her off? That Section Q had operatives in Moscow did not surprise her. But surely they had more important things to do than meddle in minor domestic matters. Yet one of them must have trailed her from the theater to Red Square and there traded his note for her gum. You sent a man to do a boy's work, Hugh, she mentally accused him. Why?

There was only one way to get an answer. She looked at her watch as she started toward the phone. Midnight in Moscow was four p.m. in Washington. He was probably in his studio and—her lips curved in a wry smile—probably expecting her call.

It would take, the operator told her, about half an hour to complete the call. Waiting, Selena sorted out her thoughts. She must accept the possibility of a listener on the line, but that would present no real problem. Hugh would know why she was calling and they were both skilled at conveying information in veiled terms. So when the connection was made they hurried through the conventional remarks expected of a tourist calling home and she waited for him to answer the questions she didn't ask.

"I visited your sick friend," he said. "We had an interesting talk."

"Really? I hope it didn't overtire her."

"Not at all. I think she was glad to see me. But you'd better stay clear of her. Her disease may be contagious and dangerous."

"You're exaggerating."

"No, I'm not. I've gotten an expert diagnosis. You'll be sorry to hear, too, about your cousin. She was caught smuggling drugs into Turkey and is likely to get ten years in jail. There's not a thing the family can do to help her."

"How dreadful!"

"She should have had better sense. Well, that's enough bad news. I miss you, darling. Please take care of yourself and hurry home."

She rang off and made translation. The sick friend was, of course, Trinka. I might have guessed his suspicions would lead him to the classmate I replaced on the tour. And when he told Trinka he was worried about me, she felt obliged to set his mind at rest by telling him all the facts—about the poem, the chewing gum, everything.

And the talk about my non-existent cousin in Turkey was meant to scare me off. He was saying that if I'm caught and put in a Russian prison, no one at home can get me out. But that's nonsense. I'm not smuggling drugs or valuables or military secrets. All I plan to carry out are a few sheets of paper that the authorities don't even know exist.

Hugh is being overprotective, that's all. He's so determined to keep me away from the kind of fire he plays with daily that he doesn't even want me to do a small favor for a friend. It's sweet of him to be solicitous, but this time he's frightened by shadows. I wonder, though, what he meant by "an expert diagnosis"?

On Sunday morning bus leaders were given two items to distribute—tickets for the folk dance and car-and-compartment numbers for the train. Selena took out a fresh pack of gum and wrote her new locations on the wrapper. The morning was, from her point of view, uneventful. But that afternoon, on the way into the huge barnlike building that houses the Soviet Space Exhibit, a chewing-gum squad approached. One of the boys zeroed in on Selena with the query, "Gum chew? You trade?"

He held out a pin bearing a likeness of Lenin. She accepted it and gave him the marked package.

"You shouldn't encourage them," the woman beside her said disapprovingly. "The ban on gum is the only good thing about Communism. My dentist says—"

Selena listened absently to the lecture as she dropped the souvenir into her purse. There was a small piece of paper on the back of the pin, but she would have to wait until she was alone to read it. Did it set time and place for a rendezvous, explain how the poem was to be handed over? Trying to guess what the message said blinded her eyes to the rocket display, deafened her ears to the glories of the Soyuz program.

When the space tour ended, she hurried to board the bus ahead of the others and, taking out the pin, slid the note free. It read: *Be patient. There are difficulties.* Be patient! She crumpled the paper. I could find better advice in a fortune cookie. Don't they realize tomorrow is my last day in Moscow?

For nearly 24 hours nothing happened. She concluded that the difficulties, whatever they were, had proved insurmountable. She must return home empty-handed. The final event was a tour of the Moscow Metro. En route to the entrance Olga, the Intourist representative, emphasized the problem of remaining together and insisted that all write down the name of the square where their bus would be parked. If any of them became separated, they should return to that square and wait for the others. Thus prepared, they went underground.

On the platform, interrupted by the noise of arriving and departing trains, Olga described the workings of the system, provided statistics, and explained the symbolism of the art on walls and ceiling. Then they were ready to ride. Since they could not all crowd into one car, they spread out along the platform with instructions to ride to the second stop, get off there, then regroup. A train stopped, the doors opened, people poured out, and others, including Selena's group, raced aboard. A stranger, following closely, nearly knocked her down.

"Quiet," he whispered. "Get off at the next stop."

He moved swiftly away from her to the other end of the car. While most of her companions found seats, she stayed near the door. Section Q again. Another message from Hugh.

The train hurtled through a tunnel, emerged again into light, and the doors opened. Selena let herself be swept onto the platform. Several people tried to call her back, but she pretended not to hear until the doors began to close. Then she looked through the windows at her fellow tourists and pantomimed dismay.

The Q-man, having left the car by the farthest door, walked past her to the escalator. She followed him up and out of the station. On the sidewalk, a few paces from the exit, he slowed down and she fell into step beside him.

"Our mutual friend," he began without introduction, "thinks he failed to make his point on the phone. He's afraid you may be going ahead with a high-risk enterprise."

"I understood what he was trying to tell me."

"Understood?" he challenged. "Or accepted?"

"It doesn't matter, since the enterprise appears to be canceled." She quoted yesterday's pinned message, adding, "In a few hours I'll be leaving town, so you can tell our friend to stop worrying."

"Mmm. Maybe. But he wants me to put you in the picture, so you'll know the threat is real. I gather this mission of yours is freelance, not for Section Q. Right?"

"That's right."

"As soon as our friend found out what you were doing, he asked me to sniff out the facts."

"An expert diagnosis?" she murmured.

"You could call it that. Here's what I found. Your classmate was naive to think she could hide inside a tour group. When her name turned up on the visa list, it triggered questions about why, after so many years, she was returning to her native land. The query was bucked to the KGB and a couple of agents visited the great-aunt.

"Communist bureaucracies move just as slowly as democratic ones, so by the time they got to her the plan had been changed. Somebody from the literary group had already picked up the poem in order to pass it on to you. The agents put pressure on the aunt to make her talk and she told them everything she knew—including the fact that the poem is pure dynamite. The invasion of Czechoslovakia touched off Korodin's outrage and it all poured out—the suppression of freedom, the silencing of artists, the enslavement of the people.

"It's a rather long narrative that starts with 1918 and, verse after verse, traces the betrayal of the Revolution. Taken alone, the words wouldn't do much harm, but in the handwriting of Communism's great prophet—well, you can see why they'd go to any length to stop the original manuscript from being taken out of the country."

"Do they know who has it now?"

"No, all the old lady knew was that a messenger came for it and said it would be delivered to the poet's granddaughter in America. You can be sure your tour was under surveillance from the moment the plane landed."

"There are one hundred and seventy-six of us," she point out, "in seven buses. Even the KGB can't watch all of us all the time."

"True. That's why I took a chance on cutting you out from the herd on the subway. I'm glad you don't have the poem, but you may still receive it before you leave Moscow. If you do, destroy it. Tear up the pages, burn the scraps, and dispose of the ashes in a way that can't be traced back to you."

"I can't do that. If the poem is all you say it is, it must be saved."

"It can't be saved. As you say, they can't watch all of you every minute. But there's one place where everybody can be thoroughly searched. That's at the Leningrad airport before you take off for the United States. If you're carrying the document, it will be found. You'll be arrested and they can convict you of stealing a priceless Korodin manuscript without revealing its contents. There's no power in Washington that can set you free, not even the President. Do I make myself clear?"

"Very."

"And you'll destroy the poem?"

"I'll probably never see it," she evaded. "Time is running out."

"A lot can happen in six hours. In six minutes even. I'll make a deal with you. My instructions are to get you safely out of the country and avoid an international incident. Section Q isn't concerned with the poem. Until three days ago no one on our side had even heard of it. But it's valuable propaganda and I hate to see it go down the drain."

"Then I shouldn't burn it?"

"Not right away. You'll receive it before you leave Moscow or not at all. There's no way they can get it to Leningrad. So I'll wait tonight at the railway station. In the dark and confusion I'll be able to get close to you. If you have the poem, give it to me. I'll keep it safe until the hunt dies down. Then we'll figure a way to get it to the poet's granddaughter. How does that sound?"

"Fine. Your facilities are certainly better than mine."

"And you'll give me the poem this evening?"

"I will," she agreed, "if I get it."

They separated and she took a taxi back to the parked bus. When the others emerged from the Metro there was much merriment over the leader's being the one who got lost and Selena expressed embarrassment at having thought they were to leave the train at the first stop instead of the second.

After returning to the hotel some tourists used the few remaining hours to buy gifts in the hotel's "hard currency" shop and others wrote and mailed postcards. For Selena it was simply a time of waiting, with each minute that passed bringing her closer to failure of her mission.

At last, when dinner was over, they boarded the bus for the station. Their luggage, unloaded from another bus, lay on the platform and the confusion the Q-man had forecast was compounded as they milled about, each traveler obliged to identify his own suitcase and either carry it to his assigned compartment or find a porter to do it for him.

A man bumped against Selena, muttered, "Quickly," and held out his hand.

"Nothing," she responded and he faded away. She found her car and compartment and carried her own bag aboard.

The compartments, composed of two upper and lower berths with a narrow aisle between them, were already made up for the night. In the one with Selena's number, three people from her bus were sitting on the lower berths—a husband, wife, and 15-year-old boy. They looked with dismay at Selena and her suitcase.

"There's no space." The wife spread her hands helplessly. "My husband put his bag and mine under the beds, but there's no room for Buddy's." She patted the one beside her. "And now one more!"

Selena, standing in the doorway as other people carrying luggage brushed past her, agreed with the assessment. While the husband poked futilely beneath the bunks as if he might magically make more room, a porter tapped Selena's arm.

"*Spassibo,*" he said. "I help."

She stepped aside. He sidled into the room and hoisted her bag into an open area above the door.

"Hey," Buddy said, "there's a big luggage section up there. We didn't even see it."

The Russian took the boy's bag from the bunk and shoved it in next to Selena's.

"Thanks a lot." The husband pulled a handful of kopeks from his pocket.

"*Nyet*." The man waved the coins away, edged past Selena, and hurried down the corridor.

It was a long and uncomfortable night. The only way four people could occupy such cramped quarters was to go to bed at once. Selena slept fitfully, burdened with thoughts of the failure of her mission. The difficulties had evidently proved insoluble. She must return to Trinka without the poem.

The train pulled into Leningrad at seven a.m. Buddy brought down his own bag, then reached for Selena's.

"Hey!" he exclaimed. "There's something else up here. Some paper."

He held an envelope toward Selena. "Is that yours?"

"What—oh, yes, it is mine." She took it from him and stuffed it in her handbag. "I almost forgot I put it up there. Thank you."

The next quarter hour was chaos as passengers and luggage debarked from the train and the tourists were once more shepherded to seven waiting buses. The envelope was like a burning brand in her handbag all the way to the hotel. Another message from Section Q? No, that connection was broken on the station platform. The number of her compartment was known, of course, to Russian underground. One of them, posing as a porter, had delivered the envelope when he lifted up her suitcase. So it must be the poem. They had, after all, found a way to get it to Leningrad.

The most beautiful city in the Soviet Union, that's what they call Leningrad—formerly St. Petersburg, home of the Czars, capital of old Russia, a treasurehouse of art and architecture. But for Selena, moving from one historic scene to another, the vision was blurred by internal debate.

As soon as she reached her hotel room she had opened the envelope and found four sheets of paper covered with closely written Russian script—the last Korodin poem. Four sticks, to follow the Q-man's metaphor, of pure dynamite. In the Hermitage she looked at Rembrandts and Goyas and Renoirs and thought, It's only four pieces of paper. There must be a way to hide them long enough to get them past customs.

In the summer palace at Pushkin she listened to the account of how artisans had recreated, down to the most intricate detail, silk screen destroyed in the war and thought, If I had their skill I'd be able to camouflage the poem and carry it away. What she needed was lab equipment that could photograph the pages, reduce them to microdots, copy them in invisible ink. But she was out of touch with Section Q. Their interest in her had ended in Moscow.

She considered phoning Hugh again to ask for help. But his order had been given—destroy the poem. And it was unlikely she could persuade him to a different view, or even explain the problem, on a line that was sure to be monitored. The decision was hers alone to make—to burn the pages and drop the ashes in the River Neva or risk her own freedom by trying to smuggle them out.

Her most vivid recollection of Leningrad was the Tuesday-afternoon tour of the St. Peter and Paul Fortress. In Czarist times it had been a prison, and after they had crowded into a bare cell the guide clanged shut the door and turned out the light. It was a moment of theatrics designed to dramatize the sufferings of the early revolutionaries, but for Selena it seemed a foretaste of her future.

That evening, as she dressed for the opera, she was aware that the articles in her suitcase had been taken out and repacked in slightly different order. Her room had been searched. Was everyone on the tour given the same attention? Or had they drawn the accurate conclusion that the person whose name was added to the visa list after the poet's granddaughter dropped out was the most likely suspect?

They'd found nothing, of course, since she carried the poem at all times in a zippered compartment of her handbag. But that would do no good at the airport where her handbag and even her person could be, and probably would be, searched.

I can't do it, Trinka, she mentally addressed her friend. I'd try, I'd take the risk if there was even a slim chance of getting through. You thought that no one else knew about the poem, that bringing it back would be easy. But now, with the authorities on the alert, I'd be bucking hopeless odds. To sacrifice myself in an effort sure to fail would be the worst kind of folly.

But even as her mind formed the argument, she saw again Trinka's ashen face and trustful eyes, heard her plead her sons' right to take pride in their ancestry. I can't let that go up in smoke. There must be a way. I've got to find it.

Wednesday was the last full day of the tour and as the time of decision narrowed she grew more desperate. In the afternoon they visited a museum where native arts and crafts were on display and she stood before a case containing a gaily painted wooden doll. It was large and bulb-shaped, and inside the doll, according to the guide, there were twelve other dolls, successively smaller in size, one within the other. It was typically Russian and souvenir shops were filled with small-scale replicas.

I'll buy one of those, Selena thought, fold the manuscript tightly, and put it inside the middle doll. Since they're bound to find it anyway, I might as well make it easy by choosing the most obvious hiding place.

That night they celebrated the trip's end with a gala dinner at the Sadok Restaurant. The tables were laden with vodka and champagne. A six-piece orchestra accompanied two singers and an acrobatic dancer. Toasts were effusive and spirits high. As a memento of the occasion the leader of each bus was presented with the window card bearing the bus's identifying number.

"Now you can show everyone that we were Number One," Buddy said while the large white cardboard was passed round the table for autographs. She caught the envious note in the boy's voice and started to say, "Perhaps you'd like—" when an idea struck her. Instead of offering him the sign as she'd intended, she finished lamely, "to be a bus leader yourself some day."

The most obvious hiding place. The concept triggered by the Russian doll summoned memory of Edgar Allan Poe's tale of the purloined letter which had been successfully hidden by leaving it in plain sight. Perhaps, just perhaps, she had the answer.

It was after eleven when the party ended. Selena pushed through the throng waiting at the coat-check counter to reach the side of Bill Parsons, leader of bus No. 4. The sign tucked under his arm was, she noted, auspiciously free of autographs.

"Hello, fellow sufferer," he hailed her. "I guess neither of us will let ourselves be conned into this job again. Rounding up stray sheep, getting blamed when they don't like their theater seats, making sure everybody gets back the right passport. It's a real headache."

"At least we've been rewarded." She waved her sign.

"Some reward! Believe me, I don't need any reminders."

"Aren't you going to take yours home?"

"Carry that back to the States? You've got to be kidding."

"In that case—" She moved closer, dropped her voice. "I have two nephews who have their bedroom walls covered with strange signs."

"Sure, I did the same thing when I was a kid. *Keep Off the Grass, Beware of the Dog*—that sort of thing. One saying INTOURIST—LENINGRAD should be a real collector's item."

"That's the problem," she said. "If I give it to one and not the other—"

"There'll be jealousy." He nodded, understanding. "But it's no problem. Take mine and make both boys happy."

"Well, if you're sure—"

"It will save the chambermaid from carrying it out with the trash tomorrow."

"That's very kind of you." She accepted the second sign. "I'm really grateful."

That night she slept peacefully for the first time since leaving Washington. Her plan was made. It might succeed, it might fail. But the time for vacillation was over.

After breakfast she used her nail scissors to loosen the lining of the top of her suitcase and pulled it free till half of the paper-backed cloth hung limp. Then she carried it to the counter near the elevators where a lady was in attendance day and night to hand out keys, serve tea, and solve minor problems. She spoke little English, but Selena's problem was clearly visible, her need for an adhesive substance apparent. The lady nodded and smiled assurance that the need would soon be filled.

Selena took the suitcase back to her room and began to copy the signatures and good wishes that the other riders had penned on the back of the bus Number 1 sign on the blank surface of the sign from bus Number 4. She was just finishing when a knock on the door signaled the arrival of a chambermaid with a tube of glue. Accepting it with thanks, Selena shut the door and placed a chair in front of it to guard against surprise interruption.

Then she took from the envelope the four pages of the Korodin poem. Placing the Number 1 sign face down on her dressing table, she separated the pages into two pairs and laid them side by side on the back of the card. They fitted easily, with a wide margin all around. Applying glue to that margin, she then put the other bus sign, with the number 4 inside, on top of the flattened pages, evened the edges, and pressed them firmly together. The result was, to all appearances, a single sign—that for bus Number 1—covered front and back with autographs. Only close inspection would reveal its double thickness.

That done, she used the glue to repair the damage she'd done to her suitcase. Then she made another trip to the service counter to return the tube. She finished her packing well in advance of the eleven a.m. deadline and went down to the lobby with suitcase and sign. Soon the buses, now minus number cards in the windows, began loading and they were on their way to the airport. And if the KGB is half as efficient as people think, she told herself, they know by now that the tourist in Room 451 ripped the lining off her suitcase and glued it back again. Let them deduce from that a belief that they've pinpointed the location of the missing document.

At the airport she held her sign with its secret pocket conspicuously in front of her and was glad to see that most of the other bus leaders were also carrying theirs. Those who still had rubles were directed to the exchange window, while the rest were channeled to customs officials who inspected luggage and packages, women's handbags, men's wallets, even clothing pockets. The search was slow and painstaking but the Intourist representative shrugged off questions and complaints, professing ignorance of the cause.

"They must have been tipped off that one of us is trying to smuggle out Russian currency," someone suggested. The rumor circulated swiftly and gained wide acceptance since it accounted for the thoroughness of the search. A few people who had planned, in spite of the taboo, to take home one or two rubles as contraband souvenirs, flushed guiltily and scurried back to the exchange window.

When Selena's turn came she laid the Number 1 bus sign on a bench, took off her coat, and gave it with her handbag to the customs man. She stood stoically while her body was patted by a woman official with head cocked and narrowed eyes—listening, Selena knew, for the telltale crackle of paper. Then she put her coat back on, slung her purse over her arm, and picked up the sign. She was starting to move on when the woman said sharply, "Wait!"

Oh, no! Selena froze, felt the blood pounding in her temples. This is it. I've been caught. Maybe the woman official is an Edgar Allan Poe fan. Selena turned slowly back, forcing an expression of polite inquiry.

"The hat." The woman pointed to her head. Trying not to show relief, Selena pulled off the knitted cap and gave it to the man to inspect while the woman ruffled her hair. In a few seconds she was dismissed. She put the cap back on, again picked up her sign, and went on to passport control. The man in the booth glanced without interest at the sign, then fixed his eyes unblinkingly first on her face, then on the pictures in passport and visa. Finding them to be likenesses, he tore off two-thirds of the visa and returned the remnant with her passport.

On the other side of the barrier the tension drained away. She sank exhausted onto a bench to await the call to board the plane. Around her people chattered angrily about the delay and promised that their first act on arriving home would be a call to the White House, the State Department, or their congressman. Selena hardly heard them. Her entire attention was focused on the journey's end.

When the boarding announcement came she was among the first out the door. And when they neared the huge Pan American jet she had to hold herself back from breaking into a run. But a few paces from the plane her exhilaration faded. Two soldiers stood at the foot of the steps checking everyone who boarded. One more hurdle.

She steeled herself and moved slowly forward. But those men, like the one in the booth, were interested only in faces. One took the final portion of her visa sheet, made sure of her identity, and let her pass.

Her seat was again on the aisle beside an elderly couple who were grumbling about the airport search.

"Such a mess," the woman said, "having everything opened and pawed through. I'll be very surprised if all the suitcases get on the plane."

"You don't have to come to Russia to lose your baggage." Her husband was more philosophical. "It's part of the flying experience."

At least, Selena mused, I can be the first one through U.S. customs since I'm certain my suitcase won't be put on board. After they tear out the lining and take it all apart, will they put it back together and send it on a later plane? Or is it lost forever?

She didn't really care. The suitcase and its contents were expendable. The valuable cargo was now on her lap. Soon they were airborne and when, a little later, the captain announced that they had just flown out of Soviet air space, Selena joined in the applause, then rested her hands lightly on the twinned cards. After I deliver the poem to Trinka, she decided, I'll look up young Buddy and give him the sign for bus Number 1.

"Q"

Jack P. Nelson

The Weasel

This is the 446th "first story" published by Ellery Queen's Mystery Magazine . . . "in which," to quote a member of our editorial staff, "a too clever criminal lawyer gets his comeuppance" . . .

66 "Will you be late?" Karen bent over the rosebush, the sun glinting in her loose red hair, her hands white against the dark green leaves and pale stalks. She did not look up at him as she spoke.

Michael paused, his hand on the cool smoothness of the car door. A miniature of the colonial house, the smooth lawn, the rose garden, and his wife was reflected in the sleek black of the automobile. He stared at the reflection as he spoke, choosing his words carefully.

"No. I'll be back before two. We can take Mary down to the lake for a while. It's going to be a hot day. You going out?"

He turned to see her shake her head. Her voice was low, almost a whisper, and there was a question in the normality of her answer. "No, I'll be here all day."

Her tone questioned him and he could not answer. He had tried to answer during the long hours of the night, but she still asked. Asked without words. Asked why an animal like Mort Janson would go free this morning because of her husband.

To Michael, the answer had been simple. Janson's freedom meant Michael's reputation. Through the long hot summer days his brilliance and wit had dazzled a courtroom of spectators, provided copy for wilting reporters jammed in the corridors, dashed the plodding competence of the District Attorney, and pushed a jury to the verge of freeing a man who was a murderer.

No, thought Michael as he slid into the car, he couldn't answer. Janson was an animal, a vicious beast. He was worse than a murderer and he was guilty. Michael had known it from the first day he had taken the case. Morton Janson had broken into the home of Daniel Frye last October, almost a year ago. He had pushed past Emily Frye on that hot autumn afternoon, had assaulted her,

174

dragged her into the kitchen, and cut her throat. Then he had stopped for a quarter of an hour while he poured and drank a cup of coffee, sitting in the kitchen near the body he had butchered.

Walking back into the front hall, Janson had seen the Fryes' four-year-old son, wakened from his nap, standing on the staircase. Janson killed the child, brutally, then walked from the house, leaving the front door open and the bloody knife on a table on the sun porch.

Now, after a short morning in court, Janson would go free.

Michael turned on the ignition and waved as Karen looked up at him. He would never be able to explain the "why" to her. Why it didn't matter whether the man was guilty or not, why it mattered only that Michael Berry had won another spectacular case.

As the car moved smoothly down the tree-shaded street, silent except for the soft hum of the air conditioner, Michael relaxed. She would forget. After a few hours at the lake they would drive back and put Mary to bed, then have a late dinner on the patio. He would keep the evening paper from her for a few days, and Karen would forget. She would forget about the Frye murders, forget Mort Janson. Before long she would remember only that her husband had won again. It had happened before. He smiled as he headed the car onto the expressway and into the heavy morning traffic.

"Congratulations!" Michael accepted his receptionist's greeting with a smile and a short nod. The morning in court had gone faster than he had anticipated, but he was still running late. The reporters crowding around him, the flashes from their cameras, the questions as he slowly made his way from the courtroom to the elevators, then down the steps of the courthouse to the parking lot and his car—he had taken it all at a leisurely pace, enjoying it, basking in the words, sensing the amazement, barely catching the cutting edge of censure in the questions that crowded down on him, overlapping and interrupting each other until he had laughed with pleasure. And the cameras had caught his laugh. Head thrown back, dark hair curling over his forehead, the brilliant flash of white teeth. It would make a good news picture.

He had seen Morton Janson only once, briefly, as the courtroom cleared. The thin weasel-like man had been watching him, his beady eyes shifting from side to side, his muddy brown hair slicked down, a crooked smile on his face. He was slumped in his chair like some noxious vermin. Michael had turned away. He needed no thanks from Janson who was merely publicity, another brick in his career. But Janson was also an animal.

Smiling, he accepted his secretary's congratulations and proceeded to sort the papers on his desk. It was nearly one P.M. when he pushed the intercom button and called Joyce into his office.

"Joyce, what's this note from Hal Speicht?"

Joyce Crowne, perfect legal secretary, flushed in confusion.

"Oh, I'm sorry, Mr. Berry, I should have mentioned it right away. I was so excited about the Janson verdict. Mr. Speicht called just before you came in. He said he had to see you and that it was very important." She indicated the note. "He said he would meet you at the Casa del Lago at one thirty."

Michael frowned. "Get him on the phone. I haven't time—did he say what he wanted?"

Joyce flushed again. "No, just that it was very important. I'm sorry, Mr. Berry, but he said he couldn't be reached this afternoon. Do you want me to call the restaurant—?"

"No." Annoyed, he pushed his chair back from the desk. Hal Speicht was an old friend, an important friend. At one time they had talked about going into partnership, but Michael had decided he preferred criminal instead of corporate law. If Hal said it was important—

"No. I'll meet him. Just call my wife and tell her I'll be home about an hour late. Tell her to have Mary ready by three and we'll stop to eat dinner on the way home from the beach."

If he hurried, he would just make it to the Casa del Lago by 1:30. Whatever Hal wanted could be cleared up in an hour, then 45 minutes if traffic was light, and he would be home by 3:15 or 3:30.

He pushed papers into his briefcase and left the cool wood-paneled office for the blazing pavements of the August afternoon. The Casa del Lago was just a few blocks from the office, but pushing through the sweating, steamy crowds on the street made it seem like miles.

Inside the dark, almost cold interior of the restaurant with its heavy wood tables, deep red-silk walls, and shaded lamps, he could relax again. The waiter showed him to an empty table in a quiet corner of the main dining room. Hal was late. Michael ordered a martini and looked around the room. Most of the noon crowd had left and few tables were occupied. The bar was empty except for one man at the far corner, half hidden in the shadows.

The martini came and Michael enjoyed the icy burning of the gin going down his throat. He glanced at his watch. 1:45. Idly he stared at the door, expecting Hal to arrive as the outside door opened, flashing sunlight into the dining area. Two young women stepped

down from the foyer. He finished the martini. The door flashed
sunlight again. A man and a woman, both elderly, came in. He
looked at his watch again. Two o'clock.

One more martini and fifteen more minutes, he thought. Then I'll
leave Hal a message and head for home. Michael looked up to signal
the waiter. The man from the bar was moving across the room
toward his table. Now that his eyes had become accustomed to the
darkness of the dining room, Michael realized that he knew the
man. He had seen him someplace. Where?

The man was coming directly to him, moving slowly, threading
his way through the tables and chairs. Where had Michael seen him
before? It was recently. The courtroom! With a shiver of recognition
he knew the man. He had seen the face often. The thin face, the
dark shadowed eyes, the shock of unruly blond hair. The man now
standing across the table from him was Daniel Frye.

"May I sit down a minute, Mr. Berry?" Frye's voice was low,
controlled.

"I . . ." Michael hesitated. "I'm sorry, Mr. Frye, but I'm waiting
for a friend. I don't think we have anything to talk about." His
forehead felt suddenly damp. Frye pulled out a chair and sat down,
his eyes on Michael's face.

"Wait a minute!" Michael half rose from his chair. "I said—"

"Don't worry, Mr. Berry." Frye smiled—a thin, humorless smile.
He placed his hands flat on the white tablecloth, pushing the sil-
verware away as he stretched out his fingers. "I haven't a gun or
anything. You can come around and search me if you wish."

"Nonsense." Michael found he had to fight to breathe normally.
There was a tight feeling in his chest and his eyes caught the gleam
of light from the butter knife as Frye's fingers pushed it over the
tablecloth.

"No, really, if you feel uneasy, I wish you would search me." Frye's
brows knit. He leaned forward and a lock of hair fell over his pale
forehead. "I haven't come to kill you, if that's what you're afraid of,
Mr. Berry."

"I am not afraid." Michael spoke firmly, meeting Frye's eyes.
Michael's stare was cold, penetrating, but Frye did not look away.
"And I have no wish to search you, Mr. Frye. I just want you to go
away. I don't want to be forced to call the waiter, but I want you to
leave."

Frye broke. His look wavered, then dropped to his hands, still
spread out, palm down, on the white linen. Michael felt a sudden

thrill of triumph, a feeling of victory. It had worked again. The stare. The long look from his eyes, which Karen had described as being like Lake Superior water, cold and blue, had broken jurors and witnesses often, until the truth they thought and spoke became stammered lies.

Meeting Frye could have been unpleasant; there could have been a scene, but now Michael knew he was in control. He knew Frye had no gun, would not pick up the knife, would do nothing but sit there, staring at his hands. I could make him break down and leave him here at the table sobbing, thought Michael. If I wanted to, I could break him. A sudden anger warmed him.

"I want to talk to you," Frye spoke without looking up. "Just for a few moments. I want to ask you something."

"I'm expecting a friend, Frye. You and I have nothing to talk about."

"You mean you're expecting Hal Speicht? He isn't coming. It was I who called your office. I used his name." Frye spoke slowly, deliberately, as though he were explaining things to a child.

"You? You arranged this?" Again the chill of fear.

"Yes. I had to ask you why." Frye looked up.

"Why?" It was Karen's question again. Always why.

"He should not have gone free. You knew it. You knew what he was. Yet you made it possible for him to go free. I don't understand why. And I have to know why, Mr. Berry. I waited for months, then I sat through the trial and watched you twist and turn things until he went free. Why did you do it?"

"I'm a lawyer. Morton Janson was my client. It was my duty."

"Duty!" A touch of anger, a hint of bitterness in the voice, then it was soft again. "You knew what you were doing. He wasn't fit to walk out free. Janson is a beast. Everyone knows what he is, what he has done. And then, at the end, he smiled. Smiled because he had killed and got away with it. The jury was all against him. They would have put him away, but you—you let him go out into the world again. You sent an animal out into the world. *Why,* Mr. Berry?"

"Mr. Frye, I sympathize with you. I know what you have been through." Michael had to end this. He had to get up and leave. The *why* again. He couldn't make Karen understand. He couldn't even try to explain to Frye. "You have to understand—"

"I came home early that afternoon. At least, I thought I had come home early. I wish I had never left the house that day. I remember the afternoon sun on the sidewalk, the chipped paint on the steps, then the door, standing open. I knew something was wrong before I even saw the knife. I think we have a feeling—something that screams out inside of us. Cavemen had that feeling when they came to the place where a wild beast had been. I sensed the beast. I saw the knife. Then I went inside, and—and I found them."

His voice trailed off. He leaned toward Michael. "Do you know what a weasel is like, Mr. Berry?"

Weasel. Janson had reminded him of a weasel. Funny that Frye should use the same word.

"A weasel sneaks into nests, into places where other animals keep their young, and he kills. The life of a weasel is to kill, and the stench of a weasel is the stench of death."

He's mad, Michael thought. The man has gone mad. He looked up and tried to signal a waiter, but there was only one in the dining room now, and he had his back to their table, bending over to listen to the elderly couple. Why didn't he turn and look at Michael?

"You could have stopped him, Mr. Berry. The cage was shut and locked. Then you began to shake the bars and brag you could open the cage. I listened to you and heard it in your voice. You wanted to open the cage because no one else could. You knew Janson. He belonged in the cage, but you let him out."

Michael shivered. He wanted to slide from the chair, walk from the room, but he couldn't. Suddenly he felt the uncomfortable trickle of sweat down his back, soaking the shirt under his jacket. His mouth was dry, and he reached for the water glass.

"There was nothing I could do," Frye continued. "I wanted to get up and shout, to scream, to let the people know the evil they were doing. But I couldn't. Janson was guilty. His fingerprints—my wife would never have asked him in for coffee—he lied. You made them believe his lies. You wanted him to go free so that you could show everyone that you could do the impossible. Is that what you wanted to do? Or did you think that Janson was innocent?"

Michael looked at Frye over the top of the water glass. He willed his hand to be steady as he set the glass down. "Yes." He spoke clearly, calmly. "I believe Morton Janson was innocent. He did not kill your wife and your child."

Frye nodded, then turned and signaled to the waiter.

"Waiter, we need a telephone here. Can you . . . ?"

"Certainly, sir." The waiter hurried across the room. The two men stared at each other over the table. Frye lifted his fingers from the table and lightly rested his hands on his knees. Michael leaned back in his chair, his fingers playing with the stem of the glass.

The waiter returned with a telephone, plugged it in, and placed it in front of Frye who waited until the waiter had left, then pushed the telephone toward Michael.

"If you believe he was innocent, don't call."

"Don't call? Don't call who?"

"Don't call your home. He's there." Frye pushed the telephone until it touched Michael's hand. Michael recoiled as if it were alive.

"At my home?" It was barely a whisper.

Frye nodded. "I bribed someone in the courtroom. They gave him a note."

"A note? What note?" Despite his efforts, Michael's voice rose.

"I asked Janson to come to your home this afternoon. For a drink. To celebrate your victory and his freedom. I signed your name. He's been there for over an hour now. Is your wife beautiful, Mr. Berry? Mine was."

Michael swallowed as his hand moved toward the telephone. He hesitated. "You're joking."

"Oh, no. It's no joke." Frye smiled briefly. "I checked on you yesterday. I got your address, the name of your friend, Mr. Speicht. I had to do something, in case—but if Janson is innocent, you have nothing to worry about. You said he was innocent, Mr. Berry."

Karen ... Michael thought of her deep red hair, her soft white skin, her tall sensual figure dressed in a bathing suit and a beach robe, waiting for him. He thought of Mary collecting her pail, shovel, and plastic animals for the beach. The white house, the cool green lawn, the red roses on their slender stalks.

Michael's fingers snapped the stem of the water glass. The crystal shattered on the table and the blood from his cut palm stained the white of the tablecloth.

Frye nodded. "Do you know that a weasel enjoys killing, Mr. Berry?"

Michael snatched the receiver and began to dial, his wound bleeding onto the telephone. He watched the blood run down the surface to the table as he listened to the first rings of the telephone.

"You have nothing to worry about if he is an innocent man. And you said he was innocent, Mr. Berry."

The telephone rang again and again. Michael looked up to see Frye smiling at him, a smile of pity, of sympathy, and the prolonged ringing of the telephone screamed in Michael's brain.

Isaac Asimov

The Cross of Lorraine

*Welcome home—hail the return of the Black Widowers inviting
you to attend another of their monthly dinner meetings. This time
writer Emmanuel Rubin is the host, and his guest is a stage
magician—The Amazing Larri. And Rubin's colleagues-in-
conundrums, his partners-in-puzzles—lawyer Geoffrey Avalon,
artist Mario Gonzalo, mathematician Roger Halsted, chemist
James Drake, and code expert Thomas Trumbull—all are ready,
willing, if not always able, to match wits with the professional
prestidigitator. (Good Lord, we've fallen into the trap of "The
Invisible Man"! How could we have forgotten the waiter, the
omnipresent, omniscient Henry? For it is The Amazing Henry
who is the master magician at these mystery meetings.)*

Here, then, is the real McAsimov . . .

Detectives: THE BLACK WIDOWERS and HENRY

Emmanuel Rubin did not, as a general rule, ever permit a look
of relief to cross his face. Had one done so, it would have argued
a prior feeling of uncertainty or apprehension, sensations he might
feel but would certainly never admit to.

This time, however, the relief was unmistakable. It was monthly
banquet time for the Black Widowers. Rubin was the host and it
was he who was supplying the guest. And here it was twenty minutes after seven and only now—with but ten minutes left before
dinner was to start—only now did his guest arrive.

Rubin bounded toward him, careful, however, not to spill a drop
of his second drink.

"Gentlemen," he said, clutching the arm of the newcomer, "my
guest, The Amazing Larri—spelled L-A-R-R-I." And in a lowered
voice, over the hum of pleased-to-meet-yous, "Where the hell were
you?"

Larri muttered, "The subway train stalled." Then he returned smiles and greetings.

"Pardon me," said Henry, the perennial—and nonpareil—waiter at the Black Widower banquets, "but there is not much time for the guest to have his drink before dinner begins. Would you state your preference, sir?"

"A good notion, that," said Larri gratefully. "Thank you, waiter, and let me have a dry martini, but not too darned dry—a little damp, so to speak."

"Certainly, sir," said Henry.

Rubin said, "I've told you, Larri, that we members all have our *ex officio* doctorates, so now let me introduce them in nauseating detail. This tall gentleman with the neat mustache, black eyebrows, and straight back is Dr. Geoffrey Avalon. He's a lawyer and he never smiles. The last time he tried, he was fined for contempt of court."

Avalon smiled as broadly as he could and said, "You undoubtedly know Manny well enough, sir, not to take him seriously."

"Undoubtedly," said Larri. As he and Rubin stood together, they looked remarkably alike. Both were the same height—about five feet five—both had active, inquisitive faces, both had straggly beards, though Larri's was longer and was accompanied by a fringe of hair down both sides of his face as well.

Rubin said, "And here, dressed fit to kill anyone with a *real* taste for clothing, is our artist-expert, Dr. Mario Gonzalo, who will insist on producing a caricature of you in which he will claim to see a resemblance. —Dr. Roger Halsted inflicts pain on junior high-school students under the guise of teaching them what little he knows of mathematics. —Dr. James Drake is a superannuated chemist who once conned someone into granting him a Ph.D. —And finally, Dr. Thomas Trumbull, who works for the government in an unnamed job as a code expert and who spends most of his time hoping Congress doesn't find out."

"Manny," said Trumbull wearily, "if it were possible to cast a retroactive blackball, I think you could count on five."

And Henry said, "Gentlemen, dinner is served."

It was one of those rare Black Widower occasions when lobster was served, rarer now than ever because of the increase in price.

Rubin, who as host bore the cost, shrugged it off. "I made a good paperback sale last month and we can call this a celebration."

"We can celebrate," said Avalon, "but lobster tends to kill conversation. The cracking of claws and shells, the extraction of meat, the dipping in melted butter—all that takes one's full concentration." And he grimaced with the effort he was putting into the compression of a nutcracker.

"In that case," said the Amazing Larri, "I shall have a monopoly of the conversation," and he grinned with satisfaction as a large platter of prime rib-roast was dexterously placed before him by Henry.

"Larri is allergic to seafood," said Rubin.

Conversation was indeed subdued, as Avalon had predicted, until the various lobsters had been clearly worsted in culinary battle, and then, finally, Halsted asked, "What makes you Amazing, Larri?"

"Stage name," said Larri. "I am a prestidigitator, an escapist extraordinary, and the greatest living exposer."

Trumbull, who was sitting to Larri's right, formed ridges on his bronzed forehead. "What the devil do you mean by 'exposer'?"

Rubin beat a tattoo on his water glass at this point and said, "No grilling till we've had our coffee."

"For God's sake," said Trumbull, "I'm just asking for the definition of a word."

"Host's decision is final," said Rubin.

Trumbull scowled in Rubin's direction. "Then I'll *guess* the answer. An exposer is one who exposes fakes—people who, using trickery of one sort or another, pretend to produce effects they attribute to supernatural or paranatural forces."

Larri thrust out his lower lip, raised his eyebrows, and nodded. "Very good for a guess. I couldn't have put it better."

Gonzalo said, "You mean that whatever someone did by what he claimed was real magic, you could do by stage magic?"

"Exactly," said Larri. "For instance, suppose that some mystic claimed he had the capacity to bend spoons by means of unknown forces. I can do the same by using natural force, this way." He lifted his spoon and, holding it by its two ends, he bent it half an inch out of shape.

Trumbull said, "That scarcely counts. Anyone can do it that way."

"Ah," said Larri, "but this spoon you saw me bend is not the amazing effect at all. That spoon you were watching merely served to trap and focus the ethereal rays that did the real work. Those rays acted to bend *your* spoon, Dr. Trumbull."

Trumbull looked down and picked up his spoon, which was bent nearly at right angles. "How did you do this?"

Larri shrugged. "Would you believe ethereal forces?"

Drake laughed, and pushing his dismantled lobster toward the center of the table, lit a cigarette. He said, "Larri did it a few minutes ago, with his hands, when you weren't looking."

Larri seemed unperturbed by exposure. "When Manny banged his glass, Dr. Trumbull, you looked away. I had rather hoped you all would."

Drake said, "I know better than to pay attention to Manny."

"But," said Larri, "if no one had seen me do it, would you have accepted the ethereal forces?"

"Not a chance," said Trumbull.

"Even if there had been no other way in which you could explain the effect? —Here, let me show you something. Suppose you wanted to flip a coin—"

He fell silent for a moment while Henry passed out the strawberry shortcake, pushed his own serving out of the way, and said, "Suppose you wanted to flip a coin without actually lifting it and turning it—this penny, for instance. There are a number of ways it could be done. The simplest would be merely to touch it quickly, because, as you all know, a finger is always slightly sticky, especially at meal time, so that the coin lifts up slightly as the finger is removed and can easily be made to flip over. It is tails now, you see. Touch it again and it is heads."

Gonzalo said, "No prestidigitation there, though. We see it flip."

"Exactly," said Larri, "and that's why I won't do it that way. Let's put something over it so that it can't be touched. Suppose we use a—" He looked around the table for a moment and seized a salt shaker. "Suppose we use this."

He placed the salt shaker over the coin and said, "Now it is showing heads—"

"Hold on," said Gonzalo. "How do we know it's showing heads? It could be tails and then, when you reveal it later, you'll say it flipped, when it was tails all along."

"You're perfectly right," said Larri, "and I'm glad you raised the point. —Dr. Drake, you have eyes that caught me before. Would you check this on behalf of the assembled company? I'll lift the salt shaker and you tell me what the coin shows."

Drake looked and said, "Heads," in his softly hoarse voice.

"You'll all take Dr. Drake's word, I hope, gentlemen? —Please, watch me place the salt shaker back on the coin and make sure it doesn't flip in the process—"

"It didn't," said Drake.

"Now to keep my fingers from slipping while performing this trick, I will put this paper napkin over the salt shaker."

Larri folded the paper napkin neatly and carefully around the salt shaker, then said, "But, in manipulating this napkin, I caused you all to divert your attention from the penny and you may think I have flipped it in the process." He lifted the salt shaker with the napkin around it, and said, "Dr. Drake, will you check the coin again?"

Drake leaned toward it. "Still heads," he said.

Very carefully and gently Larri put back the salt shaker, the paper napkin still folded around it and said, "The coin remained as is?"

"Still heads," said Drake.

"In that case, I now perform the magic." Larri pushed down on the salt shaker and the paper napkin collapsed. There was nothing inside.

There was a moment of shock, and then Gonzalo said, "Where's the salt shaker?"

"In another plane of existence," said Larri airily.

"But you said you were going to flip the coin."

"I lied."

Avalon said, "There's no mystery. He had us all concentrating on the coin as a diversion tactic. When he picked up the salt shaker with the napkin around it to let Jim look at the coin, he just dropped the salt shaker into his hand and placed the empty, folded napkin over the coin."

"Did you see me do that, Dr. Avalon?" asked Larri.

"No. I was looking at the coin too."

"Then you're just guessing," said Larri.

Rubin, who had not participated in the demonstration at all, but who had eaten his strawberry shortcake instead, said, "The tendency is to argue these things out logically and that's impossible. Scientists and other rationalists are used to dealing with the universe, which fights fair. Faced with a mystic who does not, they find themselves maneuvered into believing nonsense and, in the end, making fools of themselves.

"Magicians, on the other hand," Rubin went on, "know what to watch for, are experienced enough not to be misdirected, and are not impressed by the apparently supernatural. That's why mystics generally won't perform if they know magicians are in the audience."

Coffee had been served and was being sipped, and Henry was quietly preparing the brandy, when Rubin sounded the water glass and said, "Gentlemen, it is time for the official grilling, assuming you idiots have left anything to grill. Jeff, will you do the honors tonight?"

Avalon cleared his throat portentously and frowned down on The Amazing Larri from under his dark and luxuriant eyebrows. Using his voice in the deepest of its naturally deep register, he said, "It is customary to ask our guests to justify their existences, but if today's guest exposes phony mystics even occasionally, I, for one, consider his existence justified and will pass on to another question.

"The temptation is to ask you how you performed your little disappearing trick of a few moments ago, but I quite understand that the ethics of your profession preclude your telling us—even though everything said here is considered under the rose, and though nothing has ever leaked, I will refrain from that question.

"Let me instead ask about your failures. —Sir, you describe yourself as an exposer. Have there been any supposedly mystical demonstrations you have not been able to duplicate in prestidigitous manner and have not been able to account for by natural means?"

Larri said, "I have not attempted to explain all the effects I have ever encountered or heard of, but where I have studied an effect and made an attempt to duplicate it, I have succeeded in every case."

"No failures?"

"None."

Avalon considered that, but as he prepared for the next question, Gonzalo broke in. His head was leaning on one palm, but the fingers of that hand were carefully disposed in such a way as not to disarray his hair.

He said, "Now, wait, Larri, would it be right to suggest that you tackled only easy cases? The really puzzling cases you might have made no attempts to explain?"

"You mean," said Larri, "that I shied away from anything that might spoil my perfect record or that might upset my belief in the rational order of the universe? —If so, you're quite wrong, Dr. Gonzalo. Most reports of apparent mystical powers are dull and unimportant, crude and patently false. I ignore those. The cases I do take on are precisely the puzzling ones that have attracted attention because of their unusual nature and their apparent divorce from the rational. So, you see, the ones I take on are precisely those you suspect I avoid."

Gonzalo subsided and Avalon said, "Larri, the mere fact that you can duplicate a trick by prestidigitation doesn't mean that it couldn't also have been performed by a mystic through supernatural means. The fact that human beings can build machines that fly doesn't mean that birds are man-made machines."

"Quite right," said Larri, "but mystics lay their claims to supernatural powers on the notion, either expressed or implicit, that there is no other way of producing the effect. If I show that the same effect *can* be produced by natural means, the burden of proof then shifts to them to show that the effect can be produced after the natural means are made impossible. I don't know of any mystic who has accepted the conditions set by professional magicians to guard against trickery and who then succeeded."

"And nothing has ever baffled you? Not even the tricks other magicians have developed?"

"Oh, yes, there are effects produced by some magicians that baffle me in the sense that I don't know quite how they do it. I might duplicate the effect by perhaps using a different method. In any case, that's not the point. As long as an effect is produced by natural means, it doesn't matter whether I can reproduce it or not. I am not the best magician in the world. I am just a better magician than any mystic is."

Halsted, his high forehead flushed, and stuttering slightly in his eagerness to speak, said, "But then nothing would startle you? No disappearance like the one involving the salt shaker?"

"You mean that one?" asked Larri, pointing. There was a salt shaker in the middle of the table, but no one had seen it placed there.

Halsted, thrown off a moment, recovered and said, "Have you ever been *startled* by any disappearance? I heard once that magicians have made elephants disappear."

"Actually, making an elephant disappear is childishly simple. I assure you there's nothing puzzling about disappearances performed in a magic act." And then a peculiar look crossed Larri's face, a flash of sadness and frustration. "Not in a magic act. Just—"

"Yes?" said Halsted. "Just what?"

"Just in real life," said Larri, smiling and attempting to toss off the remark lightheartedly.

"Just a minute," said Trumbull, "we can't let that pass. If there has been a disappearance in real life you can't explain, we want to hear about it."

Larri shook his head. "No, no, Dr. Trumbull. It is not a mysterious disappearance or an inexplicable one. Nothing like that at all. I just—well, I lost something and can't find it and it—saddens me."

"The details," said Trumbull.

"It wouldn't be worth your attention," said Larri, embarrassed. "It's a—silly story and somewhat—" He fell into silence.

"Damn it," thundered Trumbull, "we all sit here and voluntarily refrain from asking anything that might result in your being tempted to violate your ethics. Would it violate the ethics of the magician's art for you to tell this story?"

"It's not that at all—"

"Well, then, sir, I repeat what Jeff has told you. Everything said here is in absolute confidence, and the agreement surrounding these monthly dinners is that all questions must be answered. —Manny?"

Rubin shrugged. "That's the way it is, Larri. If you don't want to answer the question we'll have to declare the meeting at an end."

Larri sat back in his chair and looked depressed. "I can't very well allow that to happen, considering the fine hospitality I've been shown. I will tell you the story, but you'll find there's not much to it. I met a woman quite accidentally; I lost touch with her; I can't locate her. That's all there is."

"No," said Trumbull, "that's not all there is. Where and how did you meet her? Where and how did you lose touch with her? Why can't you find her again? We want to know the details."

Gonzalo said, "In fact, if you tell us the details, we may be able to help you."

Larri laughed sardonically. "I think not."

"You'd be surprised," said Gonzalo. "In the past—"

Avalon said, "Quiet, Mario. Don't make promises we might not be able to keep. —Would you give us the details, sir? I assure you we'll do our best to help."

Larri smiled wearily. "I appreciate your offer, but you will see that there is nothing you can do merely by sitting here."

He adjusted himself in his seat and said, "I was done with my performance in an upstate town—I'll give you the details when and if you insist, but for the moment they don't matter, except that this happened about a month ago. I had to get to another small town some hundred and fifty miles away for a morning show and that presented a little transportation problem.

"My magic, unfortunately, is not the kind that can transport me a hundred and fifty miles in a twinkling, or even conjure up a pair of seven-league boots. I did not have my car with me—just as well, for I don't like to travel strange roads at night when I am sleepy—and the net result was that I would have to take a bus that would take nearly four hours. I planned to catch some sleep while on wheels and thus make the trip serve a double purpose.

"But when things go wrong, they go wrong in battalions, so you can guess that I missed my bus and that the next one would not come along for two more hours. There was an enclosed station in which I could wait, one that was as dreary as you could imagine—with no reading matter except some fly-blown posters on the wall—no place to buy a paper or a cup of coffee. I thought grimly that it was fortunate it wasn't raining, and settled down to drowse, when my luck changed.

"A woman walked in. I've never been married, gentlemen, and I've never even had what young people today call a 'meaningful relationship.' Some casual attachments, perhaps, but on the whole, though it seems trite to say so, I am married to my art and find it much more satisfying than women, generally.

"I had no reason to think that this woman was an improvement on the generality, but she had a pleasant appearance. She was something over thirty, and was just plump enough to have a warm, comfortable look about her, and she wasn't too tall.

"She looked about and said, smiling, 'Well, I've missed my bus, I see.'

"I smiled with her. I liked the way she said it. She didn't fret or whine or act annoyed at the universe. It was a good-humored statement of fact, and just hearing it cheered me up tremendously because actually I myself was in the mood to fret and whine and act annoyed. Now I could be as good-natured as she and say, 'Two of us, madam, so you don't even have the satisfaction of being unique.'

" 'So much the better,' she said. 'We can talk and pass the time that much faster.'

"I was astonished. She did not treat me as a potential attacker or as a possible thief. God knows I am not handsome or even particularly respectable in appearance, but it was as though she had casually penetrated to my inmost character and found it satisfactory. You have no idea how flattered I was. If I were ten times as sleepy, I would have stayed up to talk to her.

"And we did talk. Inside of fifteen minutes I knew I was having the pleasantest conversation in my life—in a crummy bus station at midnight. I can't tell you all we talked about, but I can tell you what we *didn't* talk about. We didn't talk about magic.

"I can interest anyone by doing tricks, but then it isn't me they're interested in; it's the flying fingers and the patter they like. And while I'm willing to buy attention that way, you don't know how pleasant it is to get the attention without purchasing it. She apparently just liked to listen to me; I know I liked to listen to her.

"Fortunately, my trip was not an all-out effort, so I didn't have my large trunk with the show-business advertising all over it, just two rather large valises. I told her nothing personal about myself, and asked nothing about her. I gathered briefly that she was heading for her brother's place, that it was right on the road, that she would have to wake him up because she had carelessly let herself be late—but she only told me that in order to say that she was glad it had happened. She would buy my company at the price of inconveniencing her brother. I liked that.

"We didn't talk politics or world affairs or religion or the theater. We talked people—all the funny and odd and peculiar things we had observed about people. We laughed for two hours, during which not one other person came to join us. I had never had anything like that happen to me, had never felt so alive and happy, and when the bus finally came at 1:50 A.M., it was amazing how sorry I was. I didn't want the night to end.

"When I got onto the bus, of course, it was no longer quite the same thing, even though we found a double seat we could share. After all, we had been alone in the station and there we could talk loudly and laugh. On the bus people were sleeping.

"Of course it wasn't all bad. It was a nice feeling to have her so close to me. Despite the fact that I'm rather an old horse, I felt like a teenager—enough like a teenager, in fact, to be embarrassed at being watched.

"Immediately across the way was a woman and her young son. He was about eight years old, I should judge, and *he* was awake. He kept watching me with his sharp little eyes. I could see those eyes fixed on us every time a street light shone into the bus and it was very inhibiting. I wished he were asleep but, of course, the excitement of being on a bus, perhaps, was keeping him awake.

"The motion of the bus, the occasional whisper, the feeling of being quite out of reality, the pressure of her body against mine—it was like confusing dream and fact, and the boundary between sleep and wakefulness just vanished. I didn't intend to sleep, and I started awake once or twice, but then finally, when I started awake one more time, it was clear there had been a considerable period of sleep, and the seat next to me was empty."

Halsted said, "I take it she had gotten off."

"I didn't think she had disappeared into thin air," said Larri. "Naturally, I looked about. I couldn't call her name, because I didn't know her name. She wasn't in the rest room, because its door was swinging open.

"The little boy across the aisle spoke in a rapid high treble—in French. I can understand French reasonably well, but I didn't have to make any effort, because his mother was now awakened and she translated. She spoke English quite well.

"She said, 'Pardon me, sir, but is it that you are looking for the woman that was with you?'

" 'Yes,' I said. 'Did you see where she got off?'

" 'Not I, sir. I was sleeping. But my son says that she descended at the place of the Cross of Lorraine.'

" 'At the what?'

"She repeated it, and so did the child, in French.

"She said, 'You must excuse my son, sir. He is a great hero worshipper of President Charles de Gaulle and though he is young he knows that tale of the Free French forces in the war very well. He would not miss a sight like a Cross of Lorraine. If he said he saw it, he did.'

"I thanked them and then went forward to the bus driver and asked him, but at that time of night the bus stops wherever a passenger would like to get off, or get on. He had made numerous stops and let numerous people on and off, and he didn't know for sure where he had stopped and whom he had left off. He was rather churlish, in fact."

Avalon cleared his throat. "He may have thought you were up to no good and was deliberately withholding information to protect the passenger."

"Maybe," said Larri despondently, "but what it amounted to was that I had lost her. When I came back to my seat, I found a little note tucked into the pocket of the jacket I had placed in the rack above. I managed to read it by a streetlight at the next stop, where the French mother and son got off. It said, 'Thank you so much for a delightful time. Gwendolyn.' "

Gonzalo said, "You have her first name anyway."

Larri said, "I would appreciate having had her last name, her address, her telephone number. Having only a first name is useless."

"You know," said Rubin, "she may deliberately have withheld information because she wasn't interested in continuing the acquaintanceship. A romantic little interlude is one thing; a continuing danger is another. She may be a married woman."

"Have you done anything about trying to find her?" asked Gonzalo.

"Certainly," said Larri sardonically. "If a magician is faced with a disappearing woman he must understand what has happened. I have gone over the bus route twice by car, looking for a Cross of Lorraine. If I had found it, I would have gone in and asked if anyone there knew a woman by the name of Gwendolyn. I'd have described her. I would have gone to the local post office or the local police station."

"But you have not found a Cross of Lorraine, I take it," said Trumbull.

"I have not."

Halsted said, "Mathematically speaking, it's a finite problem. You could try every post office along the whole route."

Larri sighed. "If I get desperate enough, I'll try. But, mathematically speaking, that would be so inelegant. Why can't I find the Cross of Lorraine?"

"The youngster might have made a mistake," said Trumbull.

"Not a chance," said Larri. "An adult, yes, but a child, never. Adults have accumulated enough irrationality to be very unreliable eyewitnesses. A bright eight-year-old is different. Don't try to pull any trick on a bright kid; he'll see through it.

"Just the same," he went on, "nowhere on the route is there a restaurant, a department store, or anything else with the name Cross of Lorraine. I've checked every set of yellow pages along the entire route."

"Now wait a while," said Avalon, "that's wrong. The child wouldn't have seen the words because they would have meant nothing to him. If he spoke and read only French, as I suppose he did, he would know the phrase as 'Croix de Lorraine.' The English would have never caught his eyes. He must have seen the symbol, the cross with the two horizontal bars, like this." He reached out and Henry obligingly handed him a menu.

Avalon turned it over and on the blank back drew the following:

"Actually," he said, "it is more properly called the Patriarchal Cross or the Archiepiscopal Cross since it symbolized the high office of patriarchs and archbishops by doubling the bars. You will not be surprised to hear that the Papal Cross has three bars. The Patriarchal Cross was used as a symbol by Godfrey of Bouillon, who was one of the leaders of the First Crusade, and since he was Duke of Lorraine, it came to be called the Cross of Lorraine. As we all know, it was adopted as the emblem of the Free French during the Hitlerian War."

He coughed slightly and tried to look modest.

Larri said, a little impatiently, "I understand about the symbol, Dr. Avalon, and I didn't expect the youngster to note words. I think you'll agree, though, that any establishment calling itself the Cross of Lorraine would surely display the symbol along with the name. I looked for the name in the yellow pages and for the symbol on the road."

"And you didn't find it?" said Gonzalo.

"As I've already said, I didn't. I was desperate enough to consider things I didn't think the kid could possibly have seen at night. I thought, who knows how sharp young eyes are and how readily they may see something that represents an overriding interest? So I looked at signs in windows, at street signs—even at graffiti."

"If it were a graffito," said Trumbull, "which happens to be the singular form of graffiti, by the way, then, of course, it could have been erased between the time the child saw it and the time you came to look for it."

"I'm not sure of that," said Rubin. "It's my experience that graffiti are never erased. We've got some on the outside of our apartment house—"

"That's New York," said Trumbull. "In smaller towns there's less tolerance for these evidences of anarchy."

"Hold on," said Gonzalo, "what makes you think graffiti are necessarily signs of anarchy? As a matter of fact—"

"Gentlemen! Gentlemen!" And as always, when Avalon's voice was raised to its full baritone, a silence fell. "We are not here to argue the merits and demerits of graffiti. The question is: how can we find this woman who disappeared? Larri has found no restaurant or other establishment with the name of Cross of Lorraine; he has found no evidence of the symbol along the route taken. Can we help him?"

Drake held up his hand and squinted through the curling smoke of his cigarette.

"Hold on, there's no problem. Have you ever seen a Russian Orthodox Church? Do you know what its cross is like?" He made quick marks on the back of the menu and shoved it toward the center of the table. "Here—"

He said, "The kid, being hipped on the Free French, would take a quick look at that and see it as the Cross of Lorraine. So what you have to do, Larri, is look for a Russian Orthodox Church en route. I doubt there would be more than one."

Larri thought about it, but did not seem overjoyed. "The cross with that second bar set at an angle would be on the top of the spire, wouldn't it?"

"I imagine so."

"And it wouldn't be floodlighted, would it? How would the child be able to see it at three or four o'clock in the morning?"

Drake stubbed out his cigarette. "Well, now, churches usually have a bulletin board near the entrance. There could have been a Russian Orthodox cross on the—"

"I would have seen it," said Larri firmly.

"Could it have been a Red Cross?" asked Gonzalo feebly. "You know, there might be a Red Cross headquarters along the route. It's possible."

"The RED Cross," said Rubin, "is a Greek Cross with all four arms equal. I don't see how that could possibly be mistaken for a Cross of Lorraine by a Free French enthusiast. Look at it—"

Halsted said, "The logical thing, I suppose, is that you simply missed it, Larri. If you insist that, as a magician, you're such a trained observer that you *couldn't* have missed it, then maybe it was a symbol on something movable—on a truck in a driveway, for instance—and it moved on after sunrise."

"The boy made it quite clear that it was at the *place* of the Cross of Lorraine," said Larri. "I suppose even an eight-year-old can tell the difference between a place and a movable object."

"He spoke French. Maybe you mistranslated."

"I'm not that bad at the language," said Larri, "and besides, his mother translated and French is her native tongue."

"But English isn't. *She* might have gotten it wrong. The kid might have said something else. He might not even have said the Cross of Lorraine at all."

Avalon raised his hand for silence and said, "One moment, gentlemen. I see Henry, our esteemed waiter, smiling. What is it, Henry?"

Henry, from his place at the sideboard, said, "I'm afraid that I am amused at your doubting the child's evidence. It is quite certain, in my opinion, that he did see the Cross of Lorraine."

There was a moment's silence and Larri said, "How can you tell that, Henry?"

"By not being too subtle, sir."

Avalon's voice boomed out. "I knew it! We're being too complicated. Henry, how is it possible for us to achieve greater simplicity?"

"Why, Mr. Avalon, the incident took place at night. Instead of looking at all signs, all places, all varieties of cross, why not begin by asking ourselves what very few things *can* be easily seen on a highway at night?"

"A Cross of Lorraine?" asked Gonzalo incredulously.

"Certainly," said Henry, "among other things. Especially, if we don't call it a Cross of Lorraine. What the youngster saw as a Cross of Lorraine, out of his special interest, we would see as something else so clearly that its relationship to the Cross of Lorraine would be invisible. What has been happening just now has been precisely what happened earlier with Mr. Larri's trick with the coin and the salt shaker. We concentrated on the coin and didn't watch the salt shaker, and now we concentrate on the Cross of Lorraine and don't look for the alternative."

Trumbull said, "Henry, if you don't stop talking in riddles, you're fired. What the hell is the Cross of Lorraine, if it isn't the Cross of Lorraine?"

Henry said gravely, "What is this?" and carefully he drew on the back of the menu—

Trumbull said, "A Cross of Lorraine—tilted."

"No, sir, you would never have thought so, if we hadn't been talking about the Cross of Lorraine. Those are English letters and a very common symbol on highways if you add something to it—" He wrote quickly and the tilted Cross became:

EXXON

"The one thing," said Henry, "that is designed to be seen without trouble, day or night, on any highway, is a gas-station sign. The child saw the Cross of Lorraine in this one, but Mr. Larri, retracing the route, sees only a double X, since he reads the entire sign as Exxon. All signs showing this name, whether on the highway, in advertisements, or on credit cards, show the name in this fashion."

Now Larri caught fire. "You mean, Henry, that if I go into the Exxon stations en route and ask for Gwendolyn—"

"The proprietor of one of them is likely to be her brother, and there would not be more than a half dozen or so at most to inquire at."

"Good God, Henry," said Larri, "you're a magician."

"Merely simple-minded," said Henry, "though not, I hope, in the pejorative sense."

Jon L. Breen

An Evening with the White Divorcees

Each new 'tec take-off by Jon L. Breen reconfirms his position as the foremost parodist and pastichist in the mystery field. This one is not only a double burlesque—double in the sense that it spoofs both the Black Widowers and their creator—but is a satisfyingly clever story strictly on its own merits.

This companion piece to the real McAsimov is the real McBreen . . .

"Now tell us please, Mr. Sousa," said Godfrey Catalina, the patent attorney, "how do you justify your existence?"

Calvin Sousa, guest of the White Divorcees at their regular monthly dinner meeting in a private room of the Garibaldi Restaurant on Fifth Avenue, had been in a surly and irritable mood all evening. Now he looked at his questioner rather unbelievingly and then transferred his gaze to the little group's other members one by one with an expression of withering disgust.

"How do *I* justify my existence? After sitting through two hours of your cutesy table talk, I am astonished you have the nerve to ask *me* that question. You supercilious jokers with your self-satisfied smirks seem to think you're the original Algonquin Round Table."

"I want to be Robert Benchley," writer Ezekiel Lubin put in.

"Which one's Dorothy Parker?" artist Grimaldo Moreno asked, leering at his fellow members.

Calvin Sousa groaned. "I give up. I sat through the first three books of the Old Testament tonight in clerihews—"

Mathematics teacher Halsey Millstead interrupted defensively. "Look, after doing *The Decline and Fall of the Roman Empire* in 185,374 haikus, I had to take on *something* challenging, didn't I?"

"Challenging, he says. I'll show you challenging. As I started to say, I sat through all that because I had been given to understand you people might be able to help me with my problem."

"Problem?" echoed Timothy Turnbull, the code-and-cipher expert.

"Now we're getting down to business. The White Divorcees love a good problem. I myself have devoted my life to a solution for the common code."

Their guest got to his feet. "That's what I mean. Look, fellows, it's been a nice dinner, and I apologize for being out of sorts, but I'm afraid presenting my story to you would be a waste of everyone's time, especially mine. I'm convinced you can't help me. Everybody here has said enough to persuade me that the kind of thinking I want is not to be found in this room. But no offense is intended—I'm sure that taken one by one, you're quite reasonable men. But in a group you're more than I can take."

"Did you say everybody?" Godfrey Catalina asked.

"Won't you have some brandy, sir?" asked Harry, the White Divorcees' regular waiter.

Sousa shook his head, looking right at the inconspicuous little man holding the brandy bottle, and said, "Yes, everybody. Not a first-rate mind in the bunch, if you'll forgive me."

"Of course we'll forgive you," said chemist Charles Gander. "But why not sit down and tell us the problem anyway? It's what we came to hear, and sometimes a person very close to a problem can miss the obvious, overlook something a fresh mind, first-rate or not, will spot at once. I mean, you've wasted two hours already . . ."

Sousa sat down again and accepted a second glass of brandy. Harry faded back into the shadows of the room, by the bar, while Calvin Sousa began his story.

"I am by profession a roboticist—president, in fact, of the United States Robot Development Corporation. I don't know how much you gentlemen know about the science of robotics, but tremendous strides have been made in recent years in the creation of humanoid robots with positronic brains. In fact, there are some such now employed in the work force, generally without the knowledge of those who work with them. I must add that they are quite illegal and have nothing to do with my company. For some reason people feel threatened by humanoid robots and it is against the law to have them operate outside certain designated, closely controlled test sites until the powers that be are convinced of their safety."

"I can see why," said Ezekiel Lubin. "The idea of machines walking around looking and acting like men scares me too."

"Why?"

"You never know what one might do."

"But we *do* know!" Calvin Sousa almost shouted. "People are detestably ignorant of the nature of positronic robots, and no amount of public education on our part seems to be able to change their minds. Has any of you gentlemen ever heard of the three laws of robotics?"

The White Divorcees all looked blank.

Harry coughed softly and said in a tentative voice, "I have, sir."

Sousa looked pleasantly surprised. "Then perhaps you can enlighten these gentlemen."

"Well, briefly, sir, the first law is that no robot can injure a human being or through inaction allow a human being to come to harm. The second law is that a robot must obey any orders given it by a human being so long as they do not conflict with the first law. And the third law states that a robot must protect its own existence as long as this does not conflict with either of the first two laws."

"Very good. That's it exactly. You can see, gentlemen, that at least some members of the public have been reached by my firm's educational and public-relations efforts. I have recently felt that the tide is turning. But now it appears that, in direct contradiction of the first law, a robot has committed murder!

"Quite impossible, but how else could it have happened? Robot training and testing at our local office is carried on in a large room something like an operating theater. Observers can watch the training take place from behind any of several one-way windows overlooking the training area. They can also hear what is being said through small speakers.

"One morning early this week I entered one of the observation boxes to watch one of my associates, Peter Griswold, working with Isaac 100, one of our newest and most complex positronic robots. For several minutes the two of them conversed quietly, neither saying anything unusual or unexpected, and then suddenly Isaac 100 raised his arms in the air and brought them down on the head of Peter Griswold, viciously, again and again.

"In a panel by the observer's chair there is a button—panic button, if you will—that allows the observer to immediately inactivate the brain of the robot in the training room. I pushed it, and the attack by Isaac 100 ceased and he stood motionless as Peter Griswold slumped to the floor.

"I rushed into the corridor and took the elevator down to the floor of the training theater. Moments later I was at Peter Griswold's side, but I was too late. He had a fractured, nay, a crushed skull—the superhuman strength of the robot had killed him. And to this moment I do not know why or how it happened.

"The accident was immediately reported to the police and the appropriate Federal agency. I requested permission to reactivate Isaac 100 and find out from him what had happened, but permission was denied. The Robotics Experimentation Board has ordered Isaac 100 dismantled before he can harm anyone else, and I fear the whole process of robot experimentation will be stopped unless I can find an adequate explanation for how this happened."

"Could Griswold have insulted the robot in some way?" Catalina asked.

"How do you insult a robot?" Lubin snorted.

"Oh, a robot can be insulted," Sousa assured them. "They have very, very complex brains, I assure you, and are subject to many surprisingly human reactions, I might even say frailties. But nothing Griswold could have said to the robot could have caused him to break the first law, let alone break it so suddenly and so decisively."

"Mr. Sousa, were there any persons at the training center that day who had reason to be unfriendly to the robot development project?" Harry asked quietly.

"Unfriendly? Well, as a matter of fact, I suppose there were. There was Kenneth Wooster, a brilliant robotic technician I had recently fired for drinking on the job, and there was also the union leader, Art Stryker, who was making a tour of the plant. He is very concerned about robots taking people's jobs away from them, but that has nothing to do with the problem at hand. I mean, Isaac 100 killed Griswold. I saw it with my own eyes and I want to know how it happened."

"Perhaps he was hypnotized," Halsey Millstead offered.

"The robot? I suppose you could hypnotize a robot, but how could you make it do something under hypnosis it wouldn't do ordinarily? You can't even make a person go against his natural inclinations under hypnosis, and the three laws built into the positronic brain of the robot are so much stronger than the most strongly entrenched human inhibitions."

"Mr. Sousa," asked Harry, "who was taking Art Stryker on the tour of the plant?"

"Why, Kenneth Wooster, as a matter of fact."

"And who else was around the training area that morning?"

"No one. It was very early in the morning. There was just me and Griswold and Stryker and Wooster—no one else could have got past the security guard. Security is very tight, I assure you."

"Did Stryker bring anything with him when he arrived for his tour that morning?"

"Just a rolled-up rug about six feet long. Look, I didn't come here to discuss trivialities with a waiter."

"You came to discuss trivialities with the White Divorcees, right?" said Godfrey Catalina.

"I didn't come here to discuss trivialities with anybody. I came here to get a solution to my problem."

"Mr. Sousa," said Ezekiel Lubin, "Harry is considered a full member of the White Divorcees."

"And that gives him a license to discuss trivialities? Do you gentlemen have any suggestions or not?"

"It was all a practical joke," offered Timothy Turnbull. "Griswold just pretended to have a crushed skull."

"It wasn't really Isaac 100 who killed Griswold," Halsey Millstead speculated, "but either Wooster or Stryker disguised as Isaac 100."

"Nice try," said Sousa. "Good to know somebody's taking this seriously. But Wooster and Stryker are both a head shorter than Isaac 100. And no human being has the kind of strength it took to kill Griswold that way, just pounding him to the floor with the hands. Besides which, you think I wouldn't recognize my own robot? It was Isaac 100 all right."

"What was the rug for?" asked Harry.

"The what?"

"The rolled-up rug Stryker had."

"Oh, I think he said he has a cousin in the rug business, and Wooster had ordered a rug for his office. When he found out Wooster had been fired, he just took the rug away with him again. Well, come on, come on, any more bright ideas?"

"Mr. Sousa," said Harry, "it would be possible, would it not, to build a positronic robot to look exactly like a living person?"

"Of course it would be possible. It's not something we've done because we've been concentrating on the brain, but it could be done quite easily. Look, I like to talk about my work and answer your questions, but this isn't—"

"I have a suggestion," said Harry. "Probably quite silly, but you might consider it."

"Better listen to him, Sousa," Charles Gander advised.

"Oh, very well. Go on."

"Suppose Stryker brought rolled up in his rug a robot built secretly by Wooster away from the plant, a robot built to look exactly like

Griswold. Stryker and Wooster waylay the real Griswold on his way to the training session and substitute for him the robot Griswold. Then the robot Griswold identifies himself to Isaac 100 as another robot and explains that an experiment is being carried on to test the strength and durability of the new model and demonstrate it to Mr. Sousa as a surprise.

"Thus they will enter the training theater and carry on as if the robot were Griswold, but on a predetermined signal Isaac 100 will see how much damage he can do to the robot Griswold. Isaac 100 would never attack a human being that way, but he would have no hesitation, if ordered to do so, to attack another robot."

"But you forget, I saw Griswold's crushed skull."

"Did you have the training theater in sight at all times?"

"Of course not. Not for the time it took me to leave the observation box, get to the elevator, and—"

"And in that period, sir, Wooster and Stryker had time to substitute the real Griswold, murdered by them by crushing his skull elsewhere in the plant earlier, for the robot Griswold, and roll the robot back into the rug. Stryker then left with the robot Griswold before the crime had been reported."

Sousa looked amazed. "I wouldn't have believed it! Who would have thought that a union leader and a disgruntled employee would get together on a scheme to discredit robotics? It just proves that you can always trust robots and never trust humans, which I should have known all along."

"Another triumph, Harry," Godfrey Catalina said heartily.

Ezekiel Lubin asked, "But how on earth did you know?"

Harry only smiled. The White Divorcees thought his smile looked slightly metallic.

"Q"

Dana Lyon

The Living End

*The story of Nell and Emma—they had been "best friends" in
high school but hadn't seen each other for more than forty years.
Oh, yes, they had kept in touch—had written to each other faith-
fully on their birthdays. But now hard times and a bleak, frightening future were bringing them together again . . .*

The living arrangements that Nell had made with her friend
Emma had not been in effect a month before she realized that
it had been a devastating mistake. Why, she asked herself, sitting
trembling at her desk while she was going over her bills, hadn't she
left well enough alone, without worrying about money all the time?
She had her little house, her so-so job with Civil Service and a
pension not far in the offing, her solitude at night, her peace and
quiet, even if inflation *was* taking a large piece out of her accumulated savings while the little apartment above was standing idle;
so why hadn't she left it that way?

Money, she thought. Worrying about the future. Seeing the savings growing smaller instead of larger, feeling the need for an increased income which she'd never get from her job now that she was
this close to retirement. So that apartment upstairs that she had
built and used herself years ago while her parents were still living
in the downstairs quarters was the answer to her need for increased
income, just sitting there waiting for another tenant.

She had tried: the nice young couple both of whom worked and
were therefore out of the house all day—until she discovered that
the girl had been three months' pregnant at the time of signing the
lease, and then there was the baby, waking Nell at night with its
incessant crying, until she had finally had to give them their notice.
What was $85 a month weighed against her peace of mind?

And then the nice-looking middle-aged woman who worked downtown and brought home man after man and was such a wretched
housekeeper that some of her roaches had finally invaded Nell's
living quarters. Notice served.

And there were others, even less desirable, particularly the ones who managed to evade rent day, and those who wanted to be sociable, wanting to use her telephone or her washer, wanting her to accept C.O.D. packages and forgetting to repay her, and always and forever the excuses for not being able to pay the rent. ("Just a week or two, Nell dear—I'm expecting a check in the mail any day.")

She had hated being a landlady, but now she was hating, even more, seeing her small savings depleted in order to take up the slack caused by inflation. Nevertheless, no more bothersome tenants—until suddenly she had thought of Emma.

Emma had been her closest friend, her chum, when they were in high school together, her confidante, nearer to her than anyone else had ever been. Arms entwined, heads together, whispering about boys, daringly discussing the origins of life—a commitment they knew would last for life. It didn't, of course.

Nell had gone her way to college and other friends, to love affairs and marriage, to divorce and finally a job with the state, and somewhere along the way Emma had been almost forgotten. Except for one definite and unfailing commitment that had lasted all these years: they exchanged long letters on each other's birthday and thus at least kept in touch once a year. But as time went on there was little to tell each other about their lives which had remained almost static in their later years.

They were both in their early sixties now, but this one contact remained; they dared not neglect this birthday acknowledgement for fear that whoever didn't write would be considered dead by the other. So they had continued writing.

Emma, Nell thought now. I know she doesn't have much money. I wonder if she'd like to take the apartment overhead. I could bring the rent down to $75, and I'd be company for her, and she'd be company for me—but not too much, not as if, heaven forbid, we had to live in the same rooms. Nell enjoyed her privacy too much, her own way of doing things—letting the dishes go if she felt like it, or flying at the cleaning chores some weekend if that was what possessed her at the time, or playing the radio late at night, or the TV, or painting in her little studio room. Snacks at any hour of the day when she was home, instead of regular meals. Quiet reading. Walks alone along the country road where she lived. Just to be alone when she wanted to be—

However, the apartment upstairs was entirely separate, and even had an outside staircase of its own, and someone like Emma, who had always been so thoughtful of others, would not make much noise. The $75 would help; it would just about take over the depletion that present-day prices had made in her savings. Well—a few more years and she'd be able to retire on her pension and what she had managed to save during the years of her enslavement. But there'd be no savings left unless she rented the apartment.

Emma was delighted. She wrote, "I have been so depressed, dearest Nell, because I thought the rest of my life would have to be spent alone, no family, even my friends here are dying off; and you make the little apartment sound so fascinating. I'll give notice on this dinky room I live in." Room, thought Nell; is that all she has?—and began to feel qualms along with the Good Samaritan warmth within her. "I'll just pack up my things and get a bus ticket and be with you in a week."

More qualms. Why was Emma in such a hurry? What was she doing that she could pack up and leave her way of life and her job and what friends she had, without another thought—too eager, perhaps, to join Nell's life? Well, no matter, they could still lead their individual lives. Emma would be getting a cheap apartment and Nell would be getting an increased income.

Nell spent the following weekend giving the little apartment—sitting-room, kitchen, bedroom, and bath—a thorough cleaning. She laundered the curtains, put everything in place, even added a little bouquet of flowers from the garden just before she went off to the bus station to greet her friend.

"I can't believe it!" Nell exclaimed over and over as they drove back to the house. "You seem just the same, dear. I just can't believe it, how long has it been, you've hardly changed at all—"

"Nor you," said Emma, beaming, both of them fully aware they were lying. "How could we ever have been separated for so long?"

"Well, like everyone else, we got busy with our own lives. Here we are," and she pulled into the carport at the side of the house. "Do come into my little nest for a bite before I take you upstairs."

"What a darling place!" Emma exclaimed, looking around Nell's cozy living room. "Don't bother with anything, dear, I won't want to put you to any trouble."

Nell beamed. "Well, if you're not hungry, how about some sherry?"

"No, thanks, but you go ahead."

They sat there, in Nell's charming little living room, and for a moment said nothing. What was left to say? They had chattered all the way from the bus station, but now there was nothing left that hadn't already been said in their long exchange of letters. They had changed, indeed: Nell, the tall, graceful, dark-haired high-school girl, was now lean rather than slender, her dark hair mostly white, her once lovely eyes shadowed by glasses, her lipstick not quite even; and Emma, the plump, plain little high-school girl was now plumper and plainer. Her faded blonde-white hair was cut in a Buster Brown fashion, making her look like a prematurely aging kindergartener, her dress was flowery, her shawl askew, and her face, as always, bland.

Out of the silence Emma finally said, "What a lovely home you have here, dear. Shall we go upstairs and look at mine?"

She exclaimed joyfully over the neat little apartment. "Just right for me!" she said. "And with you downstairs for company I'll never get lonely—"

Apprehension washed over Nell like a sudden splash of cold water. "Well, I keep pretty busy all the time," she explained hastily. "Working all day, then doing my chores at night, and I've kind of taken up painting—oh, not commercially, of course, just for my own amusement though it might develop into something someday. Now about the rent, dear. As I told you, seventy-five a month for *you,* though I usually get a lot more, but I decided I just didn't want strangers up there any longer."

"Oh, yes," said Emma. And then, "But I don't guess you want a deposit of a month's rent or a lease or anything like that, do you? Being friends and all."

"No," said Nell patiently. "I don't think a lease is necessary between us. Just the month's rent."

Emma paid her. In cash. "And I promise," she added, smiling, "that I'll be very careful with the utilities so they won't add too much extra onto your expenses."

Nell thought: Who said anything about my paying the utilities? But she kept silent, more apprehensive now than ever.

The first month was quiet and calm and Nell could now figure on replenishing her savings account toward her retirement. Except, of course, that it wasn't a full $75 since the gas and electricity and water took up well over $10.

And it soon became apparent that Emma was far from solvent herself, so she started looking for a job. She found nothing, until finally she put an ad in the paper as baby sitter, and was repaid by a rash of answers on the telephone—Nell's telephone, of course, since Emma claimed she couldn't afford one of her own. Therefore Nell gave her a key to her own apartment and Emma ran down her outside stairs whenever the phone rang.

And at night, when Nell answered, she had to go out and call Emma, who never answered until Nell had climbed the stairs and knocked on the door. If she can hear the telephone when I'm not at home, Nell asked herself, why doesn't she hear me when I call? She finally resorted to banging her broom handle on the ceiling and Emma learned that if she didn't respond Nell would simply hang up the phone.

No matter. Emma was delighted with the $2 an hour she was paid for her services, although occasionally she was called on to supply her own transportation which, of course, meant Nell's, and soon this became intolerable as Nell was expected to pick her up any time after midnight, as well as to take her earlier, and what with the telephone ringing almost constantly, Nell was soon at her wits' end. Until finally she informed Emma that she must take jobs only where transportation was provided.

"Oh," said Emma, looking downcast. "That means I'll have to lose a lot of my jobs because most of them expect me to drive myself. Maybe I could learn to drive your car?" she asked hopefully.

"No," said Nell, and that was that. Until the first of the following month when the rent was due. Emma did not offer it and finally, five days late, Nell brought up the subject.

"Oh," said Emma. "Well, dear, would it be all right if I just paid half of the rent this time and made it up later? You see, with business falling off and everything, I'm a little short of cash. Just for this month, of course," she added hastily.

Nell said, "Will next month be any better? Emma, I think you should have made your financial circumstances clearer before you pulled up stakes and came here. You told me you had an income from your brother's estate and also your Social Security that you took at sixty-two instead of waiting till sixty-five when you'd have gotten more, and that you felt you would have no trouble getting a job here. After all, dear, seventy-five dollars a month, utilities included, is very low rent for these days."

"Yes, I know," Emma said hurriedly, "but it's a lot more than I paid back home where I stayed with friends. Only I thought you needed me, that you were lonely and that's why you wanted me to come and keep you company, and then I thought how you might be pleased for me to help with the work in your dear little house, cleaning and cooking and laundering, and that would take care of the rent, and so everything would turn out fine."

Too late Nell remembered Emma's proclivities of the past that had earned her the name of Pollyanna Emma, who always knew that tomorrow would be sunny and happy and that everything would turn out right for little Emma. But it never had, because little Emma, being so sure of God's grace, had done little to prepare for the inevitable rainy day. "Oh, I'm sure everything will turn out for the best," Emma was always saying, and it frequently did but only because of the services of people around her.

So now she said, "I'm sure everything will turn out fine for both of us," and Nell could have slapped her. But she couldn't bear to come down too hard on her. After all, she'd given up what home she'd had (whatever *that* was) to do something she thought would help her friend. Emma couldn't pay, that was certain, and so Nell said resignedly, "All right, Emma, you can help with my place," and went back to it in despair.

So now, she thought, I have a dependent for the first time since I got my divorce.

Emma was always under foot and always in need—she had to use the telephone, she had to go to the library, the dentist, the supermarket, everything for which she had no transportation and for which Nell did. Nell would come home tired out from her job of coping with people, her boss, her co-workers, the public; and even though she tried to be as quiet as possible, hoping for a few moments of peace, there would be Emma on her doorstep saying, "Oh, Nell dear, do you suppose you could run me down to the store—or would you have an extra can of tuna fish?" or, "Drat it, I have to go to the dentist's tomorrow, only appointment I could get was three o'clock. Do you suppose you could take a weensy bit of time off and run me to his office?"

"Emma," said Nell, pushed to the wall, "I'm afraid this arrangement isn't going to work out very well after all—"

And then the little round face under the white bangs would grow old and pinched and frightened and Nell would sigh and say, "Well, we'll see—" and the little face would brighten with relief and things would go on as before . . .

Emma was idle and lonely. She still had a few baby-sitting jobs when the transportation was included, but the rest of her time was spent without purpose. She didn't really care much for reading, she hated any sort of handiwork, gardens did not interest her; she had no TV set nor the wherewithal to buy one since she did not even have the wherewithal to pay the rent. This last was an unmentioned, rather sordid matter that Emma refused to acknowledge, and which Nell, exhausted, would no longer bring up after the three times she had mentioned it and as a result suffered excruciatingly from guilt qualms when she'd seen the bleak frightened look on her little friend's face.

Little friend, hell, Nell said to herself. She's a *leech*! But she doesn't know it. She keeps saying that she'd do the same for me if our positions were reversed, take me in and give me a home and look out for me—she knows damn well our positions could never be reversed, but in the meantime she gets credit for being noble enough to offer her beneficence to me!

Nell was getting frantic. Emma said, at various times: The roof leaks. The heater doesn't work properly. Now that summer's here the heat is terrible, perhaps if I could have an air conditioner—?

Winter again. Emma growing plumper, Nell growing leaner. And more tired. Pitter-patter up and down the outside staircase, knocking on the door the minute Nell got home, sitting there chatting but unable to keep the disapproval out of her eyes while Nell sipped her sherry and yearned to read the paper at the same time. Why am I such a fool? Nell asked herself countless times. So, okay, I made a mistake but God knows I've paid for it over and over. Do I have to pay forever?

One wintry day Emma tapped lightly on the door and when Nell appeared she said, "Dear, could I see you for a minute?"

"What?" said Nell. "I'm busy with supper."

"O-oh, it smells wonderful. Swiss steak, is it? Haven't had any for years, it seems. Just scrambled eggs. Or tuna. Gets kind of tiresome."

The wind blew a blast of cold air into Nell's cozy living room.

"What is it, Emma?" she asked impatiently. I'm damned if I'm going to ask her *again* to have supper with me. She'll end up a permanent unpaid boarder.

"Well, it's just the staircase outside. It shakes a little when I use it. That nice Mr. Brown who brought me home the other night noticed it—you know, the one with the two children I sit for, they're really darling but they do keep me busy, they get into such mischief—where was I?"

"The staircase," said Nell with foreboding. "What about it?"

"Well, Mr. Brown noticed how it shook when he took me to my door—so polite, the other fathers never do—and he said I should tell my landlady about it."

Nell went out and inspected the staircase. It did shake. The main post holding it up was beginning to rot at the bottom. Without Emma up there, she thought, I could just let the thing go and close up the apartment. Wait till I get ahead a little with my finances, and then I'll have it repaired. But not with Emma there.

She said briefly, "I'll see about it," and went into her apartment again, ignoring the mewling plea behind her, "Oh, but Nell darling—"

Shut up, said Nell to herself. Shut up!

She sat erect in her chair and cried.

And thus Nell's life became a shambles. There was now no further talk of paying the rent—Emma was always low on funds. And there were constant complaints (delicately put) of things that should be done to the apartment to make it more habitable, other things that were needed—like transportation, telephone, air conditioning, television—that would make Emma more comfortable and happy. With always the offer to take care of Nell's house, cook her meals, do her cleaning, refusing to believe Nell when she said, in a moment of exasperation, that all she wanted when she got home at night was peace and quiet and solitude, a look at the paper, and her drink in private.

"You're just saying that," said Emma, beaming her bland smile. "But I know that you just don't want an old friend like me doing menial work for you. But honestly, dear, I don't mind. I'm very independent, you know, but I like to do my share—"

Another time, a day when Nell was more exhausted than usual, Emma was waiting for her at the door. "I could hardly wait," she said excitedly. "I've had the most wonderful idea that would do wonders for both of us! Look, dear, it's just that— Oh, let's go in first and I'll tell you while you have your little drink—it's really a solution to everything."

There's only one solution, Nell thought drearily, and that's for you to pack up and leave.

They went in.

"It's so simple," said Emma, her voice rising. "Look, I know you could use a little more money and of course I hardly have any at all, so—why don't I move into that little studio room of yours, where you paint, and rent the upstairs apartment, then we'd both be better off. We could split the rent money because I'd be giving up my own apartment, of course—"

Nell looked at her incredulously. She did not go into explanations. She simply said no, and did not speak again.

Emma left, her head bowed like a child who has been unjustly disciplined, and Nell poured herself a drink and sat trembling in her chair, her thoughts black and deep.

She spoke aloud. "This," she said, "is the living end. The absolute living *end*."

A storm rose slowly, unobserved, from the north, and then came rushing like a wild insane creature of the elements, swooping down in blackness and noise and torrents and terrible sounds until the small house shook. Nell roused and lifted her face and said, "Storm, why don't you blow off the roof of my house?" The thought felt good.

She got up finally and went outside and saw that the steps leading up to the apartment were trembling in the wind. She went to the unsteady post and examined it, the wind and rain lashing at her. Nell did not notice. She smiled and kept her hand on the fragile support, then gave it a violent shove. It moved dangerously, almost loose from its moorings, ready to go with the least pressure put upon the steps. She smiled, and went into her warm little nest, humming happily to herself.

When would Emma come? She was frightened of storms. There had been other times of wildness in the elements when she would come shivering with fear to Nell's door and plead to spend the night there. How soon? She must come now—now when the storm was raging.

Still humming, Nell went into the kitchen, got the broom, and banged its handle on the ceiling. That should fetch her.

The storm, the wild screaming wind, pounded on the small house and shook it like an angry giant and the torrents fell and the air was filled with noise and confusion and terrifying threats; and suddenly there was another sound, the wrenching crash of the steps outside as they were torn from their moorings; and then a single human scream . . . At last, as if finally satisfied, the wind held itself in abeyance for an instant, and suddenly there was no sound at all. Just silence.

And Nell sat on, drink in hand, still smiling, still humming. She was alone at last . . .

Emma did not die.

She lay in traction from head to foot in the hospital to which she had been taken. Her back had been so shattered that she was given little hope of ever being able to walk again. A wheelchair possibly, after months spent in bed.

Nell did not go to see her. Not, that is, until Emma fully regained consciousness. She went then only because the hospital called her and said that Emma was asking for her and that since she was Emma's only living relative—"I am not a relative," said Nell sharply. "I am her landlady only."

But she went. Emma smiled wanly from the bed. "Hello, dear," she said. "It's so good to see you. I'll bet you were here every day while I was unconscious."

Nell said nothing.

After a brief silence Emma said bluntly, "The bills are enormous. I don't know what I'm going to do."

"Well, I'm sure the county will take care of you. They always do in cases like yours."

"County! What do you mean, county? I have never accepted charity from anyone."

Oh, no? Nell thought. No free rent, no free transportation, no free food half of the time? "And," the pathetic little voice continued, "I don't intend to start now."

"Then what *do* you propose to do?" said Nell, monumentally uninterested. "You certainly can't pay these bills yourself."

"I don't have to!" said Emma triumphantly. "You know that nice Mr. Brown who used to bring me home after I sat with his kids? Well, he's a lawyer, and he was the one who pointed out how rickety those stairs were, so he was in to see me this morning and he told me—"

There was an uneasy silence. Then Nell said, not really wanting to know, "Well? What did he say?"

"He said," Emma explained carefully, "that you should have had those stairs fixed after I complained about them, and that undoubtedly your insurance company would come through with plenty of money to take care of me—"

There was a brief silence. Then Nell spoke. "Emma," she said carefully, "there *is* no insurance company."

"Then of course you should have had the stairs fixed. Mr. Brown inspected the hole where the post had been and he said it looked as if the post had been even more damaged than when he first saw it."

"The storm—"

"No," said Emma. "The storm knocked away the post but the hole was cement and it was broken all around the top—he said the post must have been hanging by a thread when the storm came. No insurance, hm? Well, dear, then I guess I'll just have to sue you personally."

"Sue *me*? What do you mean? You know I haven't done anything to be sued for—it would just be a waste of money on your part. You can't get blood out of a turnip. It wasn't *my* fault the storm blew down the steps, so there's no use your threatening me with a lawsuit—"

Nell's voice rose hysterically, and the impulse to murder was there in her hands. She could almost feel them moving of their own volition, twisting in her lap, struggling to be free in order to silence this hateful creature forever.

"I have nothing, do you hear?" she cried, her voice rising out of control. "Nothing!"

"Well, then, what am I to do?" said Emma helplessly. "And of course you have something, dear. Your little house—you told me once it was free and clear—and your car and your little, or big, savings account that you plan for when you retire— Oh dear me, yes, you have a lot and of course it is only fair for you to take care of me for the rest of my life since you ought to have had the stairs fixed, you ought to have had the stairs fixed, you ought to . . ." She smiled contentedly, and dozed off.

Bill Pronzini and Barry N. Malzberg

Problems Solved

"Most people have murderous fantasies of one sort or the other" . . .

D ear Mr. Grey:
Thank you for consulting me, and for your expression of confidence that I will be able to solve your problem. I do take considerable pride in "Problems Solved," my consultation service. As you know from my magazine advertisements, this service by mail has been functioning successfully for seven years (with never a complaint, if I may add proudly).

Now then, to your problem. Mr. Grey, the question you pose in your last paragraph is obviously what has really been on your mind throughout your letter. Thus, in answer to this question, let me say that I do not believe your murderous fantasies are so unusual, nor do I think that you have any reason to feel as guilty about them as you say. *Most* people have murderous fantasies of one sort or the other, sometimes toward those who are closest to them and whom they love best. These fantasies function usually as a normal and healthy outlet, since the important thing is that they will never be acted upon. Seen in that context, then, they are definitely a healthy release.

Of course, guilt can be self-destructive. I am reminded of a case many years ago in the small upstate New York town in which my wife was born: a local man murdered several strangers for the confessed reason that he had "wanted to kill people all the time lately and I couldn't stand knowing I was as good as a murderer inside, so I just went out and did it." So, Mr. Grey, I urge you to work on these guilt feelings of yours more than on the fantasies themselves. It is *only* the guilt building up within you which could be dangerous.

Your accompanying check in the amount of $50.00 is exactly double my customary fee for a consultation of this nature. Therefore, I am entering a credit of $25.00 which you may use for another consultation. I *do* hope to hear from you again, since I believe your particular problem may involve at least one and possibly two or three additional consultations before we can safely mark it "solved."

Sincerely yours,
Dr. Harold Rawls
"Problems Solved"

Dear Mr. Grey:

I am in receipt of your second letter, and I must say first of all that I am sorry you were disappointed with my initial advice. I am also sorry that you feel continually disturbed, and although I agree that there is no accounting for "the range of human pain and the desire to inflict pain," as you put it, I must strongly repeat what I said previously.

Giving free rein to your murderous fantasies may actually be counter-productive, you know. The explicitness of detail in your letter would be shocking to a nonprofessional, and while I well understand the context in which this should be placed, I must tell you that I would not, if I were you, express these details to anyone but me.

Please, Mr. Grey, you must understand that your fantasies are quite common and that you should not feel the kind of guilt which merely triggers further rage and pain. We live in difficult times, unhappy times: many of your best friends, perhaps, would secretly like to be murderers. It is the act of *commission* which makes all the difference.

This second consultation has been paid for, of course, by your $25.00 credit. When you write again, please enclose further remuneration. And please tell me something about yourself as well. You have been quite bare on personal details in your two letters to date. With more knowledge of who you are, what you do for a living, and so on, I can be much more specific in my advice.

Sincerely yours,
Dr. Harold Rawls
"Problems Solved"

Dear Mr. Grey:

I have received your latest letter and your $100.00 check for a total of four consultations. However, I am returning herewith my check in the amount of $75.00, which represents a total refund less $25.00 for this third, and unfortunately final, consultation.

You have given me no alternative, Mr. Grey. I cannot deal with you any longer. You have refused to confide any personal information beyond a name and a post office box address in upper Manhattan. You prefer to remain hidden in the shadows, as it were. As a result I have no idea of who you are or who you are talking about when you mention "this urge, this terrible, incessant urge to kill." Members of your family? Friends? Business associates? Strangers?

You seem also and for no apparent reason to have taken a dangerously abusive attitude toward me, which I will not tolerate. Violent emotional outbursts and veiled threats such as those which marked your letter are pointless, childish, and misdirected.

It is my final opinion, Mr. Grey, that you are a seriously ill personality and that you should seek a face-to-face consultation with a qualified psychotherapist before it is too late.

> Sincerely,
> Dr. Harold Rawls
> "Problems Solved"

Mr. Grey:

I suppose I should have foreseen the content of your most recent letter. That I did not is a comment only upon my heavy workload. I will say nothing about your vile and insane threat on my life. I will not attempt to reason with you, for it is obvious you have graduated beyond reason to psychosis.

I would like you to know, however, that I maintain careful files which include all letters sent to me and carbons of all my responses. These files are kept under lock and key, where no one but myself and my secretary have access to them, and in the event of harm to me they would immediately be turned over to the police.

Not, of course, that I anticipate any harm from you. Individuals such as yourself are very common in my profession. You obtain satisfaction from ventilating aggressions which you are unable to act out in reality. Thus, I am not at all frightened that you will carry out your threat. Threats such as yours do not disconcert me in the slightest, for I not only understand their origin, I have a great inner strength.

I suggest, once again, that you consult a qualified psychotherapist as soon as possible.

> Sincerely,
> Dr. Harold Rawls
> "Problems Solved"

Dear Friends,

I'm sorry for this mimeographed note, but I don't have the time or the energy to personally thank all of you who sent flowers and other expressions of sympathy on the terrible death of my husband, Dr. Harold Rawls. I know you will understand. I also know you will understand why I must go away for a while. There are too many memories here, too much sorrow—and as long as the lunatic who murdered Harold is still at large, my own life may be in danger as well.

With gratitude,
Muriel Rawls

MR JOE VINSON CRISTOBAL HOTEL NASSAU GRAND BAHAMAS ARRIVING EIGHT FORTY TONIGHT FLIGHT 62 STOP PROBLEM SOLVED STOP LOVE YOU

MURIEL

Celia Fremlin

The Magic Carpet

If this magical story gets on your nerves, it's supposed to—on your nerves and in your nerves . . .

It was not Hilda who first talked of being driven mad up there in the high flats, far above the noise of the traffic and the bustle of the crowds. On the contrary, it was her neighbors who complained to *her* about the stresses. "It's driving me up the wall!" said her neighbor on the right; and "I can't stand it any longer!" said her neighbor on the left; and "I'll go out of my mind!" said the woman in the apartment below.

But not Hilda Meredith. Hilda was the young one, the busy one. From the point of view of the neighbors it was she who was the cause and origin of all the stresses. *She* wasn't the one who was being driven mad, oh, no! That's what they would all have told you.

But madness has a rhythm of its own up there so near to the clouds—a rhythm that at first you would not recognize, so near is it, in the beginning, to the rhythms of ordinary, cheerful life . . .

"What's the *time*, Mr. Wolf? What's the *time*, Mr. Wolf?" Thumpty-*thump*-thump-thump. Thumpty-*thump*-thump-thump. The twins' shrill little voices, the thud of their firm little sandaled feet, reverberated through the door of the kitchenette and brought Hilda to a sudden halt in the midst of the morning's wash. Her arms elbow-deep in warm detergent, she just stood there, while the familiar, helpless anger rose slowly from the pit of her stomach.

She would have to stop them, of course; the innocent, happy little game would have to be brought once more to a halt by yet another "No!" And quickly too, before Mrs. Walters in the flat below came up to protest; before Mr. Peters on the right tapped on the wall; before Miss Rice on the left leaned across the balcony to complain of her headache and to tell Hilda how well children were brought up in *her* young days.

Miss Rice's young days were all very well; in those days children had space for play and romping. If they were rich they had fields and lawns and nurseries and schoolrooms; if they were poor they had at least the streets and the alleyways. But today's children, the sky dwellers of the affluent Twentieth Century, where could *they* go to run, to shout, to fulfill their childhood?

All day long, up here in the blue emptiness of the sky, Hilda had to deprive her children, minute by minute, of everything that matters in childhood. They must not run or jump or laugh or sing or dance. They must not play hide-and-seek or cowboys and Indians or fling themselves with shrieks of joy into piles of cushions. Except when she could find time to take them to the distant park, they must sit still, like chronic invalids, growing dull and pale over television and picture books.

What's the *time*, Mr. Wolf? . . . One o'clock . . . Two o'clock . . . Three o'clock!" Thumpty-*thump*-thump-thump. Hilda had a vision of the sturdy little thighs in identical navy shorts, stamping purposefully round and round the room, little faces alight with the intoxication of rhythm and with the mounting excitement of the approaching climax.

Before this climax—before the wild shriek of *"Dinnertime*, Mr. Wolf!" rent the silence of the flats, Hilda would have to go in and spoil it all. "Martin, Sally," she would have to say, "you really must be quieter. Why don't you get out your coloring books and come and sit quietly? Come along, now, over here at the table." And she would have to watch the bright little faces grow tearful, hear the merry chanting voices take on the whine of boredom, watch the firm taut little muscles relinquish their needed exercise and grow flaccid as they sat and sat and sat. It was wicked, it was cruel . . .

"Mrs. Meredith? Could I speak to you for a minute, Mrs. Meredith?"

So. Already she had left it too late. Here was Miss Rice out on her balcony, hand on brow, headache poised like a weapon, and already sure of her victory.

"It's not that I want to complain," Miss Rice began, as she began every morning, "and if it was just for myself I suppose I'd try to put up with it, but it's Mrs. Walters, she hasn't been too well either, and it's driving her up the wall, it really is, all this hammer, hammer, hammer. She's just phoned me, asked if I could have a word with you, save her coming up the stairs with her bad knee."

Bad knees. Headaches. Not-too-well-ness. These were the weapons by which happy little four-year-olds could be crushed and broken; there was no defense against them.

"I'm sorry," said Hilda despairingly; and again, "I'm sorry, I'm sorry . . ."

The twins had been settled at their coloring books for nearly an hour before Mrs. Walters below rang up to inquire if Hilda couldn't somehow stop that boom-boom noise?

"Boom-boom-*boom*," the clipped voice mimicked on the wire. "It goes right through my nerves, Mrs. Meredith, it really does. I can't think what they can be doing, little kiddies like that, I can't think what they can be *doing*."

Firing a cannon? Riding roller coasters round the room? No, it turned out to be Sally's energetic rubbing out of her drawing of a cat. It wobbled the table, it set the floor vibrating.

"No, Sally, don't use the eraser any more, just color it as it is, there's a good girl."

"No, Martin, you must keep your dinky-car on the *rug*. Mrs. Walters will hear it on the linoleum."

"No, Sally, leave that chair where it is—we don't want Mr. Peters knocking on the wall again."

No. . .No. . .No. . . Two lively little creatures reduced to tears and tempers, to sobbing, hopeless boredom.

Nevertheless, it wasn't Hilda saying, "I can't stand it!" It was Miss Rice. And Mr. Peters. And Mrs. Walters.

Autumn passed into winter, and it was less and less often possible to take the twins to the park. Their bounding morning spirits had to be crushed earlier and earlier in the day. The search for a quiet game, for something that wouldn't annoy the neighbors, became a daylong preoccupation for Hilda; but in spite of all her efforts nothing, *nothing* seemed quiet enough; for still, without respite, came the voices from above, from below, from every side: "Really, Mrs. Meredith, if you *could* keep them a little quieter. . ."

"Mrs. Meredith, sometimes I think it's a herd of elephants you've got up there. . ."

"It's not that I don't love kiddies, Mrs. Meredith, but that's not the same as letting them grow up little hooligans, is it, Mrs. Meredith?"

"It's my head, Mrs. Meredith."

"It's my nerves, Mrs. Meredith."

"I've not been feeling too well, Mrs. Meredith."

So, no...no...no...all through the gray November days. No, Martin. Stop it, Sally. *No.* No, no, no! The twins grew whiny and quarrelsome. Their sturdy little legs looked thinner, their faces paler.

And still it wasn't Hilda who said, "I can't stand it!" It was Miss Rice. And Mr. Peters. And Mrs. Walters.

It was the new carpet that gave Hilda the idea—the new square of carpet bought to deaden the sound of footsteps in the hallway. It was not really new, it was second-hand and somewhat worn, but the twins were enchanted by it. They had never seen a Persian carpet before, and for a whole afternoon there was silence so absolute that not a word of complaint came from above or from below or from either side.

From lunchtime till dusk Martin and Sally crouched on the carpet examining every brown and crimson flower, every purple scroll and every pinkish coil of leaves. Hilda felt quite light-headed with happiness—a whole afternoon with the twins truly enjoying themselves and the neighbors not complaining!

"It's a *magic* carpet," she told them hopefully, when she saw their interest beginning to flag. "Why don't you sit on it and shut your eyes, and it'll take you to wonderful places? See? Off it goes! You're flying off above the rooftops now, you're looking down, and you can see all the houses and the streets and the trains—"

"And the zoo!" chimed in Sally. "I can see the zoo and all the nanimals. I can see tigers and lions—"

"And now we're over the sea!" squealed Martin. "I can see the whales and the submarines and—and—oh, look! Look, Sally, I can see an island! Let's stop at that island, let's go and live there!"

The game took hold. The perfect quiet game had been found at last. Hour after hour the twins would sit on the magic carpet and travel from land to land, seeing strange and wonderful sights as they went. They would land in Siberia or at the South Pole or on a South Sea Island, where wild adventures would befall them, and they only escaped in time to fly home for tea.

But their favorite destination of all was Inkoo Land. In Inkoo

Land there were tiny elephants just big enough to ride on; there were twisty knobbly trees, wonderful for climbing, trees from which you could pick every kind of fruit in the world. There were wide spaces of grass to run on, there was a jungle to play hide-and-seek in, there were monkeys that talked monkey language, and Sally and Martin learned it too, with fantastic speed and ease; and then they played with the monkeys, swinging from branch to branch through the green sun-spangled forests.

But always, in the end, they had to come home; they grew tired of sitting even on a magic carpet; and the moment they disembarked and set foot on the floor the voices would start again, from all around—

"It's my head, Mrs. Meredith."

"It's my nerves Mrs. Meredith."

"It's not what I'm used to, Mrs. Meredith, it's making me ill, it really is!"

If only they could stay in Inkoo Land all day! Such a lovely game it was—there were moments when Hilda caught herself thinking how good it was for them, on the gray winter afternoons, to have all that exercise, rushing through the sunny glades, and climbing about in the forest trees. So much better for them than the steely winter park, with its asphalt paths and "Keep Off the Grass" signs.

Then she would recollect herself, smile a little wryly at her own childishness in getting so caught up in her children's fantasies, and set herself to preparing tea ready for their "return."

But at last, inevitably, the novelty of the game began to wear off: the "return" became earlier and earlier; and one day, a gray hopeless day of fog and cold, the twins refused to go to Inkoo Land. Hilda was conscious of sickening, overmastering despair. They *must* go to Inkoo Land! In vain she pleaded, bribed, even scolded. But go to Inkoo Land they would not.

"We've got nothing to *do*, Mummy," the old cry began again; and as if at a prearranged signal the voices returned—

"It's my nerves, Mrs. Meredith."

"It's my head, Mrs. Meredith."

"I don't want to complain, Mrs. Meredith, but—"

The voices seemed to go on and on, whispering in the air, sighing in through the window, seeping in under the doors—and suddenly Hilda knew what she must do.

"I'll come with you to Inkoo Land," she declared. "You must show it to me—I've never seen it, you know."

The twins' interest was at once revived; they scrambled eagerly onto the magic carpet.

"Mummy come too! Mummy come too!" they chanted; and when they were all seated on the carpet Martin gave his orders in a clear little treble. "Inkoo Land, please!" he told the carpet; and they all clutched each other against the tipping and rocking to be expected as the carpet lifted itself off the floor.

But what had gone wrong? The carpet didn't move at all! Hilda stared stupidly round the walls that still enclosed them.

"Say it again, Martin!" she urged him; and a little surprised, the child obeyed.

Still nothing happened. Hilda felt her heart beating strangely. Was it too heavy for the carpet, having to carry an adult as well as the two children? Or—why, that was it! They should be near a window! How could they expect to fly if there was no window to fly out of? Jumping up, she hurried into the living room and opened the window wide to the foggy winter air.

"Bring the carpet in here!" she called, and hurried out to help drag it in from the hall.

She was surprised to see both looking a little frightened. Sally's lips were quivering. "Play properly, Mummy," she said; and "Oooo—it's cold in here!" complained Martin, as they laid out the carpet in the living room, now slowly filling with swirls of icy fog.

"Never mind. We'll soon be in Inkoo Land," Hilda encouraged them. "Onto the carpet, both of you. We'll soon be in the lovely warm forest, with the sun shining, and all the monkeys and the elephants. Say the words, Martin; say them again."

And still the carpet didn't move. The three of them together must definitely be too heavy, decided Hilda; they would have to help the carpet. One could see how hard it must be to lift the whole lot of them bodily off the floor; but if they were to give it a start by launching it off the window sill, then it would be able to glide along easily above the rooftops.

But why were the twins crying? Backing, hand in hand, away from the window, refusing to help as she dragged the unwieldy carpet onto the ledge of the open window?

What a floppy sort of magic carpet it was! How it hung, limply, half in and half out of the window, dangling down on either side! But of course it would stiffen as soon as it began to fly. She climbed awkwardly onto the ledge and sat, as well as she could, balancing, on the carpet-covered sill.

She began to feel excited. In a minute now she would be in Inkoo Land. Instead of this chilling fog, there would be a tropic sun beating down upon her; leaves on the great trees would shimmer in the golden light; bright tropical flowers would be there, and luxuriant creepers; and she would see her little twins romping joyously at last, running, shouting, jumping in the sunshine, far, far from the complaining voices.

"Mrs. Meredith!" came the shocked voice of Miss Rice, leaning out of her window; but already it seemed far, far away, a little thread of sound from the world of fog and chill which Hilda was leaving "To Inkoo Land!" she cried to the carpet, and together they launched forth from the High Flats into the swirling silver emptiness of the sky...

It was warm in Inkoo Land, just as she had known it would be; and there was grass and great forest trees and the sun shone. The grass was like great sweeps of lawn, and once or twice the twins had come, to run about on it and laugh and shout and turn head-over-heels, just as she had imagined. But mostly it was people like herself, wandering slowly among the trees; and other people, in white coats, moving more briskly. And several times Miss Rice had mysteriously appeared, a quite changed Miss Rice, crying, and saying, "If only we had known!" and "When you come back, dear, everything will be different!"

Miss Rice, it seemed, had saved her "in the nick of time"; but somehow Hilda couldn't think about that just yet, or about the long, long problem that lay behind. Enough, for the moment, to be in Inkoo Land, and to know that, sooner or later, she would return, just as the twins had always returned, in time for tea.

"Q"

John Ball

Full Circle

When envy and hate of another person seethe constantly inside someone's mind, when resentment and humiliation are added irritants, the mixture can come to boiling point—and spill over. And in some cases the spilling over takes the form of the most drastic action man is capable of—especially if the act is safe, air-tight, and with no motive visible to the police ... John Ball, creator of Virgil Tibbs, writes in an almost documentary style, full of realistic and convincing detail, and with a deep sense of justice ...

It was three minutes to four in the morning. Lying wide-awake, Walter Kaskow watched the tip of the luminous minute hand as it reached upward toward the hour. Once again he listened to the steady, slow breathing that told him his wife was still deep in sleep. Then he turned his attention back to the clock, and waited.

At precisely the moment that the hands indicated the hour he slid noiselessly out of bed and carefully replaced the covers behind him. It was still pitch-dark, but the excitement of the day already charged the air. The time had come at last to shave, dress, leave the house as quietly as possible, meet Fred, and do the thing he had planned.

At 4:14 Walter crept silently downstairs, fully dressed except for his shoes which he held tightly in his left hand. The street light in front of the house filtered just enough light through the living-room window to show where each piece of furniture stood. With careful self-indulgence he eased himself into the one comfortable chair and put his shoes down without a sound on the ten-year-old carpet. Letting his weight settle into a position in which he could relax, Walter looked about him in the near darkness, then crinkled his face into a tight-lipped, satisfied smile.

The first move had gone precisely as he had planned; he was up, dressed, and out of the bedroom exactly one hour ahead of schedule. Mabel would sleep on now, and he would not have to resort to the thin excuse, if caught, that he had been too stimulated to sleep any longer. He had before him one clear, silent uninterrupted hour to go over every detail in his mind—to be sure, absolutely sure, he had overlooked nothing.

He began by reviewing his relationship with Fred. He tried to put himself in the position of an expert investigator. What was there to be found out?

Fred and Irma Ziegler had bought and moved into the house next door last spring. There had been no previous contact between the families. Almost from the first day the Zieglers and the Kaskows had been neighborly; by midsummer they had become good friends. Irma Ziegler would state that her husband and Walter had always been on the best of terms. So would Mabel, who was asleep upstairs.

In his hearty, blustering, loud style Fred himself would have to lay it on thick, claiming he and Walter were inseparable companions—that is, if Fred would ever have been called upon to testify, which he wouldn't since in about three more hours he would be dead.

Not once, Walter knew, had he ever given the slightest hint to anyone of his true feelings about Fred. Months ago he had realized the need to keep the secret, and he had done so. There was proof of that, because if either Irma or Mabel had had the least doubt, one of them would have said something before now. That was what made the whole thing completely air-tight; there was no visible motive anywhere.

In fact, just the opposite. At worst, Walter might be thought to have envied Fred, but many people could have done that. Fred was the kind of man who looked and acted success. He mixed easily and knew people from one end of the city to the other. Because he had his own auto dealership, he could come and go as he pleased. Walter, on the other hand, had had three jobs during the past two years, none of them very important.

When Walter had badly needed a better car, Fred had stepped in and generously sold him one of his best used cars at a giveaway price. But it was Fred who was always one notch ahead, Fred who had the bigger and better house, who cheerfully and easily won almost all the card games they played, who was clever with his hands and could make things, whose loud voice filled the room, whose jokes were always newer and funnier, who was now building an even bigger and better new house.

Walter caught himself; he sucked in a quick breath and deliberately snapped this line of thought. Danger lay that way! One single outburst, even the smallest hint, and he was finished, done for.

He looked toward the window. Outside the first gray of dawn was visible in the sky. Seated where he was, Walter could see past the street light and into the dying night beyond. It was now close to 4:30. He knew that he had to settle down and use the next 30 minutes to review every detail of his plan.

He began with the dinner party. Before he could start where he had intended, his mind jumped to Mabel's remark when they had been together at home afterward. Her voice came back to him: "Isn't it wonderful, Walter, that Fred and Irma are our friends! You can learn so much from him, and he has so many connections. He really likes you and some day, maybe, he'll do something wonderful for you."

Walter pushed back his feelings mechanically as he had done so many times before. Fred's death would wipe the slate clean; it would settle for all time who was the better man, the cleverer, the more resourceful. No one else would know, no one but he, Walter, and that was all that counted now.

Consciously he returned to the dinner party and relived the conversation. Fred, of course, was talking.

"Ever eat venison before, Walter?"

So that was what it was. The piece of meat turned into something tasteless in his mouth; he pushed it in front of his teeth and held it there where he couldn't accidentally swallow any more. Fred just sat there and grinned.

"What's the matter, Walter?" Mabel asked. "Is anything wrong?"

Walter clamped his napkin in front of his mouth and pushed the bit of half-chewed meat into it before he replied.

"I'm sorry. I don't want to eat deer meat. I—I like animals."

"Well, a cow's an animal, you know." Fred leaned back and patted his big middle. "And you eat beef all the time. You want to get over that, Walt. Wait till you've gone out into the woods, shot yourself a squirrel, skinned him, and cooked him for your dinner. Sure, I like animals too, always have, but face up to the facts of life, man. Meat is a big part of our diet. Millions of animals would never be born if they weren't raised strictly for food."

Walter picked up his fork and carefully ate a mouthful of mashed potatoes. He remembered his role, and played it carefully.

"I'm sorry, Fred. I saw a deer killed on the highway once and it kind of made me sick."

"Why, of course, Walt, nobody likes to see anything get hurt that way. I tell you what—I've been meaning to mention this anyway—how about going out hunting with me when the season opens in a couple of weeks? You'll feel differently when you've been out of doors with a gun in your hand and maybe brought in some meat for your own table. Remember, one quick accurate shot that drops an animal in its tracks doesn't hurt it."

"Go ahead," Mabel urged, "I think it's a fine idea." To her everything Fred proposed was a fine idea.

Now he must be careful! "I'd like to, Fred, for the sake of your company, but honestly I don't know the first thing about guns or how to shoot."

"That's easy. I'll lend you a book. Get it right now." Despite his bulk, Fred got up with enthusiasm and disappeared into his den. He was back in a few moments with a large volume. On the cover there was a color plate of a spotted dog, pointing.

"Here, take this home with you. It'll tell you everything you need to know. I'd be glad to lend you a gun, but I don't have a spare. Tell you what I'll do, though: you get yourself a gun and if you don't really want to keep it after you've tried it out, I'll take it off your hands. Go down to Blanley Sporting Goods and ask for Jack Marino; he's a friend of mine. Tell him I sent you and he'll take good care of you."

So it had all been Fred's idea; there were two witnesses to prove that. Walter had dutifully studied part of the book, including particularly the chapter on "Precautions in Handling a Gun." Then he had visited Jack Marino and bought a simple beginner's rifle, not too complicated, inexpensive—just the kind he would have been expected to buy.

The date had been set for this morning. Up at five, a half hour to dress and eat, then out to go hunting.

There was no flaw. It was Fred's own idea. He had planned the trip. He had recommended the gun salesman who would testify that he had waited on Mr. Walter Kaskow at the specific request of Mr. Fred Ziegler. It was well-known that Walter Kaskow was a close friend and neighbor of Fred Ziegler and indebted to him for many favors. And he had never felt, or shown, the slightest romantic inclinations toward Mrs. Ziegler.

Through the side window Walter saw a light come on in the kitchen of the house next door. Fred was up ahead of schedule, ten minutes early at least. But he didn't know that Walter had got up earlier still. For once Fred's overflowing energy had been outdone.

As he thought of Fred's energy, Walter laughed a little to himself. How much energy does a corpse have, how many people can it influence, how much money can it make? A quick, wild sense of power hit Walter like a sharp fist. He reached down and began noiselessly to lace his shoes.

It was close to a forty-mile drive to the spot where Fred planned to park the car. Through the hour-long trip Walter listened and asked questions; it was the thing he would have been expected to do. Fred drove easily as he talked about hunting as one of the great and useful sports.

"You want to understand, Walt, that wild life gets a much better break than you think. Take deer: they're protected by law throughout the year—only a few weeks are open season. If they were left entirely alone, they would breed so fast that something drastic would have to be done. The law is wise, it's set up so that the deer population is controlled and protected at the same time. And one deer can put meat on the table for a good part of the winter."

Fred paused to swing off the main highway onto a good secondary road.

"The place we're going to today is private property and posted; the guy who owns it is a good customer of mine and invites me out every year. Chances are there won't be anyone else around, so you don't need to worry that someone will take a pot shot at you."

It was twenty minutes of seven when Fred pulled the car off into a patch of hard stubble and set the brake. Then he reached for a vacuum bottle. "Let's have a cup of coffee," he invited. "Then we'll head for the woods. Got everything?"

Walter slapped his pockets for ammunition, chocolate bars, and the other things Fred had suggested. Then he accepted a plastic cup of steaming coffee and let the hot liquid run down the inside of his throat. Fred heaved his bulk out of the car.

"Come on, Walt, let's go," he said as he tucked the car keys deep into one of his pockets. Walter carefully opened the door on his side and stepped out. He waited while Fred prepared his new gun and handed it to him. Then they set off together across the open field toward the woods beyond.

Walter was thinking furiously now. As Fred strode beside him, something inside began to warn him of the enormity of the thing he had planned to do. Almost viciously he thrust the thought aside; he had gone too far, planned too well, to stop now. Of course he could change his mind and no one would ever know. He considered that for a moment—to lead Fred to the very edge of his death and then spare him: it would take a man of power to do that.

Fred suddenly slapped his heavy arm across Walter's shoulders. "Walt," he exclaimed abruptly, "today may be a big day for you. Give you a chance to prove you're a man."

A spasm of violent resentment seized Walter; he controlled himself only with an heroic effort. By the time he had himself fully in hand once more, they were close to the trees. Fred stopped to give instructions.

"Remember now, Walt, that a gun is a dangerous thing when it isn't carefully handled. Don't drag it through a fence behind you. Well, you read all that in the book I lent you. Just remember not to shoot until you're sure of your target. Normally you'll have plenty of time to spot what you're aiming at. I don't think anyone else is out here this morning—I didn't see any other cars parked—but there may be cows or other animals around.

"Maybe it would be best for a while if you didn't shoot at all unless I give the word. That way I'll take full responsibility. After you have a little more experience under your belt, you can go it on your own. Understand I'm not trying to tell you what to do, just trying to help you get started right. Okay, let's go in. You follow me."

Walter followed. He was thinking very carefully now. This was the one part that couldn't have been planned in advance. He would have to watch, wait, and be extremely cautious. When the right moment came, he would have to recognize it and act quickly, without hesitation. His mind thought of nothing else now—it closed itself tightly against any distraction. This was the beginning of the true test.

As they passed under the first of the trees, Walter could no longer fight back the cold chill of warning that was hammering inside him. He let the thought come, take possession of him, and have its say. Then he deliberately pushed it aside and concentrated on the constant humiliation he had suffered at the hands of the big man in front of him, the successful man who had everything given to him the easy way, who everyone agreed was his superior. Walter tightened his grip on his new gun. "Superior"—the word burned hatred into his brain.

Carefully Walter reviewed the remaining details of his plan. At the right moment he would shoot, calmly and deliberately. He would take the remote chance that there might be a witness, but if he could not see a witness, then a witness could only have at best a poor view of him. He could look around freely, as though he were trying to spot game, of course. And then, immediately after the shot, he would rush up, drop his gun, and cry aloud.

If there was a witness, Walter's fright and shock would be readily apparent. But more than that, if he missed, if Fred were only hurt and lived to tell what had happened, Fred himself would testify that it had been an accident, the fault of a rank beginner whom Fred himself had encouraged to come into the woods with him. A beginner who everyone would state was his close friend.

Most important of all, he must *feel* that a terrible accident had occurred. There would be police to talk to later, Irma to face. The only safe way was to believe completely in the terrible disaster; only after it was all over would he be able to begin the secret enjoyment of his triumph. Right now he wouldn't even consider the consequences of failure. He would not fail.

For nearly an hour they worked their way through the woods. Walter saw no game. Several times Fred signaled him to stop, and brought his gun up to his shoulder, but he did not fire. Each time Walter trembled in silent excitement; he wanted to hear the gun discharged, wanted Fred to start the shooting. In that way it would be partly Fred's fault. He remembered a long-forgotten phrase he had learned in his schooldays: "Those who live by the sword . . ."

Walter was ready now; the time had come. They had been in the woods long enough. If it had happened too soon—say, during the first ten minutes or so—it would have been suspicious. Now, with cold calculation, Walter began to watch for something over which he might legitimately trip. He found a protruding root, looked up, and was afraid to act. He found another, and stepped over it carefully. His nerve, schooled for so long, began to trickle away like the sands in the top of an hourglass.

Fred stopped and threw up his hand; Walter stopped behind him. They waited silently, motionless. Then, slowly, Fred raised his gun. Automatically Walter raised his too. Fred crept forward a half dozen steps as noiselessly as his bulk would allow. Walter followed more slowly; as he stopped he felt a raised tree root beside his foot.

With an electric thrill he realized this was exactly what he had planned to find: himself behind Fred, Fred's attention distracted, and something under his feet over which he could plausibly stumble and lose his balance.

Then Fred spoke: "Be quiet, Walt. I'll handle this."

As the seconds ticked, Walter let the implications soak into his mind. He was the inferior, he would always be the inferior, he would never be able to catch up, unless—unless—

The silence was shattered by the sharp terrifying slam of Fred's gun. Before the echo had died away, Fred fired again, and a third time quickly afterward.

Now!

Walter made no actual decision to do it. He had lived this moment so many times in his imagination, rehearsed it so many times in his mind, that it required no decision. The reports from Fred's gun unlocked the fear of his own gun which had frozen Walter's hands. He aimed just under Fred's left shoulder—and fired.

For an instant Walter thought he had missed; Fred said nothing and did not move. Then his knees unlocked and his big body began to fall. Fred turned, and for a stricken, paralyzing moment his eyes looked directly into Walter's. They showed pain, bewilderment, and a hopeless plea for help. Then Fred fell heavily to the ground and lay horribly still.

Walter screamed, forcing the air with all possible pressure from his lungs. He dropped his gun and rushed to where Fred lay. Dropping to his knees, he had a blinding reaction that he must do something—he must help! Fred's face was half buried in the earth; Walter tried hard to turn him over. When he succeeded, Fred's open eyes stared unseeing at the sky. A cold, gripping panic seized Walter and he wanted desperately, at any cost, to undo what he had just done. He was in trouble, terrible trouble, and he needed help—Fred's help.

Terrified and stricken, he somehow found his way out of the woods. Using the keys he had forced himself to take from Fred's pocket, he started the car with ice-cold fingers and managed to turn it back onto the road. He stopped at the first place that had a telephone and called the police.

He did not tell his story as he had planned. Instead he blurted out a confused, wild report that in every sentence seemed to be crying out his guilt. When he was finished, he put his head into his hands and knew he could never face an inquest, or a trial, and carry it off the way he had so carefully planned.

All that obsessed him was the look in Fred's eyes as he had died—the pain, the bewilderment, the plea for mercy. Mercy that Walter would have given his soul to be able to offer now. He was not sure he still possessed a soul. The triumph he had anticipated was stillborn as he was engulfed by a sense of irreparable loss. It was made more agonizing by the terrible knowledge that he had brought it onto himself. If only he hadn't! But he knew that he had; his friend and protector was gone, never to return.

Walter wept, and wanted to die.

He was not held. The quiet, friendly man who offered him his comfort and consoled him was a far keener observer than Walter had ever visualized. The man knew that Walter's shock and desperate grief were genuine, and so stated in his report. He was not clairvoyant and therefore did not sense the true reason for Walter's stricken misery. Walter was allowed to go home to face his wife, and Fred's widow, Irma.

In six months' time his wound failed to heal. Walter sat by himself and tried to lash his intellect into a sense of triumph, but it would not come. Each day as he returned home from work, knowing his job could not last much longer, he looked at the *For Sale* sign in front of the house that had been Fred's and was now Irma's. Then one day the house was sold.

Irma came to say goodbye. The whole thing had to be gone over once more—Irma's forgiveness, her understanding that it had been an accident, the reassurances they would continue to be close friends. This time she carried something in her hands. Walter looked at it and knew it was some sort of expensive camera.

Irma looked at him and spoke with quiet dignity. "Walter, I want you to have this. It is Fred's camera. It's a very fine one. Fred loved to use it and he told me more than once how he hoped to interest you in photography. He—he wasn't a very good photographer himself; perhaps you will be a better one and take the kind of pictures he always knew this camera could get. He would want you to have it, I'm sure, because wherever he is now, he feels the same way I do."

Walter took the camera in his hands and stared at it. The name Rolleiflex meant nothing to him; he wanted to throw it away, not touch it. As it lay in his hands, a new thought came to him. It was a link; the first tenuous tie back to the man whom he had destroyed. Walter's eyes turned wet. Irma pressed her hands over his, forcing the camera tighter in his grasp, then walked quickly out through the front door. The latch closed with a gentle click behind her.

Walter knew he could not go on as he was; he must recover himself, get back his composure. His job was tottering; he would have lost it long ago, but an understanding management had overlooked his sudden ineptitude for long patient weeks. But even a job as minor as his had to be done well and he had no skills to offer anywhere else. The camera might help—it would give him something new to do.

He borrowed several library books on photography and read them. He found one devoted to the exact camera he now owned and purchased a copy. Mabel encouraged him and made little meaningless suggestions with the thought that they might help him.

The camera did help. Each time the dark terrible cloud began to gather once more in his mind, Walter reached for the camera and practised with the gadgets that controlled its mechanism. Then he would take a few more pictures of Mabel with whatever light was available. The quality of his pictures slowly improved; he began to make fewer errors and gradually learned which lens openings and shutter speeds to use. He bought a tripod and the fuzziness that was evident in many of his earlier snapshots disappeared. Mabel showed some of his pictures to Irma, whom she went to see for that purpose. When she returned, she told Walter that Irma had a cozy little apartment and was very busy with her charity work.

On the first warm day of spring the idea came to Walter. It seemed strange to him that he had not thought of it before. It frightened him, but at the same time it promised him something he desperately wanted.

He knew where Fred was. Not in the cemetery where he had stood and watched his remains being lowered into the carefully draped grave. Fred was out in the woods where he had last been alive. Walter wanted to go there and commune with him. He was sure that if he went there, with Fred's camera in his hands, it would be the first step back to where he had been. Fred would not come back to life, of course, but part of the pressure that was relentlessly torturing Walter might be lifted. Fred, wherever he was, might even see to it. If he were alive, Walter knew, Fred would help. He was always like that; he liked to help people.

Walter did not want to return to the exact spot; he was terrified of that. Just the woods, any woods would do. And Walter knew where he was going. There was a low hill only a few miles away that commanded a good view from its top. At least it should, Walter reasoned. He would be able to take some fine shots with the new color film he was learning to use.

When he told Mabel, she offered to go with him. Almost harshly Walter told her he wanted to go alone and for once Mabel understood correctly. She kissed him goodbye before Walter drove off to keep the appointment that his dreadful secret had made for him. He knew he was pursuing something he could not hope to catch, but the very act of trying made him feel better.

He drove his car up to the base of the woods that crowned the hill and parked the car off the road. With a grim sense of reliving something he carefully put his car key into the same pocket Fred had put his. It helped, he felt, to tune himself to Fred's frequency, to indicate that he wanted to reach out and meet Fred halfway.

He roamed the woods all morning, feeling the yielding ground under his feet and wondering if any other human had ever followed exactly the same trail. A tiny sense of adventure came over him. He remembered Fred's instructions, "Be quiet, Walt. I'll handle this." There were no guns now, no danger, only a camera Walter knew how to use. He did not need Fred to help him here; he could go it very well on his own.

For the very first time a long dormant sense of triumph began to filter into his brain. It was all over long ago, and he *had* fooled everybody. There was no Fred now to make him walk in the rear, to be the general in command. It was an army of one now and General Walter Kaskow had assumed command. He took a few steps forward while the trees all about him stood respectfully at attention. He turned and faced in four different directions; no other human being challenged the supremacy of his position.

Walter commanded his lips to speak, to utter a phrase that they feared. "I'm glad I did it," he whispered.

In that moment a new sense of power flooded over him. Not because Fred was out of the way, but because he had done a thing few men would have dared to do, and he had succeeded. There was no way he could be found out now. He and Mabel could go somewhere else; he might even change his name to a more impressive one, one which would command more respect. Walter marched forward through the sentinel trees and felt he was discovering virgin soil.

He halted his advance when the trees abruptly thinned out and revealed a panoramic view of the countryside below. Walter looked down and smiled; there below were the thousands he had success-fully deceived, who did not know the power of the man who stood on the hill looking down at them. He had been right—coming to the woods, for the first time in months, had restored his balance and his ego.

Walter stepped back into the secrecy of the woods. He liked the idea of being out of view, someone no one knew was there. He picked a comfortable spot, sat down, and began to unwrap the lunch Mabel had packed for him. It had been a nuisance to carry, but now it had earned its passage.

Walter chewed the two sandwiches and regretted only slightly that he had nothing liquid with which to wash them down. His newfound sense of power made it a minor hardship of battle, something every great commander had to endure. It was only a slight discomfort, which made it all the better. A tiny gust of wind picked up a crumpled piece of waxed paper that lay beside him and danced it across the ground.

A scrap of paper was a clue, a betrayer of the fact that he had been there.

Amused with himself, he crept four paces on all fours to retrieve it. If he was to be the phantom of the woods, there must be nothing left to betray—

The sharp startling bark of a gun hit his ears at the same moment a stab of frightful pain paralyzed his side. Walter tried to spring to his feet, but agony conquered him and he fell to the ground.

He gasped in a hard breath and a streak of terror stabbed him; his brain would not respond to his commands. He gasped again and at that moment his stricken mind told him he had been shot.

"No!" he screamed.

With violent rage he demanded that the pain be made to disappear. He could not move. His ears told him someone was running toward him, someone who would help.

His eyes began to refuse the orders of his brain. The pain was getting worse, worse. What would heal him? He could not—could not—continue in this unbearable pain. He—

His eyes saw the blood, his blood, spreading rapidly over his shirt and the top of his trousers. A terrible, unbelievable, utterly impossible thought struck him—he might be dying.

He could not! He was Walter Kaskow, the great Walter Kaskow, the true unsuspected genius who had fooled everyone.

His brain began to swim. The woods about him grew. He was frantic now, desperate. His ego screamed at the outrage, and he knew complete and utter terror.

His mouth was open wide at the moment he died. His eyes stared up unseeing at the sky as the eyes of another dead man had done a half a year before.

A man bent over him and with expert hands checked for a heartbeat. Then he stopped, because he knew the man on the ground was dead. He turned and with the restrained pace of an elderly man made the best time he could out of the woods.

The two patrol officers stood looking down at the body.

"There's no doubt about it," the senior man said. "You can see clearly where he was dragging himself along the ground. Why he did that we'll never know. He must have known how dangerous that was with the county now open for small-game hunting."

He hitched up his Sam Browne belt as he turned toward the elderly man who still held his light hunting piece in his hands. "I'm not saying this officially, but I don't believe you need to blame yourself at all for this. It was clearly an accidental shooting. You thought he was some small game crawling on the ground. Did you know this man?"

The elderly man shook his head; he seemed completely unnerved. The other policeman laid a hand on his shoulder. "We'll have to take your name and address, of course, and it might be best if you followed us down in your car so that we can make a full report. I'll radio for the coroner's crew to come up and take care of the body."

The officer produced a notebook. "Your name?" he asked, trying to make it sound casual.

"Herbert William Sandski," the elderly man replied. He moved his lips with an effort. The officer wrote.

"Herbert William Sandski," the officer repeated. "What do you do, sir?"

The man looked down at the shape that lay before him on the ground. When he turned his back to the sight, there were tears in his eyes. Without being told, he began to walk in the direction from which the three of them had come.

The older patrolman touched his partner's arm. "Sandski, remember?" he asked.

The other officer shook his head.

"It's strange, him of all people," his partner confided. "You ought to know. He was the state executioner."

"Q"

The   Odd   Man

Once again Ellery is challenged by the other members of the
Puzzle Club; but this "adventure in deduction" offers not only
armchair detection in its "purest" sense but also "variations on
a 'tec theme" . . .

Detective: ELLERY QUEEN

One of the unique encounters in the short and happy history of
The Puzzle Club began, as so many interesting things do, in the
most ordinary way.

That is to say, 7:30 of that Wednesday evening found Ellery in
the foyer of Syres's Park Avenue penthouse aerie pressing the bell
button, having the door opened for him by a butler who had obviously been inspired by Jeeves, and being conducted into the grand-
scale wood-leather-and-brass-stud living room that had just as obviously been inspired by the king-sized ranchos of the Southwest
where Syres had made his millions.

As usual Ellery found the membership assembled—with the exception, also as usual, of Arkavy, the biochemist whose Nobel
achievement took him to so many international symposiums that
Ellery had not yet laid eyes on him; indeed, he had come to think
of the great scientist as yet another fiction his fellow members had
dreamed up for mischievous reasons of their own. There was Syres
himself, their hulking and profoundly respected host—respected not
for being a multimillionaire but for having founded the club; tall
sardonic Darnell of the John L. Lewis eyebrows, the criminal lawyer
who was known to the American Bar, not altogether affectionately,
as "the rich man's Clarence Darrow"; the psychiatrist, Dr. Vreeland,
trim and peach-cheeked, whose professional reputation was as long
as his stature was short; and wickedly blue-eyed little Emmy Wandermere, who had recently won the Pulitzer Prize for poetry to—for
once—unanimous approval.

It was one of the strictest rules of The Puzzle Club that no extraneous matters, not of politics or art or economics or world affairs, or even of juicy gossip, be allowed to intrude on the business at hand, which was simply (in a manner of speaking only, since that adverb was not to be found in the club's motto) to challenge each member to solve a puzzle invented by the others, and then to repair to Charlot's dinner table, Charlot being Syres's chef, with a reputation as exalted in his field as that of the puzzlers in theirs. The puzzles were always in story form, told by the challengers seriatim, and they were as painstakingly planned for the battle of wits as if an empire depended on the outcome.

Tonight it was Ellery's turn again, and after the briefest of amenities he took his place in the arena, which at The Puzzle Club meant sitting down in a hugely comfortable leather chair near the super-fireplace, with a bottle, a glass, and a little buffet of Charlot's masterly canapés at hand and no further preliminaries whatever.

Darnell began (by prearrangement—the sequence of narrators was as carefully choreographed as a ballet).

"The puzzle this evening, Queen, is right down your alley—"

"Kindly omit the courtroom-type psychology, Counselor," Ellery drawled, for he was feeling in extra-fine fettle this evening, "and get on with it."

"—because it's a cops-and-robbers story," the lawyer went on, unperturbed, "except that in this case the cop is an undercover agent whose assignment it is to track down a dope supplier. The supplier is running a big wholesale illicit-drug operation; hundreds of pushers are getting their stuff from him, so it's important to nail him."

"The trouble is," Dr. Vreeland said, feeling the knot of his tie (I wonder, Ellery thought, what his analyst made of that—it was one of the psychiatrist's most irritating habits), "his identity is not known precisely."

"By which I take it that it's known imprecisely," Ellery said. "The unknown of a known group."

"Yes, a group of three."

"The classic number."

"It's convenient, Queen."

"That's the chief reason it's classic."

"The three suspects," oilman Syres broke in, unable to conceal a frown, for Ellery did not always comport himself with the decorum the founder thought their labors deserved, "all live in the same building. It's a three-story house . . ."

"Someday," Ellery said, peering into the future, "instead of a
three-story house I shall make up a three-house story."

"Mr. Queen!" and Emmy Wandermere let a giggle escape. "Please
be serious, or you won't be allowed to eat Charlot's chef-d'oeuvre,
which I understand is positively wild tonight."

"I've lost track," Syres grumped. "Where were we?"

"I beg everyone's pardon," Ellery said. "We have an undercover
police officer who's turned up three suspects, one of whom is the
dope wholesaler, and all three live in a three-story house, I presume
one to a floor. And these habitants are?"

"The man who occupies the ground floor," the little poet replied,
"and whose name is John A. Chandler—known in the neighborhood
as Jac, from his initials—runs a modest one-man business, a radio-
and-TV-repair shop, from his apartment."

"The question is, of course," Lawyer Darnell said, "whether the
repair shop is just a front for the dope-supply operation."

Ellery nodded. "And the occupant of the middle floor?"

"An insurance agent," Dr. Vreeland said. "Character named Cutcliffe Kerry—"

"Named what?"

"Cutcliffe Kerry is what we decided on," the psychiatrist said
firmly, "and if you don't care for it that's your problem, Queen,
because Cutcliffe Kerry he remains."

"Very well," Ellery said, "but I think I detect the aroma of fresh
herring. Or am I being double-whammied? In any event, Cutcliffe
Kerry sells insurance, or tries to, which means he gets to see a great
many people. So the insurance thing could be a cover. And the top
floor?"

"Is rented by a fellow named Fletcher, Benjamin Fletcher," Syres
said. "Fletcher is a salesman, too, but of an entirely different sort.
He sells vacuum cleaners."

"Door to door," Ellery said. "Possible cover too. All right, Jac
Chandler, radio-TV repairman; Cutcliffe Kerry, insurance agent;
Ben Fletcher, vacuum-cleaner salesman; and one of them is the bad
guy. What happens, Mr. Syres?"

"The undercover man has been watching the building and—isn't
the word tailing?—the three men, according to his reports to his
superior at police headquarters."

"And just after he finds out who the drug supplier is," Darnell
said mournfully, "but before he can come up with the hard evidence,
he's murdered."

"As I suspected," Ellery said, shaking his head. "Earning the poor fellow a departmental citation and the traditional six feet of sod. He was murdered by the dope boy, of course."

"Of course."

"To shut him up."

"What else?"

"Which means he hadn't yet reported the name of the dope supplier."

"Well, not exactly, Mr. Queen." Emmy Wandermere leaned forward to accept the flame of Dr. Vreeland's gold lighter, then leaned back puffing like The Little Engine That Could on a steep grade. She was trying to curb her nicotine-and-tar intake, so she was currently smoking cigarettes made of processed lettuce. "The undercover man hadn't reported the drug supplier's name, true, but in the very last report before his murder he did mention a clue."

"What kind of clue?"

"He referred to the supplier—his subsequent killer—as, and this is an exact quote, Mr. Queen, 'the odd man of the three.' "

Ellery blinked.

"Your mission, Mr. Queen, if you accept it—and you'd better, or be kicked out of the club," said Darnell in his most doom-ridden courtroom tones, "is to detect the guilty man among Chandler, Kerry, and Fletcher—the one of them who's been selling the stuff in wholesale lots and who murdered our brave lad of the law."

"The odd man of the three, hm?"

Ellery sat arranging his thoughts. As at all such critical stages of the game, by protocol, the strictest silence was maintained.

Finally Ellery said, "Where and how did the murder of the undercover agent take place?"

Darnell waved his manicured hand. "Frankly, Queen, we debated whether to make up a complicated background for the crime. In the end we decided it wouldn't be fair, because the murder itself has nothing to do with the puzzle except that it took place. The details are irrelevant and immaterial."

"Except, of course, to the victim, but that's usually left out." Having discharged himself of this philosophical gripe, Ellery resumed his seat, as it were, on his train of thought. "I suppose the premises were searched from roof to cellar, inside and out, by the police after the murder of their buddy?"

"You know it," Syres said.

"I suppose, too, that no narcotics, amphetamines, barbiturates, etcetera *ad nauseam,* no cutting equipment, no dope paraphernalia of any kind, were found anywhere in the building?"

"Not a trace," Dr. Vreeland said. "The guilty man disposed of it all before the police got there."

"Did one of the men have a record?"

Miss Wandermere smiled. "*Nyet.*"

"Was one of them a married man and were the other two bachelors?"

"No."

"Was it the other way round? One of them a bachelor and two married?"

"I admire the way you wriggle, Mr. Queen. The answer is still no."

"The odd man of the three." Ellery mused again. "Well, I see we'll have to be lexical. By the commonest definition, odd means strange, unusual, peculiar. Was there anything strange, unusual, or peculiar in, say, the appearance of Chandler or Kerry or Fletcher?"

Dr. Vreeland, with relish: "Not a thing."

"In a mannerism? Behavior? Speech? Gait? That sort of thing?"

Syres: "All ordinary as hell, Queen."

"In background?"

Darnell, through a grin: "Ditto."

"There was nothing bizarre or freakish about one of them?"

"Nothing, friend," Emmy Wandermere murmured.

Ellery grasped his nose more like an enemy.

"Was one of them touched in the head?" he asked suddenly. "Odd in the mental sense?"

"There," the psychiatrist said, "you tread on muddy ground, Queen. Any antisocial behavior, as in the case of habitual criminals, might of course be so characterized. However, for purposes of our story the answer is no. All three men were normal—whatever that means."

Ellery nodded fretfully. "I could go on and on naming categories of peculiarity, but let me save us all from endangering Charlot's peace of mind. *Did* the undercover man use the word odd to connote peculiar?"

The little poet looked around and received assents invisible to the Queen eye. "He did not."

"Then that's that. Oh, one thing. Was the report in which he fingered the supplier as being the odd man written or oral?"

"Now what kind of question is that?" the oil king demanded. "What could that have to do with anything?"

"Possibly a great deal, Mr. Syres. If it had been an oral report, there would be no way of knowing whether his word odd began with a capital O or a small o. Assume that he'd meant it to be capital O-d-d. Then Odd man might have referred to a member of the I.O.O.F., the fraternal order–the Odd Fellows. That might certainly distinguish your man from the other two."

"It was a written report," Darnell said hastily, "and the o of odd was a small letter."

Everyone looked relieved. It was evident that the makers of this particular puzzle had failed to consider the Independent Order of Odd Fellows in their scheming.

"There are other odd possibilities–if you'll forgive the pun–such as odd in the golf meaning, which is one stroke more than your opponent has played. But I won't waste any more time on esoterica. Your undercover man meant odd in the sense of not matching, didn't he? Of being left over?"

"Explain that, please," Dr. Vreeland said.

"In the sense that two of the three suspects had something in common, something the third man didn't share with them–thus making the third man 'the odd man' and consequently the dope supplier and murderer. Isn't that the kind of thing your undercover agent meant by odd man?"

The psychiatrist looked cautious. "I think we may fairly say yes to that."

"Thank you very much," Ellery said. "Which brings me to a fascinating question: How clever are you people being? Run-of-the-game clever or clever-clever?"

"I don't think," Miss Wandermere said, "we quite follow. What do you mean exactly, Mr. Queen?"

"Did you intend to give me a choice of solutions? The reason I ask is that I see not one possible answer, but three."

"Three!" Syres shook his massive head. "We had enough trouble deciding on one."

"I for one," Counselor Darnell stated stiffishly, "should like to hear a for-instance."

"All right, I'll give you one solution I doubt you had in mind, since it's so obvious."

"You know, Queen, you have a sadistic streak in you?" barked Dr. Vreeland. "Obvious! Which solution is obvious?"

"Why, Doctor. Take the names of two of your suspects, John A.–Jac–Chandler and Benjamin Fletcher. Oddly enough–there I go again!–those surnames have two points of similarity. 'Chandler' and 'Fletcher' both end in 'er' and both contain eight letters. Cutcliffe Kerry's surname differs in both respects–no 'er' ending and only five letters–so Kerry becomes the odd surname of the trio. In this solution, then, Kerry the insurance man is the supplier-killer."

"I'll be damned," Syres exclaimed. "How did we miss that?"

"Very simply," Miss Wandermere said. "We didn't see it."

"Never mind that," Darnell snapped. "The fact is it happened. Queen, you said you have three solutions. What's another?"

"Give me a clue to the solution you people had in mind, since there are more than one. Some key word that indicates the drift but doesn't give the game away. One word can do it."

Syres, Darnell, and Dr. Vreeland jumped up and surrounded Emmy Wandermere. From the looped figures, the cocked heads, and the murderous whispers they might have been the losing team in an offensive huddle with six seconds left to play. Finally, the men resumed their seats, nudging one another.

Said little Miss Wandermere: "You asked for a clue, Mr. Queen. The clue is: clue."

Ellery threw his head back and roared. "Right! Very clever, considering who I am and that I'm the solver of the evening.

"You hurled my specialized knowledge in my teeth, calculating that I'd be so close to it I wouldn't see it. Sorry! Two of the surnames you invented," Ellery said with satisfaction, "are of famous detective-story writers. Chandler–in this case Raymond Chandler–was the widely acclaimed creator of Philip Marlowe. Joseph Smith Fletcher–J. S. Fletcher–produced more detective fiction than any other writer except Edgar Wallace, or so it's said; Fletcher's *The Middle Temple Murder* was publicly praised by no lesser mystery fan than the President of the United States, Woodrow Wilson. On the other hand, if there's ever been a famous detective-story writer named Cutcliffe Kerry, his fame has failed to reach me. So your Mr. Kerry again becomes the odd man of the trio and the answer to the problem. Wasn't that your solution, Miss Wandermere and gentlemen?"

They said yes in varying tones of chagrin.

Ordinarily, at this point in the evening's proceedings, the company would have risen from their chairs and made for Syres's magnificently gussied-up cookhouse of a dining room. But tonight no one stirred a toe, not even at the promise of the manna simmering on Charlot's hob. Instead, Dr. Vreeland uttered a small, inquiring cough.

"You, ah, mentioned a third solution, Queen. Although I must confess–"

"Before you pronounce your *mea culpa,* Doctor," Ellery said with a smile, "may I? I've given you people your solution. I've even thrown in another for good measure. Turnabout? I now challenge you. What's the third solution?" . . .

Ten minutes later Ellery showed them mercy–really, he said sorrowfully, more in the interest of preserving Charlot's chancy good will than out of natural goodness of heart.

"John A. Chandler, Cutcliffe Kerry, Benjamin Fletcher. Chandler, Kerry, and Fletcher. What do two of these have in common besides what's already been discussed? Why, they derive from trades or occupations."

"Chandler." The lawyer, Darnell, looked around at the others, startled. "You know, that's true!"

"Yes, a ship chandler deals in specified goods or equipment. If you go farther back in time you find that a chandler was someone who made or sold candles or, as in very early England, supervised the candle requirements of a household. So that's one trade.

"Is there another in the remaining two surnames?

"Yes, the name Fletcher. A fletcher was–and technically still is–a maker of arrows, or a dealer in same; in the Middle Ages, by extension, although this was a rare meaning, the word was sometimes used to denote an archer. In either event, another trade or occupation.

"But the only etymological origin I've ever heard ascribed to the name Kerry is County Kerry, from which the Kerry blue terrier derives. And that's not a trade, it's a place. So with the names Chandler and Fletcher going back to occupations, and Kerry to Irish geography, your Mr. Kerry becomes once again the unpaired meaning, the odd man–a third answer to your problem."

And Ellery rose and offered his arm gallantly to Miss Wandermere.

The poetess took it with a little shake. And as they led the way to the feast she whispered, "You know what you are, Ellery Queen? You're an intellectual *pack rat!*"

Robert L. Fish

In the Bag

A night on the town meant a night of safecracking to Claude, and if all went well, this night could easily be the highspot of Claude's criminal career. But Claude was to learn a lesson: "Never invent problems. Life furnishes us with sufficient" . . .

Criminal: CLAUDE BIESSY

To go back to the Rue Cologne or not, that was the problem!

Claude Biessy recognized that his appearance was a decided advantage, for he looked like a student at the Sorbonne and therefore dressed accordingly. With his student's satchel dangling indolently from one hand and his curly head obviously in some philosophical cloud, he always walked—strolled would be more accurate, though at times many miles were involved—from his small apartment in the Rue Collard near the university to and from his jobs.

His appearance may have been a bit of luck, but all else was thoroughly planned. No wheeled transportation to draw attention to the possible presence of an intruder in some untenanted-at-the-moment home or apartment; no curious taxi driver to recall a youthful fare following a safecracking in some office building or warehouse. No wallet with identification ever carried on a job, and never any accomplice. Nothing ever stolen except cash or objects easily transformed into cash without the services of a fence. No people, no chances. To date, it had worked fine.

He paused in his labors and listened. There was only the sound of rising wind rattling the windows beyond the thick drapes of the old house; he had expected no other. With a brief nod he returned to work.

The chips were wiped from the hot drill bit, the bit dipped into oil. Claude tackled the safe door again. The beginning of the hole was clearly visible in the sharp beam of the adjustable flash. He had positioned it precisely at a certain point between the combination dial and the safe's handle—he knew this vulnerable spot very well. He turned the drill on and began again, putting as much weight against the drill handle as he could muster.

He was pleased with the near-silent humming of the small powerful motor, the eagerness with which the bit ate its way steadily through the thick metal. Easy did it; there was no rush. His careful scouting had made sure that the inhabitants of the house would not return until the following day.

The safe was a LeClair, an unusually large one for home use. Most home safes were simply meant to protect against fire and they presented no special problems. A LeClair was more complex—constructed in hopes of frustrating burglars—but Claude was familiar with it. He had spent four years under the tutelage of the famous Gil Lowendal himself and he had yet to find a small safe he couldn't enter.

The vibration of the drill changed; the bit slowed and then speeded up as it penetrated the last thickness of the steel shell. He had now drilled through to the locking linkage area. The rest was simple—even though it took a little more muscle.

From his bag, he extracted a punch made of the hardest steel and inserted it into the hole. Then, reaching into the bag once more, he produced an all-steel hammer. A few sufficiently strong blows against the punch would break the safe's lock bolt—and the job would be finished.

It was not the effort of the pounding that bothered him. It was just that, when he thought back afterward, he always had a nightmare scenario occur to him. Somehow the hammer would slip and there would be a loud clang. Or, even if it didn't, the noise of the blows might, by chance, reach the ears of a person in the vicinity. That person would rise up on one elbow in bed, perhaps, and say to himself, "Odd, I thought I heard something like hammering. Yes, there it is again. It would seem to be coming from the Duponts' house. Ah, well."

Then that person, sinking back in the bed again, would suddenly reflect, "But wait! Didn't I see the Duponts leaving for the weekend? There is something very curious here. Perhaps I should ask the police to have a look."

Claude snapped the flashlight off and went to the window to survey the street. Across the way the streetlight shone on an empty garden. There was no sign of life except for the very faint sound of music coming from some house a little farther along.

He moved back to the safe and grasped the hammer. This old house would have thick walls. Besides, he counted on the fact that the listener in his nightmare—if there ever were one in reality—would hesitate a minute, would take another minute to find his slippers, would spend a little more time getting to the telephone. There would be a further delay as the policeman at the other end of the line wrote everything down.

It took a few more blows than he'd expected—each one a cannon blast to his ears—but at last the lock was broken. It was only after he had dismantled the drill and put each piece of his equipment carefully back into his satchel that he turned the handle of the safe. It moved easily.

He shone the beam of his flashlight inside. Silver plate; he pushed it aside without qualms. A jewel case; he whistled slightly as he opened it, and then closed it resolutely. A tin box! He dragged it out and tipped the cover up. Papers. He took one up. Papers? Securities! *Negotiable securities!*

He took one look at the face value of the top one and his eyes widened. A fortune! But this was no time to stand and count it. He dropped the bundle into the satchel, tossed the flashlight on top of it, buckled it hastily, and moved to the window.

He was three blocks away, his surgical gloves tucked into an inner pocket, his bag swinging negligently from his hand, when a police car passed him with flashing lights and keening siren. Claude began to look after it and then brought his head to the front. It was impossible that the sound of the hammer could have brought any investigation to the old house in that short a time.

Besides, a police car was certainly no unusual sight in Paris, even in the suburbs. Crime was certainly not limited to his small efforts, and automobile accidents were as common as the common cold. He put the police car from his mind and continued his stroll toward home. But subconsciously one ear listened for the return of the siren.

The streets through which Claude returned were not the same ones he had traversed in going to the job, but they were of the same general nature. Major arteries were avoided, as were streets that appeared completely deserted. Avenues lined with spreading plane trees and strolling couples out for the evening air were the ones he preferred. Along several he saw other students—he always thought of them as *other* students—equally hampered by bags, walking alone or together, and he felt a certain kinship with them.

He crossed the Avenue Mozambique and turned down the Rue Cologne, staying a reasonable distance behind a couple walking with their arms about each other. Here, well into the body of the city proper, traffic was still oddly light, but the night was pleasant and the breeze cooling.

Claude strolled along, enjoying the walk, when he heard the sharp clack of leather heels on the opposite pavement. His eyes came up, incurious. Marching along in the opposite direction was a uniformed policeman, visored hat square on his brow, cape swinging in cadence to his almost military step.

Claude smiled faintly, a smile that faded as the footsteps suddenly stopped. There was the briefest pause, and then they resumed, but their owner had turned and was now moving in the same direction as Claude, just across the street.

Claude frowned slightly without breaking the evenness of his pace in the least. A coincidence? Quite obviously. But, still, here he was with a satchel full of negotiable securities, not to mention a lot of highly unusual implements it would be most difficult to explain. One should be allowed a touch of nervousness, should one not? Ah, well, he thought, taking heart, one could scarcely walk across half of Paris and not run into a policeman now and then, could one?

And if that policeman was walking in the direction he was, so what? They all had to walk in one direction or the other, did they not? Obviously, they did.

Still, this one had stopped dead and turned just after passing Claude, had he not?

He had.

On the other hand, look at it this way: If the *flic* had the slightest suspicion that he was following a much-wanted safecracker (*not* following, you idiot! Because he *isn't* following; he's merely walking in the same direction!), would he remain across the street, marching along so sedately? Not likely! He would be storming over, whistle blowing like mad, baton raised for action. So forget the man, for heaven's sake! Walk along like the student he thinks you are, and stop sweating!

Curbs came and went on the Rue Cologne. Step down, step up. The couple ahead had withdrawn into a shadowed alcove; giggles came from it as he passed. Would the *flic* cross over and investigate the giggles? He did not, but it had really been a lot to expect.

Ahead, the walk was now bare, the overhead streetlights throwing the shadows of the whispering trees in wavering patches on the walk. The two sets of footsteps echoed each other, one on each side of the pavement. Claude suddenly smiled to himself. Suppose he were to cross the street and plant himself in front of the policeman? Ask the *flic* for directions, say? Settle the matter once and for all—

His smile was wiped away immediately; he felt a sudden chill. You are an idiot, my friend, he said to himself grimly, soberly. You are beginning to show nerves. That idea was strictly from nerves. Don't. It is a bad habit to get into. Try not to get any more of those ridiculous notions.

Turn down one of the small side streets? And if the *flic* merely turns down the street with you, what then, my foolish friend? What did we just say about ridiculous ideas? Just keep walking. That's right. One foot ahead of the other.

The lights of the Place Duquesne appeared before him; a deserted sidewalk café beckoned hospitably from the broad sidewalk that flanked the empty flagstoned circle. Wait a minute! Approaching the *flic* was one thing, but pausing for a brief refreshment was quite another. One thing was certain; they couldn't keep up this silly charade all the way back to the university! Who was it who had said, if war must start, let it start here?

Claude smiled faintly, slowed his steps, and dropped into a chair well back from the curb. His satchel seemed to drape itself naturally across his thighs. And then he felt his heart lurch. The footsteps across the street had also stopped!

"M'sieu?"

Claude swung about, startled, staring up at a sleepy-eyed waiter. "What?"

The waiter stared at him. "Exactly, M'sieu. What?"

"Oh. A cognac."

The waiter nodded, yawned, wiped the table from force of habit, and wandered off inside. He returned with a glass of amber liquid and placed it down. Claude turned to the glass, refusing to recognize the existence of the uniformed figure hesitating across the small *place* from him; he raised the drink and downed it in one swallow. It was a cheap cognac, an embarrassment of the vine, but its warmth was welcome.

Claude forced himself to raise his eyes. The caped figure across from him had not moved.

"Waiter!"

"M'sieu?"

"Another cognac. A double!"

It was placed before him. He twisted the glass slowly and then raised it toward his lips. About to toss it down, his hand froze on the glass. The caped officer had ceased his vigil and was slowly crossing the stones of the *place*. His baton swung restlessly at his side.

Claude felt fear evaporate as quickly as it had come. He had always known the day might come. A plan formed, as plans always formed for him. He would not answer the questions; he would pretend he had not heard. When the *flic* bent lower, he would receive a double dose of cognac in the eyes!

The policeman was big, but he did not look very fast. Off and running! Take the securities from the satchel on the run and the rest jettisoned, maybe under the *flic*'s feet! Here he comes. Claude's fingers lowered the glass slowly.

The policeman shouldered his way through the scattered tables, passed Claude without a glance, and came to rap on the bar counter with his baton. The waiter looked up.

"M'sieu?"

"Your telephone—"

Claude frowned. Calling for the wagon? His muscles tensed, prepared. The voice of the policeman came now, but it was surprisingly nervous, oddly cringing.

"Marie? Where have you been? I finished my tour nearly an hour ago . . . I've been up and down the Rue Cologne several times . . . No, no, my darling! Of course I'm not complaining . . . I'm merely . . . No, no, darling! Believe me, of course I still want . . . It's simply that . . ."

There was a pause as the uniformed man listened further. "I'm at the Place Duquesne, on the Rue Cologne . . . Ten minutes? . . . Of course, my sweet . . . No, no, I don't mind! . . . No, no, I'll wait . . ."

Claude bit back a grin, fighting hard not to burst out into nervous, almost hysterical laughter. A lesson here, he told himself, trying to sound stern, and took the cognac in his hand down in one huge swallow. He choked a bit on it but welcomed it. Never invent problems. Life furnishes us with sufficient. He swung an arm up to intercept the waiter.

"One last cognac, if you please. And the check, as well."

The policeman passed him, a foolish grin on his face, and took a stand at the curb, staring hungrily up the deserted avenue. Claude grinned in relief, gulped down the cognac and reached into his pocket. It was empty. He reached into another with equal results.

What the—

His wallet! His wallet, of course, was home with all other identification. He looked up to see the waiter's eye on him, cold as only
years of serving the public can chill an eye.

"I must have left my wallet at home . . ."

The waiter moved closer, preventing escape, managing a sneer
without moving so much as a muscle of his face. The policeman had
turned and was watching.

"Tomorrow I will come back . . ."

The waiter shrugged, caught the policeman's eye and jerked a
thumb downward. The policeman stared and then shook his head
in profound disgust as Claude sat frozen. The shoulders of the uniformed man slumped. Eight long, miserable, lonely hours on his
feet, Marie about to meet him with almost assured results, and now
this! Because of some idiot youngster who wandered off without
money, he was going to have to waste hours at the office, fill out
God-knows-how-many millions of papers—it was impossible! Would
Marie wait for him to get back? What a dream!

No, damn it, no! Not tonight! He looked down at the pale face of
the young man in the chair.

"I'll lend you the money for the cognac," he said, reaching for his
billfold. "This is my regular beat; four in the afternoon to midnight.
You can come by tomorrow and pay me back."

Claude felt his head whirling. He could not believe it. He came
to his feet. "Oh, I will, I will!"

"I'm sure you will," the *flic* said confidently and picked the satchel
from Claude's fingers. "I'll hold your books for security." He was
generous, but also cautious. "Don't worry. They'll be safe."

To go back to the Rue Cologne or not, that was the problem!

William Bankier

Dangerous Enterprise

Martin Milligan, in deep personal and business trouble, was ripe for a desperate venture. With his life a shambles, what did he have to lose? But Marty never thought negatively. With his flaming Irish temper and hard fists to back it up, Marty thought of what he had to gain in this game played for high stakes . . . a novelet, complete in this volume, that reads like a house afire . . .

It began with Milligan bringing his hand down flat on the fragile rosewood table causing a crystal wineglass to topple and fall, as if in slow motion before his glazed eyes, and smash on the parquet floor.

"Martin, don't start," Deirdre said. She went to stand beside her new man.

What Milligan wanted to say was that he was beating the furniture to avoid beating the pale young person who now stood one pace in front of Milligan's wife, his eyes wide and his mouth clenched like a small fist. Behind him, Deirdre loomed large, almost twice his size. At another time Milligan might have laughed.

He said, "You'd better listen to me because I haven't even started yet. What the hell is going on here?"

"I told you when I left Montreal I wasn't coming back."

"We told each other a lot of things."

"And I remember every single one of them."

"We've told each other worse. And got back together."

"Not this time. I'm in London to stay."

"Like hell. You're coming back with me."

"No, I'm not. I'm never coming back." Deirdre stepped from behind her lover and confronted her husband, pushing back waves of dark red hair with both hands. "You're such a fool, Marty. I don't know what else to call you. I knew you had detectives following me and that was bad enough. But here you stand, drunk

253

at two o'clock in the afternoon, smashing the furniture and pretending I'm going to come running back to you. Well, I won't."

"Deirdre, it isn't as if I'm not trying. I thought I could make it myself, but I can't. Don't make me plead in front of this jerk."

The young man spoke for the first time. "My name is Lane. And I'm not afraid of you, Milligan. We see people a lot sicker than you at the hospital every day."

"I'll plant him, so help me," Milligan said. "Come out of here, Deirdre. Come back to my hotel."

"You aren't going to plant anybody. Go back to your hotel by yourself. Put your things in a bag and catch the next plane to Montreal. I have a good reason for not coming with you."

"I don't want to hear."

"You have to hear." She put out one hand and took his wrist. Her grip was cold, as firm as a manacle. "I'm three months pregnant. I'm going to have Lane's baby."

Milligan almost collapsed. "Help me, God," he whispered.

"I'm happy, Marty. You must try to understand that. And we'll both be better off if you just get the divorce thing going and we head our separate ways. Anyway, it doesn't matter to me or Lane. Divorce or not, we're going to live together."

Milligan turned away from his wife and in doing so struck the little table with his hip. The other wineglass fell over onto a plate of salad. Deirdre steadied the table and set the glass erect. She took up a linen napkin and wiped a streak of dressing from the crystal, frowning, intent on having a clean glass.

"But it would be so much better if we could simply be divorced the way so many other people are these days. Life would go on. It isn't the end of the world."

He could not raise his voice above a croak. There was no wind in him. "Don't say this to me."

"Martin, you're such a stubborn fool. You said you wanted babies as much as I do. Well, then, all you had to do was take the test and prove why we weren't having any."

"Shut up. I feel like killing myself."

"Don't start that again. It's just talk. That's all you are these days is talk."

The young doctor said, "The fact is plenty of men are sterile. If you really want to have a family in the future, I mean with some other woman, why not consider adoption, or artificial insemination?"

Deirdre said quietly, "You always wanted to blame it on me. Well, Lane and I have proved the trouble wasn't with me." She sat down with a straight back and folded her hands across her stomach.

Now Milligan was outside walking erratically along Bayswater Road, heading west. He crossed the wide street in the middle of a block, challenging the traffic in both directions. A taxi swerved and came to a full stop and the driver put his head out of the window and yelled, "Get stuffed, you great drunken twit!"

Milligan entered Kensington Gardens through Lancaster Gate and strode across the grass. A pickup game of soccer football was in progress and he reeled through the middle of it, cursing, kicking the white ball into a tree, ignoring the cries of the offended players as he stumbled on. There were canvas chairs dotted across the lawns. He headed for one set in the shade of a chestnut tree and fell into it. The chair creaked under his 240 pounds, but it supported him. He closed his eyes.

At first thoughts of Deirdre tried to force their way to the top of his mind, but he fought against them. For months he had been running after her and, having found her today, where could he run to now?

The park was quiet. His chair was only a few hundred yards from the street, yet traffic noises were almost non-existent. Gradually one of his favorite memory sequences came back to him. He was standing on the pitcher's mound at the old Atwater Baseball Park in Montreal, wearing his Verdun Shamrocks uniform. There were several thousand people in the stands and they were making lots of noise, but all Milligan's concentration was focused on the batter. The Shamrocks were one run ahead in the ninth inning and there was a man on third base, not through any fault of Milligan's but because the third baseman had made a throwing error after fielding a routine ground ball.

There were two strikes on the batter, both blazing fastballs Milligan had thrown across the center of the plate. The catcher was signaling now for a low, outside pitch, but Milligan shook off the sign. He would do it his way. He would reach back for something even faster and challenge the man right down the middle of the strike zone.

He had pitched nine innings, but he wasn't tired. Milligan was 20 years old and too good for this league. He knew it, the major-league scouts knew it. The people in the stands knew it, too; they wouldn't have Marty Milligan to cheer for much longer. They would have to read about him in the newspapers.

His windup felt good, perfectly balanced, his cleated left shoe raised high in the air, the ball in his right hand almost touching the ground behind him. The throwing motion was all fluid coordination ending in a long striding follow-through, his eyes on the ball as it streaked toward the catcher's mitt. The batter swung hard, but he was late. Strike three, the game was over!

Milligan strode from the mound to the dugout, head down, glove dangling in his left hand. As he crossed the third-base line, he raised his head to the applauding stands and gave the peak of his cap a slight lift . . .

He opened his eyes into blazing sunlight. The shady area had fallen away onto the grass on the other side of the tree and his face was burning, his shirt sweat-soaked under his linen suit. He stood up, took off his jacket, and went looking for a drink.

Milligan found a pub on the Bayswater Road. The patio out front was full to standing and there were bodies lined up at the bar inside. He managed to reach across heads with a one-pound note in his hand and get a pint of draught Guinness which he carried to an empty space on the wall where he leaned and drank heavily. The pint went down easily and he went back for another.

Accustomed to the layout of the pub by this time, he noticed a doorway leading to a small back room. He took his beer through and saw an empty chair in the corner. Trying to get past a crowded table, he stepped on some feet. A blonde-haired girl in an expensively cut blue denim jacket drew her legs in, picked up her drink, and showed Milligan her straight, narrow back.

"Excuse me," he said.

She was listening to the conversation of a well-groomed man across the table. His face was deeply tanned, setting off the color of narrow green eyes. His mouth was narrow, too—almost unpleasantly thin—but as he spoke, he smiled and his face lit up with magnetic enthusiasm.

Milligan squeezed into the chair in the corner, taking a long pull at the mug of beer and watching the tanned man's animated face over the blonde girl's shoulder. Her hair was short and almost white, like cornsilk. Her companion leaned forward and tapped her on the shoulder. She turned; her eyes were hidden behind large dark sunglasses. Her lips were smiling at what the man across the table had been telling her.

"I said excuse me," Milligan said. His voice was loud in the tiny room.

"That's all right. Forget it."

Milligan sat back and wondered why he didn't want to forget it. He had stepped on her feet and she had said it was all right, but forgetting it seemed a lot to ask. He also wondered how he would be able to squeeze back out in a few minutes to get another beer. This one was going down rapidly.

He liked the English pub system of having no waiters, everybody getting their own drinks at the bar. It might make sense to put in a room like that at his restaurant back in Montreal. But right now it was a hazard for him to get another beer. Somebody would grab the seat the moment he left it.

As he finished his beer, Milligan assessed the table in front of him. Besides the girl and the slender sun-bronzed playboy who was dressed in expensive clothes, there were two other men at the table. One was built like a fire hydrant, squat and round in strained slacks and a black turtleneck sweater. His curly hair was greasy and his face was red and coated with sweat. He looked as if he had been holding his breath for an hour.

The other was more a boy than a man, probably no older than 18. His hair was the same color as the girl's, silky blond, and it hung straight down almost to his shoulders. Milligan guessed they could be brother and sister. He drained his glass mug and stood up, leaning over the girl and putting his face close to her cheek.

"I'm going to get another beer," he said.

She kept her face pointed across the table at the sleek playboy who turned his smile on Milligan. "Good luck," she said.

"Would you see that nobody takes my chair?"

The playboy said, "Don't worry about it. We'll take care of it for you." His voice was New York American.

Milligan went to the bar, stopping to visit the men's room on the way. When he returned with a fresh pint, he found the young blond boy sitting in the single chair. As he approached, the boy got up, grinning. "It seemed like the easiest way to protect it. Saved telling everybody the same story." Another American voice, not New York but clearly East Coast.

"Thanks a lot," Milligan said. He sat down, noticing as the boy shifted back to the table that one of his shoes had a thick built-up sole and heel.

The playboy was saying, "I want you to listen to me, Vera. We must get out of that hotel. I hate it."

The girl said, "We just checked in."

"There's no better time to check out."

The toad in the turtleneck sweater said, "You're kidding. Find another hotel room? In London? In July?" At last an English accent; the girl's speech was East Coast like her brother's.

The boy said, "You should have told Dad you were coming. I put through a call to New York this morning. He hasn't heard from you in six months, Vera."

"My father can go take a flying front one-and-a-half off the Statue of Liberty."

The boy laughed uncomfortably. "But he could have fixed you up with one of his apartments here."

Milligan's mind began to wander. He thought of his restaurant back in Montreal, wondered how it was making out without him, and told himself it was probably dying, even at the height of the tourist season. The days were long gone when the presence of Martin Milligan would bring in enough customers to make the restaurant pay. Six months more at this rate and he would lose the place. Then what would he do?

In the old days tourists would come in from all over the United States and Canada to see the young man who had been the most promising pitcher on the New York Mets' roster. There would be smiles, warm handshakes, and respectful questions about the injury that had terminated his career after only two spectacular seasons. Did he think he could ever make a comeback? Was he bothered any longer by the headaches and double vision? They loved recalling that line drive off Hickman's bat that struck him on the forehead like a bazooka shot.

There had been years of such attention with Milligan's Restaurant attracting almost as many pilgrims to Montreal as St. Joseph's Oratory. Then gradually a new generation took over and Milligan's name was no longer an attraction. He could take a taxi right now to Tower Bridge and throw himself into the Thames and he'd never be missed. In fact, he would probably be doing Deirdre and friend a big favor.

No, he would not think of Deirdre now, of the way he used to walk into the dark townhouse on Mountain Street, thinking it empty, feeling tense and lonely. Then he would hear her voice from the kitchen and all the anxiety would drain out of him and he would relax, safe at home.

For once the playboy at the next table was listening while the turtlenecked toad did the talking. His lah-de-dah English voice contradicted his burly appearance. "I know one of the lads in the Parachute Battalion on guard duty in Belfast. He says you can't turn your back without some Catholic taking a shot at you. They've got the kids involved too, throwing acid bombs. Some education for a six-year-old."

Milligan sat up straighter in his chair.

"The only thing to do," Toad went on, "is for the Protestants to show the Catholics the same treatment. Give 'em back two bombs for one. That's the only message they'll understand."

Milligan leaned forward and rapped on the table with one knuckle. All three faces turned his way. He addressed the red sweaty one. "Excuse me. Do you know what the hell you're talking about?"

Toad smiled and the crimson of his face moved one shade closer to black. "This is a private conversation. Keep out of it."

"No, I'm sorry. I am in this conversation and the thing that strikes me is some people might think you're speaking English, but what is coming out of your fat mouth is malarky."

Playboy began to say, "Now, Tony, it would be better if—"

Tony stood up and so did Milligan. "There's a space just outside," Tony said. "We can settle this without troubling anybody else."

Milligan kept his eyes on Tony's muscular body as he followed him into the alley. The toad looked solid and he walked with a lot of confidence—not a man to be taken lightly.

They entered a small paved courtyard behind the pub. Turning around, Tony began to say, "This should be—" and Milligan hit him as hard as he could right below the heart. The man's eyes widened and his mouth hung slack. Milligan drew back again and drove his right fist through the man's fat nose, thinking of the back of his head as he did it.

Tony took two short steps back against the brick wall and began to sag at the knees, blood pouring from his smashed nose over his chin and onto the black sweater. He raised his right fist and threw a round-house punch which Milligan avoided easily.

Then, drawing back his right shoe, Milligan kicked Tony's shins as hard as he could, one after the other. As he bent forward, Milligan brought up his knee, closing the man's left eye and snapping his head back.

Milligan felt a hand on his arm. Playboy had come out into the yard. "That's enough. You've done enough," he said.

"Get back," Milligan said. He turned to Tony who was bending over a dustbin and hit him on the side of the head with the heel of his hand. Tony fell, knocking the dustbin over, and Milligan stomped on his extended ankle.

"Cut it out! That's it! That's all!" The playboy's eyes were green balls on white saucers in his golden face. "He's hurt enough."

"I don't want him following me."

"He won't follow you. Go back inside. I'll get him out of here."

Milligan watched as the playboy knelt beside his friend. He heard Tony say, "Never gave me a chance, the scum."

Milligan bent close. He said, "I wanted to kill you, but your friend stopped me."

"Go on inside," playboy said, "and send out Lester, the young lad. Will you do that?"

"Sure." Milligan headed for the open doorway.

"And will you do me a favor? Stick around until I come in? I want to talk to you."

"Are you getting rid of him?"

"Yes, he's going home. It's a long way, but he's going."

"Okay. I'll see you inside."

Milligan went into the pub and told Lester to report to the back yard. The boy left the room taking uneven steps on the built-up boot at the end of his left leg.

Milligan sat down at the table. The blonde girl said nothing. She sat facing him but the dark sunglasses were opaque; she might have been observing him or she might have been looking over his shoulder.

"Your boy friend asked me to wait for him."

"Fine."

"Sorry to bust up your party."

"Tony Ackland is no particular friend of mine." She drank from a small glass that held what looked like gin. Then she said, "For what it's worth, I didn't like what he said about Catholics either."

"Are you one?"

"I'm a Muslim this week. I think next week I may be a Jew."

"You'll never make it. I hear they have tough exams."

"I'll pay somebody."

"You've got lots of money?"

"Enough for now."

Milligan reached across to his former table and retrieved his mug of beer. "Is the guy with the tan your husband?"

"Normie? Lord, no. He's just one of my habits."

"You make it sound like you've got lots of habits."

"I've tried them all. Know any new ones?"

"I used to, but I forget."

"All you need is somebody to jog your memory."

"That could take time. I've got a bad case of amnesia."

"If you get lucky, it only takes a minute." She took off the dark glasses and Milligan saw her eyes for the first time. They surprised him. They were younger eyes than he had expected to see—gray-blue, and cold as slate.

The playboy was back. "Hey, good. I see you two have gotten to know each other. I'm Norman Quast. What's your name, slugger?"

"Martin Milligan."

They shook hands. The girl said, "I'm Vera Logan," and he took her hand, too. It felt hard and small, and polished.

Quast sat down and the table seemed to adjust itself to his presence. The world always pointed his way. "Okay. What's with you, Milligan? Do you always go around trying to kill guys who say something you don't like?"

"This is my bad day."

"Vera, you should have seen what he did to Ackland. He destroyed him. If I hadn't gone out there we would have had one dead body on our hands."

"Where's Lester?" the girl asked.

"Taking Tony home in a taxi. The guy can hardly move."

"Should Lester be alone with him?"

"Why not? Tony can't tell him anything. He didn't even know what he was supposed to do yet."

"But we were counting on him."

"Never mind."

"We can't do it a man short."

"We'll find somebody else. Somebody better."

Milligan said, "If you folks don't mind, I'm going to get some food."

"Wait," Quast said. "Hang in for just a minute while I ask you something. I work on hunch, and if there's one thing I am it's a good judge of character. I've been watching you since you came in here. I spotted you for a winner as soon as you walked across the room. And after seeing how you wiped out Ackland, I know I was right. Tell me something, are you all hung up with responsibilities right now?"

"Not really."

"Are you free to disappear from London for a while and pick up $50,000 for a few days' work?"

Vera said in a warning tone, "Norman—"

"It's all right, sweetie. This guy feels beautiful to me. Yes, Martin Milligan feels exactly right."

"Tony Ackland felt right."

"Listen, Martin. I want to put a proposition to you. It's dangerous, I won't kid you about that. But it's a chance to put a little adventure in your life. And I have a hunch you're a man who could stand a little adventure in his life. Let's go somewhere quiet and have dinner and we'll talk about it. What do you say?"

Quast's eager face was suspended over the table, close to Milligan's. Vera turned away and shook her head slowly.

"You know what I say?" Milligan said. "I say I think my hand is busted."

Norman Quast charmed the whole dining room at dinner, waiters and customers alike. All Milligan could do was eat left-handed, his bandaged right hand throbbing on his lap, and stare at his host balefully through an alcoholic haze. They probably didn't realize how drunk he was; most people didn't because he could pour a lot of liquor into the large Irish head that thrust up like a fence post from his size-17 shirt collar, a cylinder of ruddy flesh and bone capped by a mass of thick black hair salted with gray.

"This remind you of anything?" Quast asked Vera after he had sent the wine steward strutting away, radiant with Quast's praise of the mediocre Reisling he had brought them.

Vera looked around. "The ship," she said.

They were dining aboard Old Caledonia, a converted paddle-wheeler tied up alongside the Victoria Embankment. Big Ben and the Parliament Buildings played the part of a tourist poster outside the window. A hundred yards away a longboat of sailors in training pulled on their oars to make some headway against the Thames current.

"We met aboard Queen Elizabeth II," Quast said to Martin. "How long ago was it, three years?"

Vera's assent was a slow lowering of the eyelids as she ate scampi. Milligan enjoyed that languorous expression. He wanted to see it again. By leaning back in his chair he could observe a few inches of dark nylon where her thigh pressed the edge of the chair. He leaned back frequently.

"I was a clarinet player in one of the ship's orchestras," Quast went on. "And here was this knockout of a blonde tearing up the dance floor every night in the Double Down. It took me till noon on the second day to get a conversation going with her and I don't think we've spent a day apart since then."

"Congratulations," Milligan said. He reached for his wine with the right hand, winced, and started over again with the left.

"You're lucky that's not broken," Quast said. "Still, I'm not belittling the injury. A sprain can hurt like hell."

Milligan had been fascinated watching Quast talk them into and out of St. Mary's Hospital Emergency in less than half an hour. Quast must have been a new experience for socialized medicine.

Vera said, "He says he was just a clarinet player but you should have heard him play. Do you like jazz?"

Milligan nodded. It was one of his beefs about Montreal, which was an okay town in most respects but was light on good jazz clubs. Years ago when he was in the Mets organization, he used to stand up at bars in Manhattan and drink a lot of beer listening to people like Cozy Cole and Sol Yaged. Now there was a clarinet player—Yaged.

"Normie used to be one of the top studio players in New York."

"Let's not open up that little chapter, sweetie," Quast said. He smiled openly at Milligan as if he was about to tell of a trophy he had won for attendance at Sunday School. "A little trouble with the musicians' union. I was producing commercial music tracks for the ad agencies and that was great until I started keeping all the money they paid me. Not paying the sidemen. That's a no-no."

Vera waved her finger like a bored schoolteacher. "You're a bad boy, Norman Quast," she said, and Milligan realized she was as drunk as he was.

"Well, what the hell," Quast said. "If they hadn't busted me I wouldn't have ended up on the QE2, and I'd never have met Vera Logan."

"And neither of us would have met Martin Milligan."

"Good girl. Precisely the point." Quast emptied the wine bottle into their glasses and signaled with the bottle for another. "It's explanation time."

"Explain me the $50,000 for a few days' work. That's what got me out here—I'm afraid of ships." Milligan glanced past Vera's shoulder at his reassuring view of the gangplank connecting the Old Caledonia with the riverbank. He could not imagine himself ever taking a sea voyage the way these two had. To be in mid-Atlantic, even in a floating hotel like their luxury liner, and unable to get off would drive him crazy. He was terribly claustrophobic. The only way Milligan could endure an airplane trip was by deadening himself beforehand with booze.

Quast laughed. "It's so easy you can start spending the money tomorrow."

"I'm surrounded by hands waiting for cash." Milligan was almost afraid to get his hopes up. If there was only some way he could find enough money to keep the restaurant going, then it followed that he could sponsor the ball team again next season. Which meant lots more of those great evenings at Snowden Park with Lucien Lacoste and Neil Coleman and the rest of the gang, cleaning up the opposition in the Commercial League. Something told him it was pathetic for a grown-up man to depend so heavily for his happiness on an amateur ball team. But something else told him why the hell not, what else was there?

"Have you ever heard of a man named Castle Logan?" Quast asked him.

"Anybody who's been around New York knows of Castle Logan. Does he still lead the big dance band?"

Vera lowered her eyelids again. "He not only leads that one, he farms out dozens of bands under his name. Half the parties in New York on any given night have Castle Logan bands providing the music." She sucked a tooth that produced a boorish snap. "Dear old Dad always knew how to make money."

"You're the same Logan?"

"She's the same Logan," Quast confirmed, "and so is young Lester, the lad who saved your seat for you back in the pub."

"My fair-haired brother," Vera droned, "the apple of Daddy's eye." She was beginning to sound like a sour old drunk, almost but not quite spoiling for Milligan the erotic effect of those silky legs and the pale sensual eyes.

"Now here's the gig," Quast went on. "We are going to kidnap young Lester. And Castle Logan is going to pay two hundred thousand bucks to get him back."

Milligan felt a slight chill along his hair line. Something made him say, "No blood?"

"Of course no blood. Who wants to hurt anybody?" Quast's tanned face reared back and regarded Milligan with amazement. "And who needs it? Listen. This will be the easiest money any of us ever picked up. All we do is feed the boy a lot of booze at a party at my place. This is no problem—all the Logans drink like fish."

His narrow green eyes darted once in Vera's direction. She didn't miss the remark; her lips, pursing to receive the wine-glass, silently formed on obscene phrase.

"Then we pound in a couple of seconals," Quast went on, "just enough to keep him under. And we take him on a plane. Where? To New York City."

"Daddy will think he's somewhere in London," Vera said. "Lester just phoned him this morning."

"Especially he will think so when he gets in his personal mail a ransom letter, postmarked London, telling him to get the money ready. To be paid to a New York representative who will contact him that day. That would have been Tony Ackland. Now it's you."

"Will he pay?"

"He'll pay," Vera said. "He'll dig into the safety-deposit boxes where he keeps the undeclared loot. For Lester baby, he'd sell his soul."

"And even mortgage his C-Melody saxophone," Quast said. "Can you see how beautiful this is, Martin? He'll be told to keep the police out of it, and he probably will. But even if he calls them in, the cops will start looking in London. But Lester will be in New York. And they'll never suspect me and Vera; we were in California yesterday and we'll be back there as soon as we split the cash. As for you—well, hell, Martin Milligan has nothing to do with anything. No connection whatever."

Something was bothering Milligan. He said, "What happens when Lester wakes up? He remembers he saw you in London. If I were you, I would have stayed out of his sight. Let somebody else get him drunk."

Quast was nodding and smiling as Milligan spoke. "You're fast," he said. "That would have been better. What happened was, this scheme only came to me today, after we ran into Lester unexpectedly. But that's what's good about it. A simple spontaneous action without a lot of complicated planning to go wrong. We just do it. We go! No problems."

Milligan couldn't help thinking of the scrub ball games he used to play in, spur of the moment, totally disorganized. But hadn't they been the most fun? He had to laugh. "It's a game," he said.

"A game. Right. For big stakes."

"But what about when Lester wakes up and blows the whistle?"

"He won't blow any whistle. He'll be so doped he won't remember a thing. So he says he saw us in London, big deal. I'm here on business, then I'm back in L.A. Go prove something."

Milligan was starting to enjoy himself for the first time in weeks. He said, "You're crazy, Quast. You know that, huh?"

"Totally insane," Quast agreed. "The mad impresario. Quast Productions presents *The Snatching of Lester Logan*. Starring a host of brilliant performers including Martin Milligan, the voice on the telephone, the innocent Lester Logan, the not-so-innocent sister Vera, with a special guest appearance by the one and only Castle Logan and his Dancing Dollars. Everything under the direction of the boy genius Norman Quast whose credits include writing, casting, directing, and pulling all the strings." He turned to the others in the restaurant and raised his voice and his arms. "Let's hear it for the Boy Genius!"

The dining room echoed with enthusiastic applause from waiters, maitre d', and customers. Milligan was grinning and shaking his head as the three of them trooped out after Quast left a generous tip on the table. These nutty people cheering and clapping, he thought. They don't even know what they're doing, they just go ahead and do it. The whole world's crazy!

Back in Quast's and Vera's hotel room, time fell apart for Milligan. Whenever his wrist watch happened to pass in front of his eyes, he would notice that 45 minutes had been cranked out, or an hour and a half. They seemed to have killed a couple of large bottles of gin and suddenly it was past midnight and Quast had sent a room-service boy to the kitchen for milk and vanilla and God-knows-what-else and he was now busy adding crushed ice to the mixture in a cocktail shaker.

"Ramos gin fizz," he said. "The way they make 'em in New Orleans. Wait till you taste this."

Milligan tasted it. It was very easy drinking, something like a vanilla milk shake with a kick. He raised his socked feet onto the arm of the sofa on which he had been stretched out for some time. He smiled into the glass. This was the night he had dreaded facing alone. Why? Life was exciting; you lost people, you stayed loose, you met other people.

Vera Logan had changed into a loose one-piece garment of sheer pale-blue nylon which gripped at the neck and wrists and ankles. When she raised her arms she was the shape of a floating manta ray, and when she passed in front of a light, her naked body moved inside a glowing, transparent tent.

She came now and took Milligan's glass from his hand and pulled him to his feet. He was a foot and a half taller than she was. When he put his arms around her and picked her up and kissed her, she was a long way off the ground.

"Carry me around that corner," she said.

As Milligan carried her to the short section of the L-shaped room and lowered her onto the bed, Quast said from the radio set where he had been working the tuner, "A little *nachtmusik*. This cat is playing good records. The next hour is going to be all John Coltrane."

Then Milligan's mind was washed in waves of harsh sound as the tenor saxophone player blew lines of angry notes that wound up and down and into areas where no musician had penetrated before.

Vera's body smelled of cinnamon and they were both wet with perspiration in this room that had never known air conditioning. Eventually Milligan must have passed out because when he rolled over, he saw Quast and Vera beside him. He watched them with dull eyes and saw Quast grinning like a Cheshire cat.

Later, with his eyes closed, he came out of a half dream to smell pungent cigarette smoke and hear Quast talking about food. "And that shrimp *rémoulade*," he was saying, "do you remember that? Man, the way they eat down there." He sighed. "I'm telling you, if I ever run away, look for me in New Orleans. In the Vieux Carré, eating sea food."

"Shut up your big yap," Vera said.

"What shut up?" Quast rumbled. "He's out like a light."

And suddenly Milligan was.

They were both up and dressed when Milligan awoke. He heard

them around the corner in the other part of the room, talking
quietly over the clink of plates and cutlery. He could smell toast
and coffee, and Milligan was reminded with a flash of anguish of
mornings when as a boy he had lain awake in bed listening to his
mother and father talking in the kitchen outside the tiny room
where he slept in the same bed with his young brother Mike.
Soon through the window he would hear the clang against the
iron pole and he and Mike would be up and into their shorts and
running shoes and off to the East Hill playgrounds for another
day in the endless summer of horseshoes and baseball, and if it
rained, everybody would jam into the old wooden pavilion with
the sides down letting in the wet green smell while somebody
hammered *Chopsticks* on the almost toothless piano.

Guilt flooded through him as he recalled last night. Then the
image of Deirdre and her doctor friend arose in his mind—Deirdre
at last with child after ten years of a marriage which Milligan
had managed to convince himself was okay. Not a great marriage,
but okay.

"God, what is happening to me?" Milligan whispered. It was
not a rhetorical question. "Help me, God, please." His lips fluttered over the words, "I'm not a wicked man. But I'm feeling
worse every day and I don't know what's happening to my life.
Help me out of this, and forgive me all my sins."

Vera's voice came brightly from her head thrust around the
corner. "I thought I heard you muttering away in there." She
looked brushed and scrubbed. "Wakey, wakey, rise and shine!"
She snapped a mouthful from the slice of crisp toast she was holding and disappeared.

Dressed and shaved, Milligan felt scarcely better, but he was
able to eat and listen to Quast's new idea.

"Came to me in the middle of the night," he said, "like the voice
of an angel. We don't take Lester to New York. Not now that we
have a new partner. We fly him to Montreal where we bed him
down and stay with him, Vera and I, in your place while you fly
to New York and pick up the money. Montreal is even better.
There's nothing to connect Lester with Montreal."

Quast was watching Milligan like a father staring at his new
baby. "Now all I need is for you to tell me your place is full of
wife and kids."

"No," Milligan said. "I live alone."

Quast turned to Vera and they slapped flat hands the way football players do when a pass is completed. "What did I tell you?" he chortled. "This enterprise is now enchanted. Milligan has brought us new luck."

They sat separately on the plane. Not having been a part of the afternoon's preparation of Lester Logan during which the boy was made drunk and later fed the seconal, Milligan was surprised to see the way he was delivered to the plane.

Had it not been for the club-foot, Milligan would not have recognized him. Gone was the slim, blond-haired youth in student garb of jeans and T-shirt. He came aboard the plane supported like an invalid by Quast and Vera, and dressed in a feminine pant-suit with a smooth black wig covering his own hair and with an expert touch of makeup on cheeks and lips.

There was an empty seat beside Milligan. Halfway across the Atlantic, Quast came and sat in it. He was smoking a thin elegant cigar and there was an exuberant puff to his cheeks. He looked closely at Milligan, who was fighting his fear of airplanes.

"Are you okay?"

"I'll make it." Sometimes Milligan wondered if he would have been able to hack all the jet travel that pro baseball players face. Maybe the hit on the head was a blessing in disguise; it got him out of baseball and back on the ground. He remembered reading about how one of his favorite pitchers years ago, Don Newcombe, had tried hypnotism to cure his fear of flying. Milligan did not believe in hypnotism. He felt God gave people these fears for a reason. But in his own case he did not want to know the reason.

To get off the subject he said, "Why the Halloween costume on the kid?"

Quast beamed. "My latest idea. Those are Vera's things, the wig and the suit. Nobody will remember seeing Lester Logan leave London."

Milligan looked at Quast. "But he's traveling on a passport, isn't he? It has his picture glued on it. How did you get him on the plane?"

"Easy. I told them my friend is a little queer. He likes to dress up in girls' clothes and get drunk."

Milligan couldn't believe this. "That's insane. You couldn't have made yourself more memorable." Doubt welled up in him like spring water, near freezing. "I want out of this game."

"Relax," Quast said. "Don't be so uptight. Remember, this is all in the family—Vera, Lester, the old man. He's got the dough, he'll

fork it over. It's like getting a loan you don't have to pay back."
Quast became serious. "Hell, it's Vera's money anyway, she's the
oldest. He should give her a lot more than he does. Stop worrying
and leave all the details to me."

Milligan said, "You're so bush league I can't believe it." But
once again, bathing in the radiance of Quast's enthusiasm, he was
beginning to feel reassured. Half in jest he said, "I bet you even
forgot to mail the letter to Castle Logan."

Quast winked and screwed a finger into Milligan's chest. It
hurt. "You lose," he said. "I mailed it yesterday. That was the
first thing Vera and I did after I got the idea to hose her old man.
We took out the old scissors and glue pot and a copy of the London *Times.*"

When Quast went back to his seat, Milligan made himself sleep
for the remainder of the flight, a trick he had learned during his
baseball days when he was traveling so much of the time. It was
more a state of semiconsciousness than proper sleep and Milligan
paid a price for it because his mind was free to roll on and feed
him all sorts of material he would have screened out if he were
awake. They were like dreams, these sessions, except they went
on for a long time and their substance was horribly close to reality.

In this trance Deirdre sat with her doctor lover, kissing him
and talking seriously about the importance of children in making
sense out of a marriage. Then she went away and came back leading their new son who walked with a limp because he had a club-
foot. The scene broadened and they were all sitting in Milligan's
Restaurant having a meal during which the doctor pushed away
his plate and said he wouldn't eat in this place. He then
apologized to Milligan who said humbly, "That's all right," after
which Deirdre said not to worry because the restaurant was being
closed anyway for lack of funds.

Milligan came fully awake just as Norman Quast was saying he
would buy the place and turn it into a jazz club featuring himself
on C-Melody saxophone and Vera Logan performing pantomimes
with her father, the unforgettable Castle Logan, star of stage,
screen, and gas chamber.

They took a taxi from Dorval all the way to Milligan's townhouse on Mountain Street. Lester Logan slept on Quast's shoulder, breathing in a slow even pattern. Noticing a wisp of blonde
hair at the edge of the black wig, Vera frowned and tucked it in

with a fierce stab of her finger. Milligan could see a white line on the boy's forehead where his sister's fingernail made its mark.

"What did you give him?" Milligan muttered, still floating close to sleep. "He's out cold."

Quast sidestepped the question. "Having a much-needed rest," he said.

While Quast paid off the cab driver, Milligan gave Vera the key and sent her ahead to open the door while he got his arms under Lester and carried him up the walk. The boy's cheek rolled against Milligan, smelling of Vera's makeup. He could hear Quast's voice inside the taxi explaining that his girl friend had drunk too much on the plane.

They tucked Lester in bed, fully dressed. Milligan began to make coffee, and Quast went into the bathroom to shave. Vera sat on a kitchen chair and smoked cigarettes.

"What's with you, O silent one?" she said after awhile.

"I'm all right," Milligan said.

"No, you're not," she said. "You hate this whole caper. Kidnaping is against the law and you're a law-abiding citizen."

"I need the money," he said. "I'm in. Don't worry about me."

She accepted a cup of coffee and a shortbread biscuit from the package he opened, apologizing for the fact there was nothing else to eat in the house.

"What are you, Milligan? What do you do?"

"Are you a baseball fan?"

"I could never get interested. My father used to go all the time."

Milligan thought about that. "I used to be a professional baseball player. Until I got hurt."

"I thought only football players got hurt."

"It was an unusual accident. Now I run a restaurant."

She was watching him. "In London I figured you for a drifter. You came on like one in the pub. Now the closer I get to you, the straighter you look."

"Maybe I'm practising to be a drifter," he said.

"I don't think you'll ever make it," she said.

Quast stuck his head in from the bathroom and said, "Where do you keep your after-shave?"

For no particular reason Milligan said, "I drank it." It was in his suitcase, but he didn't feel just then like doing Quast any favors. The men looked at each other in silence and for the first time in two days Quast did not smile.

Vera said, "Use some of my cologne. It's in my shoulder bag on the sofa by the front door."

Quast went away, muttering, "Hell, just a little after-shave."

"What's the matter with him?" Milligan asked.

"He's tired and nervous," Vera said. "We all are."

"Except Lester. He's sleeping like a baby."

Vera dunked her shortbread in the coffee. "You know something, baseball player?" she said. "With you and my brother it was love at first sight. I've heard about you big masculine athletes. He looks nice in drag, doesn't he?"

"You're one sick woman," Milligan said.

"The truth hurts, doesn't it?" Vera said. "You and my father will get along fine. He loves Lester, too. When I was nine years old and my mother put her head in the gas oven, do you know what my father said to me? He said, 'We've got to find some way to tell Lester without hurting him.'" She pushed the coffee aside. "Haven't you got any booze?"

"Just beer." Milligan opened a couple of cans and set one in front of her.

Quast came in and took Vera's can of beer before she could touch it. "Are you still here?" he said to Milligan. "I thought you were on your way to New York."

Vera said, "Norman, I don't think you should drink that beer. You're starting to sound funny."

Quast swallowed half the can, a couple of nicks showing red on his freshly shaved throat as it worked at downing the beer. "Big man with the fists," he said, turning his back on Milligan, taking a few testy steps around the kitchen. "A little after-shave is all I asked for."

"Have you taken your pill?" Vera said. "If you have, you shouldn't drink any more."

"What do you want?" Milligan said. "Shall we call it off?"

"You'd like that," Quast sneered. "Give you a chance to chicken out."

"Both of you stop it," Vera said. "We've brought Lester here, now all we have to do is go and get the money. Let's not start acting stupid."

When Quast finally quit sulking and explained the New York end of the plan to Milligan, it sounded simple enough. Even if it had sounded tough, Milligan would have gone through with it. Vera was right, he hated the whole thing. But he had come this far, and he needed that fifty grand. According to Quast, the ransom letter was frightening enough to make Castle Logan eager to pay. Vera confirmed that her father would not take any risk whatever where Lester's safety was at stake. And she knew for a fact that he always had that kind of cash available.

"It's as easy as taking the collection in church," Quast ended, the up phase of his personality suddenly taking over again from the down. "Go with confidence, come back with cash. While you're away I'll rent a car. Once we split the loot, Vera and I vanish to California. You take the car and drive Lester to Toronto where you check into any motel. Then you grab a cab to the airport, leaving the kid to wake up and wonder how in hell he got there."

"Lester won't wonder for long," Vera said. "He'll hurry home and Daddy will just be glad he's safe and sound."

"And Logan will never call the police," Quast said, "because he'd have to explain where he got all that undeclared cash."

Milligan walked from the townhouse to the Sheraton Mt. Royal Hotel to catch the limousine back to the airport. Quast, he knew, would have sprung for another eight-dollar cab ride, but this was not Milligan's way. Yet he was perfectly willing to go into the Sunset Bar on the way and set himself up a couple of double Scotches.

He was on his way out again and turning the corner at Maisonneuve and Peel when he ran into Lucien Lacoste, broadly handsome in his blue constable's uniform, his thick mustache a smooth bar of gleaming black above his slightly arrogant smile.

"Hey, Marty, where have you been? I asked for you in the restaurant, they said they thought you were in Europe."

"Just like Montreal cops," Milligan said. "Always around when you don't need them."

Lacoste studied Milligan's face. "Man, you look bad. Big Marty is not in shape."

"I just got back from England. I heard Deirdre was over there."

"Did you find her?"

"Yeah."

The men stood facing each other but a little off center, looking over each other's shoulder at traffic. A light changed and the normal minimum throb of downtown Montreal shifted up a few notches to a frantic roar. Motorcycles, taxis, buses, sports cars charged past the policeman and his friend.

"You were good last game for the first seven innings," Lacoste said. "We should have won."

"Damn right we should have won. Those were two sweet double plays you turned in the second inning and the fifth."

"Should have had another one in the ninth, if Neil doesn't drop the ball."

"Neil has got to practise his glove work," Milligan said. "Work with him, will you, Lucie? Show him how to use the glove."

"Sure." The policeman looked at his watch and said, as if the team schedule was listed there, "I guess we can't win it this year, after losing that one."

"Wait till next year," Milligan said.

Lacoste's face brightened. "Are we sticking together next year? Somebody said there'd be no team."

Milligan put both hands on Lacoste's shoulders and straightened him like a piece of furniture. "Wait till next year," he repeated.

In a way it was like going home for Milligan to fly to New York. On the bus ride from the airport he thought of all the people he could call up if he had the time. Dooner would be glad to hear from him; he had lived at Dooner's house years ago when he was trying to stick with the Mets and it was not yet certain he would make it. Or he could call Max Lowenstein, the art director from the ad agency who took the trouble to telephone Milligan the night after his first appearance in a league game when the Phillies had hit everything he threw and made a real fool of this young Canadian stepping up to the majors with all the glowing press reports behind him. A raucous voice in the stands had yelled, "Go back to Montreal, your arm is still frozen!"—and everybody had laughed at the stupid remark.

After that Milligan felt like a failure and the Met players were letting him alone, wondering if he had the moral fiber to hang in and help the team. Then this stranger called and asked him to come and see where the good jazz was, since he was going to be around New York for a long time and might as well find the right spots.

Milligan and Max Lowenstein had got pleasantly drunk together many times over the next couple of years. And Milligan had gone out once to hang around a film studio in Princeton to watch Max supervise the filming of the title sequence for a TV detective series the agency was behind. He remembered when the actor featured in the filming was asked to take off his shoes before walking on the painted cyclorama, and he had an embarrassing hole in the toe of one sock.

But there was no time on this in-and-out trip to call Donner or Max or anyone except Castle Logan. And let's hope he has the money ready, Milligan told himself, because I am sure not equipped to hang around in this kind of a situation.

Castle Logan did have the money. As directed in Quast's letter, he was standing by. As Vera had predicted, he was eager to pay.

"Cash?" Milligan asked. "In small bills?" He was calling from a pay phone in the lobby of the Roosevelt Hotel.

"Yes. I've done exactly as you said. Where is my son?" Logan's voice sounded angry with offense, like that of a housewife whose grocery delivery is one item short. "I telephoned London and there's no answer."

"Of course there's no answer. We have him."

"Is he all right? How do I know he's safe?"

Following Quast's instructions, Milligan said, "You have no choice, Mr. Logan. You have to take our word. If you hedge, you'll never see your son again. But if you play it straight, believe me he's all right and you'll have him back soon."

"Why should I believe you?"

"You have no choice."

It was ridiculously simple, as Quast and Vera had promised. They knew their man. Logan was to walk into the street with the cash in a suitcase where he would flag a taxi and proceed to a specifed intersection, to arrive there precisely in fifteen minutes, at which time the telephone in the booth on the corner would ring. Logan was to answer that phone while the taxi waited.

This was done and Milligan was able to give Logan the other half of his instructions. He was to get back into the taxi and give the driver the address of an apartment building on East 60th Street. When they reached that address, Logan was to get out without paying the driver and, leaving the suitcase of money on the floor of the cab and the back door of the taxi open, he was to run into the apartment building without looking back.

This unlikely procedure took place too, and Milligan was able to step into the abandoned taxi, slam the door, and say to the outraged driver, "It's okay, that's my crazy Uncle Joe. I'll take care of the meter. Drive me to Kennedy."

There were no police cars following as the cab took off for the airport, although Milligan half expected there would be. And there was real money when he opened the suitcase although he half expected to find torn-up pieces of newspaper. It was bizarre. $200,000 for doing almost nothing.

At the airport he called Quast as they had agreed he would.

"All done. I'm ready to fly out."

He heard Quast's excited aside to Vera, the voice of a child at a magic show. "He's got it!" Then back into the phone, "Is it all there?"

"I haven't counted it, but it looks like one hell of a lot of tens."

"Okay, now here's what you do. Check the bag at the counter—"

"Check it?"

"That's right. People check luggage every day and they always get it back. Then put the check in an envelope, seal it, write my name on it, and leave it with the girl at the Pan Am counter."

"You mean I come back and the money stays here?"

"Unless you want to try coming through Canadian Customs and Immigration with two hundred thousand bucks in a suitcase."

Milligan said, "When do I get my share?"

"As soon as you get here. I've got your $50,000 waiting for you."

Milligan stood for nearly half a minute watching a 707 take off. Quast's voice in the earpiece was saying, "Marty? Hello? Martin Milligan?"

Finally Milligan said, "Have I got any choice?"

Quast's laugh was shrill with delight. "Sure you have. You can take the whole boodle and get on one of those planes I hear taking off and head for Tahiti."

"That ain't my style, said Casey."

Quast picked it up without missing a beat. "Strike one, the umpire said. Listen, sweetheart, I trusted you, now you trust me. Come home, baby, all is well. We have made a killing."

Milligan felt inclined to make one more phone call, although it was not in the script. "Mr. Logan?" he said.

"Is that you? Where's my son? You've got your money, when do I see my boy?"

"I just wanted to reassure you that everything is okay. I've been in touch with my associates"—Milligan almost said in Montreal, but checked himself— "in London. They'll release Lester soon and you'll be hearing from him."

"I hope so. If you've harmed one hair of that boy's head, I'll spend every cent I've got to find you."

"Mr. Logan, you've been straight with us, and I want to be straight with you. There was never any intention of harming Lester. I'm sure we've caused you a lot of anguish and I want to apologize."

"Go to hell," Castle Logan said. "I don't want your apologies, I want my son."

On the flight back to Montreal, Milligan promised himself not to get into another airplane for a long time. During the brief hour in the air he closed his eyes and thought about Lucien Lacoste's double plays.

Lucie was one sweet shortstop. Milligan had only seen him play in softball games but over quarts of beer in the tavern afterward, as they sat around with the sweat drying on their jerseys, Lucien said that he was on the verge years ago of signing a contract with the St. Louis Cardinals. Milligan could believe this because U.S. scouts were always beating the bushes in French Canada, hoping to turn up another Claude Raymond.

"What happened?" he asked.

Lacoste's eyes flickered. "My father wanted me to stay with the classics course at Jean de Brébeuf College, where I was. I was smart once, eh? You din' know that." Under the influence of the beer Lucien's careful English had deteriorated. "So what happens? I get a girl pregnant, a nice Catholic girl. I leave school to get married, we raise lots of babies, I become a cop. My family is happy, Monique's family is happy. The Church is happy. Everybody is happy."

"Except the Cardinals," Milligan said. "They missed out on a Golden Glove shortstop."

Lucien Lacoste studied the beer in his glass. "You were up there, Marty. You think I could have made it in the big league?"

"Hell, yes. You could have made it."

They had ended up looking through the pictures in Lacoste's wallet—a bunch of sturdy kids with their arms around Dad's neck, and Milligan had to cough and blame the smoke in the tavern to cover up the tears in his eyes ...

The airplane landed at Dorval and for the second time in twelve hours Milligan rode in a taxi to the townhouse on Mountain Street. He let himself in with his key and knew instantly that something was wrong.

Vera's bag was not on the sofa. One of her used tissues lay crumpled on the coffee table. Apart from that—nothing. There is a feeling about an empty place, and this was it.

Milligan checked the kitchen—a few more empty beer cans, a full ashtray. He went to the bedroom door and stood outside it, feeling the same rising pounding in his chest he used to feel in the bullpen when the starting pitcher was dying out there and he knew he would be called in.

"Quast?" he called. "Vera?"

A terrible sense of trouble came over him, a genuine premonition of doom. He told himself he hoped it was all a hoax, that he was the victim along with Castle Logan. He wished as hard as he had ever wished for anything that when he opened the door he would find the room empty—that the boy Lester had been an accomplice in the trick and was now up and gone and laughing in New York, sharing the money with his sister and her boy friend.

He opened the door.

In the shadows he could see the shape on the bed. He walked into the room. It felt cold.

"Lester?"

He leaned over the boy and looked for a sign of life. There was none because the boy was dead, peacefully dead in a black wig and dried lipstick.

The telephone rang.

"Hello?"

Quast's voice came on brisk and cheerful. "Hey, baby, we're right on schedule. We must have passed each other in the air somewhere over Albany."

"He's dead, Quast. What happened?"

Quast put on a Maxwell Smart voice. "Sorry about that, Chief." Then he said, "We had to give him something extra to make sure he wouldn't wake up. He'd be an awful pain in the neck talking about us to the police.

"But what about me?"

"I suggest you get rid of Lester as quickly and as quietly as you can. Unless *you* want to talk to the police. But I don't think you're in a very good position to do that."

Milligan said quietly, "I'm not getting my money either, am I?"

Quast's laugh was exuberant. "That's the first really smart thing I've heard you say. Now, listen. Vera and I have to run. Not to California, that was also a lie. We don't stay in California. And there's no use trying to trace me. Quast is not my real name."

"Listen," Milligan said, "this is crazy. The whole operation has been insane right from the start. Just what am I supposed to do?"

The voice on the phone sounded genuinely concerned. "Martin," it said, "there are quite a few pills left in the bottle in the drawer. Why don't you swallow them and lie down there beside Lester?"

The disconnected phone buzzed in Milligan's ear for ten seconds before he put down the receiver.

There was one beer left in the refrigerator and he drank it as he thought about what to do. He was surprised to find that he did not feel frightened. The undercurrent of anxiety which had been trickling through him seemed to have been shut off.

He had to go back into the bedroom to get the suitcase that had been with him to London and back. Some of his dirty laundry was still in it. He threw these things into the wicker hamper beside the bureau, then repacked the bag with fresh shirts, underwear, socks, and a couple of pairs of slacks from the wardrobe. He worked with the light turned off and managed to get through it by telling himself the boy on the bed was asleep.

Back in the living room he checked his wallet for cash. He had been traveling the last couple of days on Quast's money and there was still a hundred of that left plus his credit cards. He could get where he wanted to go. And when he got there, if his hunch was correct—if his bleary half recollection from that distressed London morning was not a dream—then it would be Quast's turn to be surprised.

One last phone call, then one more plane trip. He sat down to dial, every muscle in his body aching with fatigue.

"Hello, is Lucien there?" He waited for Lacoste to come to the phone. "Lucie, it's Marty."

"What's up?"

"Something bad. Now just listen. I want you to come to my place. I won't be here, but I'll leave the door unlocked. In the bedroom you'll find a dead man on the bed."

"Marty, are you drunk?"

"Just listen. Write this down. The dead man is Lester Logan. He's the son of a rich guy in New York. Castle Logan is his name."

"The band leader?"

"That's right. The boy was kidnaped by me and two other people. He wasn't supposed to end up dead, but he has."

Lacoste said, "I can't believe any of this."

"Come and see for yourself," Milligan said. "The other people involved are Logan's daughter Vera and a guy who called himself Quast. Q-U-A-S-T. But that isn't his real name. Have you got all that?"

"*Oui,* yeah, but—"

"Okay. You come here first and then call in your homicide people. Maybe you'll get a promotion out of it. Now I'm cutting out."

"Hey, hey, don't hang up yet—"

"Lucie, I have to split. Listen. Practise making the move to second base, you aren't that good."

"Marty, I'm coming right over."

"Goodbye, Lucien. Goodbye."

The neighbor in the next townhouse had signed the lease simply because he liked the idea of living next door to the famous Martin Milligan. He was coming in now as Milligan was hurrying out with his suitcase. It seemed incredible to the neighbor that the big baseball player would be crying openly as he strode down the street.

The story was big in the New Orleans *Times-Picayune*. Milligan bought a copy and read the account as he sat at a mahogany table in the Desire Oyster Bar with an icy glass of beer in front of him.

It was sensational news and the reporters were making a lot out of it: *Millionaire's Kidnaped Son Found Dead In Montreal Apartment Of Former Baseball Star*. Lucien Lacoste was mentioned and quoted as saying he knew Martin Milligan and was sure that once all the facts were known, his involvement would be explained away.

But the reporters liked the idea of the boy being dressed as a woman. Hypothetical questions were asked. How long had he known the baseball star? What was their relationship? Had Lester Logan traveled willingly from London to stay with Milligan, and had he died accidentally from an overdose? In which case, was the kidnaping a hoax?

In New York, Castle Logan was reported to have said he had not seen the man who claimed the money. But he would see him now. In hell. As for his daughter Vera who was implicated by Milligan's statement to officer Lacoste, Logan could only say he had not heard from his daughter in a long time. But yes, he was sorry to say she was capable of something like this. Her mother had been irrational and Vera seemed to have inherited the bad seed.

Quast was a nonentity. Nobody had ever heard of him. Quast might be a figment of Milligan's overwrought imagination, or a cleverly devised red herring intended to complicate the police search.

There was a good picture of Milligan with the story but the photo was 15 years old, showing him lean and tanned in his Mets uniform. Now, heavier, pale and paunchy of face, and wearing the straw hat and dark glasses he had bought yesterday on arrival in New Orleans, Milligan felt he could walk the streets in safety although he knew his time was limited.

The Vieux Carré had interesting streets to walk. Milligan left the bar and kept circulating, scanning the crowds for a glimpse of the pair he was looking for. Would they be together? Would they look the same? Milligan was not worried about disguises; something told him he would detect Quast hidden inside a hollow tree. But it had to be soon.

He saw a pair of cops approaching, walking side by side, doing what he was doing. Were they always this attentive on regular duty? Sure they were; they had a whole list of pimps and pushers to be on the lookout for. Even so, Milligan stepped inside a shop and sniffed jasmine-scented candles like any other tourist until the cops had passed by.

By late afternoon he was tired. He sat on a bench in Place d'Armes for a while, watching the raggedest crowd of young people he had ever seen. Their bare feet were bruised and filthy, their overalls had belonged years ago to other people, and in Milligan's weary eyes they appeared to have been inundated with agony and disinterest. One of them stood up and from a paper bag he took crusts of stale bread and threw them to a squadron of clattering pigeons. The birds buzzed the young man, confusing the humid air around him. Finally he threw the bag away, crumbs scattering, and walked away.

Milligan left the park and walked back to Bourbon Street where he sat at the bar in Jean Lafitte's Absinthe House and drank two more beers. He would soon have to eyeball Quast or Vera, or he would run out of time.

There was a TV set above the bar. The evening news came on and Milligan heard again about his house in Montreal and the dead body of Lester Logan. Then he was surprised to see Deirdre's face on the screen. She was being interviewed in London. The setting looked like the same paneled room in which Milligan had almost upset the luncheon table. Where would he be sitting now, he asked himself, if he had done what his heart desired and had taken his fists to young doctor whatever-his-name-was?

Well, he sure as hell would not be in this jeopardy now. But a voice told him to forget it; a murder would have happened a couple of days sooner and he would have committed it.

"Yes, I saw Martin just the day before," Deirdre was saying to the camera. "He'd come to London to talk to me. We're separated, you see." Her face showed satisfied concern.

The announcer's voice asked, "Do you think the fact your marriage has broken up had something to do with what Martin Milligan did?"

"Partly. But you must understand Martin's whole life had become a total failure. His restaurant in Montreal is going under. I think he'd become alienated from most of our friends. Then, as you say, he's lost me." One of Deirdre's hands pushed back the cascade of red hair on one side. "And years ago there was his baseball career. It wasn't his fault, of course, but he failed at that too, didn't he? So I suppose he was bound to come to grief. He certainly looked on the brink of something awful when I saw him last."

"Thank you, Mrs. Milligan," the announcer said.

A thought came into his mind from out of nowhere. He paid his tab and as he did so he asked the bartender, "Where is the best place for me to get some shrimp *rémoulade?*"

"Galatoire's," the bartender said. "Just down the street."

Galatoire's looked more like a barbershop to Milligan than a restaurant, with its white enamel woodwork and the yards of mirrors down both sides of the room with brass coat hooks between them. And it was anti-class, he discovered when he ordered a bottle of California chablis and the waiter brought it to him in a yellow plastic bucket of ice water which he set on the floor beside Milligan's chair. But it was good wine, and the shrimp *rémoulade* was superb, and so was the trout *amandine* and the *crêpes maison* followed by *café brulot.*

Milligan was smiling as he finished the feast. With all he had been drinking in the last couple of days, he had only one foot in the real world. "The condemned man ate a hearty dinner."

The waiter said, "What?"

"A very good dinner," Milligan said, putting money on the table and getting up unsteadily to leave.

Vera Logan was coming in as he was going out. He might have missed her with her hair changed from blonde to black and styled differently, but her reaction to him drew his attention.

"Well now," he said, but she had turned and began to run up the street.

Milligan took off after her, almost lost her in a crowd as he turned a corner, but managed to spot her again on the other side of the road just as she darted into an open doorway.

It was a jazz club called Crazy Annie's. Milligan went in and sat at a table near the door. The place was not very crowded at this early hour, but the band was blasting away at *South Rampart Street Parade* just as if it were New Year's Eve.

He soon caught sight of Vera with her back to him at a table near the wall. He took the drink his waiter had brought him and went to sit beside her.

"I didn't know you enjoyed Dixieland," he said. "That gives us one thing on common."

"It bores me," she said. "You're a smart man, Milligan. You got here almost as fast as we did."

"I just figured the team should stick together. Where's Quast?"

"Look around."

There were three other tables with people at them and Quast wasn't at any of them. That left only the band. And there was Quast in the front row, blowing unison riffs on his clarinet with the trumpet player while the trombonist took a solo. Quast had made no attempt to disguise himself. He was wearing a blue blazer with brass buttons over a white shirt and a striped tie and with his tanned face and styled hair, Milligan had to admit he looked like a million dollars. Well, two hundred thousand.

Quast stood up as the trombone player sat down and played a clarinet solo that rated very highly with anything Milligan had ever heard. He didn't have the technique of the pros back at the Metropole in New York, but he had power. He blew the instrument harder than other clarinetists, in short bursts that fitted exactly what the band was doing. The other musicians appreciated it; those who weren't blowing listened and glanced at each other approvingly.

It was the end of the set. Quast left the stand and came to the table. He shook Milligan's hand. Milligan couldn't believe it but there it was, the warm grip of the manager welcoming back his best player at the start of a new season.

"You are one smart man," Quast said.

"I told him he was smart," Vera said.

"I mean getting out of Montreal and keeping so quiet about it. I appreciate it. You remembered New Orleans and you could have told the cops New Orleans. But you didn't. You just took a powder, and I'm going to make that up to you."

"You mean by paying me my fifty thousand."

"More than that. Much more."

"How much more?"

"Half, man. Half of the take. One hundred thousand dollars."

"Keep it, Quast," Milligan said. "Or whatever your name is."

"What do you mean?"

"I'm here to blow the whistle on you. I wanted the pleasure."

Quast looked straight at Milligan. There was a smile on his face, but the eyes weren't smiling. They were animal eyes, peering out of a dark hole, wondering whether to stay put or make a run for it. "That's crazy," he said. "They'll grab you, too."

"I'm prepared for that. I'll take what's coming. I didn't kill Lester."

"Neither did I," Quast said, "but that's no reason to run to the cops."

"You fink," Vera said. "You rotten stinking fink."

"I like cops," Milligan said. "I always have. They keep the traffic moving outside the ballpark."

"What the hell do you mean?" Quast said.

"Never mind. Come on with me." Milligan stood up, taking Quast's arm in one hand and Vera's in the other. She pulled away and fell back onto her seat. Quast was strong and Milligan sensed he would have his hands full. "All right then, Vera," he said, "stay put. You won't get anywhere by yourself."

Out on the street people backed off as the big man in sunglasses wrestled the man in the blue suit into the middle of the road. A pair of police officers saw the action and approached, walking deliberately. There was a young cop and an older cop.

Milligan spoke to the older cop. "I'm Martin Milligan, wanted in the kidnap murder in Montreal. I'm turning myself in."

The cop said, "Yeah, Milligan. I recognize you."

Quast was standing very still, but his arm was rigidly tensed in Milligan's grip. "And this is the man behind the kidnaping. You'll have to hold onto him—he's not turning himself in."

A movement in the doorway of the club caught Milligan's eye. Vera was out and darting up the street. "That's another one," he yelled. "Vera Logan. Don't lose her."

The young cop took off after the girl just as Quast, taking advantage of the distraction, twisted free and ran the other way.

Quast was fast. Milligan had trouble keeping him in sight as they raced through the streets with the older cop's running footsteps gradually fading behind them.

They were approaching the park when Milligan heard the police siren. Good. They'd soon trap Quast and then Milligan could rest. His out-of-shape lungs were heaving as they had that one time when he had fooled everybody and hit an inside-the-park home run, beating the throw at the plate. They had walked the left fielder intentionally in order to pitch to Milligan. It was a sweet memory.

Now there were other cops in pursuit. He heard yelling, then a whistle blew. Brakes squealed and the siren died like an old crow with a harsh caw.

Quast was just in sight at the far side of the park, heading for a gate. Milligan put on a desperate burst of speed.

A voice behind yelled, "Stop right there!" and at the same time a gun was fired. Milligan felt a punch in his back and stumbled, the grass floating up to buffet his face.

Somebody turned him over. He felt as though he could open his eyes if he wanted to, but he decided to just leave them closed. He heard bits of what was being said above him.

"Why did you have to shoot him?" It sounded like the older cop. "He was giving himself up. It was the other guy."

"He was running away. We'll get the other guy. There's three cars on the other side of the park."

"I got the girl." The young cop's voice.

An ambulance siren. They were lifting Milligan onto a stretcher.

"He was a great ballplayer," the older cop said. "I saw him strike out Marbeck three times in one game."

After that third strikeout you couldn't hear yourself think in the stadium. Forty thousand people were standing up and applauding when Milligan left the mound and walked toward the dugout. As he crossed the third-base line, he lifted his cap.

It was Milligan's last sweet memory.